"*The Letter Tree* is a sweet, heartfelt romance that contains all the things I love best in historical romance, including a beautiful epistolary element. Rachel Fordham writes with warmth and grace, crafting a winning love story that's sure to please. I thoroughly enjoyed it!"

–Mimi Matthews, *USA TODAY* bestselling author of *The Belle of Belgrave Square*

"Combining charming hints of *You've Got Mail* with the poignancy of *Romeo and Juliet*, *The Letter Tree* is a journey of forgiveness and reconciliation and overcoming differences. Rachel Fordham's characters are quirky and relatable, and fascinating bits of 1920s culture color the story. An enjoyable and romantic read!"

–Sarah Sundin, bestselling and Christy Award-winning author of *The Sound of Light* and *Until Leaves Fall in Paris*

"Another tender, emotionally satisfying book from Rachel Fordham. Rachel's masterful writing style and cleverly crafted storyline bring a lovely and heartfelt romance to life. Highly recommended."

–Jennifer Beckstrand, *USA TODAY* bestselling author of *Second Chances on Huckleberry Hill*

"Skillfully layered and engaging from the start, this dashing tale of secret pen pals and forbidden romance set in the 1920s is sure to win the hearts of readers everywhere. An absolutely delightful read!"

–Nicole Deese, Christy Award-winning author

"*The Letter Tree* is a little bit *You've Got Mail* and a little bit of Hallmark's *Signed, Sealed, Delivered* and all sweet, immersive romance. Using delightful and beloved tropes to spin her own unique historical tapestry, Fordham's latest character-driven historical is destined to enthralled readers of Robin Lee Hatcher and Gabrielle Meyer."

–Rachel McMillan, author of *The London Restoration* and *The Mozart Code*

challenge anyone to finish reading it and not feel uplifted. Perfect for fans of Karen Witemeyer and Jennifer Deibel."

—KIMBERLY DUFFY, AUTHOR OF *THE WEIGHT OF AIR*

"'Two houses' is how Shakespeare's *Romeo and Juliet* begins and Rachel Fordham has captured the essence of that classic in *The Letter Tree*— but oh so much more. With wit and imagination, Ms. Fordham brings us a refreshing view of family mysteries, misunderstandings, and the hope of forgiveness in even the most dire circumstances. I loved this story that is an inventively told and deeply considered romance. It is a joy to read and remember. Best of all, *The Letter Tree* has a much happier ending than that other work of 'Two houses.'"

—JANE KIRKPATRICK, AWARD-WINNING AUTHOR
OF *BENEATH THE BENDING SKIES*

"What a true delight! I couldn't wait to return to this gem of a novel and see what the next page held. I've never read anything quite like it, so I never knew what was coming next. The charming premise drew me in, and then I was hooked, and couldn't wait to see what would come of these letter writers stuck in an impossible situation, and how they would each find out the true identity of the other. This is the sort of timeless love story that charms you immediately and remains with you for a long time."

—JOANNA DAVIDSON POLITANO, AWARD-WINNING AUTHOR
OF *THE LOST MELODY* AND OTHER HISTORICAL FICTION

"*The Letter Tree* transported me to a place where characters feel real, dreams come true, and happily ever after is actually possible. It's everything I love in a book."

—SHELLEY SHEPARD GRAY, *NEW YORK TIMES*
AND *USA TODAY* BESTSELLING AUTHOR

"*The Letter Tree* is a charming and captivating romance that reminds us of the transformative power of love, hope, and the written word. Palpable chemistry, complex familial relationships, and shared dreams that transcend barriers blend beautifully in this ambitious offering from Fordham. It was worth every emotional second from start to finish."

—RHONDA McKNIGHT, AWARD-WINNING
AUTHOR OF *THE THING ABOUT HOME*

THE LETTER TREE

A NOVEL

RACHEL FORDHAM

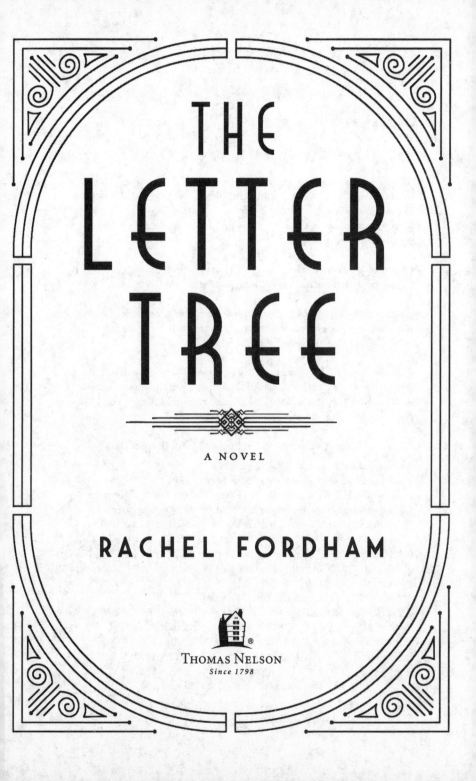

THOMAS NELSON
Since 1798

The Letter Tree

Published in Nashville, Tennessee, by Thomas Nelson. Thomas Nelson is a registered trademark of HarperCollins Christian Publishing, Inc.

Thomas Nelson titles may be purchased in bulk for educational, business, fundraising, or sales promotional use. For information, please email SpecialMarkets@ThomasNelson.com.

Publisher's Note: This novel is a work of fiction. Names, characters, places, and incidents are either products of the author's imagination or used fictitiously. All characters are fictional, and any similarity to people living or dead is purely coincidental.

Library of Congress Cataloging-in-Publication Data

Names: Fordham, Rachel, 1984- author.
Title: The letter tree: a novel / Rachel Fordham.
Description: Nashville, Tennessee: Thomas Nelson, [2023] | Summary: "Romeo and Juliet meets You've Got Mail in 1920s New York when hidden letters change everything for two lost souls and the community around them"—Provided by publisher.
Identifiers: LCCN 2023012080 (print) | LCCN 2023012081 (ebook) | ISBN 9780840718426 (TP) | ISBN 9780840718563 (epub) | ISBN 9780840718730 (audio download)
Subjects: LCGFT: Romance fiction. | Novels.
Classification: LCC PS3606.O747335 L48 2023 (print) | LCC PS3606.O747335 (ebook) | DDC 813/.6—dc23/eng/20230316
LC record available at https://lccn.loc.gov/2023012080
LC ebook record available at https://lccn.loc.gov/2023012081

Printed in the United States of America

23 24 25 26 27 LBC 5 4 3 2 1

For Nichole:
No matter how long it has been, we always
pick up right where we left off.
Love ya.

The course of true love never did run smooth.

—SHAKESPEARE, *A MIDSUMMER NIGHT'S DREAM*

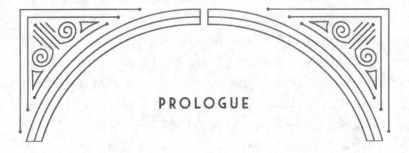

PROLOGUE

F airy tales," Laura Bradshaw mumbled as she ran her fingertip along the embossed letters on the newly purchased book, wishing it were a different title. Years ago, she'd loved the stories of Rapunzel, Briar-Rose, and the little cinder girl, but at nearly fourteen, she found her interests lying elsewhere—Shakespeare, animal care, and poetry.

"The illustrations are lovely," her mother said, unaffected by Laura's tone or the slight chill in the air. "Besides, only stuffy old people stop believing in happy endings."

Her mother's kind, gentle lips rose high in the corners, creating creases of infectious happiness. Suddenly Laura did not feel too old for stories of princes and princesses. Instead, she felt the familiar longing to curl up and fall asleep to the sound of her mother's voice reading story after story.

"I don't suppose I'm too old," she said, not wanting her mother's smile to fade or this perfect day to end. "It's a beautiful book."

"I hoped you'd like it." Laura's mother squeezed her hand before looking at the tall downtown building that loomed before them, ominous and bulky. Then she sighed deeply. When she smiled next, the expression was different—more forced. "You're growing up so fast. Everything is happening so fast."

"I'm almost fourteen." Laura stood a little taller. All day they'd been together, shopping and eating. She didn't want this mysterious final stop to darken the day. "Why do you have to go to the war office? Couldn't Father just come?"

"No," she said sharply. Gone was the lightheartedness of moments before. "I have to do this." She shook her head, then wrapped her fingers around Laura's arm. "It's up to me to make this right. Wait here. Read your new book until I get back. I won't be long."

"What do you have to make right?" Laura asked, but her mother was already three steps away. Laura's words drifted in the air like smoke pluming from a chimney with no destination. Eventually, the smoke would grow so faint that it seemed never to have existed at all. Left behind, she leaned against the wall of the nearby restaurant to wait. Her eyes and thoughts remained with her mother, who stood a few yards away, waiting to cross the street. What did her mother have to make right? She had never done anything wrong. She was perfect—wasn't she?

Unaccustomed to being alone, and burdened by her questions, Laura opened the book of fairy tales and thumbed through the pages, pausing to admire the illustrations of handsome princes. Their well-drawn faces proved somewhat diverting, though she would have rather had Isaac Campbell here for company than pictures, no matter how skillfully rendered. If Isaac were here, beside her, she might have been able to forget about the war office and the worry lines around her mother's eyes. The dashing fair-haired prince on the page in front of her was not nearly as handsome as her childhood friend. His dark hair, his eyes . . .

She snapped the book shut. This train of thought would lead nowhere. Isaac Campbell was little more than a dream or a fancy. He was kind, a bit of a tease, but at two years her senior, he still treated her like nothing more than the daughter of his father's business partner. Other girls caught his eye—she'd seen him flirt with them—but not her. She and Isaac were chums, nothing more. But maybe one day . . . *No, don't start that,* she chided herself.

A shriek pierced through her rambling thoughts. Laura looked up, instantly back in the present. Tires squealed. She dropped her book, all romantic thoughts vanishing as she moved toward the scene in disbelief, pulled to it like a magnet to metal. She ran, pushing through the crowd, then stopped. It couldn't be real. No. It couldn't be.

A second shriek. This one came from inside Laura, rippling through her young body with so much force that she fell to her knees. The image of her mother crumpled and broken in the street burned itself in her memory, and with it came the knowledge that this moment changed everything.

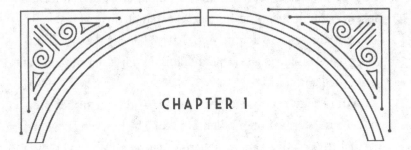

CHAPTER 1

Buffalo, New York
1924

Laura tightened her grip on her beaded handbag as she walked the maze of paths through the zoo, bound for *her* tree. Big Frank's enclosure, with its elephant sculptures and proud stone edifice, caused her to pause, but only for a moment. Today, not even the waving trunk of her elephant friend could entice her to stop. She would have time to say hello to her four-legged friends later.

Before reaching the sea lions, she turned left and slowed her pace. Her heartbeat did the opposite, quickening with each cautious step as she approached the most awe-inspiring feature of the entire zoo—the letter tree, or so she called it—tucked in a corner that had once been part of the nearby park. It had been easier to get to the maple before the zoo expansion claimed this section of land a year ago. Since then, she'd had to enter the zoo, pay admission, and work her way through the crowd to get to her unconventional mailbox.

Today her quest would have to wait, seeing as she was not alone in the normally quiet corner of the zoo. A woman clinging tightly to a man's arm stepped into the shade of Laura's maple.

She giggled. He worked his hands around her waist and leaned closer. Without meaning to, Laura stared at the lovely couple, both tall and with matching dark hair. The way they looked at each other left Laura gawking and longing for a man to look at her in such a way.

Afraid they would take their escapade too far in her presence, Laura stepped on a fallen branch. The cracking of wood startled the couple, who, to Laura's great relief, stopped ogling each other and, without so much as a word, turned their backs on her and walked toward the crowd and the animals.

Laura looked down at her polished Bradshaw black-buckle pumps while she waited for the pair to disappear from her sight. Her father's shoe factory made the finest shoes, though those who favored Campbell shoes would argue theirs were superior. It seemed a lifetime ago that Bradshaw and Campbell had been united.

She ought to be proud that her father was such a successful factory owner. And, on occasion, she was. But those instances were rare; normally, the well-fitted shoes only reminded her that she would always be second in her father's eyes. His tenderness had been tossed aside in his tireless pursuit of success and vengeance. She buried the toe of her glistening shoe into the soft dirt until it lost its sheen.

"Excuse me, miss, have you dropped something in the dirt?" She took a quick step backward. In front of her stood a white-haired man with rosy cheeks and a welcoming smile. "I can dig around for you so you don't have to muddy your shoes."

"No!" Her voice came out an octave higher than normal. "I haven't lost anything. I was merely . . ." She scrambled for an excuse. None came. "I like this corner of the zoo."

"You've a keen eye. This tree is magnificent. Most everyone comes for the animals." He put his hands in his pockets while his eyes traveled the trunk of the tree. Her gaze followed his, admiring the vast array of branches and lush, vibrant spring growth. Her maple was beautiful. Magical. Large, proud, and old enough to have seen history she'd only heard of in whispered stories.

"It's a fine tree," she said, loving the maple, the animals of the zoo, and the inkling of joy she felt while within these fine gates. Paying admission was a difficulty, but the zoo itself was an oasis in the doldrums of life. Here, she felt connected to the world outside her father's home and nurtured her dreams of a life of freedom.

"I'm told this beauty was almost cut down a few months back."

She gasped. "No!"

"Lost a big branch in the first snowstorm of winter."

"I remember. But I didn't know there was talk of cutting it down."

"One of our donors demanded we leave it be. He made a big fuss. I guess we're not the only ones who love this tree." The man pulled his hand from his pocket, and with it came a pocket watch. "I'm to feed the bears in a few minutes. I suppose if you come to the zoo often, you've already met our fine bears."

"I have." She smiled. She'd spent many mornings watching the bears put on a show for their food.

"It'll be my first time doing the feeding on my own. My friend's a guard here. He helped me get this job. He told one of his friends about my work as a veterinarian. I treated mostly livestock before coming here, but I'm well read on the workings of other animals."

Her breath caught in her chest. Where once he'd been a stranger, she now saw a man who shared her interest in animals and their care. "The polar bear is my favorite. I have watched his feeding many times. He seems a well-mannered fellow. You'll do well, I'm sure."

"Don't go telling the other bears, but he's my favorite too."

"I won't tell." She grinned. Each animal felt like a friend to her. On her loneliest days, she could come here, look over the railings, and observe the vulture, tiger, or meerkat, and the day would improve.

"We've baby foxes, born three weeks back," the zookeeping man said. "They aren't coming out much, but you might want to take a look, see if you get lucky. I caught sight of them myself the other day."

"The baby animals have always been my favorite."

She'd been seven years old the first time she came to the zoo. Big Frank didn't have an elephant house back then, only a ball and a chain. Her fingers tingled, pricked by the memory of her mother's hand in hers, and she clenched her fist, wanting to cling to the feeling as much as she wanted to drive it away. The place where her mother ought to be had been empty for so long.

She fidgeted with the beads on her handbag. Her tongue burned, wanting to pepper this man with questions about animals and veterinary work. But she was better off remaining forgettable. There was less chance of word getting back to her father that she was at the zoo without his permission. Women no longer needed the ever-watchful eye of a chaperone, but her father had not embraced their newly granted freedom.

From beneath his white brows the elderly zookeeper studied her. What did he see when he looked at her? Did he see her fashionable straight-cut dress, with its scalloped hem, and assume her a modern woman? He couldn't know that she was anything but modern, preferring comfort over fashion and never caring if there was dirt beneath her nails.

Laura touched a hand to her hair, smoothing the waves as she searched for the right words to end this unexpected exchange and escape his inquiring gaze.

He spoke first. "I've been wondering how I know you . . ."

Oh dear.

"I've got it—"

She shook her head. "We've not met. I believe you're mistaken."

"You're a Bradshaw, aren't you?"

Laura sucked in her bottom lip and chewed on it a moment. "I am."

"Best not look at my feet. I'm wearing a pair of Campbell boots today." His dark eyes twinkled with a spark that would have been welcoming had she not felt the sting of nerves racing up her spine at his recognition. She preferred, no, she needed her anonymity. Without it, her visits to the zoo could be in jeopardy. "You've the same auburn hair and blue eyes as your mother. Same small frame. It's been a long time, but it's like looking at your mother."

"My mother," Laura whispered, suddenly cold despite the warm sun. Talk of the feuding shoe companies riled her spirits, but talk of her mother left her out of sorts. She needed to get away from this man and the memories that were sure to assault her and leave her hollow, empty, and begging for answers.

"It looks as though everyone is headed toward the bears," she said, desperately hoping to end the conversation.

"You're right. I've dawdled too long. Before I go, I should have introduced myself. It's not fair that I know you're Catherine Bradshaw's daughter but you don't know I'm Brent Shaffer."

Polite manners required her to share her name. "I'm Laura Bradshaw."

"It's been a pleasure meeting you. Perhaps if I see you again, we can talk more. It would do this old fool well to hear how Catherine Bradshaw's daughter is faring." He looked again at the moving crowd before stepping away. "Good day, Miss Bradshaw."

She offered a brief farewell, then stared like a ninny as he walked away. His gait was slow; she had time to run after him and ask how he knew her mother. If she pried, perhaps she could find a clue that explained her mother's death and answered one of the many questions that haunted her.

Her father refused to speak of his wife's accident, brushing it under the rug as though their loss were an irrelevant piece of old factory equipment or unimportant bit of dust. But understanding what had happened was important to Laura. She wanted to tear the rug away, dig through the pile, and discover what led to her world falling apart. Perhaps then she could put things back together.

A gust of wind rustled the young spring leaves of the maple, reminding her of her quest. Now was not the time to dwell on a past she did not understand. Now was her chance to get to the tree.

Laura let her fingers graze the ridges and valleys of the maple's bark. Over her shoulder she looked at the crowd, with their peanuts and popcorn in hand, that migrated like a flock of wintering birds toward the bears, leaving her unnoticed. A moment like this was what she always waited for. She stepped closer to the maple that was, in many ways, more than a beloved tree. It was memories. It was comfort. It was hope.

Like a ballerina, she popped onto her tiptoes and reached into the hollow opening. The moment her fingers touched paper, warmth raced to her heart, and nothing else mattered. She took her prize, wishing she could open it immediately, devour its contents, and escape into the world of words. But caution kept her from acting impulsively. Instead, the paper went into her handbag, and then, just as quickly as she'd retrieved the waiting letter, she placed her own carefully penned words into the tree.

For seven years, this tree had been her mailbox—the gateway connecting two worlds. She'd been fourteen when her unusual correspondence began. Now, at twenty-one, the letters were a solace, providing a reprieve from her many woes and a touch of excitement and mystery to her often dull life. Like her very own fairy tale, this secret exchange felt magical, whimsical—and hopeful.

She stepped out from under the shadows of the branches, smoothed her drop-waist dress, and, with head high, walked back through the zoo, stopping only briefly to look for the baby foxes, wave at the swimming sea lions, and admire Big Frank's leathery skin. The stench of elephant manure hovered in the warm, humid air, but the onlookers' excitement remained unfettered.

Big Frank's eyes found hers, and she could almost believe he recognized her. An unusual friendship, to be sure, but one she treasured. Big Frank, with his wise eyes, saw her come and go, and when there was no crowd around him, he listened to her worries, her dreams, and her secrets. He even knew about her letters, a secret she'd not shared with anyone else.

A crowd began to gather at the elephant enclosure, so she waved goodbye and made her way to the zoo's exit and the grounds of the adjoining Delaware Park, mindful of staying on the side of the park that faced her home so she could look for the warning crystal prisms Mrs. Guskin hung in the window whenever her father came home early. There would be no going to the lake or to Spire Head; it was better to find a quiet spot in view of the parlor window to read the letter and soak in her last bit of freedom before returning to her oversize and ornate prison, so effective at cutting her off from the world that it may as well have been Rapunzel's tower.

Sweet old Mrs. Guskin, who worked under the title of housekeeper but was more like a grandmother to Laura, encouraged her to go out nearly every day, even if only briefly to stretch her legs. On that account, Laura fared better than Rapunzel.

"Go on now," Mrs. Guskin had said earlier that day as she waved a hand toward the door, behaving as though Laura were a rambunctious child and not a grown woman of twenty-one. But there was nothing condescending about Mrs. Guskin; she was all goodness and warmth. "Go breathe the fresh air you love so much. See the animals. Those books of yours will never compare to the real thing. Your father made no mention of coming back early, but be sure and check the window." A throaty laugh followed. "As soon as I believe I know what to expect from your father, he does something unexpected."

"I'll check the window." Laura grinned, grateful that Mrs. Guskin had no fear of undermining her father. "I don't want a lecture from him today."

Mrs. Guskin adopted the deep voice she used whenever she mimicked Laura's father. "How many times must I tell you—how you behave affects the factory. No one needs to see my daughter running around like a tomboy." She laughed, and her voice returned to normal. "Go on. Put on a decent dress in case someone spots you. Enjoy yourself."

Laura hadn't needed to be told twice. She'd readied herself and scurried out.

When Mrs. Guskin first arrived, shortly after Laura's mother died, Laura had been leery of trusting the older woman. Then one night Mrs. Guskin came to her rescue, interrupting Laura's father when he'd had too much to drink and his temper was high. She claimed he'd received a telephone call and then gave Laura the *go on, get out of here* look. They'd had an alliance ever since.

Laura inhaled, her lungs filling with the damp spring air. She looked around the meadow-like park. The people of Buffalo could almost believe themselves far from the city while walking the paths of Delaware Park. In truth, she often imagined herself far away, in some distant country, a breeder of the finest horses or a country lass caring for her flock of overly pampered chickens. Her dreams were always simple—varied, but full of freedom and fresh air.

An open bench invited her to sit, providing a perfect spot to read her letter. She traced her finger over initials carved into the bench's worn wood. *RB + TF.* Who were they? Were they married now, with a houseful of children? Were they deeply in love, devoted to each other? She closed her eyes, blaming the many novels she read for her active imagination and incessant longing for companionship. How lovely would it be to be a woman in love, sitting beside a handsome suitor? She imagined what it would feel like for a kindhearted man to take her hand, to have eyes for only her, to carve their initials for the world to see . . .

From within the confines of her handbag, she retrieved her letter. Her reality was not all bad; her letters were better than any dream. After all, this secret friend was real, and he was hers.

Dear Wishing Girl,

She paused, smiling at the silly greeting. When she'd been fourteen, still grieving her mother's death and feeling stifled by her father's controlling hand and spike in temper, she'd escaped to the park with pen and paper. Near the letter tree—only it hadn't been the letter tree then—she'd penned a poem, trying to capture in words the tumultuous feelings warring inside her. When Mrs. Guskin put the hurry-home prism in the window, Laura had panicked, afraid her father would catch her out of the house and read her words, brow furrowed in disappointment.

In desperation, she'd looked for a place to stow her writing, and her eyes had landed on the maple with the narrow hollow. Two days later she'd returned, eager to recover her words and dispose of her novice attempt at poetry for good. But her poetry had not been there. Instead, she'd found a letter.

She'd read it a thousand times since. Even now, she could quote it by memory.

Dear Wishing Girl,

I found your poetry and I have kept it. You didn't want squirrels using your words for their nests, did you?

You must be wondering how I came upon your words, and so I will tell you. I was at the park with a couple of my chums. We had no plans, and

according to my father, it is not good for boys to go about with no direction.
He says trouble always follows. My father is never short on advice.

She'd smiled at his mention of his father. Her own father also had a great deal to say about her every move. Reading these words, she felt a connection, like a thin thread linking her and her mystery pen friend together. Over the years it had grown thicker, stronger and more binding.

The lot of us were aimlessly passing the time when we spotted a couple sitting on the grass, staring at each other as though nothing else in the world existed. I thought I might get a laugh if I tossed a pinecone or two at them. I flicked one and hit the man on the leg. He flinched but didn't take his eyes off the woman. I threw another and another. When I had thrown seven or eight of them, the man jumped from his spot and came chasing after me. His face was all red, and he was scowling. How was I to know that a little fun would rile him up? My pals ran off in different directions, but it made no difference—it was me he wanted.

I ended up climbing the big maple tree and hiding there until he gave up. When I finally came back down, a scrap of paper caught my eye. I thought perhaps I'd found a treasure map or a letter sent between secret lovers. But it was neither. It was your poetry I found, and a great many questions. Who was the writer? Had we ever met?

I think it's a funny story, don't you? My father would disapprove; he'd hate knowing that I found a magic mailbox after causing trouble. I suppose it will only be a mailbox if you find this and write back. Otherwise, I am writing to no one. I will call it an act of faith and believe that you will come back and find this and that you and I are meant to be friends. When you find this, write again. Tell me why you left your poetry and why your words have me believing you are sad.

My curiosity is piqued and is begging to know who the mysterious writer is.

Until I hear back, I remain,
Your pinecone-throwing friend

Seven years later, she was still the Wishing Girl and he was still her pinecone-throwing friend, that and many other titles. His writing skills had only become more refined with time, but his letters retained their humor and heart. When she wrote him back the very first time, she told him little about herself. She'd insisted they not use their names, declaring it far more enchanting if they remained anonymous. In truth, she'd feared her father's reaction should he ever discover their correspondence. She'd already lost her mother. And because of the shoe factory divide, her interactions with her childhood friends were severed. She hadn't wanted to lose anyone else.

Laura pulled herself from her musings, unread letter still in hand, and glanced toward the window. Her heart stopped. The prisms were in the window, glistening like a beacon. Her father was home.

She leaped to her feet and, like the sly foxes at the zoo, dashed for the servant's entrance so she could slink inside and pretend nothing was amiss.

CHAPTER 2

Isaac Campbell's sizable donation to the zoo gave him the ability to visit the grounds nearly anytime he wanted to. Often he came in the evening or at night when only one guard was on duty. With such a well-known name and recognizable face, thanks to his uncanny resemblance to his father—both tall, broad, and with strikingly dark hair and equally dark eyes—coming at night was the easiest way to get to the tree unnoticed.

Besides, animals never inquired after the Campbell shoe company's affairs. They didn't bombard him with gossip about their rival company or pretend to know what happened seven years ago between his father and his father's former business partner. They didn't ask him his feelings on prohibition, recount memories of the Great War, or whisper about his bachelorhood. Animals were far less meddlesome than people.

Isaac shoved his hands in his pockets and meandered slowly along the stone paths of the zoo, whistling to the tune of "My Little Dream Girl." The evening air was crisp but not bitterly cold like the winter nights had been. The temperature was comfortable enough that he could stay all night if he wished.

Outside these gates, he was a different man, but in here, he felt free. Liberated from the struggle to prove himself to his father. Here no one knew he was a sought-after bachelor who felt no inkling of desire to date the women who batted their eyes at him. Here he was free to think of the woman behind the letters, or to think of his uncle who'd died in the war and long for days gone by. The buzzing world outside the gates could wait; he was in no hurry to return to it. His mind wandered in whatever direction it chose, carefree as the spring breeze.

The guard, Bill Turner, an old friend, waved as he made his rounds. "That's a fine tune you're whistling."

"It's playing on the radio all day long. It gets stuck in my head."

"I thought maybe you were dreaming about a lady." Bill stopped his march around the zoo. "We had hundreds of folks here today. The warmer weather is filling these grounds."

"There's nothing like spring in Buffalo. Makes you want to get out of doors and celebrate."

"Sure does," Bill said. "Even Big Frank's been livelier. I suppose seeing the grass after all these months has him excited. It's going to be a good spring."

"What makes you so certain?"

"The war's been done long enough that folks is smiling again. Times are good—seems everyone is prospering." He shrugged. "Everyone's back to being plumb crazy, and I s'pose that's better than being sad and worried all the time. Time's healed a lot of wounds."

Isaac leaned on the railing of the sea lion enclosure. The big male waddled from his rock to the water and slid in, sleek and smooth. The zoo's electric lights danced across the ripples the sea lion made, giving the scene a majestic feel. Isaac kept his gaze on the animal, watching the sea lion's acrobatics in the water. "I think you're right. The war's reach is fading. It'll be a good spring."

"I hear there's talk of an exhibition at Niagara Falls. Some fool plans to go over in a rubber ball. Read about it in the paper. Should be happening in a few weeks, or maybe it was months, I can't remember for sure."

Years ago, Isaac may have aspired to something so reckless as riding over the falls in a barrel. He'd wanted so badly to make his own mark on the world, one not connected to his father or their business. Now he wasn't sure what he wanted. He'd stayed home when his friends went off to college, just waiting for his turn to make decisions at the factory, but at twenty-three he found that time still hadn't come. "I may have to go and watch the exhibition. Sounds more entertaining than spending my days trying to take down the Bradshaw shoe factory."

Bill's rumbling laugh earned him a smile from Isaac and a sleepy-eyed look from the nearest animals. "Is your father still giving you . . . interesting assignments?"

"I'd hardly call them interesting." He kept his tone light despite the angst he felt. If only Bradshaw would close his factory doors, Isaac would be free of him, and then perhaps Isaac's father would give him real responsibility at the Campbell factory. His hands tightened on the metal railing. "There's a new supplier of raw goods. Word is he inherited a business from his late father. There's talk that he's brilliant and incredibly wealthy—I believe he deals in investments as well, but I don't really know much about him. It is now my father's hope that I will befriend the man and get him to work exclusively with Campbell shoes. He's convinced that this man is the secret to him becoming bigger than Bradshaw and putting Bradshaw out of business for good."

Isaac's jaw clenched. He wanted to open new markets or design a useful shoe, but his father was forever telling him to run along as though he hadn't been learning the business for years. When he begged for responsibility, his father gave him trivial tasks, like befriending a man. But Isaac knew numbers were what ought to sell contracts.

"Someday..." He trailed off. All this talk of work left him feeling like an impish child, trying desperately to prove himself. He had everything... and yet he always felt something was missing.

"You're ambitious. I'm sure your father is proud of you." Bill grinned, his crooked teeth showing. "Might as well enjoy all the time you have. Someday you'll likely have more work than you'd like. I say, take a woman with you to the falls. Watch the spectacle. Enjoy life—the rest will work itself out." Bill winked before starting on his rounds again.

Take a woman. Every time Isaac heard those words, his thoughts went to his letter girl. She may not know his name, but she knew him better than anyone else. How many letters had he composed asking to meet her, begging to know her name? But he never left them for her. He tore them up, threw them in the fire, and went on as they had for so many years. Talking about books, the weather, and the happenings of Buffalo. They wrote of dreams and sorrows, fairy tales and hopes. Always careful and cautious, sharing details that filled his mind and heart but never enough clues to put a name or a face with the words. She'd made it a rule from the start: no names. And he'd complied, despite his curiosity.

Once, when they'd first started writing, he tried to catch her leaving a letter. He spent hours in the tree, even clinging to its branches during a rainstorm. But his efforts were fruitless, and after that he decided to embrace their unique friendship and the gift of namelessness.

Why had he never asked her to change her rule? The part of himself that wanted to ask ached to know her completely. But if he did ask to meet her, or for her name, then he would have to decide what to do with her answer. What if he met her and found her unattractive or abrasive? Either possibility was hard to imagine. Still, there was a risk that what they had would end. And if he no longer had the letters to look forward to, he felt certain a void would form in his life that would be impossible to fill. Theirs was something steady, predictable. In the ever-changing landscape of a bustling city, he wanted to keep for himself this one unchanging pillar.

A wolf at the other end of the zoo howled. He turned toward the noise but saw nothing more than dark shadows. The half-moon and a few electric lights offered enough illumination that he could easily make his way through the maze of pathways, but the night still wrapped everything in a blanket of near darkness. He tossed the scraps of jerky he'd brought for the foxes to find later, when they left their den to stretch their weary limbs.

From there to the letter tree, he needed no light at all. He traveled the path now on his long legs, one step after another, until he'd arrived and was reaching inside the maple.

He smiled. She'd written. And soon he was whistling "My Little Dream Girl" again.

———————•———•———————

"Your father's in ill spirits. That man can growl louder than the devil in a thunderstorm." Mrs. Guskin smirked while she helped freshen the waves in Laura's hair. "He's bringing a guest and has told me twice to make sure you're dressed in the latest fashion and don't have dirty nails. He mumbled something about you playing in the dirt."

"He knows I'm not playing in the dirt," Laura said. "He used to like the flowers in the back before Mother died."

"He's a stubborn man, and he's convinced himself that hating everything that has to do with your mother will somehow make things better."

"And he calls me foolish." Laura balked. "Being mad at a dead person never got anyone anywhere."

Mrs. Guskin's tight bun gave her a deceptively stern look. "That may be, but it won't hurt to give your hands a good scrubbing. I believe this dinner has something to do with business, and there's no reason to rile up your father."

Everything her father did was about business or social standing. He dressed each morning with the sole purpose of impressing others. He ate at the finest restaurants and even attended speakeasy gatherings at green-door locations, all for the purpose of bettering the Bradshaw shoe brand and ensuring Buffalo—and the whole world, for that matter—knew Bradshaw shoes were superior to Campbell shoes. Even her pet macaw, Tybalt, was the result of his vanity. He'd bought the red bird only because it was exotic and something few others had. He'd bragged about it until he grew annoyed with Tybalt's sea slang and smell, at which time Laura claimed the bird as her own.

Tybalt's birdcage was in the far corner of her room where he could see out the window. He was a delightful, albeit stubborn, creature, who had completely stolen her animal-loving heart. He always paraded back and forth across his roost, red feathers puffed and head jutting forward and back.

"Storm's coming," he squawked as he pranced, mimicking a sailor she'd come to know in voice only. "Storm's coming."

Laura snickered at the words he'd learned to mimic while traveling from South America, but inside she squirmed. It was only old ship talk. She knew that. Yet an eerie chill raced down her spine as though Tybalt's words somehow carried truth. Could a storm be coming? She longed for change, but not the vile, chaotic sort. What her heart and soul yearned for was change that brought escape from the monotony of her life.

"Perhaps you could tell my father I've a headache, and then I would not have to sit through a business dinner at all." Laura's eyes connected with Mrs. Guskin's through the mirror, and a knowing look passed between Mrs. Guskin's motherly brown eyes and Laura's younger blue ones. "I promise I'd stay in my room."

"I know what you'd do. You'd pore over your veterinary books or lose yourself in one of your well-loved fairy tales while missing your mama."

"If I promised to help you, would that change anything? I'd dust every inch of this floor."

"Tempting—I do love it when we work together—but I think it best you save your headache for when it is truly needed, don't you? You'll only have to sit there until your father pulls out the brandy and insists you leave so they can talk business."

"I don't see why I need to be there at all. He'll simply talk numbers and complain about Campbell and claim the man is stealing his designs. It's the same thing every time."

"That may be. But I think it wise to appease him. I don't blame you, but for now wear the green dress—the color is stunning, and it's so fashionable. And remember if the dinner drags on that it *will* end, and your books will be here, hidden under your bed like they always are. And I'll be here, ready to hear how it went."

Laura scrunched up her nose. She never felt completely at ease in the green dress, striking as it was. The plunging neckline and fringed skirt left her feeling as though she were pretending to be someone she was not. Why could a man not appreciate her in something more comfortable? But her father cared about appearances, and if he wanted the latest fashion, then the green dress it must be.

The old stubbornness that she was forever burying and trying to ignore fought like a seedling struggling to burst through the soil, only to find itself covered again. She was a grown woman, old enough to decide what to wear and how to fill her day. She did not work at her father's factory, but in many ways, she felt as though she were his employee. Always subject to his commands and scrutiny. He claimed it was all for her good, that his quest to best Campbell, his tireless work at the factory—all of it—was for her. And his demands on her, likewise, were meant to protect her. But from what? He kept her from the socials, the roller rinks, and the dance halls. The heaviness in her chest increased.

Laura's eyes went to Tybalt, trapped in his cage, dependent on her. *"You wouldn't survive out there,"* she'd told him many times. *"The cage is for your safety."* She turned away, hating cages in all their forms. Hating her restless heart, wishing it weren't there. If she weren't such a dreamer, perhaps she could be content with her stifling life.

She gritted her teeth and pushed the obstinance back down, knowing that, like Tybalt, she would not survive on her own. The thought made her feel weak and small. With no means of income, few connections, and her father's commanding voice in her head, so much seemed against her. Her gaze landed on the fairy-tale book and then on Mrs. Guskin. At least Laura was not alone in a tower. For that, she would choose to be thankful. "I'll wear the green. But only if you promise to listen to me complain about every detail of the night."

"My ears are already burning to hear how it goes." Mrs. Guskin pulled the elegant garment from the wardrobe and ran her hand across the black beadwork that crisscrossed the front of the dress. "You'll look lovely."

Laura exhaled, resigned to her fate. Soon enough she would be back in her room with her matronly housekeeper, her bird, and her box of letters. Today's missive had been two pages of nothing and everything all at once. Talk of the theater he'd attended, the baby foxes he'd been able to catch a glimpse of at the zoo, and how he'd stood near the spot where President McKinley was assassinated during the Pan-American Exposition.

I wonder whether you and I ever cross paths when we stroll through the park. Have our eyes met, and we did not know it?

How often had she wondered the very same thing? Whenever a stranger's eyes lingered on her, she searched her heart for a gentle flutter, something to confirm that the man in front of her was not truly a stranger. She wanted to meet her letter friend, but in all these years he'd never asked, and so her rules from the beginning remained, protecting them both from her father's sure disapproval. At times she'd been tempted to ask him personal questions, but fear, the ever-present sentinel, stood close, holding her back. Fear whispered doubts and taunted her with the idea of losing her letter friend all because she wanted too much.

"If you'd cut your hair into a bob, it'd look even more modern," Mrs. Guskin said, interrupting Laura's thoughts.

"I prefer the faux bob." She touched the small, tight buns at the nape of her neck, carefully twisted to give her the appearance of a bob without requiring she cut off her dark auburn tresses. "Mama always loved brushing my long hair."

"You poor girl." Mrs. Guskin's thin lips drooped down in the corners. "I remember my own mama brushing my hair when I was a girl."

"She's been gone for years," Laura said, trying to appear unaffected despite the sting of loss that lingered like a bullet embedded in her chest. "I do wonder why she was there that day." She fidgeted with the hem of her shirtwaist. "I met a man at the zoo today. He said I look like my mother. I suppose that is why she is on my mind."

"You don't have to be so brave." Mrs. Guskin planted a motherly kiss atop Laura's head. "A woman is allowed to miss her mother every day of the year. She needs no reason for it."

"That day, she said she was going to go and make things right. I've always wondered . . ." Laura closed her eyes, not wanting tears to come now. "I don't want to keep seeing the accident in my mind. But it is still there."

"You shouldn't have seen that," Mrs. Guskin whispered, a reverence in her tone. "I wish I could wipe it away for you and all the fears that came because of it. You were just a child."

Laura blinked quickly. "I imagine the old zookeeper knew her from church or some social committee she was on. There was a time when everyone knew her." She took a slow breath, steadying her voice. "I almost wish he'd not said anything. Mama's gone, and talking about her won't bring her back." A quiver of emotion crept into her voice, betraying her desire to appear nonchalant. "My mother is gone, my father cares only about making thousands of shoes, and I must get ready for dinner."

"Your father treats you like a pawn in his game of chess. He shouldn't ignore you so often, nor expect you to always be there at his beck and call."

"He's never said he blames me for that day, but—"

"He'd be a fool to blame you." Mrs. Guskin's voice was soft yet full of force. In books housekeepers were often docile, present but quiet. Mrs. Guskin broke the mold, and Laura was glad of it. Their gazes met once again in the mirror and held. Mrs. Guskin delivered her next words slowly and with emphasis, her gaze never wavering. "You are not a game piece. And you are not responsible for your father's choices. Don't forget that."

"I'll do my best," Laura whispered back, as though her words were a vow.

"The war changed a lot of people. It's no excuse, but it did."

"My father didn't go to war. He made boots for soldiers. They called him a hero because he kept our boys' feet dry." She turned her attention away from her mirror. "It doesn't matter."

"*You* matter. All of it matters. But right now, your father expects you." Mrs. Guskin backed toward the door, giving Laura time to sort out her feelings. Before leaving, she said, "I'll go and let your father know that you'll be down shortly. Take a moment if you need it."

Alone, with only Tybalt, Laura pulled on her green dress, careful to preserve her hair. Then, rather than hurry downstairs, she walked to the window and pushed the curtains aside. It was dark out, and only a few couples still strolled the park. Was her letter-writing man among them?

"Do you suppose he's feeding the ducks?" she asked her bird. "Or staring off at the sky and wishing I was there with him?"

Tybalt wrapped his beak around the bar of his cage and gnawed at it, paying her little heed.

"He's probably down there, looking at every window, wondering where I am. Maybe someday he'll see my window, and he will just know that it's me in here. He'll climb up." She opened the curtains as wide as they would go and then waltzed away from the window. "And we'll dance, and the rest of the world will disappear. His arms will be large and strong, and I'll feel completely safe in them. We won't have to hide anything because we already know each other's hearts." She closed her eyes, wishing she knew his face so she could picture him looking at her. "And then he'll lean in close and kiss me."

Tybalt flapped his wings, distracting her.

She stopped dancing, the illusion fading. "Do you not think that is what he'd do?"

Tybalt let out one of his ear-piercing screams that had gotten him banished from her father's presence.

"It doesn't matter what you think," she said to Tybalt. "I don't actually expect him to come climbing up like some lovesick suitor. I know one day the letters will stop. He'll fall in love and marry, and it will all end. I'll be left with only a box of words."

She got a cracker and reached it through the bars of his cage. "It's been fun, dreaming that one day he'll fall in love with me. You don't begrudge me a few daydreams, do you?" Tybalt cocked his head to one side and then the other. "It's silly, I know. No one falls in love with a person they've never seen. And even if we did declare ourselves smitten, Father would find a way to come between us. He'd claim there was a better match out there." She imitated her father's deep voice, not matching the timbre as well as Mrs. Guskin had. "Laura, I forbid you from seeing your Pinecone Man and insist you marry a stuffy old businessman."

She rolled her eyes, a childish act she would never do in front of her father. "Perhaps you and I should sneak off to the jungle together. I think I'd make a fine jungle woman, don't you?"

A laugh bubbled through her when he nodded his head up and down. There was no friend like Tybalt, no one she'd rather sneak away with.

"A jungle woman would have to be brave." She tapped her lip. "I will practice my bravery tonight as I endure an entire dinner with Father and his work associate. When I come back, I will tell you how I faced the enemy, never wavering. I might even use some of your favorite sea language when I do."

CHAPTER 3

M y dear, you look lovely." Laura's father, Stanley Bradshaw, stood when she entered the dark wood-paneled parlor with its crimson curtains and crystal lighting, as did the man seated near him. "Mr. Fredricks, this is my daughter, Miss Laura Bradshaw." He turned to her. "Laura, Mr. Abel Fredricks."

"Very nice to meet you," she greeted him, offering her most appealing smile while also trying not to gawk at this unexpected guest.

"The pleasure is mine." Mr. Fredricks was not the weathered old man she had expected to meet when she descended the stairs and stepped into the parlor. He looked to be in his mid- to upper twenties, with light hair and clear blue eyes—an alarmingly handsome man. "It was good of your father to invite me to dinner. You've a beautiful home. I have always been fond of parks. Surely there's no finer place in all of Buffalo."

"There are a few families on the shores of the lake who claim their view superior to ours, but they have not had the luxury of waking to the sound of exotic animals." She glanced at her father.

Stanley Bradshaw nodded his head. She relaxed a little, and then he said, "We can discuss the merits of living parkside over dinner. If you'll follow me, we can all go in and dine."

The small party of three left the parlor and moved to the dining room with its tin ceiling and twinkling chandelier. The home clung tightly to its Victorian charm; apart from the radio and other modern novelties, the décor was almost entirely how it had been when her mother was alive. On occasion, Laura could recall a pleasant memory or two by simply walking the halls or looking at her mother's favorite chair. It was always a battle, the tension between yearning for the past and wanting to wash it away altogether.

Her father sat at one end of the large dining room table, Laura to his right and Abel to his left. Candlesticks and full place settings gave the dining room both an intimate and formal feel. The fringe on Laura's dress tickled her legs when she sat, and though it was not the dress she would have chosen, she could not help but wonder what Abel Fredricks thought of her appearance.

She kept her back straight and readied herself to seem far more interested in the conversation than she felt. Her father brought business guests to the house from time to time. Whenever he believed her presence would contribute in some way, she was asked to join them. Some contracts were easier to secure if her father could present himself as a family man. As a result, she knew all too well how *dull* talk of production numbers and competition could be. And she had mastered the art of thinking about other things while nodding her head at the right moments.

To her great astonishment, Abel said little about business. She gathered that he was a supplier of raw materials for shoes and a man eager to grow and invest. But he said little else about his trade, asking instead about their life in Buffalo. He often held her gaze, and when he spoke, he smiled. In the book she had received the day her mother died, there was a drawing of a prince whose mouth was shaped just like Abel's.

"Have you lived here your entire life?" His blue eyes searched hers rather than her father's.

"In Buffalo, yes." She dabbed the corners of her mouth with a napkin, giving herself time to calm her quivering heart and instruct her mind to banish all thoughts of princes and fairy tales and happily ever afters. "I was born at Sisters Hospital and have rarely had cause to go farther from home than there." She chose not to mention her father's heavy hand in regard to her schedule.

"Ah." He nodded, seemingly engrossed in her words.

"My parents bought this house when I was six," she said. "I don't remember living anywhere else."

Abel set down his fork. "How have we not met? I've been living only a few blocks from here since arriving in Buffalo. Our proximity should have brought us together."

"Even a few blocks could put thousands of people between us. Surely you do not know all five hundred thousand people who live in the City of Light, do you?"

His face dimpled. "No, I can't say that I do. But I do try to know the most important ones. I am certain had we met, I would have remembered you. And now that we are acquainted, I won't forget you."

Something inside her leaped. No one had smiled at her like that, not ever.

She was not minding this business dinner as much as she'd feared. Laura opened her mouth, ready to continue their conversation and search for a connection with this young and handsome man, only to have her father interject himself into the discussion, steering it in other directions. While he boasted about his business, Laura snuck glances at Abel Fredricks.

The time flew by—not once did it lag. His laugh, his easy conversation, all of him seemed to fill the room in an exhilarating sort of way. She knew little of him, but so far, she saw nothing that did not recommend him. He seemed to be the very embodiment of perfection, almost too perfect to be true, like a hero in a story, flawless and ready to save the day. When he left, she watched his back, wishing he'd lingered a little longer.

"Very good." Her father clapped his hands once they were alone. "Aligning our business with Abel's could cut our costs. He says he has investment opportunities the likes of which this decade hasn't seen. A good price for materials, and a few good investments, and I could put Campbell out of business and the market would be ours. We'd be too big for him to compete with."

The magic of Abel and his presence vanished at the mention of Campbell and the never-ending rivalry between the companies. She was the princess of the Bradshaw company, heir to the feud, yet she did not understand where the hatred came from. Were there not enough feet to keep both companies busy?

Regardless, she knew she was to hate Campbell and everything and anyone connected to him. And she did—she hated them. Not because of any business dealings but because Campbell's shadow seemed to touch everything. Her throat tightened. She hated how the feud had changed her life, and she hated Campbell's son, Isaac, who had once been a friend. He'd turned his back on her like everyone else when the company split. She saw his name in the society pages from time to time. He was leading his life, giving no thought to her. A sudden weariness crept over her, replacing the contentment of moments before.

"I think I'll go to my room. I've a book I wish to read." She inched away from her father.

"You're twenty-one," he said, causing her to stop her retreat. She waited, braced for whatever he would say next. He was in his late forties, with silver hair and creases near his eyes. These signs of age softened some men, but her father only grew more intimidating with each passing year. "You sit around reading books all day, digging in the flower beds, unless I happen to bring a business associate to the house."

"I paint. I play the piano. I attend church." She sighed. "I asked to attend the socials there, but you thought it unwise. You said it wouldn't do for the daughter of a factory owner to mingle with the children of our workers. Is there something else you wish me to be doing? I assure you, I am eager to fill my days with worthwhile pursuits."

He ran his finger over the rim of his glass. "I've taken care of you. Given you the best of everything."

She dared not argue. Nor mention that the role of a father was to care for his offspring, not only in material ways but also nurturing their hearts and minds. On those accounts, he'd stopped trying years ago.

He took a long, slow drink. Her father was quite the opposite of a teetotaler, and only pretended to be if his audience expected it of him. He set his glass down with more force than necessary. The amber liquid sloshed from side to side, but he gave it no mind. His eyes were fixed on her. "I intend to have Abel over again. I want you to spend as much time with him as you can. Get close to him."

"You've always preferred I not socialize . . . or at least socialize very little." Her voice was barely above a whisper. "You said only trouble would come of it. You said it was not befitting—"

"Forget all that. I didn't want you making a fool of yourself or traipsing about like the ridiculous women who do whatever they please. And I certainly couldn't have you mingling with Campbell sympathizers. It wasn't wise."

"You kept me from everyone—"

"Court Abel. Marry Abel. It's your chance to give something back to the company that has taken care of you. An alliance with him . . . it's a good match."

"And if I don't want to?" she asked, though she instantly regretted it. Abel could be her key to a different life. Running off to the jungle wasn't practical, even if it was appealing, but marrying a wealthy, handsome man . . . there were worse fates. He could be her way to liberty outside the walls of this mansion. He could be the cure to her loneliness, and Lord willing, he may even permit her control over her life. "He may not want to marry me."

"*Be* what he wants. Your mother proved to be nothing more than an actress. Certainly there is a part of her in you."

"What?" Laura's hands shook, and her knees quivered. "What did you say?"

"Go on," her father snarled, no longer the professional man he'd been through dinner. "Go read your books. But when he comes again, be ready to impress him."

When he poured himself another full glass, she left. There was more to say, but not now—not with his eyes growing blood-shot and his temper growing shorter with each sip. Now was the time to raise the white flag, keep the peace, and escape to the refuge of her room.

Mrs. Guskin, true to her word, was waiting for her with a bit of embroidery in hand. She pulled the thread up from the bottom, wrapped it around itself, and then stuck it back through the fabric and set it aside. "Cook says he was a young man?"

"Yes." Laura sat on the edge of her bed and unbuckled her shoes, buying herself time as she wiggled her feet free. "He was not at all awful. And yet . . ."

"Not awful is good, isn't it?" Mrs. Guskin left her seat in the corner and sat beside Laura on the bed, making it sway with her weight. "Tell me more."

"Do you think that love could grow between two people even if they are cajoled into being together? Father practically insisted that I impress Abel and try to woo him with my charms." She chuckled. It was laughable, the idea of her being able to entice a man like Abel Fredricks. "I know Father only wants me to court Abel for business reasons." She pressed a hand to her forehead, but it did little to steady her thoughts. "I don't know what to make of it. I dream of love, but not like this. It's a scheme, and if I were to go along with it, someday Abel would see through it. Wouldn't he?"

"I suppose real love can come about in many ways. You ought to know that. You've been reading about love for years." Mrs. Guskin put a hand on Laura's shoulder. "My John was a quiet man. We spent months doing nothing but stealing glances at each other."

"If he never talked, how did you come to love him?"

Mrs. Guskin's eyes twinkled with a youthful gleam. "I was sitting on the same blanket as him at a church picnic. He was looking at me, like he so often did, and I decided to find out what it was he was trying so hard *not* to say."

Laura laughed. Knowing her housekeeper as well as she did,

she could easily imagine Mrs. Guskin accosting the poor man and demanding he speak to her. "What happened then?"

"I may have been overly bold." She pressed her lips together, her eyes dancing. "I grabbed his hand and said, 'John Guskin, you have been staring at me for long enough. If you have something to say, say it.'"

"The poor man." Laura pulled at the pins in her hair as she listened to the tale. "Did he declare his love for you right then?"

"No, he looked at my hand on his and then turned redder than any man I've ever seen. I think I petrified him. When he finally spoke, he stuttered and tripped over his words, but with enough coaxing, he asked to court me. I suppose I cajoled him. I loved every moment with him, peeling back the layers and discovering who my quiet man was." Mrs. Guskin twirled the simple band she still wore, despite the long-ago passing of her husband. "Someday, you'll be telling your own story. I wonder whether it will begin with reminiscing about a forced business dinner, or perhaps something else."

"I do hope my story has as happy an ending as yours. It seems like all I've done is wait for something to change. I've been nothing but a dreamer."

"You've done more than wait and dream. It's been a quiet life, but you've been learning on your own. You know about animals, you're a talented artist and musician. You've kept the garden beautiful. And through it all you haven't lost your spunk. Those are good things, and the right man will see them." Mrs. Guskin stood and crossed the carpeted floor to the door. "I was able to save a dollar at the grocer. That ought to get you into the zoo a few more times. I also went to Lafayette Square—"

"You went to the library!"

"Yes, and I found a whole stack of veterinarian books and plant books. And I found us a new recipe to try. It was in a magazine, which says that everyone is talking about how good it is. Pineapple upside-down cake. With a name like that, it seems worth trying. We'll have to convince Cook to let us into her kitchen."

Laura's worries over Abel and her future faded. "Someday I'll find a way to thank you. God must have been looking out for me when he sent you."

"Coming here and working for your ornery old father . . ." Mrs. Guskin sniffled back a tear. "You don't need to thank me. You've been good for me, like the child I never had." She wiped at her eyes. "Enough of this nonsense. It's late, and we ought to be sleeping."

Laura left her spot on the bed and grabbed Mrs. Guskin's hand. She pressed her fingers around those of her motherly friend and said, "Thank you for the books and for telling me about John."

Mrs. Guskin patted her hand before leaving.

When the door closed, Laura's large room felt eerily quiet. Even Tybalt slept. So much for shouting sea slang and sorting through her tumult of feelings together. She wished Mrs. Guskin would come back and tell her more about her courtship or her years as a maid, or tell her where the library books were—anything to save her from the silence.

She sat on her window seat and looked out at the now vacant park. Was Abel her knight, come to rescue her? Questions settled all around her like dandelion seeds swirling on a breeze. Could love blossom from such beginnings? And what had her father meant when he called her mother an actress?

When no answers came and the flood of questions continued, she left the window and went to her closet, where her hatbox full of letters was hidden, and attempted to hush her racing mind with words from a friend. With great fervency, she read here a little and there a little.

> . . . *I listened to a man at the park talk of the Great War. He looked weary, but he said for freedom, he would fight again. And I wondered, if I were faced with the same decision, whether I would be so noble . . .*
>
> . . . *I came upon a bird knocked from his nest. I wished you were nearby. I feel certain you'd have known how to treat him. The poor fellow was still alive, so I climbed the tree and put him back. I hope that was the right thing to do. A small crowd watched. They all probably thought I was very foolish, climbing up a tree in my suit . . .*
>
> . . . *Do you ever feel like everyone else has a plan for your life? I keep wondering what my life would look like if I were born to a different family or in a different time. I know it's a useless thought. We have great control in this life, but not in regard to how we enter this world. But I do wonder . . .*

She leaned her head against the wall and pulled the letters to her chest. So often she, too, had wondered about such things. Then, out of nowhere, tears came. Tears for her bleak future. Tears for the love she longed for that may never come. Tears for her father, for her mother, and for herself. As a child she had friends, and the future had seemed full of possibilities. Now she had nothing but letters to turn to and orders to obey. She looked at her green dress and saw Abel's face in her mind. She knew what she had to do. It was time to escape—not with a ladder, but by trying her hand at romance.

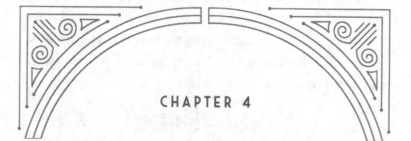

CHAPTER 4

Isaac sat near the entrance of the Albright Art Gallery. The Greek revival–inspired building with its fine columns of stone provided an ideal setting for pondering life's complexities. He should have gone home hours ago, but he'd strolled the park instead, eventually sitting on the steps of the gallery, staring out at the moonlight and wishing his letter from the tree had been longer.

He fidgeted with his pocket watch, a gift from his father on his eighteenth birthday. His father had been uncharacteristically teary eyed when he placed it in Isaac's hands. Isaac's mother stood nearby, dabbing at her own eyes, though her tears were not as shocking. She cried often.

"For you," his father had said, patting Isaac on the head before pulling a handkerchief from his pocket and blowing his nose. Isaac hadn't known how to respond. He'd been given many gifts before, but something about this watch felt different. "It was meant for your uncle."

"Uncle Morton?" Isaac brought the watch close with reverence. Uncle Morton had been like a brother to Isaac before going off to war.

"He'd want you to have it," his father said. A shadow befell his features before he stepped out of the room, leaving Isaac to read the inscription alone.

Even apart, we battle together. He read the words a thousand times, picturing his uncle on the battlefields of the Great War and his father at home. When he later inquired after the inscription, asking his father why he'd picked those words, his father had shrugged, giving him only half answers.

Isaac absently opened and closed the cover, the slight creak of the hinges providing background noise for his many jumbled thoughts. He'd spent years in school, but there had not been lectures on understanding one's father. Excelling at writing and arithmetic had not in any way helped Isaac understand why his father often had a faraway look on his face. Or why he went from one emotion to another so quickly, always landing back on ones Isaac couldn't decipher. Isaac closed the pocket watch like one would slam a door, with force. Did all sons feel confused about their fathers?

Isaac was the prince of Campbell shoes and ready to take his place as such, but his father seemed determined to treat him forever like a seventeen-year-old boy instead of a grown man.

"There's no need for you to still be here," his father had said, urging him from the factory early in the day.

"I don't mind staying—"

"Go on—you're young. Enjoy life."

And so he'd gone, rather than have the same disagreement over his role that they'd rehearsed so many times before. One in which Isaac pushed for purpose and his father encouraged him to while his time away.

Isaac stood, too restless to sit. How could he love a man who exasperated him so much? Somehow he would show his father that he was mature, responsible, and capable of knowing not only his mind but also his heart. He was tired of waiting off to the side for something to happen. His father seemed to care about only three things: Isaac having the best of everything, the factory's success, and tirelessly hating Bradshaw.

Isaac didn't mind having nice things, but that wasn't all he wanted in life. He was grateful his father worked hard and for the factory's bounty. As for the Bradshaws, he'd obediently followed his father's lead and done his best to hate them all these years. No company wanted competition, especially from former friends. He kicked at a loose rock on the path. Yes, Isaac had always been on his father's side, even agreeing to never see the Bradshaw daughter again. Why, then, did there still exist a chasm between father and son?

If only he could explain his situation in greater detail to his letter friend. Surely she would have advice for him. He'd mentioned many times the struggle to understand his father, and she had expressed her own struggle with her father. It seemed fathers today were all complicated. They blew steam about the younger generation, but they were not as easy to understand as they believed themselves to be.

If Isaac knew where she lived, he'd bang on her door and beg her to walk beside him so he could draw from her wisdom. He closed his eyes, wishing he could picture her face and hear her voice. But though he believed he knew her heart, he could not see her in his mind.

For a half hour more, he paced the park, the night air biting his cheeks and nose as he roamed. He gave it no heed, his attention now drawn to the stately homes that guarded the boundaries of the park and zoo. Dimly lit windows evidenced the lives within. Strangers—or were they? He knew one house. His gaze landed on the Bradshaw mansion. As a child and youth, he'd been there many times. In an upper room giving off a soft yellow light, the curtain pulled back, he saw the silhouette of a woman looking out at the park. It was too dark to make out her face, but he could almost believe the woman was Laura, his old childhood friend. The one he'd spent so many afternoons with before latching onto his father's hate. He raised a hand as if to wave to her before quickly pulling it back, knowing that the gesture would be traitorous. She made no indication of seeing him. It had been years since they last locked eyes or confided in each other. He'd lost her years ago. The blow was cushioned only by the comfort of his letter friend.

Where did she live? Beautiful, large houses bordered the park—was one of them hers? Would he ever know?

Tomorrow he would talk to his friend Charles about his growing frustrations and hope to garner some advice worth heeding. And then, when the moment was right, he would return to the tree and find solace in whatever words awaited him.

As expected, he was back at the tree the very next day.

Dear Letter Friend,

Isaac smiled at her greeting. He felt calmer just reading her words. She'd never called him by name—she didn't know it. But she'd created an abundance of endearments for him.

I've found myself reflecting on the many years we have spent writing to each other and all that has transpired in that time. I was only fourteen when you first found my poetry. In many ways it feels like a lifetime ago. We've grown up together, without ever meeting. No one would believe us if we told them we'd written for so long without divulging our names. It's been delightful, and comforting, knowing that you were always there. What a treasure our many letters have been.

His grin widened. The letters had been a comfort to him as well. They'd been there on the best and worst of days. When he'd been off visiting family and traveling, he'd missed them more than he'd missed his own bed. He never felt at home until he came to his tree and found a letter from her.

Can you believe that the war was not over, and prohibition was not a law, when we first wrote to each other? So much has come and gone and changed. Your words have brought me laughter and happiness, and, of course, I have loved the flowers you've tucked inside. I thank you for all of it.

I am not the same girl I was seven years ago. I have let many of my ambitions go. I used to dream of leaving the city, writing a novel, or any number of romantic notions. I suppose it is normal to realize that life is not as rosy and simple as one believes it capable of being in their youth. I clung tightly to the hope that one day my father would see me as a treasure, like he once did. I will always hope for that, but I cannot wait forever for him to delight in my happiness, or for him to encourage me to find my place in the world.

Where once I dreamed of a match built on love, I now spend my time dreaming of little more than having a home of my own away from my father's home. I want to believe that once I am free, I will again be able to dream of other pursuits, and that my path will lead me to love—even if it is a love that is fought for and earned over time. I tell you all this because I may have found a way out. It is not the key I imagined, but I am going to see if it will open the door.

He brought the page closer to his face. His pulse picked up, warning him something wasn't right. What was she saying? He saw her words, but their meaning evaded him. A "key"? A "way out"?

This all must sound rather cryptic and a little dismal. For that, I am sorry. I don't want you to ever worry about me. I have a godsend of a housekeeper for company, and my needs are all met. In those regards I fare well, but I long for something more.

One thing has me perplexed. It is a question that weighs on me. How does our friendship go on? And if it cannot, how does one say goodbye to someone they care so much for?

His breath caught in his chest. She couldn't be going away. She couldn't be, could she?

It would be unfair for us to continue writing if we become attached to another. The very thought of reaching into our tree and finding it empty makes my heart ache. I don't know how I will bear it. But it seems wrong to write to you and at the same time entertain the idea of forming an attachment elsewhere. I believe it is time for us to end our correspondence so that I might more fully live the life in front of me and you may as well.

Isaac tore his eyes from the tear-rippled paper. She'd cried while penning her parting words. She'd cried, and he had no way of comforting her. His fist clenched around the letter, wrinkling the page.

Goodbye! How could she even think to say such a thing? *Court another.* Selfishly, he'd always believed their letters would go on and on. They were to be the steady constant of his life. No matter what came, he had believed she would be there for him. They'd traveled so much of life together. How could they walk alone now? How naive, how foolish, how stupid he'd been.

He was on a wooden bench at the zoo, surrounded by a crowd. Now he wished he'd read the missive in private. Had he suspected something tragic in the letter, he would have hidden himself away with it so he could wallow in misery.

There was no brushing away reality, no matter how many times he wiped his hand across his face. Penned in ink, dried and real, she was saying goodbye.

Today he'd learned of his old chum Charles Redd's engagement to Elsie Maddox, and he'd been eager to check the tree for a letter. He'd assumed he would be reading about spring flowers and thoughts about the mayor's softness on prohibition, or perhaps a lengthy discourse on the sermon she'd heard on Sunday. He would have welcomed it all. Then he would have written her back and discussed how odd it was that everyone around him was pairing off and settling down while he was still being treated like a child. He was happy for Charles. Of course he was. Yet Charles's happiness and pending nuptials left Isaac unsettled, aware of how unattached and directionless he was. So he'd run to his tree and her waiting words—he'd come to her, like a man to his vice, hoping her words would somehow fill the hollowness in his heart.

But her letter hadn't helped. The confusion swirled faster, like a northeaster blowing out of his control. *Goodbye.* The word struck anew, bouncing around inside him, chinking away at his innards. With each thud, the hollow in his chest grew larger and larger. She couldn't say goodbye. Not after all they'd shared.

He stuffed the letter into his pocket and left the bench. A woman's eye caught his. She pursed her lips and waved. Did he know her? His mind was fuzzy, refusing to focus on anything but the possibility of *goodbye*.

He had planned to write his letter friend back while still within the gates of the zoo. But now, writing about his engaged friend or the pastry he'd had on Elmwood seemed trivial. Unimportant news would not convince her to continue writing him. How did one beg a friend to remain when they wished to go? And what if she never came back and checked the hollow of the tree? Was he too late?

Near the fox enclosure, he paused. Only one of the female fox's ears was visible, the rest hidden by mounds of dirt and grasses. He watched, waiting for something to change. Minutes passed, and nothing moved. Then the ear sank lower until it, too, was out of sight. Gone.

A lump formed in his throat, making it hard to swallow. What a fool he'd been, expecting everything to always stay the same when everything was always changing. He should have begged for her name. Begged for her presence. A new thought struck him, hard and powerful. He should have begged for a chance to court her. But like the fox now out of sight, she was going to disappear, and he would lose his dearest friend and confidant.

He'd known loss before. When Isaac was a child, his parents were always with the Bradshaws, and their daughter, Laura, had been his quiet friend. Her nose was forever in a book, but when she spoke, she was witty and intelligent. He found her intriguing and different and teased her relentlessly, loving the way she scrunched up her nose and glared at him. He believed they'd always be friends. Then the single shoe company split . . . and he lost her. One day they'd been together; the next, he'd been forbidden to see her, and he'd not fought back. He'd accepted his father's wishes, joined his side, and lived with that choice. He'd not seen that day coming, and he'd not seen this one, though reason should have warned him that someday someone so clever and thoughtful would find herself the object of a man's affections.

Blast it all. There had to be another way. His heart beat faster. An urgency filled him. There *had* to be a way to hold on. This time, he had to fight.

He left the foxes, no longer caring if they reemerged. Quick as he could, he stepped away from the crowd, pulled from his pocket the paper he'd brought, and began writing. He prayed he wasn't too late and that his words would somehow set things right.

Dear Wishing Girl,

Don't say goodbye. That can't be the right course of action. It feels terribly wrong to me, and I can't help but believe it must feel wrong to you as well. The possibility of courting another is not reason to banish a friend. Agree to meet me, and let us find a way to go on with our futures without parting ways and never knowing each other's names. You write of dreams falling away and choices being few. I understand your sentiments. My life is not what I imagined it would be. But perhaps there is another key that could unlock your cage. What if there is another choice? Would you not want to consider it?

Meet me. I'll be at the Quarry Garden in Delaware Park on Friday at noon.

I beg you, don't do something rash. Meet me first.

Yours,

The boy with the pinecones

He tucked his request in the letter tree along with the hope that in three days' time, he would no longer think of his pen friend as a nameless confidant—but as ever so much more.

CHAPTER 5

I don't understand why you've agreed to go." Mrs. Guskin *tsk*ed as she flitted about Laura's room. "It'll be a smoke-filled gathering full of men drinking bathtub gin. Everyone knows a club card is a ticket to smuggled alcohol."

"He says it's a respectable place. Besides, I can't live here forever, and no one else is calling on me."

"So you're going to dress up and put on makeup and a show for Abel so he'll help you escape, is that it?"

"I thought of running off to the jungle with Tybalt, but with no money to board a ship . . ." She brushed a piece of fluff off the shoulder of her knee-length black dress. "Abel has invited me, and Father has not only consented but as good as told me I must go." She shrugged as though it had all been an easy decision, when in fact she had wrestled with accepting the invitation and dealt with a nasty batch of nerves. But in the end, she was set on going. "There are worse men he could be aligning me with. I should consider myself lucky. At least he's not a crotchety old man."

"It is 1924. No woman should be coerced into marriage, even if the man is decent."

"What options do I have? I have no money. Women may finally be allowed to vote, but that doesn't mean all of us are free.

I have no means of sustenance without a man. I may as well be a mail-order bride, but at least with Abel, I don't have to travel on a dusty road hoping he'll meet me at the end. He's right here, and if I can convince him I'm worth looking twice at, I'm going to do it."

"What of the other man? Is he not an option?"

Laura's eyes shot up. "What other man? If you mean Tybalt, he's a bird. I intend to take him with me should I ever marry, but he can hardly be expected to earn a living."

"You're especially funny today. You know I meant the one you've been meeting at the zoo this last year. The animals, I know, intrigue you, but I always imagined there was more to your escapades." Mrs. Guskin flashed Laura a sly smile. "I figured you knew your own heart and mind. I always imagined one day you'd come home and tell me you were running off with your love."

"No, it was never like that." She sank into the chair near her dressing table, every bit of air in her chest leaving in one surprised breath. Her hand shook as she reached for her brush. No witty jokes fell off her tongue, only the truth. "I wasn't meeting a man."

"What were you doing all this time? You can only learn so much about an animal from behind a fence. I've been saving you grocery money for a year. What have you been spending it on?"

Laura tilted her head back and closed her eyes. She'd already written a goodbye. What good could come from dredging up the past now? Yet she'd wished so many times for the bravery to share her secret with someone. "You'll think it all very childish."

"It can't be more childish than talk of running off to the jungle. Tell me so I can decide for myself."

"Very well. When my mama died, Father changed, and then the shoe factory split, and he only got worse. Everything felt wrong." She swallowed and paused, trying to keep her voice from quivering. "I felt so alone. I was suffocating. You came, and for that I was grateful. But still, nothing felt right. I remember praying that something could happen. Something good."

"And . . . ?"

"I went to the park when my father was gone, and I wrote a few lines of poetry. Just innocent rambling." She exhaled, hoping Mrs. Guskin would not mock her for this truth. "I left them in a tree. Someone found them and wrote me back. We kept writing all these years. Our letter tree used to be in the park, and now it is in the zoo. For a year now I've had to pay admission to get to it."

Mrs. Guskin's spine straightened, and her face filled with motherly concern. "You've been writing a stranger?"

"He's not a stranger anymore."

"What's his name? Where does he live? Do you know about his parents?" She rattled off a string of questions, each one making the room spin faster and faster.

"I don't know his name or much about his parents," she whispered. If only she could shrink away and hide in a corner. How humiliating it was, hearing the tale aloud. The exchange of letters had always felt like a gift from above, but in this moment it all sounded trivial. "I was afraid Father would find out and become angry. I wrote in the first letter that we were not to use our names. He has simply been a friend to me. It's unconventional, but it's never been improper. Don't worry." The tears came now, streams of heartache. "I have told him that I can't write anymore. I intend to court Abel, and it wouldn't be fair—"

"Oh dear." Mrs. Guskin put a hand on her forehead. "This is not what I expected."

"You thought I was cavorting about with a man. It seems

to me a letter friend is a far lesser travesty than that." Her in-
jured pride resurfaced. "I've done nothing wrong. There's no law
against writing to a man."

"It's not that. I've never questioned your morals. I do find
it all a bit shocking, but it is also terribly sweet." Mrs. Guskin
stepped near Laura and took her hand. "If you had been meeting
a man and strolling the park with him, then you would know if
he were a better match for you than Abel. But a pen friend could
be anyone. He could be someone devious, or someone entirely
perfect for you who would never tire of your talk of animals or
expect you to wear"—she motioned toward Laura's sparkling
dress—"this. He could be a man who loves books and would buy
you a house in the country."

"I suppose that part will always remain a mystery. He's never
asked to meet me, not in seven years. I can't wait for him. If I do,
I could end up trapped here forever." She dabbed at the corners
of her eyes. This exchange accomplished nothing except to rattle
her spirits and feed the longing to write that she'd been battling
to stifle.

"You could ask to meet him, could you not?"

"I can't throw myself at a man. If it must end, I want it to end
in a way that allows us to always remember each other with fondness. We will always have the letters." Her eyes went to the closet,
toward her treasured hatbox. "Abel is here now. I can't turn my
back on him in hopes that this man might someday show romantic interest in me. Abel is the first man to want to see more of me.
Besides, he didn't just talk about business when he was over. He
spoke of other things. And Father likes him."

"Your father would like any man who has money. Don't settle
for a man you don't love to appease your father."

"I don't know him well enough to know if I love him or not. I want to believe that I could. What I do know is, if I can find a man interested in me, one who has money, converses easily, and has Father's approval, I ought to count myself lucky and do what I can to hold on to him. It may be 1924 for most women, but not for me. A man might be my only way to escape this life." She pushed away from her dressing table and smoothed her dark dress. "How do I look?"

"You look . . . like a flapper."

Laura didn't allow herself to dwell on Mrs. Guskin's forced smile. After all, she wanted to look like the other women in the club, even if that meant not recognizing herself in the mirror.

"I do want you to have a good time." Mrs. Guskin picked up a flowered hairpin and tucked it above Laura's ear.

"I will," she said, looking away from the mirror and the unfamiliar woman staring back at her.

"You've never been one to do something halfway." Mrs. Guskin put a hand to her chest. "Tell me all about it when you get home. I know I fret, but it's only because I want the best for you."

"I know you do," Laura whispered, warmed deep inside by the sincerity in Mrs. Guskin's tone. "I don't know what I would have done without you."

"Oh, pishposh. You'd have managed fine." Mrs. Guskin shied away from the praise, batting it away as she always did, as though it were undeserved. "Will you ever check for letters again?"

Laura squirmed. Already she felt the ache to reach her hand into the tree. "I don't think it would be wise. It's time for me to let that go and grab hold of something else. Moving on is the right thing to do."

"You know what's best." Mrs. Guskin patted Laura's cheek. "Trust that heart of yours, and you'll be just fine. You'll get your happy ending. I'm sure of it."

Laura's heart pounded. She could only guess if it were a cautionary beat or a confirmation as she opened the door and stepped away from her room, away from Mrs. Guskin's watchful eye, and toward Abel Fredricks.

⸺ • ⸺

Hours later, when the sun had long since gone away to shine on other lands, Laura sat on the edge of her bed, then let out an audible sigh and fell backward in a heap of exhaustion. She closed her eyes and reflected on the night, reliving each detail and calling back every feeling, every color, every smell she could.

Abel had been so dapper in his pin-striped suit and ivy cap. His Nash touring car had gleamed in the evening light, parked outside their home. She'd felt her heart skip a beat at the thought of sitting beside him in such close quarters and suggested they walk instead, claiming the evening too fine not to enjoy. Without so much as a sideways glance, he agreed, offering his arm like a suitor in a Jane Austen novel. Like a dream, they entered the club, where they were greeted by a haze of smoke and jazz music. The band played their notes quickly, and the excitement in the room increased. They slowed their tunes, and couples stepped into each other's arms. Fast or slow, she was a part of it all, never slipping out of character—she'd been a modern woman.

Abel kept her near him, smiling at her whenever their eyes met, and when the music was so loud she struggled to hear over it, he leaned in close, and his breath tickled her ear. No man had ever noticed her like he had. Even now, she felt different having had his eyes on her. She felt seen . . . and yet, had he really seen her?

She rolled to her side, still wearing her dress that carried the scent of smoke from the crowded gathering. The night had been exhilarating. Different from any night she had ever lived before. She'd talked and laughed and blended into the crowd. The dance lessons Mrs. Guskin had insisted upon were finally put to use. She had been in the arms of a man, dancing with him, the fringe on her dress swaying with every step. She'd smiled through the night, letting her red-painted lips tell the world that she was away from home and that she was brave. Even when doubt crept in, or the soft whispering in her soul told her she was a fraud, she kept smiling and playing the part of a high-class woman on Abel Fredricks's arm.

An unsettling heaviness replaced the elation. She felt the old pull to her desk, the nudge that often had her scribbling notes about her day, eager to share with someone she knew would care. Tybalt was a good listener, but after a night like she'd had, she longed to draw the scene out in words and to ask her letter friend if it had all been real or merely a grand farce.

She curled into herself, resisting the urge to run to her pen. The adrenaline slowed in her veins, no matter how hard she tried to hold on to it. The dream, like all dreams, faded, replaced by reality—and the truth was, she missed her friend already.

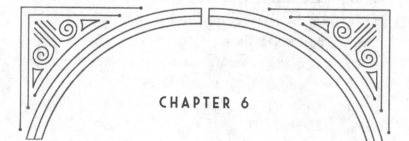

CHAPTER 6

Isaac stood beside Charles, looking down at the production floor as hundreds of workers made shoes at a rate his father had once believed impossible. Like cogs on a wheel, everyone moved about in an organized way—raw materials, machine maintenance, packaging. They made shoes in every color and style, hundreds a day. The machines clicked and whirred, proof time was passing, bringing him closer to the moment when he would at last meet the one woman who had consumed his mind and heart for years.

"Your father got the better deal when the factories split," Charles said, completely unaware of Isaac's wandering thoughts. "Bradshaw's factory isn't nearly as nice. I heard they had to make major repairs this week just to stay open."

"Good, I hope it shuts them down. It seems every time there is a new contract to negotiate, it is always Bradshaw we are trying to outbid. I wouldn't be surprised if he is trying to convince Abel Fredricks to work with him. He's probably dangling a carrot in front of Abel's nose."

"I don't know how Bradshaw manages to make as many shoes as he does. His numbers are bound to top off before long. With the new repairs, maybe they'll plummet. Besides, he's getting older, and everyone says he's a crotchety man with no one lined up to take over for him. I heard he threatens his employees. He tells them that if they so much as fraternize with a Campbell employee, he'll replace them."

"He may be stern, but we lost five employees to him last month. He's doing something to lure them."

Charles snorted. "He'll crumble one day. Campbell will come out on top of this."

"I do hope so. The man has caused enough trouble for us. If my father would let me do more, perhaps Bradshaw could be gone sooner. I could have us shipping shoes all over Europe."

"You've got everything, and your father asks you for nothing in return. I wouldn't complain so much. If I had a father insisting that I went bowling and watched the Buffalo Bisons, I would count my blessings. You're always so restless. You should enjoy it, not spend so much time trying to find work to do or trying to figure out what happened between your father and Bradshaw."

So much for Charles understanding. It wasn't that Isaac didn't appreciate leisure. But he wanted to know he played a vital role in providing for himself, and that his hands and brain were making a difference. And who wouldn't want to understand why the company he worked for had split? But he'd never made any headway. No one knew what happened, and his father wouldn't talk about it.

"Nothing wrong with a man wanting to earn his own way or understand the past," Isaac mumbled, ready to change the subject.

"Keep trying to meet with Abel. Maybe that will open the door to more work for you. I've heard people talking. They say he's a brilliant businessman. He knows all about stocks and the market, and the business he inherited is thriving."

"If he ever returns my telephone calls, I'll tell him you'd like to be his apprentice. Seems everyone is talking about him, but I can't get a moment with him." Isaac shrugged and stepped near the desk, pretending to busy himself with paperwork that didn't involve him. He shuffled a few papers around, stacking them into neat piles. Orders, shipping manifests. He paused when an unopened personal letter fell out from among the business correspondence.

"Do you know a Mary Kensington?" he asked, tempted to open the letter right there and distract himself with its contents.

"No. Probably someone wanting a custom order. It's ridiculous what some people will pay to have a pair of Campbell shoes made to their specifications." Charles moved for the door. "I'd better get back to work. Your father is keen on you loitering about, but not me. And soon I'll have a family to take care of." He puffed out his chest, the thrill of his engagement still new and exciting.

Charles left the office and returned to the production floor, leaving Isaac alone to look again at the letter before tucking it into his pocket for later. A custom order was something he could easily handle, but not right now. The hands on the clock were at last approaching noon. His time for dallying was up. The Quarry Garden beckoned him to come and see the face that went with the words.

———•———•———

Laura awoke to sunlight streaming through her window, her dark dress from the night before twisted around her and the stagnant smell of smoke clinging to her skin. She sat up, stretched, and winced when her tight muscles screamed back at her, begging her to stay in bed. Tybalt tore at his breakfast, cocking his head when she forced herself to rise. Her rumbling stomach convinced her to leave her room. In the hall, before getting to the dining room, she came upon Mrs. Guskin dusting the sconces on the wall.

"Your father was in good spirits this morning." Her hand stilled. "He said to let you sleep as late as you needed. I had no idea you'd sleep the entire morning away."

"The walk home seemed much longer than the walk to the club." She covered her mouth as she yawned. "I don't know why he cares when I wake. Abel says Father is a brilliant businessman. I should have told him I know firsthand how good he is at giving orders."

"I thought I told you to leave your sass at home." She winked. "Did you enjoy yourself?"

Laura scrunched up her nose in thought. The night before had been new and intimidating, but she'd faced it head-on. She kept up with the music and giggled at the right moments, and when Abel brought her home, he asked to see her again. The night had been a success. She nodded slowly, still unsure how to put all she felt into words.

"You're allowed to have enjoyed yourself, even if the night was your father's idea." Mrs. Guskin's gentle words comforted her.

"I thought I did . . . I think I did enjoy it." She groaned. It seemed nothing was simple. "I did enjoy it," she said with more confidence. "It was thrilling. I've never seen so many elegant women in my life, and the men were just as fine." For one second, she was back in the club again, looking around at the scores of beautiful people all laughing and smiling and free as birds with no cage. "It was like going to the theater, but rather than watching, I was part of the show."

"And Abel was the leading man?"

"He stayed beside me the entire night. He was a gentleman."

"Ah, so will you be seeing Abel again soon?"

Laura nodded, unsure why she felt any reservation over it. He'd been so kind when he brought her home. At the doorstep he put his hand on her waist, letting his touch linger as they said their farewell. Before she stepped away, he brought her a little closer and asked if he could see her again.

"I know we don't know each other well, but I'd be honored if you'd dine with me again this week," he'd said. And then he flashed his perfect grin, and her stomach filled with butterflies. She almost stepped closer and tipped her head up, like a princess to a prince. But when she went to put her hand on his arm, a small stain of dirt on her thumb caught her eye, and she wondered if he would want to kiss her if he knew she was still growing into the fashionable woman he believed her to be.

"I want to know him better," she said to Mrs. Guskin. "And I want him to know me better." Likely it was simply lack of sleep that had her confused.

"Excellent plan. Two people courting ought to ask a thousand questions of each other and spend as much time together as they can."

"He's going to take me out tomorrow night. We're going to Valentino's on Wellington Avenue. He says their Italian food is the best in all of Buffalo. That it's equal to, if not better than, Chef's on Seneca. It'll be like a true trip to Italy. What do you suppose I ought to wear?"

"You could wear your beige. It's flattering but not as ostentatious as some of your other dresses. I think you'd be comfortable in it."

"I do love that dress. I don't know why all dresses can't be so simple."

"It is a shame," Mrs. Guskin said, almost absentmindedly. Laura looked closer at Mrs. Guskin. Something was different. Their conversation was light, but there were worry lines between her brows.

"Do you think it is too soon for us to be going out again?"

"No. A smitten man should want to see you any chance he can."

"What is it then? Something is bothering you."

"You are an observant girl." Mrs. Guskin sucked in her bottom lip. She gnawed on it for a moment before saying, "Well . . . I . . . I don't know how to tell you this, but I have a confession to make."

"Did you tell my father about the letters?" Laura pressed her palm to her forehead. "Why? You know he'll be furious. It's over, it's done with. He doesn't need to know."

"It's not that. I would never—" Mrs. Guskin reached into the pocket of her apron. "I went to your tree."

"I don't understand." It was Laura's turn to stare like a dunce.

"You said it was in the part of the zoo that used to be in the park. I went early this morning and was able to find it. I was careful; I thought I might run into the zookeeper you told me about, but no one saw me. I hated the idea of you never going back, and I kept thinking about your letter friend. I worried that his response was just sitting there. I meddled, and I am sorry. I should have told you I was going."

"You went to my tree." Laura's voice was breathless. "And he wrote?"

"It did take me a bit to locate your hiding spot. Seems providential that you ever found each other in such a way. I'd say the good Lord must have had a hand in it."

"I know—it's hard to believe." Laura had often thought that a higher power must have known she needed a friend. She took the letter, holding it gingerly. "Did you read it?"

"No, though I wanted to." Mrs. Guskin picked up her dusting again. "It's your letter. Not mine to read."

The letter dangled in Laura's hand. She stared at it, afraid to open it. "I don't know what to do with it. I am going out with Abel again. I closed this door. I already said goodbye. It'll only hurt if I have to say it again."

Mrs. Guskin held out her hand. "Give it to me then, and I'll throw it in the fire for you. You can pretend you never saw it."

"No!" She drew it to her chest. "I . . . I'll take care of it."

"Thought so! Go on, enjoy it." Mrs. Guskin turned back to the sconces, but her shoulders shook. Laura retreated to her room, her treasure held tight. He'd written, and no amount of laughing from Mrs. Guskin could distract her from the fact. Like a bird in flight, her heart rose and sank, soaring high and drifting low. How could she ignore his words? But then how could she ever be done with him if his words kept coming?

She set the letter on her desk and scowled at it.

"You weren't supposed to write," she mumbled to no one. "You were supposed to go and live your life without me."

Likely this was his farewell, she reasoned. She nibbled her thumbnail as she paced from window to closet, back and forth, mulling over what to do. Her eyes continually darted to the letter.

"I suppose you are entitled to a farewell letter. I said my piece. It's only fair . . ."

More pacing. More inner wrestling. More pull to open it. More fear. More longing.

Don't be a ninny, she instructed herself, stilling her restless feet. Reading a few more words would change nothing. One more letter read did not make her unfaithful to Abel, with whom she'd shared no promises. In a swift motion she picked up the letter and settled herself on the window seat. Open curtains revealing the glistening green park below provided the backdrop for her final letter reading. It was decided. She would read his words and allow him his goodbye. And then she would stop thinking of him, and both would lead their own lives. This was the end.

No more waffling. She tore it open. Her hungry eyes raced across the page, skipping over words and freezing on others.

> *. . . Don't say goodbye. That can't be the right course of action . . .*
> *Agree to meet me, and let us find a way to go on with our futures without parting ways and never knowing each other's names . . .*
> *Meet me. I'll be at the Quarry Garden in Delaware Park on Friday at noon . . .*

He wanted to meet her. *Oh goodness.* He wanted to meet her!

"Mrs. Guskin!" She ran for the door, reacting rather than thinking. "Mrs. Guskin!"

"I'm right here. What are you fussing about?"

"I have ten minutes to get ready to go to the Quarry Garden." Her eyes found the housekeeper's. "Help me."

CHAPTER 7

Isaac stood hidden among the trees at the edge of the Quarry Garden, near the large stone bridge that crossed the rocky pond, and waited in eager anticipation. This moment, so long in coming, felt dreamlike. After years of correspondence, he and his Wishing Girl would finally be more than letter-writing friends—a moment from now, they would be face-to-face friends. He smoothed his dark hair, tugged at his jacket, and ran his hand over his freshly shaved jaw. Composure was not normally something he lacked, but in this instance, he felt entirely at a loss. Should he rush to her side, take her in his arms, and tell her how her letters had changed him from a reckless youth to a man seeking purpose? Was that too bold?

Then there was a more harrowing possibility: What if she did not come?

Of course she would come, he reasoned. She must be as curious about him as he was about her. More than curious, he was intrigued—dare he say, enamored—by her words.

This moment could only be lived once; he wanted it to go well. No, he needed it to go well. If she was considering another man, this could be his only chance to convince her that what they had shared all these years had been real. And, if they chose, it could be lasting.

At the sound of footsteps, he put a hand on a nearby rock and waited.

A woman stepped past the big boulder and into view. Was it her? His Wishing Girl. Her soft blue dress swished with each step she took. Before even seeing her face, something inside Isaac whispered, affirming that this was not a stranger but the friend of his heart. She looked to her left and right, searching. He swallowed. It was him she sought.

There she was. Standing before him. His mouth dropped open like a fool. He stared from his hiding place as he watched her walk among the Onondaga limestone. Everything about her was as beautiful as he'd imagined, and seeing her now at the Ledges felt too good to be true. She was an illusion; she had to be. But she wasn't. His confidant and friend . . . she was here, standing mere feet away from him.

He took a step closer, still unsure what he should say. One more step and he would be visible. He ought to move forward, go to her and make his presence known. But something stopped him. A gust of wind whooshed through the deep cliffed garden, blowing strands of the woman's hair across her face. She put a hand to her head, tucking the hair back in place.

A recognition he had not expected stole his breath and set alarms ringing through his mind. He looked harder. That face—he knew it, but from where? Or rather, when? He retreated a step, giving himself time to piece together where he'd seen her before.

Memories flooded back, afternoons at the Bradshaw home when his father and Stanley Bradshaw were still business partners and friends. Afternoons at this very park when the two families had shared a deep bond. Outings to the lake. Moments in the library where she kept to herself, lost in a book. And then he knew. His letter girl was not a stranger. She was the daughter of the enemy. The one person he'd been forbidden to see.

"You so much as knock on her door and you'll lose your role in this company. No traitor will ever have a piece of what I've built," his father had said when Isaac asked to say goodbye. Isaac had withdrawn his request and submitted.

And now here she was. It couldn't be. He blinked. He looked away. He tried to deny it. But there was no refuting the truth. There before him stood the quiet girl he'd known in his childhood. His heart lurched. She'd been much younger the last time he saw her. They'd been at the factory, trying on shoes together. She put on a fancy pair and wobbled around the smooth floor, claiming to dislike them. He teased her about not wanting to be a high-class woman and called her a tomboy. She took off the shoes and said that someday she'd find someone who liked her just the way she was. He'd been too caught off guard by the lump that formed in his throat to speak and say that he liked her just fine as she was. Then the moment passed, and there was never another.

Contention between their parents spiked, and boundary lines were drawn. The children joined ranks with their parents, dutifully rallying for a cause they didn't understand. He'd not seen her again; in his mind and heart she'd remained fourteen. But the Laura in front of him was only a shadow of his childhood friend. Gone were her round cheeks and impish grin. She was taller now, and lean, and her hair was darker. But even so changed, he could not deny that there before him stood Laura Bradshaw, the reclusive daughter of Stanley Bradshaw.

Laura put a hand to her heart, her eyes still searching. Isaac remained in the shadows, trying to make sense of this turn of events. How could his letter friend be Laura Bradshaw? He sighed, realizing no matter how he fought it, she was here, and in many ways, it *did* make sense.

They'd played near the letter tree many times. Pieces of the puzzle he'd ignored came together. Clues that had not meant anything filled his mind. Her wistful poetry, which had first appeared near the time the company split. Her many mentions of her busy father. The lines about her mother being dead. Her love of reading and fascination with animals.

Blast it all. He should have seen this coming. Had he been an ounce more perceptive, he could have stopped this moment from ever happening.

He raked a hand through his hair, no longer caring about it being parted and slicked. What was he to do? Go to her, make his identity known, and accept whatever reaction she had? Risk his father's threats to cut him off, not knowing how she even felt? Or use caution, protect her from any chance of word spreading that Laura Bradshaw and Isaac Campbell had shared a secret connection for years?

He waffled. If he went to her, what would she think of him? For seven years their families had hated one another. He shifted his weight, uncomfortable about the hate he himself had harbored. He clenched his fist; he needed more time. Rescinding the introduction would not be an option once he made his presence known. The best course of action was to walk away and go on as before, only without his letter friend to buoy him onward.

If only he'd never asked her to come, then he could have kept her memory untarnished, and she could have remained the mysterious woman behind the letters. She'd said her goodbye; he should have let that be enough. But even now, he felt an unwelcome pull to go to her. And he found it increasingly hard to cling to hate when there was nothing menacing about her doe-like eyes and lovely frame.

Why couldn't she have been a factory worker, a maid, or the daughter of the owner of a diner? His father would have detested the idea of a disadvantageous match, but he would have come around, especially if it meant his son's happiness. If she were any-one else—anyone but Stanley Bradshaw's daughter—she'd be in his arms already.

"The Bradshaws are conniving and manipulative. They think of nothing but themselves." His father had said as much only the day before when he'd gotten word that Stanley Bradshaw's latest shoe looked nearly identical to one of their designs.

Nothing about the lovely woman in front of him screamed conniving . . . but things were so often not as they seemed. He wished once again that he understood the true reason behind his father's anger. Never had the rift affected him so personally as it did in this moment.

Laura Bradshaw. Her name rolled through his mind like thunder booming through the night sky. He stilled his worries a moment and gazed at her heart-shaped face and innocent eyes. She was beautiful. So often when he'd read her letters, he tried to imagine what her face looked like. But his dreams were no comparison to reality. And he already knew from her letters, and his past, that she was smart and witty. Her merits seemed endless, but his father would never permit their union. He would use it as fuel to ignite the flames of loathing deeper, and Isaac could not let Laura get burned. It was only right for him to walk away, let her free herself from her cage with the other key she had found.

With a heavy heart, Isaac turned, hoping she would somehow know that his not coming was a noble act. He didn't go far. He might never be so close to her again; he could not get his legs to take him out of the park. Just outside of the Quarry Garden he sat, remorseful, pensive, and in paralyzing agony. When his uncle Morton died, Isaac had believed nothing could match the pain he felt. But this moment rivaled it.

Two torturous hours later, he saw her leave the garden. Her shoulders were stooped, her face red and streaked with tears. He turned his head away, hating himself for being the cause of her pain.

She stopped outside of the Quarry Garden, ten feet away from him. From within her handbag, she pulled out a piece of paper and scribbled a note. She put it near the garden's entrance, placed a rock on it, and walked away.

It was over.

Finished.

The final blow stole his breath and pierced his heart. Their relationship had been years in the making, and now, in an instant, everything they had built crumbled. He'd failed her—not by choice, but all the same, she'd walked away alone, with tears marring her perfect face. Because of him.

Anger burned inside, fueled by the injustice of it all. With his jaw flexed and his step clumsy, he staggered from his spot, cursing the day he found the first letter, wishing he had never come upon it. So often he'd believed their unlikely friendship an act of divine intervention, but after seeing her tears, he felt certain it was nothing but a cruel joke. He was done with jokes. There was no humor in this. Not for him.

When the ever-fervent storm of emotion turned his anger

back to sorrow, he slid to the ground, back against a giant rock, and tipped his head up to the sky. He closed his eyes, and as if the very sky were crying, rain began to fall. He did not turn from it but let it wash his face. If only the rain could wash this all away, turn it into nothing but a figment of his imagination, he'd beg for a downpour.

A cluster of women started for the garden. Umbrellas overhead, they walked straight toward him. He wasn't ready to leave, nor was he ready to face an inquisition. Reluctantly he stood, knowing gossips spreading word about Isaac Campbell crying at the park would only make matters worse. Prepared to go and revel in his sorrow somewhere else, he turned away from the garden only to remember her note. He stepped in front of the women, offering no apology, and retrieved the damp paper.

Ducking under a tree, Isaac let the canopy of leaves provide some shelter as he read.

If you find this, know that I came, and that I waited.

Each word was a dagger to his heart. And each blow went deeper.

You never came. I will choose to believe you wanted to come, but saying goodbye was simply too hard. I accept your silent goodbye and pray you lead the sort of life you have often written about.

Be safe, dear friend. Be happy.

All the air in his lungs pushed through the thin slit between his lips in one raw gush. He had disappointed her. He knew it before when he'd seen her pacing near the rocks, but now, reading her words, he felt the pain all the way to his core. How could he make it right? He clenched his fist around her words, crumpling her message into a mass of wet paper. He threw it on the ground, turned, and walked away.

There was no making it right.

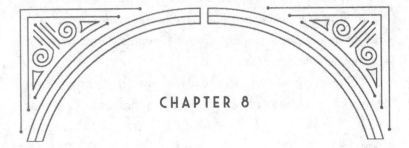

CHAPTER 8

Isaac's wet clothes clung to him, reminding him again and again of the pain in Laura's eyes. He fought against the memory, ripping off his jacket the moment he stepped inside his family's home and then throwing it over the back of a chair—only to have it slide off into a heap on the floor.

He didn't care about the mess or the letter from the office he'd tucked in his pocket. None of it mattered. Not now.

With long, swift strides, he made his way through the house, past his father's office, and up the stairs to his room, where he shed the damp shirt. He wished he could tear the memory away as easily.

A rap on his door had him groaning deeply. He didn't want to see anyone, and he certainly didn't want anyone asking if anything was amiss.

"Isaac." His mother's voice sounded through the door.

He pressed his lips into a tight line and stood still in the center of his large bedroom, as though silence would make her go away.

"Are you ill?" She jiggled the handle on his door. "I saw you rush up here. Open the door. You don't want me to be sick with worry, do you?"

"Everything is all right," he said, keeping the pain from his voice the best he could.

The handle jiggled again, more urgently now. There was no fighting it. Her concern would have her plowing through the door if he did not admit her himself. He pulled on a dry shirt and opened the door. "I'm not ill."

"Something is wrong." She looked him over, her frantic eyes assessing him the same way his father appraised a new shoe design, critically and looking for flaws. "Are you working too hard?"

"No!" His voice came out sharp and terse. "I don't do any real work. I pace around the factory. I sign a few papers. I try to make friends with Abel Fredricks but can't even do that. Nothing about my work is taxing. Father treats me like a child. He—"

"Be careful." Her tone changed from that of a fidgety woman to a loyal wife. "You sound ungrateful. Would you rather your father put you on the production floor? He could be paying you a few pennies an hour to stitch shoes together. Is that what you want?" He flinched like a rebuked child. "He wants to give you everything. Can't you see that? He wants you to enjoy your life." Her voice faltered. "Not everyone gets that."

If Isaac's frustration were not so great, his mother's display of genuine emotion may have startled him. Was she thinking of Uncle Morton and his life cut short by war? As it was, he snapped back at her, "Why did the shoe factory split? What happened between Father and Bradshaw? I've asked before, and no one has ever given me a straight answer."

It was the piece of the puzzle he needed, the one that had kept him from being able to show his face to Laura and declare himself the letter writer. Every oddity of his life, his father's incessant demands that he while away his time—all of it seemed to go back to the factory split. He was ready for the truth. "If this is to be my factory someday, then I ought to know where it came from."

"When you were young, you only wanted to play. And now you claim to want to work. Will you ever be content?"

"Why did they split?" he asked again, his voice a low growl. He wanted answers, and he wanted them now. He'd been *patient* for years, doing nothing but waiting for his chance at something. "Why does Father hate Bradshaw?"

"Bradshaw was your father's friend. For years they were as close as brothers." The creases near her eyes deepened, revealing a weariness, as though the memories were painful. "They both believed in their factory."

"I know that much. I remember the two of them laughing; they were as close as Charles and me. Something changed. What happened?"

"Bradshaw lost his way. Business was all he cared about. It became everything to him. After—when things didn't go well, it ruined him."

"I still don't understand." Isaac gritted his teeth. These weren't answers. "All Father cares about is business too. There must be more to it than that."

"Your father cares about more than the factory." She took a step into his room. "He cares about you, about me. He cares."

"That doesn't explain what happened."

"Where is this coming from? Has someone been talking about your father or his business? Has Bradshaw gotten to you somehow?"

Her desperate eyes searched his. This conversation was unnerving her, stealing from her usual lighthearted approach to life. It took effort to swallow the questions he so badly wanted answered. But Isaac had already hurt one woman he cared about today. He couldn't bear to hurt another.

"Charles is getting married," he said, deflecting and falling back into line. Playing the part of the dutiful son. Was there no way to have answers *and* familial peace? "Everyone is leading their own lives. They're buying houses, making business decisions. And I'm . . . bowling."

"You're restless." Her face softened; the worry lines relaxed. "Of course you are. With everyone marrying, you must feel eager to settle down yourself." She clasped her hands together. "We'll have a dinner party. We'll make it the talk of the town. We can fill this house with eligible women. Spend a little time with the right woman, and you'll be as happy as Charles and all the others."

He forced a smile. She was going to *fix* everything without fixing anything. They would be exactly where they were before, where they'd always been, with questions between them.

"A dinner party sounds nice," he said for her sake, hoping the conversation would end and he could wallow in his misery alone.

"I'll go right to work on it. Perhaps we can invite Abel Fredricks. I know your father wants the two of you to become better acquainted. You could kill two birds with one stone."

Isaac stepped toward his mother as though he were herding sheep, steering her for the door. "Invite whomever you like."

"It'll be a fine party. It'll be just what you need."

"I'm sure it will," he lied, feeling sick as he said it. "I'd best change and get ready for the evening."

She left, and he was again alone with his thoughts and memories. Facing a mental crossroads, he fought with his sparse list of choices. He could go after Laura, but he had nothing to offer. He had possessions in excess but no means of income outside his father's factory, and his father had told him long ago that Isaac would lose his position as future owner if he ever associated with Bradshaw. Besides, even if he went after her, when she saw his face and knew his name, she might hate him as passionately as their fathers hated each other.

What other choice was there? He could go to his mother's party and find a woman to court, settle down, and be exactly who his parents always wanted him to be. Laura had found someone else; she wasn't going to be alone, pining over him. He ought to do the same. Perhaps it was time he accepted his lot in life and stopped pretending there was something else out there for him.

The reality was that he was Isaac Campbell, son of William and Helen Campbell. A man with hours in his day to spare and a company that he would one day inherit. Women told him he was handsome and practically swooned in his presence. He ought to find a way to embrace what he had and stop dreaming about what would never be. The past made little sense to him, but did it have to make sense? His future was here, with his family, with his inherited hate for Bradshaw, and at this moment, the only demands that anyone had made of him were to befriend Abel Fredricks and attend a dinner party.

There was no other option. He would accept his fate and hope that the constant niggling desire for something else would eventually go away.

***

Laura blew her nose for the hundredth time and with a clean handkerchief wiped at her eyes. Her cheeks were extra red, and her eyes were puffy, but at least she did not look half as bedraggled as she had the day before when she'd first returned home from the Quarry Garden. The humiliation, the broken heart—she shuddered. It'd been awful.

A fresh bout of tears came the moment she let her mind wander back to the limestone setting. She wiped at the river of tears, but they continued to run in trails down her face. It seemed they were endless.

Mrs. Guskin had said nothing when Laura flew through the side door and ran for her room, but the look in Mrs. Guskin's eyes had instantly gone from a pleasant greeting to deep concern. Laura wanted arms to fall into and a shoulder to cry on, but she did not know how to voice the pain that ravaged her. He'd rejected her. He hadn't come, and though she wanted to believe he had a compelling explanation, it did not change the fact that she waited. For two hours. Her hopes had floated to the tip of the sky only to plummet whenever a man passed by without so much as stopping to greet her.

"He didn't come." She forced the sour words out of her mouth just loudly enough for Tybalt to hear. If only her bird could grow large enough that she could climb upon his back and fly away from everything. "I'm to go with Abel to dinner." She sniffled in an unladylike fashion. "Everyone leaves," she whispered through her tears, thinking of her mother's death, of her father's changed demeanor, and of her letter friend, who would remain a faceless memory. "Will Abel stay? If I am what he wants, will he stay?"

Tybalt stretched his wings out wide and pumped them twice before tucking them back by his sides.

"Laura Fredricks." She said the name aloud, wanting to love the sound of it. Wanting to believe the future held promise. This was the only key she knew of, and so she must take it. She nodded and wiped at her face once more, determined this time to be done crying over a man who hadn't shown. "Abel's handsome, and he's been kind. We will walk on the bustling streets together. I'll be on his arm, and I'll be free of this house for the evening. I'll smile and flirt, and someday he may take me away for good."

Tybalt squawked.

She slid a cracker through the cage to him. "Don't worry. I will do my best to make him fall madly in love with me, but I will only marry him if he promises to be good to you." She swallowed against the tightness in her throat. It all sounded good enough, but she knew little about making a man fall in love with her. She was quiet. She loved books and gardens and animals. She was a self-taught woman. These traits were natural. Being what Abel wanted, whatever that may be . . . she could only hope she was capable of becoming it. She would have to try. Becoming an old spinster in her father's house was not an option. Anything at all was more appealing.

"No matter what, I won't leave you." She took another cracker from the tin box. "I wouldn't do that."

By the time Abel arrived, Laura had regained her composure and thickened her resolve, though her heart was still raw.

"He's downstairs," Mrs. Guskin said. "You were right. He's a handsome man."

Mrs. Guskin had been careful to give her space and had refrained from asking too many questions. An understanding existed between them, born of mutual respect and admiration and a keen sense of timing. The questions would come later, but not until Laura was ready. For now, Mrs. Guskin offered strong, quiet support.

"Go on and have the best time you can," Mrs. Guskin said.

Laura nodded, then left the oasis of her room and descended the stairs toward Abel, who stood waiting at the bottom in a finely tailored suit. He'd put effort into his appearance. Surely it meant that this dinner mattered to him. She smiled. He cared enough to show up, and there was a chance he would care enough to stay. When he offered his arm, she took it, ready to be with someone who wanted to be with her.

"You look stunning," he said as they stepped away from her home. "I've thought of you often since we went out last. The hours between then and now felt especially long. Twice as long as normal."

"And how does time move now that you are with me?" She'd spent hours looking out her window, watching couples in the park stroll together like she now strolled with Abel. The women always laughed and clung to their companions' arms. She did her best to mimic what she'd seen.

"I hope it moves slowly, only so I can enjoy it all." He grinned, his row of white teeth catching the light of the evening sun. "Are you hoping the night drags on or rushes by?"

"I am hoping . . ." She paused, searching for the right and truthful answer. "No matter how fast it goes, I hope it takes us somewhere."

"Well, my lady, your carriage to somewhere awaits." He opened the door of his Nash touring car for her as though escorting a princess off to a ball. "We'll fill ourselves with Italian pasta and then go wherever you like."

"Thank you," she said, doing her best to still her quivering nerves. Something about being in an automobile with a man made her nervous. Perhaps it was all the newspaper articles she'd read about automobiles changing the world of courtship. "I thought we were walking."

"If we drive, then we can go somewhere else after we eat."

"You're right." She forced a smile as she slid into the seat.

Abel didn't seem to notice her jitters as they drove to the restaurant. The park, the zoo, her home—they disappeared. Even her abysmal afternoon at the Quarry Garden seemed to fade with each turn of the wheel. Like a nightmare that weakens with the rising sun, she could almost believe her hours of aimless waiting were nothing more than her imagination playing tricks on her. With every passing block, she relaxed a little more.

Abel stopped the car to wait for an old couple crossing the street. The woman had a bent back and slow shuffle. The man was tall and lean, except for his thickened waist. He walked slowly, his hand on her back.

Laura watched them with unfettered attention, loving the way they moved together in slow but perfect unison.

Abel mumbled under his breath about their slow pace. He started to drive before they were all the way across. Her heart reacted, beating faster and faster, and she gripped the handle of the door with all her might and pressed her eyes shut. Since her mother's death, she'd often felt her heart jump and lurch in fear when an automobile crept too close to someone on the street.

She tried to ignore Abel's frustration. After all, he'd not lost a parent in the way she had. She breathed easier when the couple were safely across the street. And as soon as the automobile was back up to speed, Abel smiled again.

"You must be hungry," she said.

He turned and looked at her. "I'm eager to see your reaction to the pasta. It's the best I've ever had. You'll love it."

She smiled back, forgetting the old couple and thinking only of her and Abel. This was real and important. As best she could, she engaged in conversation, nodding and smiling at all the right moments. Abel grinned back and even stretched his arm behind her like a movie star would in one of the moving pictures she'd snuck into on rare occasions with Mrs. Guskin.

Abel opened her door after parking the car, and once again she found herself on his arm, floating beside him. On the way to their table, the eyes of the other couples in the restaurant found her. She could feel their scrutiny. Did they know she felt unnatural in her short dress?

All through dinner couples whispered, but Abel paid them little notice. He smiled whenever someone caught his eye, but his attention remained fixed on her.

"Does everyone know you?" she asked as she leaned closer.

"I'm new in town, but rumors spread fast. There's talk of my investments and business, but I think it's you who has everyone looking."

"Me? But why?"

"You're the rarely seen daughter of Stanley Bradshaw, and now you have been spotted out twice with me. Can you blame them for wondering about us? They are no doubt curious how I came to be lucky enough to have such a rare beauty on my arm."

"That's silly." She felt heat race to her cheeks. "I get out . . . I go to church every Sunday. I'm not some princess trapped in a castle."

He threw her a crooked smile. "You're the daughter of an

incredibly successful factory owner. In Buffalo you may as well be a princess. And the way you've kept to yourself has only made you more intriguing. You're elusive. They can't help but wonder why."

"What do they say? They must have some explanation they believe to be true."

"Some say you still grieve your mother. Others say it's because your father has someone lined up for you to marry and doesn't want to risk you tarnishing yourself and ruining his business alliance."

She felt her jaw drop open, horrified that such talk was about her.

"Others say you keep to yourself because you've some dark family secret or that you believe yourself superior to others."

"I had no idea." She put a hand to her chest. It had never occurred to her that her quiet life was the topic of gossip. Her father must not have known either, or he surely would not have stood for such talk. *Would he?*

"Wagging tongues need something to keep them busy. And it only adds to your charm. I wouldn't worry about what others say. Besides, I'm glad to be the one who was able to lure the princess from her castle."

His words startled her. He was describing what she'd always wanted, a man eager to rescue her, to take her away. Yet the victorious smile on his face left her rattled.

He wiped a napkin over his mouth and patted his stomach. "Have you ever tasted anything so good?"

She did her best not to care that her name was on strangers' tongues or that the companion across from her looked like a man gloating after a victory. Fairy tales were full of stories of men setting off on quests for their fair maidens. And the endings were always happy. "It was delicious. You were right—I felt swept away to Italy."

"Where would you want to go now? Anywhere in the world."

Anywhere? She'd never been far. "I would go . . . to South Dakota."

He laughed. "I wasn't expecting that. I thought you'd want to see the pyramids in Egypt or something else spectacular. Why so far west?"

"My mother spent her childhood there. I remember her telling me about the quaint little town she was from. She would talk of the animals she had and of her family. I wish I could have known her then, and I would like to see the mines and the train tracks she spoke of. The way she talked about her hometown . . . it filled my imagination." Suddenly afraid her answer was wrong and far too personal, she busied herself by smoothing the napkin in her lap. "I think the pyramids would also be exciting."

"What was her name? I have only ever heard her referred to as the late Mrs. Bradshaw."

She felt her eyes grow large and her heart skip a beat. He wanted to know about her mother, the subject she'd so often been told to avoid. If she was going to trust this man, and she wanted to, she may as well begin now. "Her name was Catherine. She came to New York to go to school and become a doctor like her father, but she met my father instead."

"A love match?" His perfectly handsome grin was so big and broad that her worries from before went away.

"I believe so," she said. "Either way, she never went back to South Dakota."

"I am sorry for your loss."

When she squirmed uneasily in her seat, he stood and held out his hand. "I can't take you to South Dakota, at least not tonight, but I could take you for a stroll near the water. We could pretend it is the Mediterranean Sea."

She took his hand. If he'd asked, she may have run away with him. "Forget going west. It is the Mediterranean I very much wish to see."

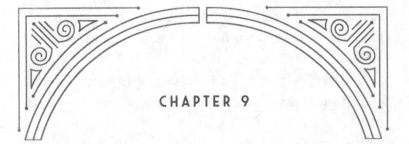

CHAPTER 9

Charles tugged at the bottom of his well-worn, too-small mohair jacket. "Do you think your mother will kick me out of your matchmaking party if I go dressed like this? I do want to be there to witness her throwing women at you."

Isaac looked up from the newspaper he'd been distracting himself with. "I think she's more worried about my lifelong happiness than she is about what you wear."

"If she could find a way to get you to wedded bliss and me to run along, I think she'd take it." Charles looked at the length of his tie. Seemingly dissatisfied, he pulled it off to tie it again.

Charles wasn't entirely wrong. Isaac's parents tolerated Charles and even acknowledged his work ethic, but they still viewed him as an employee more than a friend. Isaac himself found it strange, seeing as his father got his start by being friends with the well-known Bradshaw family.

Isaac set his paper down in a messy heap beside him. Headlines about the mayor's confrontation with the growing KKK group were more disturbing than distracting. He would never understand such evil. "I've seen my mother's guest list. She worked on it for days. And every time someone let her know they were coming, she acted as though wedding bells were already ringing. I'm surprised she hasn't taken out an advertisement in the paper letting every eligible woman in Buffalo know I am in need of a wife. Like a mother from a Jane Austen novel."

"A Jane Austen novel?" Charles balked.

Drat, he could kick himself for his careless words. All these years, he'd kept his letter writing to himself, and now when the letters were nothing more than a box of memories, he'd gone and said something so thoughtless. He reached for the newspaper again, flicked it open—not caring which page he was staring at—and hid behind it. "My parents have all sorts of books in their library."

"That doesn't explain why you've read one."

"Honestly, Charles, it's not as though the books are labeled for female readers only." He'd read them on Laura's suggestion years ago. Their letters back and forth about the Bennet family and Darcy's aloof personality had made for an excellent summer of entertainment.

Charles crossed the room and looked over the top of the paper. "They don't have a label because everyone knows they are for female readers."

"Don't women want men who are willing to share their interests? Seems to me it will be easier to carry on a conversation if I am not so far removed from what they care about."

"You might as well start wearing feathered headbands too." Charles snickered at his own joke. "They'll find you charming because you are the son of William Campbell. Say whatever you like in conversation, and they'll swoon. I never would have thought you'd be reading—"

"Everyone is allowed some mystery." He smirked. "Your tie is still too short."

Charles looked at his tie and groaned.

With Charles distracted, the itch to write a letter surfaced against Isaac's will. It was so natural, this urge to write Laura whenever an interesting thought crossed his mind. And at this moment, he very much wanted to discuss secrets, friendship, and his good-hearted mother's uncanny resemblance to the matron Bennet in *Pride and Prejudice*. In response he knew he would receive paragraphs of thoughts on the matter, all of which would be music to his ears. But such letters were not to be. The urge would simply have to be ignored.

"A few more attempts, and that tie might actually be hanging where it ought to," Isaac teased, doing all he could to stay in the present and remember his plan. Tonight he would search for a woman who spoke to his soul like Laura had.

"I should simply call it good enough. I am not the one about to be surrounded by starry-eyed women. Elsie has already seen me in far worse. All eyes will be on you."

"Don't remind me."

"Having your choice of women is not the worst trouble to have." Charles walked to the mirror and looked at his reflection. With one hand he smoothed his obstinate red hairs into place. "The party will probably be written about in the society section of the paper, and your family's popularity will grow. As if the Campbell name isn't already big enough."

"Why must you always spin my misery about in such a way that I feel guilty for feeling it? When I was determined to make sense of the business split and could not, you said it was probably easier to embrace the future of the factory without being burdened by details of the past. And now here I am wanting to complain about a roomful of women, and you're turning the conversation upside down."

"You do want to marry someday, don't you?"

"I am not opposed to marriage, only to this obsession my mother has recently developed. I am not in favor of having a bride foisted upon me. Everything Mother says and does is for the purpose of settling me down as though I can't find a wife on my own."

"She may believe that to be true. You've practically ignored the fairer sex for years." Charles laughed, likely remembering the many mischievous deeds of their youth.

"I should scour the room for the most unruly woman and see what my mother thinks of that." In truth, Isaac felt an inkling of eagerness for the night, clinging to the small hope that someone would catch his eye and help him forget about Laura. He hadn't been back to the zoo in two weeks. He'd thrown himself into the little work he had and done what he could to clear his mind, but so far, he'd not been able to stop wondering if he did the right thing when he walked away. He'd believed his act noble and necessary, but the ache inside begged to differ.

"I heard Abel is coming." Charles leaned against the wall, no longer tugging at his clothes.

"My father has told me a dozen times that this is my opportunity to befriend him."

"This evening you could find yourself a wife and a new best friend."

"Who said I have an old best friend?" he teased, grateful that Charles and Elsie would be at the party. "My mother said he was not coming with a guest. He may be my competition tonight."

"I know you're not fond of gossip, but I hear he's been seen with the same woman on his arm more than once. He may already be spoken for."

"Perhaps his mother is pushing him toward marriage too."

Charles's shoulders rose and fell. "Could be. He's a bit of a mystery. Don't you think it's strange how he arrived out of nowhere and is already a sought-after bachelor? I've been here my whole life, and no one notices me."

"Elsie did."

Charles beamed. "You're right. I don't need anyone else talking about me. I'd rather spend every evening with Elsie than go to parties and drink bathtub gin in smoky rooms. Abel can enjoy his popular bachelor status—I'm content."

To be so satisfied . . . Isaac could hardly imagine such bliss. "Not all women are as pleasant as Elsie."

"Very true. But there must be a woman out there you could tolerate." Charles, not one to sit still, paced around the bedroom. His green tie, which he still fiddled with, was a near perfect match for the dark wallpaper. He paused by the window, pushing the window coverings aside and looking out. "There are so many people in this city, and somehow we manage to find someone who stands out from the crowd. Love is an odd thing."

"I hope to share the sentiment someday." Isaac's freshly pressed white shirt felt tight in the collar. All this talk of love left him uneasy and made avoiding thoughts of Laura extra difficult. Their lives had miraculously crossed, first as children and then again in a most peculiar way, and yet they could not have a happy ending. Isaac hoped his friend's marriage proved simpler than his letter-writing venture had. "Tell me, have you decided when your wedding will be?"

"A month from now." Charles grinned. "I'd marry her today if she weren't so set on having a dress made."

Their conversation moved away from matchmaking, and

for the next half hour, Isaac let himself believe this day was like any other—filled with nothing more than two friends enjoying each other's company. But their casual conversation was cut short when his mother knocked on the door and asked Isaac to meet her in the parlor before the guests arrived.

"I suppose it's time," Charles said, a mischievous grin on his face. "Your bachelor days are about to come to an end."

Isaac's mother pulled him aside the moment he stepped into the front room and reminded him that this was not a speakeasy gathering or petting party, a ghastly term Isaac hadn't realized she knew. His reassurance that he not only had no desire to attend such parties but also would never want to tarnish her good name seemed to ease her worries.

"I'll be a perfect gentleman," he said.

"That's my boy. I've heard such terrible things about parties these days." She patted his arm and then began flitting about the room in nervous anticipation, straightening frames on the wall and arranging pillows. She stopped only at the sound of approaching footsteps.

"They're arriving," she screeched in a sharp whisper before smoothing her hair and making sure the bobble that hung from her headband was just how she wanted it.

The first to arrive were the Lowry sisters, Maude and Myra. He'd met them on several occasions. Their father owned two hotels near the waterfront and made sure everyone around him knew how successful his business ventures were. His daughters loved fur; even in the heat of a Buffalo summer, Isaac had never seen them without a skin dangling around their necks or an overly conspicuous hat perched atop their heads. Tonight they wore dresses trimmed in fur. For the sake of his well-meaning mother, he greeted them and did what he could to carry a conversation, despite knowing he would not be singling either woman out. Even as he politely welcomed the sisters, his eyes traveled to the large front door, anxious to see who would arrive next.

Abel was the twelfth guest to step over the threshold. He drew all eyes with his sweeping entry. Abel smiled, earning a sigh from Myra and an inward groan from Isaac. He hadn't known what to expect from Abel Fredricks and was determined not to judge Abel too quickly, but Isaac found himself instantly skeptical of the man and his boyish grin. Abel's fedora perfectly matched his suit. His tie was more colorful than anyone else's, which ought to have made him an oddity but seemed simply to make him shine in the crowd.

"Welcome to our home," Isaac said, sticking out his hand and playing the part of amiable host, despite his initial resistance to the man. "We're glad you could make it."

"How could I say no? It's not every day you get an invitation to a party with so many lovely guests." He dazzled the women near him with his lingering gaze before turning his attention back to Isaac. "I'm honored by your invitation. Being so new in town, it is most appreciated."

"We've been looking forward to meeting you. I tried your office several times—"

"Yes, I saw a note about that. I've been busy. I assume you want to talk business, but I hope you won't mind waiting until another time. I find I am eager to settle in and become acquainted with Buffalo and its fine citizens. You don't mind, do you?"

"Of course not," Isaac said, still trying to size Abel up. He could appreciate a man who wanted to relax and who cared about relationships. "I see you did not come with a guest."

For one split second, Abel's composure slipped. "I hope your numbers are not uneven."

"Not to worry." Isaac chided himself. Surely he could manage being civil for an evening. Perhaps a friendship with Abel was not impossible, even if it was the result of his father's insistence. "Allow me to introduce you to everyone."

Once the other guests arrived and the formality of introductions was over, the party began in earnest. Conversations took off in all corners of the large room, music played in the background thanks to the radio, and food was eaten off silver trays. Isaac, determined to engage, conversed with Ruth Bagley about the Allendale Theatre and the rise in moving pictures.

"I do wonder if the theater will remain open," he said before taking a sip of his drink. "There is something timeless about the theater."

"I don't care whether it stays or goes. I like the glamour of motion pictures." She leaned close to him. "My mother finds them scandalous, but I can't get enough of them. The older generation is so stubborn about change."

"I wonder if someday our children will feel the same about us." He winced. That had sounded presumptuous and entirely different from what he intended.

Ruth let out an airy giggle, and then her hand was on his arm. He almost flinched and pulled away, but instead he let the contact linger, hoping her touch would trigger something inside him. All night he'd been waiting and wondering if someone would make him feel something, but so far, he'd felt like a man moving blindly through the motions of life, numb. He cleared his throat. "Do you go to the theater often?"

"I go to the movies. We could go to a picture together." She batted her eyes. "There's so much happening in the city these days. Pole sitting, dance marathons, and the nightclubs. We must do it all."

Isaac eased his arm from beneath her touch under the guise of scratching his shoulder. He shifted a few inches away. "I hardly think I would find flagpole sitting entertaining."

"A man has done it for more than thirteen hours. The crowd went wild." She sighed. "There is to be another flagpole competition soon. If you are wanting to go, I could go with you and tell you how it all works."

He wasn't dim-witted. Comprehending the ins and outs of pole sitting on his own seemed reasonable. Most likely he would find attending the competition dull and an odd use of time. Dallying over his response, he sipped his drink as slowly as possible. From above the rim, he caught his mother's pleading look. He set his drink down.

"I do believe I would enjoy watching a daredevil . . . and . . ." Why was it so difficult to invite Ruth along? She was beautiful, with her blonde bob and feathered hair clip. Her family was prominent, and she seemed eager to know him. On all accounts, she was exactly the type of woman he intended to marry. He needed to throw himself into life, take a leap and see where he landed. "I'd enjoy your company."

She grabbed his hand and, in a voice three octaves higher than she'd used before, squealed, "We're going to have the best time!"

Then she left him, stepped across the room, and told her friend in a not-at-all-subtle tone that she'd be going about town with Isaac. His mother smiled victoriously, her hands clasped as if in a prayer of thanksgiving.

From the corner of his eye, Isaac saw Charles snicker. Isaac shot him a quick glare, which only made Charles laugh louder. *Let him enjoy his mirth.* The entire evening felt like a joke. There was nothing natural about a room full of carefully selected women in fancy dresses parading about his house.

As the evening moved along, he stole opportunities to observe his familiar and yet foreign setting. The room boasted a few more flowers than normal and the finest serving dishes were in use, but the paintings on the wall were the same as always. The couches were the same ones he'd sat on for years, only now they sat in different places, creating more room for the guests to mingle.

The people were new to him—not all of them, but at least half were young people he'd never met before. Children of his father's business friends. They were all dressed up for the occasion, the women with makeup and carefully coiffed hair. Abel knew no one upon arrival but had quickly made himself at home. He sat close to whichever woman was nearest him. He laughed and smiled and flirted, and twice Isaac saw him lean near a woman and whisper something in her ear that brought a blush to her cheeks. A ladies' man. Isaac felt half appalled and half jealous that this man was so at ease, so capable of making women smile and swoon.

He chided himself, wondering why he lacked such expertise with women. When they came close to him, his heart thudded uncomfortably in his chest. He felt the urge to pull back, not lean in, always afraid he'd cause a woman to believe there was something substantial between them when there wasn't. Where he fell short, Abel seemed to excel.

When the furniture was moved once again, this time to the

edge of the room, a record began playing, and soon everyone was dancing. He could dance the Turkey Trot or Charleston as well as anyone, his feet quick and agile. Finally, Isaac was truly enjoying the evening. The music was so fast, there was no time to think of letters or to wonder about his place in life. No chance to worry over which woman was in his arms.

"You're showing us all up," Abel said in between songs. "I haven't seen a fella dance like you since my last business trip to Boston."

"Elsie gets Charles and I to go to the dance halls. It passes the time."

Abel slapped him on the back. "Keep dancing with Ruth and you could have a double wedding with your friend."

"Another one is starting," Isaac said, grateful that the music made conversing difficult. "Find a partner and see if you can keep up."

"I'm no match for you." Abel grinned. He had his arm around a tall woman named Susan. "But I'll do my best."

Soon they both had women in their arms and were laughing as they danced faster and faster. Isaac looked over his partner's shoulder as he kicked up his legs for the Charleston and observed the man he was meant to befriend. Sweat beaded Abel's forehead and his cheeks were flushed, but he was smiling. Isaac still wasn't sure what to make of Abel Fredricks, but he knew one thing: he was a better dancer than this fair-haired flirt.

Late in the evening, couples sat around tables and played Parcheesi, backgammon, and checkers. The electric lights lent a soft yellow glow to the room, and the hushed conversations gave it an intimate feel. Memories of playing games with his uncle before he died and with his father before the company split came back as Isaac moved his pieces across the board. Those carefree days had come and gone all too quickly, his younger self too unaware to savor them when he had the chance. It felt good to be playing again, even if his current companion struggled to comprehend the most basic game rules. Isaac did his best to ignore his parents, who watched from the shadows as if searching for proof that this party would leave their son more content.

He moved a piece. "Your turn."

Abel was a table away, playing checkers with Myra. "If you could go anywhere, where would you go?"

Isaac tried not to eavesdrop, but it was impossible to avoid hearing the exchange.

"New York City, or to the ocean," Myra said, staring dreamy eyed at Abel. "My father promises to take me on a grand tour one day."

"I'd like to meet your father."

"You would?" She looked ready to fall into his arms.

"Yes, and spend more time with you, of course. Maybe sometime we could go to the lake. If we tried real hard, we could pretend it was the ocean."

Abel may have been spotted with the same woman more than once, but he clearly wasn't ready to be tied down. The way he held Myra's gaze was nauseating.

"I went," Isaac's partner said, forcing his attention back to the game board. "It's your turn."

Abel stood a few moments later after besting Myra. "I do believe this has been a most delightful evening. I've a full day of work tomorrow, and though I hate to go, I must. Thank you for your hospitality."

"We hope you'll come again," Isaac's father said. He had

arrived late to the party after an overly long business meeting.

"I would like that."

"Isaac is going to watch flagpole sitting with Ruth. You ought to go along," his mother chimed in. "You'd have the best time."

Abel nodded. "I'll phone, and we'll make arrangements."

"You will bring someone with you," Ruth said. "It'll be great fun going as couples."

"Of course," he said, avoiding the eyes of the many eager women in the room. "I look forward to it."

A date with Ruth, Abel, and whomever Abel brought along—apparently, his mother's matchmaking scheme had worked. It wasn't as though Isaac was a homebody. He went out with Charles and a few other chums. They even went to dances and the theater, bowling and socials, but he hadn't had eyes for anyone, and he hadn't ever gone steady, much to his mother's chagrin.

Isaac said goodbye to each guest. The women were slow to go, lingering as they put on their cloche hats and gloves. One woman was even so bold as to ask whether he intended to court only Ruth or if they were simply going out together once.

"I can't say." He opened the door, hoping she would leave it at that.

"You ought to take us all out and see who you prefer the most."

The newspapers often wrote about the liberated, modern woman. He'd never batted an eye at such sentiment, grateful women had the vote and a voice. But in this moment he felt ill-equipped to answer such boldness.

"Perhaps I will," he said, not sure where the words came from. And then he said the quickest goodbye he could and walked straight for his room, his pace swift and troubled. He was not a shy man, but over the years he'd become more thoughtful and cautious. He wanted closeness and craved a confidant, but not just anyone.

Laura and her letters were a tough act to follow. They had left him scarred. It was the only explanation, and one he knew not what to do with.

CHAPTER 10

Laura walked quietly through the halls in hopes of reaching her home's well-stocked library without having to explain herself to her father. There were times when their paths crossed and he almost seemed like the man she knew in her childhood—still ambitious, but with kinder eyes. Those moments were fleeting and rare, and over the last few months his focus had been narrow, rarely straying from devising how to best Campbell or inquiring about her relationship with Abel.

As she neared the heart of the home, her favorite room, with its floor-to-ceiling bookcases and seemingly endless volumes, her worries dimmed. Her mother had been a great lover of books, bringing home new treasures nearly every time she went out. Stepping into the magical room was like stepping into her arms. In the library, when the sunlight filtered through the curtains and spilled across the floor, she was often able to remember more than her mother's death. She could recall what life had felt like when her mother was alive.

"The contents of this room alone are worth a small fortune." A man's voice drifted into the hallway, warning Laura that the room she so dearly loved was not empty. "It could take me a couple weeks to find the right buyer, but within the month I could get you the cash you need."

Laura pressed herself against the wall in the hall, every muscle tense. With her breath trapped deep in her chest, she listened.

"Yes, well, it's not as though I have time to read all these old books anyway." She couldn't see her father, but she knew him well enough to know he was looking down, away from the walls as he betrayed his late wife. The tone, though strong, was also reluctant. "Do what you must. And as quickly as possible."

"I'll get right to work on it."

"Remember to keep this matter between us. I don't want anyone thinking Bradshaw shoes is struggling. We're not. My funds are simply tied up in equipment and stockpiles of materials. This deal won't wait for me to liquidate business assets."

"I understand. I never make assumptions about my clients' finances. If that is all, then I'll be going."

Laura wanted to linger and hear more so she could make sense of the conversation, but there was no time. Footsteps were already approaching the library door. She started to retreat, then, afraid she would be caught running away, turned back.

"Oh, Father," she said when her path and his nearly collided. "I did not expect to find you in the library."

Novels had never held his interest, or perhaps he shied away from the memories the books evoked. He preferred his study or the parlor, where he holed up with his crystal glasses and forbidden gin.

"I was showing Mr. Stevens our home. No tour would be complete without a perusal of the library."

Laura and Mr. Stevens acknowledged each other. "Mother was a fine collector of books."

"It's an impressive assembly." Mr. Stevens pushed his glasses up on his nose. "I have work waiting for me. It was a pleasure seeing the inside of the Bradshaw mansion. I'll get back to you soon."

After his brief goodbye, Laura was left alone in the dim hallway with her father. So much for avoiding him and burying her nose in a book.

"I don't believe I've met Mr. Stevens," she said.

"We were meeting about business. Nothing to concern yourself over."

She made a sweeping appraisal of her father. His brow glistened with perspiration, and his hands were fidgety. Most would overlook these small tells, but Laura knew they were sure signs that his exchange with Mr. Stevens had been upsetting.

"Is everything all right?" she asked, not expecting him to divulge much but wishing for a way to bring back the father of her childhood, the one who used to hold her hand when they walked in the park and smile when she threw bread at the ducks in the pond. The one who had grinned at his wife when she brought home a new book for the library.

His Adam's apple bobbed. "Business is trying. That's all. You're going out with Abel tonight. That's all you need to worry about. Try to hurry things up between the two of you. A formal agreement with Abel would be helpful."

Any hope of meaningful conversation vanished. Alarms sounded in her head. It was time to flee or else subject herself to hearing his demands. "We're watching someone sit on a flagpole. I don't think it'll be a romantic outing."

She looked past her father to the library, her original destination. An adventure, a romance, a book on animals—she was itching to lose herself in the written word, but instead she took a step away from the library and from her father.

"I know you have business to conduct," she said. "I didn't mean to interrupt. I'd better find Mrs. Guskin and get ready for tonight." With that she escaped, empty-handed but filled with questions she hoped her housekeeper might be able to answer.

"Mrs. Guskin," she said as soon as she spotted her. "Do you know who Mr. Stevens is?"

Mrs. Guskin looked up from the grocery list she was compiling. "I saw his name on your father's schedule, but I don't know what they were meeting about."

"They were in the library, talking about finding buyers for . . . I think for the books." Her chest hurt just saying the words. "Why would he sell them now?"

Mrs. Guskin tapped the pencil she held to her lip. "He never goes in there. I'm surprised he even remembers they exist."

Laura threw her hands to her sides, free to show her true feelings. "He can't do that. The library is the one thing that has felt like mine. I love the books." Her normal forced composure left in an instant, replaced by a fiery indignation that had long boiled just below the surface. "He knows I love them. He knows that. How could he—how could he be so awful? I've done everything he's asked, and still he'd do this? He's hateful." Her hands shook. "I can't lose them. I've already lost the letters."

Mrs. Guskin pushed back from the desk and went to Laura, wrapping motherly arms around her. Laura crumpled into the embrace.

"Oh dear," Mrs. Guskin whispered as she patted Laura's back and swayed slightly from side to side as though she held a restless infant. "We'll find a way to make things better."

Mrs. Guskin soothed her, mumbling reassuring words about a bright future and freedom. If her beloved library, and solace, was to be sold off, a piece of her limited happiness would be gone. Laura needed to break away. Staying here to watch this treasure fall apart piece by piece was too much.

"Help me," she said when the anger burned out. "I need to look beautiful tonight."

"I don't know anything about flagpole sitting," Laura said as she walked beside Abel, bound for the square. The late afternoon sun was bright in the sky, and her white chemise dress swayed with each step she took. The bustle of the crowd gave the world a dash of energy.

"I'm told it's happening all over the country." Abel looked at his watch. "In less than an hour's time, Silas McCoy will have set a new record. A band is going to be playing, and there will be dancing." He put his arm around her and eased her closer to his side as they walked.

They'd never talked about the terms of their relationship. Were they a couple or something less than that? But here they were in public, his arm around her and a million prospects ahead. "I don't care what we will be watching. I'm just glad for the excuse to be with you."

She leaned into him, trying to enjoy his closeness. He was strong and handsome. His tales of travel and flattering words tickled her senses, yet she still found it hard to be at ease in his presence. Not that she wasn't grateful. She was. With him beside her, she was free to leave the house, liberated like she'd long dreamed of being. In every logical way, Abel was exactly what she needed in her life. But years of solitude had left her unsure and tempted to cower under his touch and retreat to the isolation she knew so intimately. She fought off her insecurity, reminding herself that things at home were deteriorating. With Abel, her life could have new opportunities.

"Do you suppose there will be a large crowd?" she asked as she looked ahead through the buildings, trying to catch a glimpse of the square.

"Could be. It's Isaac and Ruth we've got to look for. They said they would meet us near the café on Clinton Street." He slowed his pace. "I did tell you we were meeting another couple, didn't I?"

She shook her head. "No. I didn't realize . . ."

"Don't worry. It's just a business connection and his date. I've got a big deal in the works. It could make all the difference for me." An older man walking toward them waved a hand in the air. Abel grabbed Laura's hand and pulled her into an alley. Everything happened so quickly, she wasn't sure what was going on.

"Abel, what are you doing?"

"I saw someone . . . just someone I knew when I lived in Baltimore." He spoke in a hushed tone as they stood in the shadows. "He was a friend of my father's. I don't want to spend all evening catching up with someone I don't care about. I want to spend it with you."

"I'm flattered. But I wouldn't have minded saying hello. I want to know more about your past." She took a step back toward the main street, but Abel stopped her. He pulled her near him and put a hand on her shoulder. It seemed an intimate gesture, but she couldn't help thinking it was merely a means of keeping her in the alley. "Don't you want to go to the flagpole sitting?"

"I do," he whispered. "Let's wait a minute, and then we'll go. We are not alone enough, and when we get in the crowd, everyone will be vying for your attention."

"I doubt that."

"I've seen how all the men stare at you. You're stunning." He looked at her with his pale blue eyes.

She swallowed, but her throat was tight. Here they were, in the shadows together. If she crept closer and ran her hand up his arm to his neck, she could lure him in and kiss him. Her father would be pleased.

A man with a cart rattled into the alley. She pulled away and forced a smile. "Let's go and watch the spectacle."

Abel nodded and followed her out of the dark alley back into the light. Twice he looked over his shoulder, and Laura tried to follow his gaze. Was it his father's friend he looked for? She couldn't make sense of the change in his countenance. Thankfully, the jovial Abel returned after he'd looked in front of and behind himself.

"How are your business deals coming along?" she asked as they made their way toward the square.

"Too many men are tight with their pocketbooks, but in time I'll earn their trust, and it'll prove profitable."

"My father can be cautious. You can't blame a man for being careful with his livelihood."

"Your father is not a problem. He is willing to invest. And he's eager to work with our raw-goods company."

"He must believe it'll give him an advantage over Campbell." She didn't understand all her father's dealings, but on this account she was confident. "I'm sure others will follow his lead. He knows most every businessman in the city."

"I'm glad of it." Abel pointed through the buildings. "Look carefully. I can see the man on the pole."

She followed his finger. Sure enough, a man sat high atop a pole on a small platform that swayed slightly in the breeze.

"I wonder," she said, her eyes never leaving the man on the pole, "how he meets his needs up there."

"I'm told he has coffee and cigarettes sent up by a pulley. And as for his other needs, he simply asks the crowd to turn away and relieves himself through a tube."

"Oh my." That was more than she wanted to imagine. "It seems awful. Why would anyone want to do such a thing?"

"Everyone needs a dream. Fools like him give the rest of us something to talk about." They stepped around an aged man with a stand full of vibrant flowers. Two steps past it, Abel stopped. "Wait here."

He dashed away from her, back to the man and his stand. A warm tingle of anticipation raced through her. Novels and fairy tales all featured men performing romantic gestures. Now it was her turn, only this wasn't a story. It was her life. Abel came back, a yellow rose in hand.

"For you," he said, holding out the perfect bloom to her. "Yellow, like the summer sun."

"It's beautiful." She brought it close and breathed deeply. "I'm told yellow flowers are a sign of friendship."

"Not this one." Abel stepped closer. His hand went to her waist. It was coming, a moment she'd dreamed of, daydreamed over, and prayed for. Not in a back alley but in the open, with nothing to be ashamed of. Her eyes wandered from the yellow flower to his lips. She stepped further into his arms, not caring that they stood under the G. Elias & Bro., Inc. sign or that automobiles roared down the street beside them. A handsome, important man was looking at her, moving closer. A petty worry crept in. *He doesn't know the real you*, it said, but she gave it no heed. Instead, she tried to remember how the women were pictured in her fairy-tale books. She did her best to gaze up invitingly.

"What does *this* yellow flower mean?" she asked. Their faces were so near each other, she needed only to press herself up on her toes and their lips would meet. She swallowed, nervous and eager at the same time. A kiss from Abel meant one step closer to freedom.

He moved a fraction of an inch closer and then another. She closed her eyes in anticipation of her first kiss and the turning of the key that would change everything. Like a fool she waited, feeling his breath on her face and his hand on her waist.

"Abel!"

His body straightened at the sound of his name, and his hands moved from her waist. Her eyes popped open as she tried to make sense of what had happened—and what had not happened. Taking a step backward, away from him, she fought her racing heart, grasping for calm in a sea of confusion. He'd nearly kissed her. Why hadn't their lips met? She looked around. Where had the voice come from?

"It's Isaac and Ruth. They're coming." Abel waved at a couple headed in their direction. "I don't know why he had to yell from so far away. He seems a peculiar fellow, but it's a good business connection for me, and it saves us from having to track them down. Let's just pretend to all be friends tonight."

"Oh," she managed to say, still trying to appear unaffected by her near kiss. "I'm happy to meet them. I don't have to pretend."

Her vision now clear, she focused on the approaching couple instead of dwelling on what might have been and how foolish she must have looked, ready to melt in his arms only to have nothing happen. The woman, Ruth, wore a red afternoon dress with a matching headband and high-buckled Campbell shoes that, for some, would have been hard to walk in. But she was all grace as she glided closer. A natural beauty, she was the type of woman who reminded Laura how out of place she was, trying to play the part of a carefree flapper. Laura looked at the man. He wore a pin-striped suit and stylish gray derby hat. His face, at first darkened by shadows, came into the light. *Oh dear.* She knew those dark brows and that handsome face.

"Abel, is that Isaac Campbell?"

"Yes," he said, waving at the incoming couple again. "I'm not going to give his family as good a deal as I'm giving your father, but I still need the connection. It's important for business that I stay out of your family's little feud."

"It's not a little feud." She drew back, nearly stumbling on the sidewalk. Her heart beat faster, wildly thumping inside her chest. She could not be seen with Isaac Campbell. If she were in the park, where there was open space and room to run, she might have fled. But here between the thick brick buildings with autos filling the streets, there was nowhere to hide. "Abel, I can't spend the evening with him. My father would never stand for it. He's fired employees for dating employees of the other factory. My being seen with Isaac could . . . it could be awful. There have been riots at the factories over less than this. You don't understand. Our parents hate each other. They go to great lengths to try to destroy the other. I can't just pretend none of that exists."

"You're not dating the man." He put a possessive arm around her. "You're dating me. And Campbell is good for *my* business."

There was no time to dwell on the implication of his words. Isaac and Ruth were drawing closer. She touched her hair and smoothed her dress. She'd not seen Isaac Campbell in years. It didn't matter what he thought of her—of course it didn't. And yet . . .

"Stop fretting. Your father needn't worry. I won't let Isaac Campbell sour our night." His arm around her waist tightened ever so slightly. "Your father wouldn't want to lose my business. Trust me, I can convince him that this doesn't matter."

How quickly the mood shifted. She'd been ready to believe herself in love and had nearly kissed Abel when he wooed her with a flower. Now she felt weak in the knees and nauseous with nowhere to turn. The enemy, Isaac Campbell, approached. The boy she'd stared at over the tops of her books, who had disappeared and joined ranks with the adversary, never looking back. He'd fled like everyone else, and she'd despised him for it. And now there he was, grown and handsome, with a beautiful woman beside him. He hadn't needed her, probably hadn't even missed her.

The sting of loss returned, and with it, her pride bristled. She stood taller, determined to face Isaac Campbell head-on and show him that she was leading an interesting and full life. She did, after all, own an exotic bird and Abel had just . . . almost kissed her. Her life wasn't entirely dull.

"Isaac Campbell," she said the moment his eyes locked on hers. "It's been a long time."

CHAPTER 11

Isaac's heart lurched. It took great effort to control his response. He reminded himself that Laura did not know he was the letter writer, nor did she know he'd seen her tears in the Quarry Garden. It was better, for both their sakes, if she never knew, and yet it proved difficult to look at her and not see the tear-streaked face from weeks ago or hear the many lines he'd memorized from her letters.

"Laura Bradshaw," he said, stretching the syllables in her name. "What a sur—"

"This is Laura Bradshaw?" Ruth interrupted. Her free hand went to her hip as she looked Laura over. She leaned closer to him and said, "Why is he with *her*? This can't be good."

"Abel's allowed to bring whomever he wishes," Isaac said, confident his voice was loud enough that Laura could hear him. He shook hands with Abel. "Good to see you again." To Laura, he nodded his head in greeting. There was so much he wanted to say, but not here in front of Ruth and Abel. In a different setting and with different company, he would find a way to assure himself she was well.

An awkward silence fell as they appraised each other. He opened his mouth, only to close it again. It was important that Ruth did not walk away with undue gossip and that Abel did not sense the depth of discomfort his choice in companionship evoked. Unsure how to proceed, Isaac looked past them at the gathering crowd in the square.

"This is unexpected, but I say we all go and see the daredevil on the stick. And get on with the night."

"I agree," Laura said. Isaac's eyes went involuntarily to the arm she had wrapped around Abel's. With palpable tension they walked in twos toward the bustling square, surrounded by hundred-foot brick buildings topped with decorative finials and hand-carved trim.

Young people filled the grassy center, some paired off and others in large clusters. With a crowd this size, going unrecognized would be difficult, though Laura might fare better than him. She was well known in name but not so well known in the flesh.

Still, chances were good that by tomorrow, there would be chin-waggers wondering what was going on with Campbell and Bradshaw. He'd have to rehearse an explanation for his father, and it would have to be good. For all these years, he'd managed not to cross paths with Laura, and now they were only five feet apart. But he knew businessmen; some could think only of the bottom line. Was Abel one of them—determined to make an extra dollar at any cost with no regard for how his choices affected others?

He'd recognized Laura instantly, the moment he caught sight of her in Abel's arms. She'd been about to kiss Abel, and Isaac had impulsively called out, knowing his greeting would draw the two apart. Ruth had blushed, embarrassed by his behavior, but he'd had to do it. Laura would undoubtedly fall in love and marry eventually, but he had no wish to witness it happen. If possible, he wanted to forever remember Laura as his childhood friend and the woman whose words had cushioned his heart through years of tumult. Laura and Abel . . . he didn't want to see that. He scowled.

Abel had been a work project, an assignment from his father, one Isaac hadn't wanted. But now it mattered. He wanted to know what sort of a man Abel Fredricks was and whether his interests in Laura were genuine, or if she was just one of many. How he'd go about learning that, though, Isaac wasn't sure. For now, he would observe.

Below the man on the pole, a jazz band played "A Little Bit of Heaven" for the crowd of onlookers. Laura was busy looking around, seemingly oblivious to the music. Ruth, who stood beside him, hummed along, swaying to the music as it played. "You will dance with me later, won't you?"

"Yes, of course," he said as they waited for the man on the pole to break his record. Laura was not far from him, but it was Abel she talked to in a hushed tone—not Isaac. Staring wasn't polite, but he found her far more intriguing than the bearded fellow who sat perched like an eagle on the small platform above them.

Charles had mentioned Abel being seen out with the same woman. Was Laura that woman? Was Abel the key on which she'd rested all her hopes? The thought of Abel Fredricks being the reason their letters ended infuriated Isaac. Since then, he'd half composed a dozen letters, each one a pathetic attempt to return things to the way they were before. He'd torn them up and put his efforts into forgetting Laura and their years of confiding in each other. But there was no forgetting her, or diverting his attention from her, when she stood so near.

In all regards, this was bad. If Abel were to marry the daughter of Bradshaw, then Isaac's mission to befriend the man and get him to work exclusively with Campbell shoes would be impossible. Worse, Abel could refuse to work with Campbell altogether. And what of Laura? Was this union truly what his thoughtful, intriguing friend wanted? Abel hadn't exactly been a rake the night of Isaac's house party, but he'd flirted with the women there, even inviting them to see him again. Could a man who loved such attention know how to care for a woman who was so tender, who loved animals and the less showy things in life?

Then again, she looked fashionable standing beside him, clinging to his arm. It'd been years since they talked in person—she could have changed. He rubbed his chest. He believed he knew her, but did he?

"You're scowling." Ruth tugged on his sleeve. "Abel should not have brought her. Her family is so wretched. And their shoes are terribly ugly."

"They aren't so different from ours," he said, still scowling, uncomfortable with the idea of Laura and Abel. "We blame them for stealing our designs, but it goes both ways."

"Stop being so nice. I hate that she is here and going to ruin our first date. We could leave them and just be together."

He shook his head. "It'd be rude to leave Abel. It's important we stay. Besides, you wanted to dance," he said, hoping she would relax and the night could pass quickly. "It's only one night."

"You must tell Abel that we will not go out with her again. We'll spread the word, and everyone will know that this was not your idea. We could even try to find a way for this to work in your family's favor." Ruth pursed her red lips and tilted her head. "What if we . . ." She paused, a roguish gleam lighting up her expression. "My uncle doesn't live far from here. He's practically a bootlegger. We could sneak off on our own, come back with a bottle, and put enough in Laura's drink that she'll make a fool of herself. She's such a naive thing, I doubt she's ever had a taste before."

Isaac shifted uneasily. Pranks directed at the Bradshaw side of the feud had often entertained him, but this didn't sit well. It seemed far more wicked to toy with Laura than it had to sneak into the Bradshaw factory and switch a few drawings. Even those old pranks had lost their appeal as he aged and better understood the consequences of his actions.

"Clever," he said. "But if we spend too much time scheming, we might miss the moment when Silas McCoy breaks the record."

"I certainly don't want to do that."

Silas McCoy sat perched on the pole high above them. "He looks like a gargoyle perched on Notre Dame."

"What is Notre Dame?" Ruth asked while waving to someone in the crowd.

"A famous cathedral. They say the gargoyles scare off evil spirits and protect churchgoers." She made no response to his bit of trivia, her attention elsewhere. In this moment of distraction, she'd likely forgotten all about Laura. But he hadn't. Laura and Abel stood a few feet away, their heads tucked near each other, engaged in conversation. The yellow flower she held twirled slowly in her fingers.

"I'm going to go and say hello to Hannah. I haven't seen her in months, and I have so much to tell her. You don't mind, do you?" Ruth asked and then left before he could reply.

Like a dunce Isaac stood staring after her. In a crowded square, he was a lone man. Where was Charles when he needed him?

He thought of moving closer to Abel and Laura. After all, the couples had come together. But their hushed chatter left him uneasy—was he the subject of their discussion? Time ticked by at an abnormally slow rate until the band silenced their instruments and the murmur of voices died down. A plump man with a megaphone stood up on a small platform.

"You are all about to witness history in the making. Silas McCoy"—he raised his voice and pointed upward—"is about to set a record. He remains firm in his resolve, swaying in the wind, but not once has he thought of coming down. This, ladies and gentlemen, is a feat, and he is conquering it. Join me in counting down, and then you will all be the first to congratulate our very own flagpole champion."

The crowd erupted in applause, hooting and hollering as though McCoy had done something truly remarkable. The man with the megaphone silenced the crowd again, and then he commanded them to count down from sixty. This time when the crowd roared, there was no stopping them.

Isaac looked away from the fool in the air and found himself once again drawn to Laura. He could only see her profile, but her lips were turned up in a smile, and she clapped with the crowd. Every part of him wanted to go to her and ask if she truly thought pole sitting an achievement worth such a fuss. But Abel's arm was around her, the possessive touch an infuriating deterrent. Ruth, meanwhile, was gone; they'd come to see this moment together, and she'd scampered off. So much for the adage that "a shared memory is twice as sweet."

Standing around twiddling his thumbs wasn't proving an adequate distraction. Needing to get away from the whispering couple, he cleared his throat, gaining their attention, and said, "I see food and drinks are being set up for the dance. I think I'll go buy Ruth something for when she comes back."

"Excellent idea. Do you want anything?" Abel asked Laura.

"Perhaps something to drink."

Abel pulled money from his pocket. "You don't mind bringing a drink back for us, do you? We would hate to lose this spot. We've such an excellent view of McCoy."

"I don't mind at all." Isaac took Abel's money and then, as slowly as he could, because he was in no hurry to return, made his way through the crowd. He stopped here and there to make small talk. Luckily, no one asked about Abel and Laura.

"There you are." Ruth's voice startled him just as he neared the refreshment table. "Wasn't the countdown spectacular?"

"Who doesn't love counting backward from sixty?"

She raised a brow, his sarcasm leaving her perplexed. "It wasn't the counting. The moment he broke the record was what I loved. Hannah and I could hardly contain our excitement. To think we were here at the perfect time to witness such a profound moment."

"It was . . . memorable, I suppose."

"I'll have to find a much more exciting event for us to attend next time. It'll be my goal for you to be utterly swept away by whatever we are witnessing."

Guilt awakened his senses. Ruth was, after all, his date for the evening. "I'm sorry. I am enjoying this outing. I was about to get drinks. Do you want to join me?"

She smiled, all signs of offense gone. "Let me carry back Abel's and Laura's. I haven't made a very good impression on them and want to make up for it."

With Ruth choosing to be more agreeable, the night might pass without incident. Isaac ordered four Vermont coolers, and soon they were each holding two glasses of sweet maple-flavored drinks. Isaac's mouth watered. Finally, here was something he could enjoy about the outing.

"I forgot to tell Hannah something," Ruth said. "If you don't mind, I'll dash over and talk for a moment and then bring Laura's and Abel's drinks."

"I can wait."

"No, go on ahead. I'll only be a moment."

Strange, he'd expected Ruth to be by his side all evening, not rushing off to see her many friends. How had his mother thought an evening like this would help him settle his unrest? Everything about it was off-putting. Walking the zoo alone would have been a better use of his time. The old guard Bill Turner usually had a piece of advice for him, or at least a listening ear, the animals were more reliable than Ruth, and the quiet there was more soothing than the hustle of the square.

When Ruth returned, she was all smiles and kindness as she handed Laura her drink and then Abel his.

"One good thing that has come from prohibition is the sudden interest in drinks with unusual flavors," Ruth said before taking a long sip of her drink. She looked at Laura. "What do you think of the maple?"

Laura, who hadn't tried her drink yet, took a sip, only to sputter. She looked up, wide eyed, before taking another sip. "It's different from anything I've had before."

"There are so many excellent drinks these days," Abel said. "Drinks are being made in every flavor. Though, I confess, I am not opposed to a little bathtub gin from time to time."

Isaac looked from Abel to Laura. She seemed oblivious to Abel's confession. Her eyes remained fixed on her glass.

With Ruth's hostilities toward Laura tamed, the four were able to have a nearly normal conversation about flavored drinks. Montclairs, juleps, and creams were among the group's favorites, though Laura had little to add to the conversation—she hadn't tried many of the new drinks. When they'd sipped away their Vermont coolers and were ready to try another of the fancy concoctions, Ruth offered to go and fetch them. Isaac reminded her she would not be able to carry them all, but she said she'd make two trips and that she wanted to talk to some of her other friends she'd seen arrive.

True to her word, Ruth made two trips, and soon they had juleps in their hands, tickling their senses while they watched couples head for the dance floor in front of the band. The sun sank lower in the sky. Silas McCoy, still up on his pole, was now half in shadows.

"Why have we not seen you at the parties?" Ruth asked after Laura had finished her second drink.

"It's my father's fault," Laura said, giggling softly. "He's always telling me what I can do and what I can't do." She yanked on Abel's arm. "But he likes Abel, so I can go and do what I want now, so long as Abel is with me."

"You know I love being with you," Abel said, looking at Laura with raised eyebrows.

Ruth shot Isaac a sideways glance and a wink. "You must have been terribly lonely. Living in that big house all alone."

Laura swayed, like the man on the pole, a little to the left and then back to the right. "I wasn't all alone. I have a bird named Tybalt. A housekeeper. And lots of books." She giggled again. "And I had a friend. We would wri—"

"Laura," Isaac interrupted her, knowing where her loose

rambling was taking her and that such talk would only leave her with regrets. Something was wrong, and he had a good guess what it was.

She looked at him with lost-kitten eyes. "What? You don't want to hear about me because I'm a Bradshaw? Because my father hates your father and now we hate each other? You want me back in that old house, too, don't you? Locked away like Rapunzel, only you don't want anyone to come for me."

Abel should have been the one jumping in, rescuing her, but he was staring off at the crowd, distracted by something else. Isaac would have followed his gaze, tried to guess what he was looking at, but Laura needed someone to save her from herself.

"Actually," he said, scrambling for a way to distract her, "I was wondering if you . . . if you wanted to dance."

CHAPTER 12

Isaac tried to avoid Ruth, but even from the corner of his eye, he could see her stiff posture and popping eyes. How dare she. He gritted his teeth, appalled but unable to do anything about Ruth until he'd somehow assured himself that Laura was home and safe and away from the crowd.

Laura wavered, staring at his hand before finally taking it. One day, likely tomorrow, he would wish he'd not acted impetuously, but for now, he only felt the warmth from her hand racing from his fingertips straight to his heart. Where only moments before he'd believed himself numb, he now felt very alive. This was the hand that had penned him countless letters, words that had changed his life and endeared her to him.

Laura walked with a clumsy tread as he led her toward the other dancers. He winced whenever she struggled for footing. Ruth, that conniving woman, and her bootlegging uncle had to have been responsible for Laura's sudden lack of balance.

"I wanted to dance with you." She stumbled closer, an uncanny boldness in her swaying step. "When we were younger, I thought someday you'd dance with me. I used to dream that we'd grow up and fall in love." She giggled, and he remembered that this was not a clearheaded Laura. "You were always teasing me, but I didn't care."

"That was a long time ago." He looked past her as he steadied her. Questioning eyes met his, but he gave them no heed. Laura's unsteady gait worried him. Her normal restraint was gone, and if she wasn't careful, she'd hurt herself with her words, or worse, do something that would haunt her.

"Why aren't we dancing? Is it because I'm not as beautiful as Ruth? I tried to be beautiful. I wanted Abel to think I was." She stared up into his face, an unmistakable yearning in her gaze. His heart pitched. He'd never seen a woman as beautiful as Laura. At the Quarry Garden he'd wanted to take her in his arms, and he'd dreamed of doing so ever since. But not like this, with a crowd and Laura acting against her own consent.

"This dance floor ain't that big," someone near them said. "If you're not dancing, get off and make room."

It was the nudge Isaac needed. He put one hand on her waist and took one of her hands in his other. She responded. Her free hand went to his shoulder as she stepped closer.

"Listen to me, Laura," he said, lowering his head near her ear. "We need to get you home. You don't know what you're doing."

"I do. I'm not stupid. I'm dancing with you," she whispered, her eyes suddenly filling with tears. He'd never known her to be so changeable. How desperately he wanted to carry her away and hold her close as she fought off the effects of the liquor. Never had he felt the desire to care for another more strongly than he did now, with her in his arms. "You left. Everyone did. You hate me, I know you do, and I'm supposed to hate you too."

"It wasn't like that." He looked away. Her tears threatened to pierce the weak locks that kept him from telling her everything. For her safety, he couldn't budge. He shouldn't even be dancing with her. Then again, how could this be wrong when it felt so right? He'd danced before, many times, but no woman had ever felt so perfect in his arms. He took a deep breath—he had to think clearly. "My father wouldn't let me see you. Something happened between our fathers and we just . . . we were torn apart. Do you know what happened between them?"

She shook her head with more force than necessary. "No. My father wouldn't tell me anything. Well, he tells me to date Abel and to hate you." She covered her mouth, briefly aware of her slightly slurred words. "Don't tell Abel. I want to like him—it's only that dating him wasn't my idea. But love can grow . . . It can. Mrs. Guskin even said it could. And then I can get away."

"I'm sorry," he said when no other words would come. He'd spent so many years angry with Bradshaw—for reasons he didn't understand—that he hadn't thought about what she'd endured. Only when he connected her to the heartfelt letters did he begin to understand that life for Laura had not matched his carefree experience in the years following the company split.

She sniffled, making no attempts at silencing her emotions. "I don't know why I'm crying so much. I don't know what's wrong with me." She pressed a hand to her forehead. Her appearance grew more disheveled with each passing moment. Tears streaked her face, loose hairs fell free, and the rose she'd held so dearly had fallen to the ground. "It's not so bad. I have a bird. He's awful, but I love him."

"A bird," he said, stalling as he looked for the quickest way out of the square. With each circle she grew more awkward on her feet.

"His name's Tybalt from Shakespeare. Have you read Shakespeare? It's a tragedy, two people are in love, but their families won't let them be together." Her garbled words grew more difficult to decipher. "They both die."

"It's only a story." He pulled her a little closer, knowing this moment would be short lived. All the while, his mind raced. He could tell Abel and Ruth that Laura was sick, that he had to take her home, but that excuse wouldn't make sense. Why him and not Abel? He looked over his shoulder. Abel and Ruth were talking. Isaac still had time, but not much. He could take her home, then come back and make an excuse. Even if they doubted him, it would be too late for them to intervene.

"Laura, I'm going to take you home."

"But I like dancing with you."

"Someday we'll dance again." He shouldn't have said it, but he wanted it to be true. Someday, somehow, he wanted her back in his arms, not because she was drunk but because she wanted to be near him. A dream, that's all it was, but what was life with no dreams? He loosened his grip on her. "Let's go quickly. You can tell me about your bird, or whatever you like, while we walk, but we need to go now."

"I had one friend," she mumbled as she walked by his side. "He was there for a long time, but he's gone."

"One friend?"

With the back of her hand, she wiped at her nose. "You don't want to hear about him."

"Why not?"

"He's a better man than you. He's not full of hate. He's a good man." She nearly stumbled. Her balance was precarious.

"But he's gone," Isaac said, wanting to defend himself against . . . himself.

"He didn't want to go. I know he didn't want to." More tears.

He quickened their pace—this was more than he could bear. They were in the heart of the square now, weaving through the crowd.

"He wanted to stay," he said. "I'm sure he did."

"Isaac—" The color left her face as she stopped their forward motion. She let go of his arm. Her hand went to her stomach. "I'm going to be sick."

There was no escape. He'd tried to save her, but all he'd done was lead her to the center of the large crowd, where hundreds of eyes could watch as the contents of both her drinks resurfaced. Those dancing near her stopped. And then those just out of view turned, curious about the commotion. Soon the square was filled with silent onlookers. An agonizing groan pierced the air and hurt his heart. If only he could scoop Laura up and carry her away. She teetered backward. He tried to reach for her, but she'd moved too far from him. She went to her knees, hands still on her stomach, and then it was Ruth's voice he heard, loud enough for all curious ears to hear.

"Is that Laura Bradshaw, drunk in public?" She towered above Laura, the faintest smirk bringing up the corners of her red lips.

"Ruth," he said, but she ignored him. "Don't do this."

Whispers began all around him. A dull murmur filled the square.

"What are you trying to do?" Ruth said, her words not only meant for Laura. "If you can't control yourself, why even come out? Everyone here came for a good time." Ruth turned to Isaac and pulled on his arm, but he brushed her off. She stayed by his side, smiling for the crowd as though nothing were amiss between them. Then she leaned closer. He pulled away, but not so far that he couldn't hear her say, "I know you hate the Bradshaws. This will keep her away from you for a good long time."

Isaac made no response. He took one step past Ruth, ready to go to Laura's aid, but stopped in his tracks when he found Laura's eyes and saw her glaring at him. "Go away. I don't need help from you. I should have known . . . Go be with Ruth."

"Let me help you," he said. She pushed at her hair that had fallen loose, but it only fell askew again.

"No." She stood on wobbly legs. "Go on." She waved her hand at the crowd. Tears ran down her face. Her expression was that of a helpless animal, cornered but not ready to give up the fight. "There's nothing to see here."

Abel stepped past Isaac, playing the hero. He took her arm and, in his jaunty way, silenced the crowd. "Seems you and I had better call it a night," he said, earning a hearty laugh from onlookers. "I suppose seeing McCoy up there on the pole could make anyone a bit tipsy. Let's go."

Abel turned Laura away from the crowd, and from Isaac.

⸻

Laura stumbled through the front door, eager to toss herself onto her bed, close her eyes, and pretend the entire night away. The details blurred together, giving her hope that it was all a bad dream. Isaac Campbell taking her in his arms, her retching in front of everyone, and Abel bringing her home in near silence—none of it could possibly be real. The toe of her perfectly polished Bradshaw shoe caught the edge of the floral rug, and she landed facedown in a heap. With her pounding head on the floor, she found it much more difficult to deny reality. This night had been no bad dream. It was all wretchedly, horribly, awfully real.

"Laura, is that you?" Mrs. Guskin called from the dining room. "You're home early."

Laura pushed herself up off the floor. "I'm home and about to go to my room."

Mrs. Guskin's feet shuffled closer. "I thought you'd be out until all hours, dancing and enjoying this fine weather."

Had the weather been fine? She could hardly remember. In this moment she felt clammy and hot. What she wouldn't give for a gust of winter weather to blow through and cool her off. "It wasn't what I expected."

Mrs. Guskin popped from around the corner. "Oh dear."

She stepped past Laura to the radio that Laura hadn't realized was on, turned it off, and then took Laura by the arm. "Let's get you upstairs before your father sees you like this."

"I was out with Abel. Father told me to go. It doesn't matter if he sees me." She stepped away from Mrs. Guskin's touch and sat in a wingback chair. "I was where he wanted, and then I got sick. He shouldn't punish me for being sick . . . That's mean."

"Yes, well, you were drinking, and I am certain he will punish you for that."

"I only had two of the fancy drinks they had there. Prohibition drinks—that's what they called them." Why wouldn't her head stop pounding? She closed her eyes, trying to block out the electric lights that seemed to be making matters worse. "I saw Isaac Campbell. He was there with a woman in a red dress. I don't think I like red dresses."

"Did he do this to you?"

"We danced, and then I vomited." She leaned forward and,

with her elbows on her knees, buried her head in her hands. "I don't know what I said to him. He's probably dancing with the girl in the red dress right now." She moaned. Her pounding head and thoughts of Isaac with the girl in red were enough to make her nauseated again. He'd gotten through their family feud unscathed. He'd come out dashing and with women eager for his arm. It wasn't fair.

"Come on." Mrs. Guskin pulled on her arm. "Let's clean you up. You can tell me all about it while we get you ready for bed. No dallying in here, moaning about life. There will be time for that later."

"I wasn't moaning. I don't care if he's with her, or if he's kissing her. I don't care at all." Laura stumbled to her feet.

"I had no idea you harbored such feelings for Isaac Campbell."

"I don't. I hate him, just like I'm supposed to."

"Uh-huh."

Why didn't Mrs. Guskin sound convinced? Laura wanted to ask, but the stairs were in front of her, and there were so many. With Mrs. Guskin beside her, she managed to make her way up. At the top of the stairs, she went right for her room and her bed, only to have Mrs. Guskin stop her. "Sit down. I'll help you wash up. And while I'm doing it, I want you to tell me everything you remember from the night."

As best she could, Laura recounted the evening, sparing only the details she could no longer remember. Mrs. Guskin gasped several times but did not interrupt.

"I don't know what happened to the flower Abel gave me. I must have left it. And he hardly said a word on the way home. He was so somber, and when he said goodbye, he didn't even try to kiss me. I was sure he would because he nearly did earlier, only mean old Isaac interrupted us. It's his fault I didn't get kissed tonight."

"Can't blame the man for not wanting to kiss you on the way home. You certainly aren't smelling your best." Mrs. Guskin rubbed her hands on her brown skirt. "You're saying you drank what everyone else did, but then later you were accused of being intoxicated?"

"The woman in red, Ruth or something like that, was with Isaac, and she brought me my drinks. I can't remember the names of them, but one was maple and the other was . . . they said it was citrus, but it tasted different. And then when I was sick, Ruth said I was drunk. The way she looked at me . . . and Isaac, he was there. He must have been behind it all. They came to the square together." She ran her hand back and forth on the arm of the chair. "Is this what it feels like to be drunk?"

"I can't rightly say."

"What do I do now?"

"Your father needs to know this was not your fault, but Campbell's, and he needs to learn about it here first. The papers and gossips won't get the story right."

The thought of telling her father made Laura's already sick stomach twist into a tighter knot. She left her chair and made her way to the bed, tucking her pillow under her head and curling up on her side. "I can't believe Isaac would trick me like this. He used to be funny, but he was never mean." She buried her face in her pillow. "It's so embarrassing. More people were looking at me than were looking at the man on the pole."

Mrs. Guskin came to the bed and rubbed Laura's back. "People will forget. Don't you worry. And by morning you'll feel like yourself again. It'll be easier to make sense of all this then."

"What if Abel doesn't want me anymore? Father told me to *be* what he wanted. No one wants what I was tonight. And then I'll be stuck here forever, and I won't even have the books."

"Let's worry about that later." Mrs. Guskin's soft, motherly touch soothed some of Laura's worry. "Rest up. Tomorrow you can decide what to say to Abel and make a plan to get back at Isaac, if that's what you wish."

"I thought you hated the feud as much as I did," Laura said into her pillow.

"I do hate it, but I won't stand for someone sabotaging you like that." She kissed Laura on the cheek. "In the morning I'll bring you a hearty breakfast that will chase off whatever headache you have."

"And Father?"

"I'll talk to him in the morning for you. Now get some rest." Mrs. Guskin stood and stepped away from Laura, leaving her to sleep. But sleep did not come easily. Her head wouldn't stop throbbing, and every time she closed her eyes, she saw herself in the middle of the crowd, and the sour taste of bile returned. The voices, the murmurs, and the laughter—like demons, they tormented her.

Silently, she pleaded that somehow tomorrow would be a better day. Then, when sleep still evaded her, she went to her desk and wrote. She didn't care that she'd already said goodbye. Tonight, she needed a friend. So she ran back to the man who had left her at the Quarry Garden and chose to believe he still cared.

Dear Friend,

I stood in a crowd tonight, and I felt completely alone . . .

CHAPTER 13

Excuse me." One of the maids tapped on the doorframe of the study where Isaac sat scowling at the wall. He'd been melancholy since returning home the night before, his heart and mind heavy with regrets. He'd handled everything poorly.

A young maid, new to the household, stood in the doorway. She'd come only weeks ago, and though he made a point of getting to know the staff, he'd not yet learned this woman's name.

"I've come to apologize." Her cheeks went from pale to crimson. "I was the one who cleaned your wet jacket a couple weeks back."

His wet jacket . . . from the day in the rain at the Quarry Garden?

"I found a letter in your pocket and set it aside. I meant to bring it to you right away, but I forgot." She stepped closer, her hand shaking as she reached into her apron pocket and brought out the letter he had assumed was for a custom order. It was poor business to put off responding for so long. There would be one unhappy customer out there, but no real harm done. Shoes were trivial things, at least compared to the more important matters that plagued him.

"Not to worry." He took the letter and set it on the large oak desk in front of him. "It was nothing important."

She brightened. "I'm glad. I've been worrying since I saw it again this morning."

"I'll take care of it." Before she left, Isaac asked, "Has my father seen the paper yet?"

"I don't think so. I heard he was feeling unwell and resting late this morning." She quickened her words. "But don't worry. I'm told it's nothing serious."

"I'll stop in and see him when I can. Will you have someone send the paper?"

She nodded. "I'll bring it myself."

She left, and the water-stained letter from Mary Kensington caught his eye. He touched the rippled paper, remembering how the rain had pounded against him while he waited for Laura to leave the Quarry Garden. So much had changed that day. Fulfilling a custom order today held little appeal, but he couldn't sit around all day, bemoaning the night before. And already this customer had waited long enough.

With a silver letter opener, he tore through the envelope and removed a single sheet of paper. He'd not read a letter in weeks, and though this one bore a different signature than the stack of letters he had saved in his closet, he felt a familiar inkling of anticipation as he began reading.

Dear Mr. William Campbell,

Someday, business correspondence would be addressed to Isaac rather than to his father. Custom orders were often passed along to Isaac or another employee; he'd handle this himself, and his father would never have to know that the request was neglected for so long. He read on, grateful now that he had something to think about other than Ruth's cruel prank or Laura's pained eyes.

My name is Mary Kensington, and I am searching for the relatives of Morton Campbell.

Isaac drew back. Morton had been his uncle—his carefree, always-up-for-a-game-of-chess uncle who left for the Great War years ago and never returned. Isaac remembered Uncle Morton, with his dark Campbell hair, dimpled grin, and playful disposition. Isaac looked away, the sudden rush of emotion unexpected. It'd been years since he shed tears over his uncle, but now, seeing Morton's name in ink, he was filled with yearning for the man he'd idolized as a boy.

"*I've always wanted to go overseas, but I never thought it would be like this . . .*" Uncle Morton waved with an army bag over his shoulder. "*Don't worry about me. It'll be an adventure.*"

Isaac closed his eyes, and for the first time in years, he saw his uncle's face clearly.

"*What's the first thing we should do when I return?*"

The much younger Isaac had said the first thing that popped into his mind. "*We should sneak into the zoo and take a ride on Big Frank.*"

Uncle Morton's hearty, deep laugh was the last sound Isaac ever heard from him. After that had come only letters, then silence. The whole world seemed to forget Morton Campbell had ever existed . . . until now. With all his might, he fought to hold on to the sound of his uncle's laughter and the warmth that filled him because of it.

Isaac brought the letter closer and read on. The water had

damaged the rest of the missive, leaving only a few words readable.

He deciphered what he could.

> *I found a box in my attic . . . letters . . .*
>
> *And if you . . . know . . . Bradshaws, or Isaac Campbell, I have . . . them as well.*
>
> *I am sorry that I did not find . . . My sister was a nurse in the war. . . . spent her time in France with our boys . . . home ill . . . No one ever knew what was wrong. She never recovered. . . . never looked through her belongings until now. I pray . . . bring comfort and not additional grief.*
>
> *If you are not the William Campbell who is related to Morton Campbell . . . inform me and I will continue my search. I feel compelled to find . . . My sister would have wanted it so.*
>
> *Send your correspondence to the following address.*

He held the letter to the light. He bent near it. He tried everything he could, but despite his efforts, there was no making sense of it. Bradshaw's name was there, clear and begging for an explanation. There was the promise of letters, but what they contained, he could only guess.

He tried to remember the sequence of events that led to his uncle's death. Uncle Morton was drafted, and Isaac overheard him begging for a way to avoid the war, but he'd ended up going. The family had bid him farewell. Isaac rubbed his chin. After Morton left, things deteriorated at home. He'd never thought of it before, but could Morton's departure have contributed to the stress at the company? He wasn't sure. What he did know was that it had been a season of great loss, one painful event after another.

He'd long believed that the older he got, the more the world would make sense. But it seemed the opposite was happening. Each day he felt less confident in his understanding of the past and less sure of his future.

The address inside the letter was impossible to read, and it had not been written on the outside of the envelope. He groaned. Mary Kensington's name, and the fact that her sister was a nurse, seemed to be the only clues that could help him track her down—and they weren't much. Isaac drummed his fingers on the desk, the tips of his nails tapping an anxious rhythm.

The notice that Uncle Morton died came years ago, formal and with few details. But all the important information had been there—killed by the enemy. Nothing else mattered. Morton was gone, and there was no bringing him home. But now there was more. A piece of Morton was still out there, and Isaac wanted it.

He tapped faster, more frenzied. Would his father invest the time or money needed to find Mary Kensington? There was a chance he would, but the higher likelihood was that he would simply tear up this letter and tell everyone to leave Uncle Morton's death alone.

"Here's the paper." The maid slid it across the desk, startling Isaac from his unsettled thoughts. "I meant to come back sooner. Mrs. Kline stopped me. She had a question about the vases your mother plans to put on the table at dinner."

"At dinner?"

"She's invited Ruth and her family over for dinner. I thought you knew. Everyone is talking about what a fine couple the two of you make."

"We are *not* a couple. I had no knowledge of this." He folded the letter and put it in his jacket pocket, undecided about how to handle the unexpected correspondence. "Tell my mother I won't be at dinner tonight."

"But—"

"Please."

She nodded.

He pushed away from the desk, grabbed the paper, left the room, and walked straight out of the house to read the society page by himself.

Laura sat with her back against the letter tree. She'd come hours ago, leaving the very moment her father stormed from the house. Dear Mrs. Guskin had fought Laura's battle for her, for which she was incredibly grateful. But the kindness had made Laura all too aware of her own weakness.

"It wasn't her fault," Mrs. Guskin said loudly enough for Laura, who stood in the hallway, to hear. "She ran into the Campbell boy. He must have had a hand in this."

"The papers aren't saying that," her father raged. Paper rustled, and then she heard him read. "'Stanley Bradshaw's rarely seen daughter lost her composure in front of the large crowd of spectators. It's believed that despite prohibition, she chose to consume alcohol at the square to the point of inebriation.' It's right there for everyone to see, and no mention of Campbell."

"They got it wrong." Mrs. Guskin kept her voice strong. "You know her better than that. She's never been one to lose control of herself. It's a cruel joke."

"I thought I knew her mother too. And she proved disloyal."

Laura covered her mouth. What was he saying? Had her

mother, who'd married for love and given up her dreams of returning to South Dakota, lost her way? It couldn't be.

"You can't blame her for her mother's choices, whatever they may have been."

Laura pressed closer, not wanting to miss a single word of the conversation. Eavesdropping had never held much appeal to her, but as of late, it had become a necessity. Her father's reaction now would determine how tightly her cage was locked.

"She looks just like her," he said in a voice that lacked his normal authority. There was a heaviness behind his words. "If anyone calls the house, tell them that this is all hogwash. I have to be at the factory—I don't have time for this nonsense." He slapped his hand against the desk. The sound vibrated through the atmosphere. Laura could only hope that he did not dismiss Mrs. Guskin for forgetting her place. No employee should talk to their employer in such a way, but Mrs. Guskin was not like any other employee. She was as good as, or better than, the fairy godmother in the childhood story Laura had read. "I can't have this nonsense affecting business. I should have kept her away from society. She's too naive."

"You're wrong. She's smart."

"Don't talk to me as though you know more about my daughter than I do."

"It would not be a bold assumption for me to say that I do know her better. I know she has dreams. She's clever and caring. She is going to make a life for herself. And if you aren't careful, she'll leave this house and never come back."

"She'll stay inside this house—"

"You need to get her out again, and quickly. You can't have her hiding away as though she is guilty of something she didn't do. The city is curious about her now. She needs to show them she is a fine lady. You need to stand by her."

"That's for me to decide." His voice became deeper and gruffer. "Blast it all. I needed her to impress Abel, and now this. I've asked nothing of her . . ."

"I would hope Abel is capable of seeing past one social blunder. Surely if he is interested in her, he will not let someone else's cruel deed sway him."

Abel had hardly looked at her as he led her from the crowd. He'd smiled at the onlookers, even laughed it off, but to her he'd been indifferent. The hand he'd put on the small of her back had been stiff and unnerving.

If she were any other woman, her mishap would soon be forgotten. But Laura was not another woman. She was a part of the great feud, and everyone was always watching, eager to know what would happen next between Bradshaw and Campbell. Last night, the coals of curiosity were stirred. Only this time, the people's curiosity wasn't over shoe designs, or profit margins, or who could sway the loyalties of the other's employees. It was her they'd focused their attention on.

"She tarnished our family name."

Laura gnawed on her cheek. How desperately she wanted to remind him of the many times he'd lost his temper, drunk too much, or made a poor business decision. But fighting with her father was a losing battle. If he believed her guilty, swaying him would be nearly impossible.

"Abel is a savvy man. He's not going to marry a woman who will prove a liability," her father said. "I only hope he will stay around long enough for me to close my deal."

"Campbell did this. It is his fault, not hers." Mrs. Guskin

stood her ground. "Abel and everyone else should know that. Campbell sabotaged the poor girl."

Laura knew her father was never one to admit when someone else was right, so she only hoped he would change the subject and let the matter go.

"I'll be gone all day," she heard him say. The sound of his chair sliding across the wooden floor accompanied his words. "Do what you must here."

"I'll take good care of her."

"I don't care what you do—just don't let her embarrass us again."

"Of course not."

Careful to make her stockinged feet silent, Laura stepped away from the conversation and back to her room, where Tybalt squawked a greeting.

"I think the jungle may have been a better choice," she said to her red-feathered friend. "Last night may have ruined my chances with Abel. But I did get mentioned by name on the society page. I ought to tear it out and frame it. What do you think—shall I hang it by the window or above my bed?"

She let out a terse chuckle, but it lacked any real humor. No matter how she tried, she could not make light of the night before. No matter how shrewd her imagination, this reality was beyond its reach. Last night had been awful. There was no pretending it away.

On her desk lay the letter she'd written the night before. Folded and waiting for her to decide what to do with it.

"What if I took it to the tree? It would be nice to have someone listen. He may never write back . . . but if he did . . . maybe he'd have advice," she said, more to herself than to Tybalt.

"Maybe he could even think of a way for me to humiliate Isaac like he humiliated me. There's no harm in asking a friend for help," she reasoned. "Besides, there may never be a promise between Abel and I. He may never even call on me again."

Tybalt cocked his head.

"I don't even know if I want to see Abel again."

He reached his beak through the bars and opened and closed it until she took a cracker from the tin box and gave it to him.

"I thought for a moment that Isaac was not so terrible." She frowned, remembering more and more of the night before. "It was clever of him and Ruth," she said, the woman's name coming out with an extra layer of disgust. "I took those drinks like a trusting fool, and then he led me into the crowd. I melted in his arms. How childish of me to believe that this boy from my past could suddenly reappear, and all the mess in the middle would just go away."

A fiery resolve born of shame burned in her chest. "I'll get him back."

Moments later, she'd composed a new postscript. If anyone could help her return the injustice, it was her letter friend. He'd been the king of mischief in his younger years. Surely he would have an idea for her.

PS: Does the boy who used to throw pinecones want to help me? I am in want of ideas. There is a man out there who needs to know I am not a woman to be toyed with.

And now here she sat, back at the zoo, beneath her beloved tree with her letter still in hand. Her name, like always, was not on it. She knew that when she put it in the tree, there was a chance he would write back, but there was also a very real chance it would sit there, waiting and waiting, never to be answered.

In this moment Laura wanted nothing more than to know how to handle Isaac Campbell and for someone to tell her they were really and truly her friend. Clinging to those desires, she stood, slipped the letter into her beloved mailbox, and brushed her hands on her dress. It was done. The door she'd closed was now cracked open again.

CHAPTER 14

Isaac hadn't returned to the zoo in weeks, but after aimlessly trudging along the busy streets and still refusing to go home to dine with Ruth's family, he found himself standing outside the gates. They beckoned him, welcoming him with arms of homecoming, and he answered the call, stepping into familiar territory.

"Big Frank," he said to the first animal he saw. "Did you miss me?"

The elephant went right on eating. He didn't so much as raise his trunk in Isaac's direction. Isaac deserved that; he'd kept away too long.

"Go on, ignore me. I understand." He looked around at the lush patches of grass, saw the popcorn dropped on the paths, and breathed in the familiar scent of animals. He should have come sooner. Being back in the tranquil setting, and experiencing anew the peace he felt on these grounds, he regretted staying away. Even if he and Laura never exchanged another letter, this place would always feel like home.

"I've got a bit of trouble to sort out," he said, slipping back into his old habit of telling the animals his woes.

An older woman leaned closer. He shut his mouth. This

wasn't one of his evening visits to the zoo, where he could sit on a bench and tell his life story to whichever animal he pleased.

He reached into his pocket, where he normally had treats for his four-legged friends, but found nothing. He'd left in such a hurry, and with no direction, that he'd not thought to bring vegetables and jerky. Mary's letter was the only thing he'd brought with him. "I'll come back soon and bring you a carrot."

Big Frank wiggled an ear, likely batting at an obnoxious fly, but Isaac chose to believe it was an acknowledgment. "That's better. I'm glad you haven't completely forgotten me." He turned to the woman. "Good day."

She *humph*ed before stepping away from him.

A family approached the fence. The smallest child, a little girl, climbed on it and waved her hand at the elephant. Big Frank looked up, and this time, he waved his trunk back.

Isaac laughed as he walked deeper into the zoo. Big Frank knew how to put him in his place. With hours still to go before he could return home, he walked slowly. The hot Buffalo sun beat against his neck. He stepped under the overhang of the monkey house, grateful for the little shade it provided, but it wasn't an ideal place to think. The crowds were thick and loud. Excited children squealed as they moved from one animal to the next. Their delighted chatter was a welcome sound, but he craved quiet, hoping that solitude would help him embrace a plan of action. There had to be some way to apologize to Laura without making matters worse between their families.

The letter tree became his destination. It was the most serene spot in the zoo and an excellent source of shade. His long legs took him toward the sea lions, who waddled on land but moved smoothly through the water. A woman sitting on a bench near the watery enclosure stilled his feet. It was Laura; one glimpse of her profile and he knew. He'd wished for a chance to make things right, silently prayed for it. Was this his moment? His mouth went dry. He had no words prepared, nothing thought out or rehearsed. He retreated, hiding from her again.

How alike they were, both running to the same place after a night gone awry. Her hair, woven in a loose braid, hung over one shoulder, simple and lovely. Her hands were nestled in her lap, still and calm. The zoo suited her. She looked more at ease here than she had clinging to Abel at the square in her fancy duds.

Had she seen the article in the society page? He winced, knowing he was in part to blame for the slanderous words. Ruth had been his date, and though he never believed her capable of such malice, she'd been on his arm. When he confronted Ruth after Abel had escorted Laura away, she simply smiled and told him she'd done it for his own good.

"You can't have everyone believing the two of you are friends. I was protecting you," she said, leaning in close. "I'm loyal to the Campbell side. I always will be."

The quarrel belonged to his family, and Ruth naively believed that he would find her loyalty attractive. She'd been wrong. But could he blame her when, for years, he'd talked against the Bradshaw name and factory?

"I never see her," he'd said. "It would have been better if we'd just gotten through the evening and parted ways. There was no need for a scene."

"You were dancing with her. You looked at her . . . You looked like you cared about her," she said, her lips pulled into a straight red line. "You were not thinking clearly."

"I . . ." What could he say? She was right. He'd wanted to take

Laura in his arms and forget the chasm between their families. It'd been foolish, an impulse to keep her from telling secrets. No—that, too, was a lie. Asking Laura to dance had been about more than keeping secrets. He'd wanted to hold her in his arms, and heaven help him, he'd loved the way she felt there. "Let's forget it."

"It's forgotten." Ruth practically skipped beside him, behaving like a toddler who had closely escaped punishment. "I want to talk of other things. We've seen Silas McCoy. What do you want to see together next?"

He'd swallowed. "I'll have to think on it."

It took great effort to get Ruth home without committing to seeing her again. Little good it had done, since his mother went and invited her over. Ruth was probably primping for him right now, expecting a private evening together. Her mouth would dip at the sides the moment she learned he was not home. His mother would make excuses, declaring him unavoidably detained. Depending on Ruth's perceptiveness, she may believe it. He grimaced, knowing that when he did return home, his mother would scowl and make a fuss over the mess she'd had to deal with because of him.

It was not an appealing thought, but there was no way he would go home until he was certain Ruth was gone. After reading the paper, he was not convinced he could keep his biting remarks to himself. He would face off with his mother later. For now, he was here, with the animals nearby, the most magnificent tree just steps away, and the woman who consumed his thoughts close enough that he could see the Bradshaw red leather Mary Janes she wore, a design his father mimicked only a season later.

A gust of wind sent a strand of Laura's hair blowing across

her face. She stopped the wild dance it had begun and twisted the hair around her finger. Absently, she toyed with it, and for a moment he could believe himself looking at the younger Laura. The one he'd talked to at the factory and chased through the park.

Their parents had brought them together—he had not chosen a friendship with her. Rambunctious children always lured him in. Laura had been different, steady and kind. He'd taken her gentle ways for granted. The friends he'd found after the split were good pals; they'd caused mischief together, even sneaking into the Bradshaw factory to leave it in disarray. But no one had ever been as constant and steady, or easy to talk to, as she had been.

She stood and looked over her shoulder at their tree in the distance, her gaze lingering. His heart leaped. Had she left a letter?

She turned from the tree, then her eyes found his and grew large and round.

"Laura," he said, feigning surprise. "What are you—"

"Why are you here?" she snapped, no longer looking like the docile girl he'd known in his childhood. Standing before him now was a stunning, feisty woman. "Was last night not enough? You've come back to further embarrass me?"

"No, I was . . . I was looking at the sea lions."

"I don't believe you." She folded her arms across her chest and scowled. "Tell me, was Abel in on your joke?"

"No . . . I mean, I wasn't eith—"

"Is it because I was out with Abel? Are you afraid if he cares about me, then your factory will not get raw materials as cheaply? Or that your father will miss out on some grand investment? It is always business—no one seems to care about people anymore." Her voice cracked, and his heart with it. "How dare you."

"I . . . look, last night . . . I didn't know Ruth would do that."

She shook her head, her loose braid swaying with the movement. "It was your fault."

"It was Ruth, she—"

"She was with you." She pointed a finger at him. "I thought it was only my father's feud, but I was wrong. I used to think that someday it would all go away. I thought that we would . . . that we would move past it. But I was wrong."

"Laura, I'm sorry." His shoulders fell. Every part of him felt deflated. "I'm sorry."

"You hurt me."

Unsure whether she spoke of last night's pain or of the many injustices she'd suffered over the years, he struggled for words.

"I didn't mean to." He rubbed at his sun-warmed neck. "You said we were friends once. Last night, you said you always wanted to dance with me, and . . . let's talk about this."

"No. Whatever I said, it wasn't me talking. You'd better watch out, Isaac Campbell. I'm tired of everyone thinking me incapable of making decisions on my own. I'm done with that."

"You've decided something?" He shook his head, confused. "What have you decided?"

"That I don't ever want to see you again." Putting weight on her heel, she spun away, leaving him to stare after her again. He watched, hoping she would look back, but her shoulders were squared, and she held her head high. It seemed this was to be the new normal between them. He would hurt her, and she would leave him. He watched her go, realizing the quiet girl he'd known had grown into a spirited woman who would forever leave every other woman lacking.

●————————————————————————————●

Laura stomped to the edge of the building, where she stopped to catch her breath. Her loose tongue scared her. She'd never spoken so plainly and with such venom to anyone. What was it about Isaac Campbell that freed her voice?

She peeked around the corner of the building, wanting to know where Isaac was so she could avoid him and any future outburst. He was no longer at the bench or the railing near the sea lions. She stepped out of the shadows and peered further, searching for the brown jacket he'd been wearing. She spotted only one man wearing a similar color, but his girth was too wide to be Isaac.

Another man resembled Mr. Shaffer, whom she'd met weeks ago. She was tempted to chase after him and use him as cover while she retreated from the zoo. But he stepped out of sight too quickly. Taking two more steps closer to the bench she'd been sitting on moments before, Laura could see past the enclosure in the direction of her tree.

There she spied a brown jacket, on a tall, broad man whose dark hair poked out beneath a bowler hat. She swallowed. It was him, and he was going for her letter tree. Had he seen her visit it earlier? He must have. That dirty rotten scoundrel, spying on her. How dare he? She never would have guessed that he'd become such a devilish fox of a man.

He paused at the tree, his hand on the bark, and looked up into the green canopy. For a time, he stood just like that, as though staring at a majestic mountain or ornate church steeple. Her breath caught in her chest, and her mouth fell open. And then he did no searching; he reached in as though the movement were all too familiar. He took out her letter—her letter!—tucked it into his jacket pocket, and patted the spot that held it.

She forced air back into her lungs. He was walking away from her tree. He was smiling, and he had her letter. Her heart lurched with anger. He couldn't take it. He couldn't have her words—they were meant for her letter friend.

Oh dear. She stepped back into the shadows on unsteady legs, her breath ragged.

No. A new thought took shape against her will, an idea that twisted inside her. She tried to reject it; surely there was another explanation. Sickened, she pressed her palm to her forehead and did all she could to think clearly. What if he hadn't been spying on her? What if he came here often? What if he loved this tree as much as she did?

Isaac Campbell could not be her letter friend, could he?

She leaned against the nearest building for support. Everything in her wanted to scream that it wasn't true, but the evidence demanded consideration. The way he'd taken the letter, the stories of mischief in his younger days . . . it fit. Like an ugly shoe, it fit, even if she had no desire to wear it.

Isaac walked out of sight, his gait easy and countenance content. No longer afraid of an encounter, she walked to the nearest bench and replayed a million moments from the past. Recalled words exchanged in letters and saw again the way his eyes had softened as he looked at the large maple.

And then she fought a laugh. It was him. It had to be. All these years, it had been Isaac writing her. No twist of fate could have been more shocking. What would he do if he knew she was behind the letters? Well, she wasn't going to tell him. For once she had an advantage over the slick, well-loved Isaac Campbell, and until she knew what to do with this knowledge, she'd keep it to herself.

CHAPTER 15

Affair of the heart, seven letters." Charles sat beside Isaac in the factory office, pencil in hand. "Could be *passion* . . . no . . . doesn't fit in that spot. I'd have to change six across, and I know that one's right. Hmm . . ."

"Romance," Isaac said.

"You got that easily. Does this mean that something is going on between you and Ruth? Is that why you've been happier?"

Isaac rolled his eyes. "Everyone needs to stop playing matchmaker."

"I heard she's been over to your house."

"My mother has invited her over twice, but I have been gone both times, so I don't know what they talked about. Aren't you the one who ought to be answering questions? Why has your wedding been put off?"

"Elsie's mother is sick. She's been in bed for two weeks now. The doctors aren't sure what's wrong, but they are hopeful she will improve soon."

"I'm sorry to hear it."

"We're both anxious to be married, but as her mother's only daughter, it's important to Elsie that we wait until her mother can be there. In the meantime, I'll have to entertain myself with stories about your romance."

"No romance here. Go on, give me the next clue."

"Not so fast." Charles set down the newspaper puzzle. "Something *is* going on."

Isaac pulled his pocket watch out and absentmindedly opened and closed it. *Even apart, we battle together.* The inscription could have been written for him and Charles. Charles had always been there for him. Isaac could trust Charles with anything. They had battled together many times . . . He set his watch aside and laced his fingers together. He ought to tell Charles about the water-damaged letter that had consumed much of his thoughts. But Charles wanted to know why he was happier and more jovial, and Isaac couldn't credit Mary's letter for that.

"It's not Ruth." His voice cracked. "It's someone else."

Charles scooted his chair closer. "Someone else?"

"You have to promise not to tell anyone."

"What sort of trouble have you gotten into? You've done some thoughtless things, but don't tell me you've been off having a tryst with some woman no one knows a thing about."

Isaac leaned across the desk. "You met Elsie at a cemetery. That's hardly conventional."

"She was in tears. It was only right for me to comfort her. Tell me about your mystery woman."

"You haven't promised you won't tell."

Charles narrowed his eyes. "Are you guilty of something?"

"It's complicated." Isaac grabbed the crossword from across the desk and studied the words, or rather, he looked hard at them without actually reading them. When he spoke again, it was more of a mumble. "It's Laura Bradshaw."

"Laura . . . what are you talking about?"

There was no turning back now. Isaac told Charles about the letters and how he'd discovered that Laura was behind them. He was candid and vulnerable.

"I never imagined it was her. I knew the woman behind the letters was . . . wonderful. I knew so much, but I didn't know it was her . . ." His voice trailed off. He sounded like a lovesick puppy, but he couldn't help it. She did something to him. The mere mention of her kindled a burning desire to be with her. "She's writing again. I still don't know what to do, but I know that I missed her when she stopped writing."

"You have to end it," Charles whispered, as though the walls could hear. "You can't date Laura Bradshaw. You can't fall for her or marry her. It's a road to nowhere. Your father would disown you. Turn back now—it's what you've got to do."

"I'm not courting her. We're talking . . . We write letters, that's all. I know that's all it can be."

"You're all red faced and flustered. You should hear yourself. It is more than letters, and you know it. You are madly in love with her." Charles groaned like a man in agony. "You've never talked about a woman like this. You've hardly noticed the women around you. It makes sense now, but the two of you can *never* be. As your friend, trust me, you must write her and tell her it is over."

Isaac left the desk and looked over the production floor. "And if I don't want to?"

"What then? Sneak off and have no means to support her? You didn't go to college; you have no skills other than what you've learned at your father's shoe factory. Your father will cut you off, and then you'll have nothing. What kind of life could you give her? Besides, she may not want you once she knows you're the letter writer. She didn't exactly fall head over heels when the two of you saw each other at the pole sitting."

"Circumstances were against us."

"And at the zoo? You said she never wanted to see you again."

"At the zoo she was angry about the pole sitting and the article in the paper. It's a misunderstanding. I blame myself for Ruth's behavior. But it can be sorted out."

"Everyone's been talking about her since. She's got money, so that keeps people interested, but she won't even have that if she courts you. Her father isn't any less stubborn than yours. You'd be ruining things for her too. Nothing good could come from this. I doubt she wants to have her name slandered in the paper again. You should just stay away from her."

"I've been thinking about that. I'm going to write and request a retraction and send it to the paper. It'll be anonymous, but it's the least I can do." He rubbed his forehead. Why did this situation have to be so complex? There was a chance he could convince her that he had not put alcohol in her drinks, but that didn't change who his parents were or his inability to support himself outside of the factory. "You once said that it is amazing how, in a sea of people, we find someone who is different from all the others. If someone asked you to walk away from Elsie, would you? Even if it were complicated?"

"No." Charles lost his cheeky grin. "I would not. I believe providence brought us together. I would find a way to be with her no matter the cost. She is all that is good."

"As is Laura. But . . . I don't know what to do about it." He frowned and shoved his hands into his pockets. "She's been asking me for ideas of how to embarrass a man who embarrassed her."

"She's talking about you." Charles laughed. "This is far more interesting than meeting a woman at a cemetery. What have you told her?"

"I suggested she stick a feather in his hat so everyone would whisper about him as he went about town."

Charles shook his head. "That was a weak suggestion."

"What would you suggest? That she burn down the factory? I told her that perhaps the man who embarrassed her didn't do it on purpose and suggested she forgive him."

"I bet she loved that suggestion."

"She wrote back and told me that it would take a great deal of groveling for her to ever consider it. That's the problem. I can't grovel because she doesn't know who I am. I can't tell her who I am because our families hate each other. You do feel sorry for me, don't you?"

"Not a bit." Charles stole the crossword back. "I'm grateful."

"What sort of a friend are you?"

"A selfish one"—Charles's jolly expression made it hard for Isaac to hold his frown—"who is grateful to have something so entertaining to keep him laughing until his wedding day."

"I'm glad someone is enjoying my misery."

Charles, still chuckling, read from the paper. "Four letters, a house divided."

"A feud." He rolled his eyes. "A word I have always hated, but never as much as right now."

Neither spoke. The cheery conversation had taken a serious turn. There were no easy solutions, nor was there any point in rehashing the unlikeliness of it all. After an exceptionally long pause, Charles said, "You will have to find a way to bridge the feud."

For a week now Laura had been plotting ways to get back at Isaac, and at the same time, she'd been writing to Isaac and enjoying every word of every letter. Her head spun whenever she thought about their strange relationship. Isaac had given her a few ideas for revenge, but nothing as clever as she would have expected. Mostly he wrote of other things—the animals at the zoo, a strange letter he received that had him perplexed, and how sorry he was he'd not met her at the Quarry Garden. He offered no explanation as to his whereabouts that day, but his remorse seemed sincere. When she told him she feared her father might sell her mother's book collection, his sympathetic words comforted her. They slipped back into their relationship seamlessly.

"It's so confusing," she said, opening the door on Tybalt's cage and letting him step onto her hand. "I don't like him . . . and yet I do like him. Well, I like him in the letters."

"Like who?" Mrs. Guskin stood near her open door. "I came to hang your clean dresses in your closet and overheard you."

Laura ran her hand over Tybalt's smooth feathers. "I've been writing to my letter friend again. Please don't judge me. After the crowd at the square laughed at me, I wrote to him. I knew he would be kind. And now . . ."

Mrs. Guskin had a gift for saying a great many things without saying anything at all. She looked at Laura with high brows and questioning eyes until Laura finally squirmed and said more. "I know who he is."

"You do?"

"I saw him get one of my letters. And I've read back through all the old letters. I'm certain I know him."

"And?"

"It's someone I used to know. A childhood friend."

Mrs. Guskin covered her mouth. "It's Isaac Campbell, isn't it?"

"Shhh." Laura put a finger to her lips, crossed the room, and closed her door. "I don't want Father to hear."

Tybalt walked up her arm to her shoulder, his claws holding tightly but not digging through the fabric of her dress. When she'd first claimed Tybalt as her own, she'd felt like a pirate at sea every time he perched on her shoulder. Now it felt normal, having a bird nearby. He'd listened to many of her secrets, and today he was listening again.

"Oh dear," Mrs. Guskin said. "Have you thought this through?"

"I have thought about little else. I think about it all the time. I hate him for embarrassing me, but I still don't know what role he played in that. I know that I have loved his letters over the years. I can't decide what sort of a man he truly is. I want to know. But how can I?" She sank into the chair near her mirror. "I should stop writing him. I know that, but . . ."

"But you'd miss him."

"I would. I feel like an awful person. I want to humiliate him in real life and then run to him in letters. It doesn't work like that—I know it doesn't." She leaned back in the chair and tipped her head toward the ceiling. Tybalt pranced on her shoulder, trying not to lose his balance.

"How does Abel fit into all this?"

"I don't know." She frowned, pouting at the predicament. "I don't know how any of it fits. Abel hasn't so much as kissed me, and I don't know that I want him to. He said to me only yesterday that he's forgiven me for my public display at the flagpole sitting. I suppose things may move along now . . . but then I start thinking that I have nothing to be forgiven for and that he's a cad for saying such things."

"And you certainly don't want to marry a cad."

"No! Of course I don't."

"What *do* you want? If you could have anything at all, what would it be?" Mrs. Guskin stood beside her, looking at her through the mirror. "You've been set on trying to break free from here for so long, I wonder whether you've considered where you're running to. What good would it do to trade one set of problems for another? You've got to know what it is you want— not just what you don't want."

Laura looked into her own eyes, searching their blue depths for answers. "I want a library full of books, a yard full of animals, and people around me who don't think I'm odd because I have a bird on my shoulder. I want to go to church socials and to the zoo without worrying that my father will rebuke me for loving animals and flowers and for having dirty hands." She sighed. "I want peace. Everything has felt unsettled since Mama died. I want to reclaim the joy that I felt when she was nearby. And I want to find a man who loves me with no reservations."

"Those are good dreams," Mrs. Guskin said.

"And wherever I go, I want you and Tybalt with me."

"I would like nothing better." Mrs. Guskin went across the room and picked up a spare chair from its spot near the desk. She brought it over to Laura, sat beside her, and took her hand. "Now you know what you're running toward. No more thinking about just running away—think about where you're going. If Abel can't take you to those dreams, then find a different way. God gave you good desires. Aim for them."

Laura pressed her hands firmly around Mrs. Guskin's. "With Abel I'm always so worried about being who *he* wants me to be. But I'm scared to close that door. At least with him, there is a chance for a dream or two to come true."

"A good man will want to share about himself and know everything about you. When you see him next, give him a little piece of your heart and see what he does with it. He may love the real you. If you don't show him, how will you ever know?"

"And Isaac?"

"That's a bigger problem." She tsked. "He's the opposite of Abel. He knows your heart but not your face. At least, that's true of the Isaac behind the letters. That is confusing, isn't it?"

"Yes," Laura said as she stroked Tybalt. "I wonder what my mother would say about all this."

"I think she would say how proud she is of you for facing every day with courage. And of course, she would praise you for all you've learned. She'd declare you a very modern woman, in the best of ways. It takes gumption to wake up and choose to use your time the way you have. You're bright and talented." Mrs. Guskin let go of Laura's hand and patted her cheek. "She'd tell you she loves you exactly how you are."

Laura blinked her eyes quickly, grateful for Mrs. Guskin, a true angel in her life. "Would she tell me what to do?"

"No." Mrs. Guskin shook her head. "She'd tell you she trusts you to make the right choice. She'd probably take your hand and say that the road might be bumpy, but it'll get you there."

A grin spread across her face, so big that creases formed in the corners. "And then she'd tell you to go clean off your shoulder because Tybalt has made a mess on you."

Sure enough, he'd left a mark on Laura's shoulder. She laughed as she put Tybalt back in his cage and changed out of her dress and into a clean one. "Tonight I'll show Abel something real about me. He might surprise me."

"He might."

"He did come back, even after the awful night at the square."

Mrs. Guskin clicked her tongue. "I overheard him talking to your father about an investment opportunity. Make sure he's coming back for the right reasons."

"It's not a bad thing if my dating Abel helps Father too. I may want to leave here, but I don't wish ill on Father."

"You've a generous heart, but you don't have to make Abel fit into it. Some shapes are not meant to stack together. And as for your father, he'll have to decide to be happy again—you can't force it. Whatever happened before, it wasn't your fault." Mrs. Guskin tucked a piece of Laura's hair back into place. "You go and have a good time. And remember: the right man will want to know *all* of you."

Laura nodded. "I'll do my best."

Not long after, Abel opened the door to his automobile, and Laura found herself sitting beside him, debating which part of her heart to share. She was anxious to discover whether he would embrace it or leave a sore mark of rejection. But love required vulnerability and trust, so tonight she would give what she could. She took a deep breath.

"I get nervous when I see someone cross the street," she said, avoiding his eyes and focusing on a crease in the leather seat. "My mother died near the war office. She was crossing the street. I was there—I saw it happen."

Abel scratched his head. "Why were you there?"

"I don't know. We were shopping, and she left me at the corner and told me to wait for her while she ran inside. She never told me her purpose in being there. Ever since then, there are times when I see someone walking across the road and my hands shake. Sometimes it's hard to breathe until they are across. Sometimes I feel as though I am living that afternoon again and seeing it happen all over."

"What are you saying?" he asked. "Do you not like going out because of it?"

"I . . . I wanted you to know." She shrugged. There was no real reason for telling him other than her desire to share something personal.

"All right then—I know now. Let's get going." He started the engine. "*The Thief of Bagdad* starts in fifteen minutes. I've heard it's an excellent picture."

She forced a smile, her mind immediately trying to rationalize his response. *No, not tonight.* She wouldn't rationalize it. She'd given a piece of herself, and he'd cared little for it.

"Laura," Abel's voice rumbled beside her. "You can't be scared forever. People are always going to be crossing the street. It's not going to go away."

"I know," she whispered, locking the other parts of her heart away for safekeeping.

Later in the evening, when she had another opportunity to share, she stifled the urge. Her love of animals, her abhorrence for fashion, her lonely home . . . there was so much she could tell. But she kept it all to herself, remaining a docile, agreeable companion on the outside and a bitter one on the inside.

In her room that night, she pulled out her box of letters and read through several, enough to see the many times she'd poured out her heart in earnest. She'd been so vulnerable, so real. Her secrets, hopes, and disappointments were all there.

And then she poured out her heart again.

Dear Letter Friend,

Have you ever been afraid of something? Not a nightmare, but a fear that takes hold of you and comes back time and time again——even though it shouldn't?

I saw my mother die. She was waving to me one moment, and then an automobile hit her, and she was gone. Ever since, I have felt the pinch of fear whenever I see someone cross the street. Against my will, it grabs hold, only letting go when the person is safe on the other side.

Writing the words to him was easy, and she felt certain he would respond with compassion, advice, and understanding. Did that mean he was a better man than Abel? Or did their unusual friendship simply make conversing easier? If they were face-to-face, would they share so much?

CHAPTER 16

The days following her weak attempt at sharing her heart with Abel passed slowly, each day nearly the same as the one before.

Laura expected this day to be as uneventful as the past few days had been. But at breakfast her father read the paper aloud.

In a previous article for the society page, Laura Bradshaw was unjustly accused of becoming inebriated. Accusations of poor behavior were made without the full details of the events. A source now tells us that her consumption of alcohol occurred without her knowledge and that the blame should not be placed on her. As a newspaper, we do our best to present the facts, and thus, due to the discrepancy between sources, we politely ask our readers to disregard our previous story and ask that Laura Bradshaw accept our apology.

"This is hardly a retraction," her father said as he threw the paper on the table. "News these days. It's nothing but a lot of sensationalism. They should have named Isaac Campbell and let him see how he likes having his name dragged through the mud."

Laura ignored him and let herself feel the sweet comfort that came from knowing someone had spoken on her behalf. Ruth? Abel? Both seemed unlikely. Isaac? She took a bite of her toast, too lost in thought to even taste it. Someone out there wasn't whispering gossip about her but defending her, and she felt certain she knew who it was.

"I'm going to Albany for a couple of days, and then I may go on to Boston. I don't know when I'll be back." He set his napkin on the table and stood. "While I'm gone, I need you to remain close to Abel. It's been long enough—see if you can get him to commit to you. An engagement would be helpful."

Unsure whether he expected a response, Laura moved her breakfast around on her plate with a fork.

"I can't make things go faster with him," she said when it became apparent that her father was indeed waiting for a reply. She'd yet to decide how to tell him that she felt no growing attachment to Abel and that she wondered when their relationship would end and he would leave her for a more fashionable woman.

"We're closing on a business deal soon. It's an investment opportunity, and because Abel is so fond of you, he's let me invest more than anyone else." He never shared such information with her, choosing to keep business decisions to himself. She watched him, trying to understand. His brow bore a light sheen of sweat. He was nervous—but why?

"Does your trip to Albany have something to do with the business deal?" she said cautiously.

"There's a shoe distributor there who hasn't paid his bill. I want to see him in person and get the account settled. The more money I have on hand, the more I can invest. It's why I've had to make some difficult decisions." He rubbed his hands on his sides. He was uncomfortable; all his tics were showing. "The return will be worth it. We'll be bigger than ever. I've a source that tells me Campbell is trying to get Abel to work with him too." He ground his teeth. "You can't let this fall through. This is my chance to get ahead and prove that I know best how to run a factory."

"I'm not sure I know what you want me to do. I don't talk business with Abel."

"He has to care about you." He bobbed his head, encouraging her. "He's got to. Campbell can't sway him. Do you understand?"

"He's told me before that he does business with anyone who can prove a good business opportunity. He doesn't care about the company split."

"Then you must convince him to care. Do you understand?"

"Yes," she whispered, wishing she could tell her father no with the same force with which she'd told Isaac off when they ran into each other at the zoo. Where was her boldness now, when she needed it?

Abel had been so dashing and handsome the first night she'd seen him, and though she still knew he was a handsome man, he'd faded in her eyes, remaining appealing in outward appearance only. For a man supposedly smitten, he hadn't made any true shows of affection. They went out, they watched moving pictures, they danced, but they did not talk of the future, and there was no growing trust. Why he continued calling was beyond her understanding.

Laura excused herself from breakfast as quickly as she could. She paced the halls, only stopping when Abel phoned, letting her know that his work had detained him and they would not be able to go out that evening. Laura assured him that she understood.

"I'm going to the zoo," she said to Mrs. Guskin.

"You're awfully cheery."

"Father is on his way out of town, and Abel has cancelled our dinner tonight." She grinned. "I feel free as a bird."

"Go on then."

Minutes later she was headed for her oasis. It would be a good day; she could feel it in the air as she walked from her house to the ticket booth and into her beloved sanctuary.

"Miss Bradshaw!" Brent Shaffer, the zookeeper who had known her mother, waved. Laura waved back, eager to ask whether he knew what animal they were getting ready to bring into the back corner.

"Mr. Shaffer, it's good to see you. How are the bears today?"

"We put a big barrel in with the polar bear, and he's been rolling it around all morning. He's never been happier."

"I'm glad to hear it." She pointed toward the area of the zoo that was under construction. "What will go there? More bears?"

"No, they plan on bringing in a pair of giraffes."

"Wonderful." She'd devoured several books on African animals over the winter. "Did you know giraffes only sleep for a few minutes a day? They spend almost their entire lives standing." Unable to hold back, she went on, "They're such fascinating animals. None of them have the same spots. They're all different."

Mr. Shaffer wiped a hand over his mouth, but there was no blocking his grin. "You're an animal lover, aren't you?"

"It started when I was a child. Once, I found a kitten that still had its eyes closed. I remember reading the kitten fairy tales and feeding it one drop of milk at a time. My mother helped me take care of it. We took turns getting up at night to feed him. I had him for six years, before he snuck out one day. My mother and I looked everywhere. We never found him. I think a hawk may have gotten him. We both grieved him." She paused. "You said you knew my mother?"

"I did. Not so well as some, but when she first came here from the west, we both frequented the same diner. She'd talk about back home, and I'd listen. After that I didn't see her much. She got married and didn't go to the diner, but she did bring a kitten to my veterinary office a couple of times a few years later."

"A little orange fella." Laura smiled, remembering his whiskered face. "We named him Romeo."

"That's a good name. I'm told the giraffes who are coming have been named Arthur and Joanne. I am expecting them to be an adorable old couple."

She laughed, picturing gray-haired giraffes with low spectacles. "I can't wait to meet them." Mrs. Guskin's advice came flooding back—that she should find a way to run toward her good dreams. "Would you . . . do you ever let volunteers help with the animals?"

"Well, as a matter of fact, we do. Would you like to help with them?"

"I would, if you could use me. I have been reading about animals since I was a child. I dreamed of being a veterinarian, but I know there aren't many women in the field. It's not so much the title I want. It's the animals I love."

"We're always looking for volunteers. It's not fancy work— we do a lot of shoveling manure—but I could talk to the director and get permission for you to help. I'll tell him that you're a student of animal care and a regular patron of the zoo."

Speechless, she nodded. "I would like that."

"Will your father be in support? Some men don't think it fitting, the way women are stepping into so many jobs."

"I'm twenty-one years old," she said. "It's my choice, not his."

"You sound just like your mother. I remember her telling me she was going to marry your father. She sounded just as determined." His voice grew wistful. "Come back tomorrow, first thing. I'll meet you at the gate, and we can put you to work." His eyes made a quick appraisal of her. "It's dirty work, so come prepared for that."

"I will."

When he left her, she stood for a long time doing nothing but feeling sweet gratitude warm her soul. The logistics of her bold decision were still to be determined, and perhaps regretted, but in this moment she was simply happy.

The patrons began leaving, and the carousel stopped running. Soon night would settle. She hurried for the letter tree, determined to check it quickly before she was shooed from the zoo.

Isaac had written, just as she'd hoped. And just as expected, he addressed her fear and memories with gentleness.

. . . I am sorry to hear of your painful memories. I cannot imagine how difficult it must be to relive that moment over and over. I don't know how one overcomes such a thing—perhaps by dwelling on the good moments you shared with your mother. It seems to me that if light pushes out darkness, the same may work with memories. It is only an idea, but when you are watching someone cross the road, you could try to think of the many times you walked hand in hand with your mother as you safely traveled to the other side. Did she talk to you when you walked? Did she tell you secrets? If you think very

hard, can you see her smile? I would hold tightly to that, but even if it does not work, I do not think a fear is something to be ashamed of.

She paused her reading, closed her eyes, and searched her memory until she found a moment worth clinging to: her mother holding her hand, looking down at her as they crossed the street, bound for the zoo. Her mother's smile was bright, radiating like the rays of sunlight that crept through the canopy of leaves. The light from that moment seemed to creep straight from Laura's mind to her heart, warming it with the fine glow of motherly love.

She read the rest of Isaac's letter with a smile on her face, and then she wrote a response. She told him that his advice was helpful and that she wanted to learn to live free of the dictates of fear that had so often guided her choices.

. . . A friend told me that I've spent too much time thinking about what I want to get away from and that I should instead consider what I want to go to. I'm not sure how to get where I want to go, but I've been clinging to her words ever since. Just as I will cling to your words, which remind me to remember more than just the death of my mother. I want to remember her life, and I want to live mine . . .

She wanted so badly to write him about working with the zoo animals. She wanted to shout it from the rooftops for everyone to hear. But what if he figured out who she was because he saw her mucking out pens? She both welcomed the idea and dreaded it.

. . . I've been thinking about other good dreams that are written on my heart. I'll be taking steps closer to those dreams as well . . .

Isaac knocked on the door of Clifford Cannon's detective agency. He'd made an appointment after finally confiding in Charles about Mary Kensington's waterlogged letter, and today was the day. The small office was on the back side of the Ellicott Square Building. He had entered the building through a discreet, narrow door and then stepped through an unremarkable hallway before coming upon an office door labeled simply *Detective*.

"Do you have an appointment?" a raspy voice asked from behind the wooden door after he knocked.

"I do. It's for Isaac Campbell."

The door flew open. An old man grabbed Isaac's hand, pulled him inside, and then closed the door just as quickly. "Get in here. We don't need anyone seeing you standing around in the hall."

Charles claimed that his aunt had used Mr. Cannon's services to find her husband after he disappeared. Her husband had been found five days later near Albany, singing in a nightclub. Yet it was hard to believe this man, with his unkempt white hair, bulbous nose, and erratic ways, was an expert sleuth.

"Mr. Cannon." Isaac held out a hand to the man. "As I said, I'm Isaac Campbell."

"I don't take all cases." The man shook his hand quickly, then went around his overly cluttered desk and sat on his low chair. "Sit down and tell me exactly what you want from me, and I'll think about it. And I charge for my time, so don't go thinking you can use my brains and pay me nothing."

Isaac had been worried about payment, knowing he could not turn to his father for aid. He'd considered selling some of his belongings and would if it came to it. But only recently a new idea had surfaced. The editor of the paper had been impressed by him when Isaac requested the retraction. They conversed easily, and Isaac confessed to having a love of writing. He'd written so many letters over the years that the written word was like a friend to him.

"We have people who work here permanently, but we pay for stories too. If you feel inclined, write something and bring it by. We'll look at it," the editor had said before thanking Isaac again for coming.

"Payment won't be a problem," Isaac told Mr. Cannon. He'd write a thousand stories if he had to. He'd find a way.

"Very good. Go on then, tell me why you're here."

Abrupt and to the point—Isaac could work with that. "Two reasons. First, I received a letter. It's important, but the address is unreadable. I asked the post office, but they said there was no way they could help, seeing as I don't even know a state or region to begin looking in. Plus, since it was successfully delivered, it isn't considered a lost letter." He pulled Mary's letter from his pocket and slid it across the desk. "It's in regard to my uncle who died in the war."

"The war's been over for years." He picked up the envelope, inspecting it first. "This has water damage."

"The water damage is my fault. I realize it's been a long time since the war, but my uncle was my friend, and I always wanted a chance to talk to him again. This letter leads me to believe that he left something behind for me and others. It's important to me."

"A treasure seeker." Mr. Cannon frowned. "You think you've missed out on an inheritance?"

"No. I never considered that. I was hoping for a parting letter, something of that nature."

There wasn't much else he could add to strengthen his case, so he sat in the straight-backed wooden chair and waited as Mr. Cannon pulled the warped paper from its envelope.

"This is addressed to William Campbell."

"That's my father."

"The William Campbell who makes shoes." He looked down below the desk. "I got a pair of Campbell's on today. Might have Bradshaw's on tomorrow. I never understood the hatred between the companies. You both make equally good shoes."

"I don't understand it all either," he confessed.

"What does your father think of this letter?" Mr. Cannon wasn't taking notes on paper, but it was easy to believe he was already looking for clues as he searched the paper, turning it this way and that.

"He doesn't know." Isaac cleared his throat. "I intend to handle this myself and then present my findings to my father."

"I already told you I don't take all cases. I'm an old man. I don't have the time nor energy to get between a father and a son."

Isaac scratched his cheek, searching for a way to convince this man to help him. "You may be an old man, but you must love a good mystery. Isn't that why you became a detective?"

"Go on."

"I believe my uncle's death may have something to do with the Campbell-Bradshaw feud. When this letter came, I started thinking back on everything that has happened. I know my uncle was nervous about going to war. I overheard him asking my father how he could get out of the draft. In the end he went, but things unraveled. I was young and didn't pay enough attention, but the company split not long after. Bradshaw's wife died, and that may be a clue too."

"Died? What happened to her?"

"She was hit crossing the street."

"An accident and a soldier's death. And you think they're related?"

Isaac gnawed on his cheek. "It sounds far-fetched but, well, Bradshaw's name is in the letter too. I want to retrieve the letters this woman has, not only so I can read my uncle's last words but also to see whether he wrote anything that might help me understand. Everything changed when the company split. The effects of that split are still being felt." He tapped his foot on the worn wood floor, anxious for Mr. Cannon to agree to help. "I can't ask my father. He's never wanted to tell me what happened, but I need to know. It affects me."

Mr. Cannon's white brows came together. "There are no secrets in this room. Tell me how it affects you, and then if I'm convinced, I'll work with you."

A fly buzzed above the old man's head. He reached his hands up, clapped them together, and killed it. Isaac liked the man more with each passing moment. He was straightforward, peculiar, and spry.

"There's a woman—"

"There's always a woman." He slapped his thigh and hooted. "Now we are getting somewhere."

"This woman is special." He took a deep breath, and then he told the detective more than he'd ever told anyone. He started at the beginning, sparing no details. He talked of their letters, their childhood, and his fear that Abel Fredricks would marry Laura before she ever knew who Isaac truly was. Then, having exposed his heart, he waited.

Mr. Cannon stood up and crossed the disheveled room to a

bookshelf. He retrieved a photograph, brushed the dust from it, and held it out to Isaac. A woman in a dark dress, with curled tendrils framing her face, stared back at him.

"Love's a good reason," Mr. Cannon said. "It wasn't mystery—it was love. That's why I'm a detective. This here's Darla. She came to me at church one Sunday and asked if I'd help her discover who was stealing from her father's apothecary. She said I was so smart, she was sure I could help. I worked around the clock, looking for clues. We were married a couple months later, and I've been looking for clues ever since."

"That's a fine story."

"Yours will be too." He stuck his hand out. This time when they shook, it was an agreement. "And your second request?"

Isaac leaned closer before asking Mr. Cannon if he knew how someone would go about buying or selling a collection of books without advertising such a sale. His details were sparse, but Mr. Cannon offered to see what he could discover. On both accounts, Isaac left feeling hopeful.

CHAPTER 17

"W ear this." Mrs. Guskin pulled out an old dress that looked like the calico dresses pioneers wore as they crossed the plains moving west, before the invention of the train made travel easier. It was nothing like the straight-cut dresses with fancy beadwork that women wore today. This dress was practical and very unfashionable. "You can get it as muddy as you wish, and it won't matter any."

"I don't suppose anyone will recognize me in it." Laura laughed as she pulled it over her head. Mrs. Guskin was not a large woman, but her hips were wider than Laura's, and her chest was larger. The dress was ill fitting, hanging on Laura in all the wrong places.

"You know," Mrs. Guskin said, "there is a box in the attic full of dresses that were your mother's. They may fit you better than this dress. I've heard you're the spitting image of her."

"I'll be shoveling manure. No one will care what I'm wearing."

"I won't be doing the wash often enough for you to wear that dress every day."

Laura looked in the mirror. Vanity was not a sin that plagued her, but she had to admit this dress made her look both comfortable . . . and homely. "When I come back, we could go to the attic together and see if there are dresses that will work."

"Excellent plan. I've packed you a lunch since we don't know how long you'll be staying." She sighed. "Are you sure this is a good idea? I'm worried your father will find out."

"I'll never have another chance like this." She brushed at the side of the wrinkled dress. "I'm doing it. I'll keep to myself, but if he does find out, so be it. What is the worst he can do, banish me to my room? I've been there for years. Sell off the books in the library? He's already planning on that. I heard him talk to Mr. Stevens on the telephone. There's not much left for him to take."

"Oh dear, he's really going to sell the books," Mrs. Guskin said. "He'd better be truly desperate to do such a thing."

"His bootlegged alcohol hasn't run dry, so I have trouble believing we are so close to desperation. My guess is it's greed making the decision. He wants more and is willing to use Mother's collection as collateral. I don't think my dreams need to be sacrificed on the altar of business as well. I'm going to the zoo, and nothing can stop me."

"I've wondered when that strong spirit of yours would break free." Mrs. Guskin smiled like a proud mother. "Go on then. Enjoy every moment of mucking stalls, come what may."

Laura floated on a cloud of happiness as she made her way to the zoo. Mr. Shaffer was waiting, as promised, near the front gate, a friendly smile on his face. "I've talked to the other zookeepers. They said if I was willing to keep an eye on you, they'd gladly welcome you. I thought we would start at Big Frank. I like to clean up his pen before folks start coming."

"Big Frank and I have been talking over the fence for years."

She fought the urge to skip like an excited child, a difficult task when this day felt as thrilling as Christmas morning had when she was small. "I've dreamed of knowing him better."

"He's got big tusks, but he's a friendly old man. There's a wheelbarrow stored behind the elephant house—we'll be needing that and a shovel."

Laura ran ahead and fetched them. Jittery with excitement, she tipped the empty wheelbarrow over twice on her way back.

"He's not too skittish, but I like to put my hand on his side if I have to walk beside him so he knows where I am. When it gets warmer, we'll get buckets and give him a bath."

Laura pinched herself. This couldn't all be real. She followed Mr. Shaffer into the elephant house where Big Frank stood waiting for them. She stepped near his side and put her hand on his leathery skin. "Hello there," she said near his ear. He curled his trunk up and put it on her shoulder. "Thank you for listening to me." She kept her voice low, just for him. "You've been a good friend."

"He likes you," Mr. Shaffer said. "I'll feed him if you want to start shoveling."

Laura patted Big Frank's side again before stepping away and getting to work. Her book learning could not have prepared her for the mountain of manure that awaited her or how the muscles in her back would scream at her for using them in such a way. But the old stubbornness, which Mrs. Guskin had said would help her one day, proved useful. She shoveled and shoveled while talking to Big Frank and Mr. Shaffer, stopping only occasionally to stretch her tight muscles. When they finished the elephant house, they started right away on the bears, hopping from one dream to the next.

"We can only go in with the black bears. They're from a circus and friendly as house cats. Be careful, of course, but you won't have any trouble with them. Other bears we will lock out while we clean their pens."

While she was in with the black bears, the zoo opened and the first patrons arrived. The back side of her dress was filthy from a fall she'd taken while dumping the wheelbarrow, and her hands were red and popping with blisters. She was a ghastly sight for anyone who bothered to look. Luckily, most people were more drawn to the animals than to her. Most, but not all.

"I didn't know they hired women to clean up after the animals," a man with a cheek full of tobacco said as she bent over with a shovel in hand.

"They haven't hired me. I'm a volunteer." She kept right on working. Mr. Shaffer had gone back to the main building to get feed for the bears, leaving her to deal with this unruly patron on her own.

"Can't find yourself a place in the kitchen? Must be that dress—it could scare most any man off. Underneath it, you might not be so bad." He sneered and then spit a long string of tobacco on the ground. "All this talk of modern women. I had no idea what your sex really wanted was to shovel manure. Had we known, we would have let you do that years ago."

"At least the animals in here are better behaved than the ones out there." Her eyes found his, and she challenged him with her glare. "If you'll be on your way, I'll get back to work."

The man released another string of spittle before he stepped away, muttering something about women under his breath.

She grinned, unable to stop herself. She'd scared him off. She hadn't known she could be like this: speaking up, daring to take opportunities—choosing bravery. Rapunzel may have been free of her tower much sooner had she only tried climbing down herself.

"Do you always smile while shoveling manure?"

She knew this voice. It was as deep as the other man's had been, but without any spite. Isaac Campbell stood with his arms resting casually on the fence, looking handsome as ever. "I've always wanted to get behind the fence. How did you manage it?"

"I asked."

"No—it was that simple?"

Was he the man from the letters or the one who had embarrassed her at the flagpole sitting? Nothing about his cheery expression seemed malicious. His perfectly attractive face matched the kind words so well. The flutter in her stomach quickened, telling her to take a chance on him. "There was a retraction printed in the paper. Do you know how it got there?"

"I suppose someone went to the paper and demanded it."

Her hands burned from their constant grip on the shovel. She set it down, leaning it against the wheelbarrow, and took a step closer to him. The black bears sat a few feet away, warming themselves in the early morning sunshine. She'd been afraid when she first set foot in the enclosure, but already she felt comfortable in the presence of these old circus bears.

"Did you demand it?" she asked, hoping and silently wishing he had.

"What happened to you was wrong. I didn't know it was going to happen, but I still blame myself. I should have stopped it." He didn't look away. He stood by his answer, and she believed him. "I couldn't put my name as the source."

"Because of your father?"

He nodded, and an understanding passed between them. Their fathers' fight affected everything. It was a germ, taking but never giving.

"I wish I could do more to make it right." He asked, "Can you forgive me?"

She nodded, tears threatening. She'd written that she'd only forgive a man who groveled, but looking at him now, she knew he spoke the truth, and there was nothing for him to apologize for. They were both victims. Casualties of the same war. "I blame our fathers, not you."

"I have been thinking about that." He stopped talking for a moment while a family stepped near and waved at the lazy bears. She resumed her shoveling. With her wheelbarrow full, she felt guilty dawdling, so she followed Mr. Shaffer's careful instructions on how to leave safely. There were two gates. She was to go through one, then stop in the middle and make sure the first gate was closed before going through the second. Once out, she pushed the wheelbarrow as carefully as she could through the now busy zoo to the pile behind the elephant house, where she dumped her load.

Isaac found her there, away from the crowd, surrounded by the stench of manure. He wore a suit, pin-striped and perfectly cut. She looked at her ill-fitting dress and shrank back a step. No one was supposed to recognize her. She felt sheepish in her old raggedy dress and with a dirty rump.

"How did you know I'd be at the zoo?" She picked at a loose string on her sleeve.

"Bill Turner is a friend of mine. He's a guard here and knows everything that goes on. I came in late last night—"

"They let you in at night?"

"I talked my father into making a donation a while back. It was big enough that they don't seem to mind when I come. They even listened to some of my suggestions about what trees to keep and such."

Her tree! He'd saved it. It must have been him who spoke up and asked for it not to be taken down after the branch broke. If circumstances were different, she would have jumped into his arms and thanked him.

"I enjoy it here at night. It's peaceful. It was Bill who told me there was a woman wanting to volunteer."

"And you knew that it was me?"

"Lucky guess, I suppose." He took off his hat and ran his hand over his hair, only to replace the hat again. "I remember you having a kitten and loving it. And you live so close. It only made sense."

It didn't ring true. They hadn't really talked in years—not in person, at least, and he didn't know she was the letter writer. Her skepticism must have shown on her face, despite her efforts to remain expressionless. Such curiosity was hard to hide.

"He may have mentioned your name." He shifted his weight. Was he as uncomfortable as she was? "Look, I wanted to say I was sorry. But I also wanted to talk to you."

She looked over her shoulder. They were still alone by the giant mountain of animal dung. The sight and smell of it created a barrier from the bustling zoo. Manure was hardly an attraction that drew a crowd. Still, she couldn't be too careful. It was best if she didn't linger. "I told Mr. Shaffer I'd meet him when I finished with the bears. What did you want to talk about?"

"I want to figure out what happened between our parents.

But they can't find out that I'm digging around. I want you to help me."

"Why?" She looked at her muck-covered shoes. "What could I do?"

"You can get information that I can't. Don't you want to know what happened?"

She nodded. "I don't know how much help I'd be. But I could try. What do you want me to look for?"

"Can I trust you?" He stepped closer and pulled a letter from his pocket. "I know you're a Bradshaw, and we're sworn enemies, but what if we called a truce and worked together on this? You can hate me again after if you want. But I just think if we knew what happened, then we could set it right. Or at least . . . we could understand."

"You're not secretly trying to sabotage me, are you? I'm not going to agree to this and then find that it's some wicked prank?"

"No." He shook his head. "I'll prove it."

He came close and held out the letter, offering it to her. She reached for it with blistered hands. He took hold of her right hand before she could take the letter and turned it palm up. Her tender skin came alive as his thumb roamed softly across her blisters. "You're hurt."

"It's nothing." She could barely speak. His touch was so gentle, so alarmingly, perfectly caring. She pulled her hand back, tucking it at her side, wishing the warmth from his touch could stay forever and also aware of what could never be. "I asked to help with the animals. Mr. Shaffer let me in with Big Frank. I got to pet him, and later I'll get to bathe him. Blisters are a small price to pay."

"I was the one with rough hands, not you. I was climbing

trees while you were reading books." His chest filled with air, then slowly deflated. "I've been thinking about all that since seeing you at the square."

"About us as children?"

"About how things used to be and how they are now. And how they might have been." His Adam's apple bobbed. "I guess this letter and seeing you, it has me wanting answers."

She took the letter from his hand and read it quickly. "I don't know what this means. Why does it say Bradshaw?"

"I don't know. But there must have been some reason my uncle mentioned your father. Think about it. Things fell apart at this same time."

"How will you write back? The address is washed out."

"My father can't know, but . . . I've hired a detective to help. The minute I opened this letter, I knew it was important. I'll find her, even if he can't."

"Does the detective think he will be able to track her down? There's so little information here."

"Yes, he has already begun. He intends to look through nurse records and find ones that match up with where Uncle Morton was serving. He told me to find any other clues I could and bring them back. I told him about the factory split and how I think this might connect somehow. He isn't sure it's all related, but he's willing to help me look into it."

"That's why you came to me? To see if I might know anything about why your uncle Morton mentioned my father?" She wanted to help. It didn't all align in her mind, but she'd lost someone she loved and not been able to say goodbye. If she could help Isaac make peace with his uncle's death, she would. And if they found answers along the way, she'd welcome them.

"My father is gone. He's in Albany for a few days. I'll look in his office and see if there is anything that mentions Morton there." The thought of entering his office sent a chill racing up her spine. She avoided his space, but she would do it. "I don't know when he is coming back. I'll do what I can. If I find something, how will I get it to you?"

"I'll meet you back here tomorrow morning at nine o'clock."

"The dung heap." She smiled. It was the last place she'd ever imagined having a rendezvous with a man. "I'll be here unless my father returns much sooner than expected. He doesn't know that I am volunteering here."

"Will he stop you?"

Isaac had known her father before he changed. Back then, her father might have been concerned about her safety near the animals, but he'd been indulgent and always eager for her happiness. Now he'd have nothing but purely selfish arguments against her choice. A woman of her station did not stoop so low as to work with animals. He would declare it beneath her.

"I know he'll tell me I can't come. He doesn't want me out unless it somehow helps his business."

"And Abel?"

"Abel was his idea." She looked away. "I shouldn't have told you that. I intend to see Abel again. For now, my plan is to not mention the zoo to him."

"We have a truce—you can tell me whatever you wish. I won't tell him or anyone else."

"I don't have long. Forget I said anything about Abel. He has nothing to do with why the factory split or your uncle. None of the answers you seek are there."

"What if—" He pressed his lips together, stopping himself from saying whatever it was he longed to say. "I won't say anything about Abel."

"And my father can't know that we've met. No one can."

"It'll be our secret. One of our secrets."

"We have no other secrets," she said. That wasn't true. They shared years of letters. But he didn't know that, and here, by the manure, did not seem the right place to tell him.

"Do you remember the time we were in the factory? We were not even ten, and we saw your parents together. They were kissing each other. They didn't know we were spying on them."

Her mouth went dry. The memory was so deeply tucked away that it hurt to dig it up. Her parents had been happy, standing in each other's arms, embracing and kissing. Their smiles were so genuine. "I used to believe my parents the most blissfully married couple in all of Buffalo."

"I asked you if I could kiss you. Just for practice."

Oh dear, she remembered. She'd been so young, her rebuff had been instant. "I told you no."

"I said someday we'd practice."

"That was just childish talk—that's not a secret." The wind picked up, sending the pungent smell of composting dung in their direction. "I told you I was never going to kiss a man if it didn't mean something."

"Have you kept your word?"

"That is none of your business." She folded her arms across her ill-fitting dress, not ready to admit her lack of experience with courting and romance to the first and only boy, now man, she'd ever truly cared about. "I have to get back to work."

"Want help?"

"No. I want to do this on my own. Besides, there has already been enough talk about the two of us."

"Keep working at the zoo and you'll have a new headline before long."

She smiled, despite the possibility that she would once again be a headline worth laughing over. "'Stanley Bradshaw's daughter has once again proven her lack of social grace by wearing an archaic dress covered in elephant dung.' Maybe I should write it for them and save them the time. Or you should, since you're the one demanding retractions."

He put his hands behind his back and walked a few steps to the right and then the left, his eyes studying her as he went. She tried not to shy away from his inquisitive gaze. "'Stanley Bradshaw's daughter makes bold statement by following her heart, proves that a woman in calico and dung can be exceptionally beautiful.'"

Their eyes met. She searched his, looking for the humor that so often danced there, but she saw none of it now. For a moment the chasm between them became infinitely small. There was no teasing—only sincerity. It didn't make sense. She took a deep breath, telling her senses to calm down and stop acting as though this were a fairy tale. It wasn't. It was a farce. Because no matter the letters or the compliments, Isaac was still Campbell's son, and therefore untouchable. They could toy with each other if they chose, but it would never be more than a passing game.

"The editor would surely tear that up. It's not believable." She grabbed hold of the wheelbarrow handles. "I'll be here tomorrow."

Dear pinecone-throwing friend,

I don't think it right that a man toy with a woman's heart. Compliments should always be honest and thoughtful. Don't you agree? For example, no man should ever call someone beautiful if he doesn't mean it. It may seem flattering, but it's cruel to toss around words that aren't genuine. Men should not flirt with women they never truly intend to court. It's dangerous. Women's hearts are not meant to be played with. They are fragile and can be hurt by thoughtlessness.

You asked in your last letter what I planned to do to the man who humiliated me. I meant to torment him back, but now I am considering becoming his ally.

CHAPTER 18

need your help," Laura said to Mrs. Guskin upon returning late in the afternoon.

"You need a bath."

"It will have to wait. I have to find out if either of my parents had a connection with Morton Campbell." She sucked in her bottom lip as she unlaced her boots. "I suppose I'll have to look in my father's office."

"Did the monkeys at the zoo whisper this new plan to you?"

"No. I saw Isaac Campbell. He was at the zoo. He has reason to believe that his uncle's death might have something to do with the factory divide. Like me, he wishes to know why things are the way they are."

"You seem to have gotten awfully brave all of a sudden."

"You're the one who told me to think about what I want. One of the things I want is to understand what happened." She went to the sink and washed her hands and arms as far as her rolled-up sleeves would allow, then splashed water on her dirty face and neck. "That will have to do for now. Will you help me?"

"Your father will know someone was sneaking around his office if you leave bits of manure all over it. Let's change your dress, and then I'll help you." She led the way up the stairs. "You do know that we'll both be in a heap of trouble if we get caught."

"I know. But I've asked him before, and he won't tell me." She began unbuttoning the soiled dress the moment she entered her room. "I'm not interested in his business papers or discovering how much he spends on gin. I want to know why my world fell apart so I can see whether it's possible to put a few pieces back together. I have a right to know. It affects me."

Mrs. Guskin went to Laura's closet and brought her a fresh dress, simple with a collar and bow at the neck. "I knew when I took this job that you and I would be in for an adventure."

"How could you have known that? I was nothing but a sad child. I was only fourteen."

Mrs. Guskin worked her hands through the dress and held it up so Laura could slide in. "You were a sad girl. And I was a sad woman. John had died a year before I came here, and nothing was right. When I saw you so brokenhearted, I knew we needed each other. And that we'd both find something to look forward to. We've got a lot ahead of us still, and—"

"Storm's coming," Tybalt interrupted her. "Hurry up, you rum gagger."

"If a storm's coming, we'd best be ahead of it," Mrs. Guskin said. "Hurry up."

Laura tugged her dress into place. "I'm ready."

They made their way through the large house to the office, where they stood at the threshold a moment before stepping into the room they both tried so hard to avoid.

Built-in bookshelves lined one wall, though there were few books on them. Catalogs that contained advertisements for Bradshaw shoes filled most of the shelves. Framed photographs hung from nails in the wall, and there behind the desk was the large leather seat where her father spent so much of his time, the headrest dented from its many hours of use. She looked away from his chair, and the image it conjured of his intimidating eyes, and stepped near the far wall. Frozen memories in decorative frames caught her eye. It'd been years since she paused and looked at them. Her father with his siblings beside him, young and happy. Her father in a baseball game, wearing a jersey with a large *T* on it. A framed newspaper clipping about the opening of the Bradshaw-Campbell factory, praising her father for his bold business decisions and fine footwear. Happier days.

On a shelf more frames were stacked upside down and covered in dust. She picked up the first one and brought it closer. Her mother stared back at her. She wore an elegant dress, longer than the current style, coiffed hair perfectly framing her face. Beside her stood a younger version of Laura's father, equally dashing in his sack suit. "It's my father and my mother. They were so young."

Mrs. Guskin looked with her. "She's beautiful. They were a fine-looking couple."

"They were happy. I can remember them strolling the park at night, hand in hand. She never had a bad thing to say about my father."

The next one in the stack featured her father and William Campbell together, each with an arm around the other. They looked like a couple of school chums. "I used to think the Campbells would always be in my life."

She set the photographs down—she'd seen enough. The images served as reminders of what could have been, and the avenue of *if only* led to nowhere but the land of aching hearts. There wasn't time for melancholy. She needed to search the room and be on her way. A cabinet next to the desk seemed a logical place to look for . . . whatever she might find.

The first drawer contained nothing but invoices, bills, and drawings of shoe designs. The next drawer proved only slightly more interesting—newspaper clippings, a bill of sale for their home, and old account books.

"We aren't going to find anything here." Laura closed the drawer. "It's nothing but dusty old paperwork. Knowing that shoes are shipped to Azure Springs, Iowa, and Springfield, Virginia, doesn't help me at all."

"Open the last drawer, and I'll look at the desk."

The bottom drawer groaned as Laura pulled it open. She held her breath, desperately hoping to find something of importance as she peered inside. Then, with more force than necessary, she pushed it closed again. The bottles of liquor she'd discovered clanked together, then went silent.

"There's nothing." Her whispered voice cracked. "I'll never understand what happened. This hate will *always* be here."

"Don't give up so fast." Mrs. Guskin shuffled through the desk drawers. "I don't see anything here either. But that doesn't mean we won't find clues."

"I don't even know what a clue would look like." She stepped away from the desk, back to the wall and the photos, but found no solace in her new vantage point. "I think I'll go look through the dresses in the attic. I want to be ready for the zoo again tomorrow. Mr. Shaffer said he intends to check the health of the foxes and that I can help him."

It was best to cling to tomorrow and not dwell on her empty hands.

"I'll come with you. I want to hear all about your day at the zoo." Mrs. Guskin led the way to the dust-laden attic, where they stepped around traveling trunks and broken furniture, oil lamps and old toys. Some discarded items she remembered, and others were unfamiliar, but all were covered in dust and spiderwebs. Forgotten remnants of earlier days.

"Your father had me carry some of your mother's old things up here right after I took the job. It was so heavy I needed help to get it up those stairs." She pointed to a large metal storage trunk with leather latches. "I fit in as much as I could. If the pieces are too gaudy, I could try to alter some. Seems a shame, though, to take a fancy dress and make it suitable for the zoo."

"They aren't being used how they are." Laura unlatched the front of the trunk and pushed it open. Where the attic was nothing but dull colors, muted by their film of dust, the trunk was the opposite, filled with bright and beautiful dresses in every shade and color. The first dresses were far too fancy to wear to the zoo, even with altering. Unless she hoped to impress Big Frank or the family of foxes, they would do her no good.

She held up a yellow satin dress with white lace on the sleeves and bodice. A lovely dress. She brought it close to her nose and took a lingering breath, searching for the familiar scent of her mother. But there was no hint of the rose water she'd so loved. "I remember my mother wearing this one." She kept it pressed to her cheek. "She looked so fine, like a queen."

"You'd look just like her if you put it on. Oh my, look at this one." Mrs. Guskin held up a delicate pink evening dress. "I don't think I've ever seen a dress so delicate. The fabric is soft as butter."

"I wonder when she wore that one?" Laura had no memories

of the pink, but other dresses brought whispers of her mother back. "She wasn't always dressed in evening gowns. There must be skirts and shirtwaists somewhere. There must be something simpler that I could use."

Mrs. Guskin dug to the bottom of the chest, pulling out several sturdy skirts. Though they were cut with more flare than was in fashion now, they were thick and perfect for work. Laura held them up against herself. "I think they'll work."

Satisfied, they left the attic.

Laura's only regret from the nearly perfect day was that she had nothing to report to Isaac.

———•———

Isaac finished a letter to Laura, discussing the appropriate times to flatter and flirt. He was careful when he mentioned her newly formed alliance, not wanting her to know that it was him she'd sided with. Imagining her reading his words only made the act of writing more enjoyable. He knew which lines would make her smile and which would make her laugh. And which would, he hoped, make her heart flutter.

> *You, I am certain, have been called beautiful by many men, each meaning the compliment with true sincerity. I have no doubt your outward appearance is as stunning as the inner part, which I feel I know so well after all these years of correspondence. If a man calls you beautiful, know that you are.*

Since his first letter to Laura, writing had become a comfort in Isaac's life. He'd turned to it many times, grateful he'd been blessed with such a diversion. But now, with pen in hand and letter to Laura finished, he set his sights on writing an article.

For a long time he stared at the blank paper. When writing to Laura, he'd never worried about his words being well received—they always were. But writing an article that others would read with a skeptical eye had his nerves on edge.

All day he'd contemplated what to write about. He knew a great deal about shoes . . . but as a novice journalist, he wasn't ready to tackle something as large as the feud, and a simple exposé on shoe design might draw the attention of his father, which he could not risk. He thought about an article comparing the theater to moving pictures or one on the inadequate parking throughout the city. He had strong opinions about both, but neither seemed intriguing enough to prove that he was a writer worth paying.

"Isaac." His mother's voice beckoned him. "Ruth is here. She surprised us all by showing up. I'm so thrilled that you are both here at the same time."

He cringed. He ought to write a story about overly forward women and the impossible situation they put men in. Or meddling mothers. No matter what he wrote about, writing would have to wait, but it did have to happen. Mr. Cannon was busy tracking down Mary Kensington and deserved payment for his time.

"I'm sure she came to see you," he said, knowing it would agitate his mother. "Why don't you take her for a walk, and I'll manage things at home."

"Oh, don't be such a dunce. She's here to see you, and I raised you to be a gentleman. Don't keep her waiting."

He obeyed, leaving his room, but only because he wanted to

get this over with as quickly as possible. Ruth stood in the foyer, where she greeted him with a winning smile. "I'm so glad you're home. It's been far too long since we've seen each other."

"I've been busy."

"I know." She smiled over at his mother. "You don't mind if I steal your son away, do you? The weather is so fine. I've been longing for a walk through the park, and I thought, *Who better to walk with than Isaac Campbell?*"

"You're such a dear girl. I don't mind one bit. Go and enjoy the weather. The fresh air will be good for Isaac."

He gritted his teeth, biting back words that would only cause a scene. Instead, he held out his arm and led Ruth from the house. Their home was several blocks from the park. They could walk there, but if he drove, he could get back sooner. He opened the door to his Ford and helped her inside.

"I told Myra when I saw her that we were still seeing each other. She didn't believe me, but now she will." Ruth put a hand to her perfectly waved bob and tilted her head in a way she likely believed alluring, but it only annoyed him. "We must see each other more, or the gossips will start talking."

Isaac started the engine. "We went out once. You can't claim a man after one night."

"Have you had a hard day? You're not usually so terse."

"It has nothing to do with the type of day I've had." He drove toward the park, though it felt wrong taking her to a place that made him think of Laura. The grassy lawns, the zoo—it was here he'd been swept away by Laura's words.

"When I dined with your family the other day, your father mentioned that you insisted on becoming a donor to the zoo."

"It's good for business to support worthy causes," he said,

speaking the truth. "The zoo is a fine place. It has animals from all over the world."

"I didn't realize you had such a fondness for animals." She squinted against the bright sun. "If I were to donate money to a cause, it would not be the zoo."

"What would it be?"

"A dance hall, or funds to start an improvement society. I have heard of ladies' organizations that put on the fanciest dinners."

"What do they improve?" Isaac asked, genuinely curious what the benefit of such a society would be.

"They improve the lives of the members. It's the perfect opportunity for women to gather." She giggled like a much younger woman. "It's a chance for women to talk. There's value in that."

"You would donate to a ladies' society so you could meet together and gossip?"

"You make it sound so awful." She nudged him in the shoulder. They were still in the automobile, parked but not getting out. He couldn't bring himself to step out with her. Ruth's slight against Laura was still too fresh, too personal.

"There's nothing wrong with a little gossip." She kept talking as though nothing were amiss. Her hands ran easily along the door of his car. "It keeps life exciting. You should have heard all the fun we had after the night at the square."

That did it. The scab on the still-fresh wound came off. A keen awareness that humans were capable of immense cruelty, and that this cruelty had brought pain to someone he cared for, burned in his chest. In the moment, when he had struggled to make sense of what transpired, he'd not spoken up as he should have. He'd been tongue-tied instead of bold. But he would not make the same mistake again.

"Ruth," he said. "You and I are not well suited for each other. Nothing about the night at the square amused me. I don't care for gossip, and I happen to think the zoo worthy of a donation."

"Are you saying you don't want to see me again?"

"I think we would only be wasting our time if we continued this." He started his engine again, ready to pull away from the park, take her home, and be done with Ruth Bagley. His mother could fret over it if she wanted, but Ruth would never make him happy or soothe his restless spirit. "I wish you happiness in all your pursuits. But I have no respect for someone who would deliberately intoxicate another. It was cruel."

"But you hate Bradshaw."

"It's more complicated than that."

"Everyone talks about how you're the bachelor who won't be tamed. Are there no women who appeal to you?"

She had not endeared herself to him enough to be privy to his secrets. He steered his Ford away from the park. "When I leave my bachelor ways, if I do, it will be because I have found someone who . . . who finds the zoo as peaceful as I do."

"You're a fool." Ruth opened the door to his automobile the moment he stopped and, without waiting for a goodbye, stepped away. Her disdain for him was evident in her swift, angry gait.

Sweet relief followed her exit as she grew smaller and smaller and then disappeared around the corner. Such content was short-lived, however. His mother greeted him with an ear-piercing rebuke.

"She was perfect. You let her get away." She huffed about the room like an angry peacock. "You could have been married in a month."

"I don't want to marry Ruth," he said, as he walked past her toward his room and his pen and paper. "I don't love her."

"Love!" she shrieked. "Ruth was beautiful, wealthy."

"Stop," he said. He couldn't have ever loved her. Even if she'd been kinder and more thoughtful, his heart belonged to another. Isaac left his fuming mother. He had an article to write.

The Buffalo Zoo

As the third-oldest zoo in the nation, the Buffalo Zoo is home to more than just animals. It is home to memories. Were you a child with one small hand wrapped around a parent's larger one and popcorn in the other? Do you remember the first time you saw Big Frank?

The zoo is a pillar of this great city. It is a place to go when you want to remember how big and grand the world is . . .

CHAPTER 19

Nine o'clock each morning quickly became Isaac's favorite time of day. He'd meet Laura, and they would begin by discussing anything they'd learned about the past. She hadn't come up with any clues other than a few obscure conversations she'd heard over the years—pieces that neither knew where to place.

On their fourth meeting he'd seen Mr. Cannon again and was pleased to report to Laura that the detective had been successful in some regard. He now believed that Mary Kensington lived in Niagara Falls, New York, just north of them.

"That's less than thirty miles from here. You could go there and meet her and save yourself from having to communicate through the mail," Laura said when she heard his news. "Are you done with Mr. Cannon?"

"No, not yet. He said to wait to pay him until after I have retrieved the letters. He said if they were full of clues about what happened with the factory, he'd help me try to sort them out. I thought he was a gruff old man, but he's not so bad, and he seems to want to see this through." He pulled the paper from behind his back then. "I brought this for you."

"A paper?" She took it and skimmed over the front page. "Thank you. I'll read it after I'm done here."

"I wrote about the zoo. It's on page four."

"You wrote about the zoo?" Her eyes lit up, and her fingers quickly turned the page. "This is you?"

"I had to use a pen name. Seemed safer that way."

"Why did you choose Frank Mapleton?"

He shrugged. "I had to come up with it in a hurry. I thought Big Frank wouldn't mind me using his name, and, well, I'm fond of maple trees."

"You are?"

"Who isn't? It's harder than you think to choose a name to go by. Even that took me a good half hour of chewing on the end of my pencil, at which point I decided it was good enough."

"I like it. I can't believe you told me though. It's not secretive if everyone knows."

"I haven't told everyone. Only you."

"Only me." She looked up from the paper, an adorable half smile on her lips. "What if I tell everyone?"

"You won't because we called a truce, and you wouldn't want to break it."

"That's true." She pulled her mouth to one side, her eyes dancing with playful humor. "But when it is just you and me by the pile of manure, can I call you Frank Mapleton? I don't believe there is any rivalry between the Mapletons and the Bradshaws."

"So you're saying you could be friends with a Mapleton?"

"Yes, I suppose I could."

"And . . . could you date a Mapleton?"

She laughed and swatted his arm with the newspaper. "It would depend on whether I liked the man."

He loved every moment of this exchange. "You may call me whatever you like."

"That's awfully daring."

"You were never very good at thinking of mean names to call me when we were children. I'm not too worried."

"I remember calling you a meanie once, and didn't I call you an ogre?"

He put a hand on her shoulder. He'd meant to nudge it play-fully, but he let his hand linger. "Neither of those names are very terrible."

"Ogres were always bad in the stories I read with my mother." Her voice was still playful, but it took on a breathless quality.

He found it hard to swallow. This proximity, his hand on her . . . afraid he'd do something she wouldn't welcome, he pulled his hand back. "I have to pay Mr. Cannon and don't want to have to borrow from my father. Writing for the paper . . . it was about money at first. But once I started writing, a whole other part of me came alive. Since writing this, I've been keeping lists of ideas I could write about. They want me to write more. The editor told me to stop by anytime with new articles."

"When we were children, I don't remember you having a love of writing."

Her words challenged him, daring him to tell about the letter tree and how their shared words had inspired him. He nearly did, but what they were rekindling was still fragile. It was mere coals, barely warm enough to ignite. "I have done a bit of writing over the last few years. Correspondence, mostly."

"It must have been an excellent teacher." She held up the paper. "You're in print now. It's wonderful."

Each day they shared a little more with each other. Rem-iniscing about old times, wondering what their lives would have been like if the factory hadn't split, and laughing over the dirt that was under her nails.

"What will Abel think of your new look?" Isaac asked at their sixth meeting without thinking first. Talking about Abel always widened the canyon between them.

"He's been busy working on some investment opportunity that is supposed to close soon. I don't know much about it, but it seems to have him occupied all day. I would have thought a supplier of raw goods would be consumed with managing shipping invoices and sending out notices for payment. But he rarely talks about that." She stuck her hands in the pockets of her skirt. "I've been so busy here at the zoo, I haven't thought much about Abel. I'm sure he'll call when he wants to."

Isaac rubbed the back of his neck. He didn't want to be nosy or appear as though he were out to drive a wedge between Laura and a man she could end up sharing her future with. But there were so many things he wondered about. Abel had been coming by his house over the last few days, presenting investment plans to his father—and Isaac, too, if he was present. Abel had properties in Florida that he planned to sell all at once to interested buyers.

Once, Isaac had even heard Abel speak in a low voice about how the right investment could put the Campbell factory ahead of all other companies. Were they empty promises?

"When you see him, you ought to ask him about the deal. You're smart enough to teach yourself about animal care. I am sure you could understand what he is working on."

She reached for her wheelbarrow, a sure sign she was about to tell him she had to be going. He wanted more time with her.

"Wait," he said. "You said no talking about Abel. I broke your rule. I'm sorry."

Her hands stilled on the handles.

"I don't know what he sees in me," she said in a soft, vulnerable voice. "I'm not glamorous like the women who wave and bat their eyes at him when we go out. I pretend to be what he wants, but he must see through it." She looked at her dirt-stained hands. "This is more who I am. I'm happier here than I ever was when we were at the clubs."

"And what do you see in him?" He moved closer, his voice careful. "Don't you think he wonders why you're with him?"

"He's . . . he's attentive, and he's different from my father." She fidgeted, refusing to look him in the eye. "It's not so simple."

"I remember your father—"

"He's not how you remember him." She pushed the wheelbarrow a foot before stopping again. "He cares about business, that's all. When Abel came over, and Father approved of him, I thought maybe . . . I thought he could give me a life away from . . . everything."

"What about love?"

"I hoped . . . but not everyone gets that luxury."

"Abel is a flirt. I've seen it myself. He's fond of having many women shouting his praises and hanging on his words. Don't you want to be in love with someone who has eyes for only you?"

"Yes," she said with tears right at the surface, pooled and ready to fall. "I do want that. But we don't get everything we want. I knew that the day my mother died. We can want something, we can long for it. That doesn't mean we can have it. I'm trying to sort it all out. Right now, I have to get back to work."

She started away from him, the wheelbarrow bouncing along the uneven ground.

"You deserve better," he said to her back, but she didn't hear, not with the noise of the rickety wheelbarrow.

He left the manure pile and found a corner to write in. At least on paper, he seemed to be better at communicating. Someday, if he was ever brave enough and certain they could be together, he would tell her that all the words he had written were still true, and even though he'd never signed his name to them, his heart had been there for her to take and do with as she pleased.

> *Dear Wishing Girl,*
>
> *It's a strange stage of life we are in. Everyone is dating and marrying. Some settle for someone who simply provides for them; others wait for someone they feel speaks to their soul. I wonder: What is it that you hope for in a man? . . .*

Laura walked beside Abel, doing her best to honor her father's wishes and not disrupt their relationship, at least not until it no longer affected her father's business dealings. It seemed old-fashioned, dating a man because it benefited her father. She felt small, and of little worth, to think she could be so easily traded for a contract signature.

When she saw Isaac next, she would tell him to write an article reminding society that it was 1924 and, in such modern times, marrying for money or family gain ought to be outlawed. She'd open the paper and put it next to her father's breakfast when he returned from his rather lengthy business trip, and per-haps Frank Mapleton's words would give him something to think about.

"You've been awfully quiet this evening," Abel said after they took their seats for dinner.

Laura opened her napkin and laid it across her lap. "I've been wondering . . . When was the last time you went out with a woman other than me?"

For a moment his eyes grew large, but then in true Abel style, he smiled roguishly and said, "I've found the changes in courting and dating hard to keep up with. It used to be a man sat in a woman's parlor, he spoke to her father, and the terms were clear." He tapped his forefinger on the table. "But now the rules are not so well defined."

"What are you trying to tell me?" She was not so naive that she did not know how dating had changed. The invention of the automobile liberated couples in ways they'd never known before. Women worked and attended college, and they were free to make choices about the men in their lives. But she had believed that it was still right and proper to date only one person at a time.

"Young people are going out every night, dancing, skating. I have embraced this movement toward socializing with a wide range of peers."

She stared at his smug face. "You didn't answer me."

"Let's talk of other things. When the time is right, we can define our relationship. You know I'm fond of you."

"Very well," she said, dissatisfied by his half answers. "I'd love to hear more about the business that has kept you so busy."

"You would find that dull."

"I don't think I would." She dared him to go on, emboldened by the taste of freedom she'd had these last few days. "It seems your investment opportunity is taking up more time than your delivering of raw goods. It must be an important endeavor. Tell me about it."

"I warn you it's dull." He picked up a fork and fiddled with it in his hands. In this moment, she wished she knew his tics like she did her father's. "I inherited not only the raw goods factory but also the deed to my father's other investments. He owned land in Florida that is on top of oil. He'd planned to have it worked, but with his declining health, he never did."

"What does that have to do with my father?"

"I've asked some of my business friends if they'd be interested in buying a portion of the land. I don't want the hassle of having it worked and can use the funds to grow my other businesses. They can choose how much they want to buy, use a bit of cash to get drilling going, and then they'll have a massive return in weeks. Your father is a special friend, and I'm happy to let him buy as much as he wishes."

"If the deal is so grand, why sell it?"

"My father left me other businesses and investments. Don't you worry—I've more money coming in than I know what to do with. In fact, I'm considering buying one of the mansions on Seneca Street. Selling off a few properties doesn't hurt me. It's good for everyone. I especially want to please your father." He set down the fork he'd been twirling in his fingers and reached a hand across the small table, palm up, inviting her to take it.

He was rich, more so than she had expected. The homes on Seneca were four stories tall, with gardens and carriage houses. All she had to do was take his hand and beg him to choose her above anyone else. But she couldn't take it.

Abel withdrew his offered hand and picked up the menu. "Go ahead and order whatever you like. I didn't mean to be presumptuous. Once the deal is done, you'll see that I'm genuine. Until then, we will pace ourselves. There's no need to rush our budding feelings."

She managed a weak smile. An awkwardness settled over the evening like a dense fog. What were she and Abel? A couple? They'd rarely called themselves one, and he'd as much as admitted to taking other women out. Friends? She did not feel the bond of friendship with Abel. They were not strangers. They were more like acquaintances, doing an unfamiliar dance together. When the business deal closed and her father relaxed, she would ask Abel why he'd called on her and what he saw in her. Until then, she remained the quiet, mostly agreeable date, cautious in every way so as not to find herself bound by new chains in her escape from the old ones.

Later, when she found Isaac's letter, she pondered what she would hope for in a man. And the description she penned in reply did not match Abel, not even a shadow of him.

. . . If this life were a fairy tale and I could have my choice of men, I would want a man who did not find me odd for having a pet bird or strange for dreaming of country living. I would want a man who was not afraid to laugh, and who was patient and kind. He would want none but me. I think I'd like him to have a mischievous side, but only act on it on rare occasions. And I would want him to love pineapple upside-down cake as much as I do and to climb up to my window and beg me to go away with him . . .

CHAPTER 20

After seven more days of nine o'clock rendezvous, Isaac, who had believed himself smitten before, was entirely, one hundred percent, head over heels for Laura. Yet neither of them addressed the sparks that flew when their hands brushed together, or the harmony of their laughter when an old memory came to the surface.

If today followed their quickly established pattern, and he hoped it would, they would begin by discussing Mary Kensington and the split in the factory. After all, that was their justification for meeting. Once any new details were brought to light, their exchange would take a natural turn and become delightful conversation, the type of banter and fun that he wished could go on unceasingly.

He paced back and forth, careful not to step on the bits of manure that had rolled down the side of the mound. The thought of going to Niagara Falls enticed him. He wanted to go, but he did not know how long these meetings with Laura would continue, and he couldn't pull himself away from her—not yet. Her father could return at any time. Already he'd been gone longer than they expected. When he returned, everything would be more complicated, and the blissful tête-à-tête they'd been sharing could end. For now, he was more than content having an early morning rendezvous with Laura, followed by a bit of menial work for his father, and then finishing his days scribbling articles for the newspaper.

Writing was proving more fulfilling than he had anticipated. Where his father had often found him inadequate or not ready for a job, the editor of the paper was thrilled with his work, begging him to write faster. Frank Mapleton was already making a name for himself. The harder he worked and faster he wrote, the more money he collected for his efforts. He patted the pocket of his pants, grateful that the money in his billfold was all his own and ready to help him reach not one but two important goals—finding Mary Kensington and buying Laura a gift.

His father had stopped pressuring him to befriend Abel Fredricks and had taken over negotiations himself. Normally such an act of dismissal would have left Isaac fuming for weeks, but not this time. He was happy to wash his hands of Abel and let his father broker whatever deal he wanted with the smooth-talking man. It was simpler that way. When Laura asked about Abel, he could honestly say he knew little of the relationship between him and Campbell shoes.

Isaac held a slice of carefully wrapped pineapple upside-down cake in his hand as he meandered around the manure, waiting for Laura. When he'd asked the cook to bake it, she'd turned up her nose, declaring it an atrocious newfangled recipe. He'd had to go to the store himself to get the canned pineapple, a luxury that had excited all of Buffalo when the Dole company first started shipping them around the country. With the cans already purchased, he'd been able to convince her to try something new, but it had required begging and a promise to sneak in after dinner and help with cleanup.

It'd been worth it. The cake was delicious, mouthwatering in all the right ways. The idea of bringing a slice to Laura had excited him, but now as he paced, he worried she may find it an odd gift. He would have to keep a straight face if Laura asked how he knew it was her favorite. He forced his lips into a straight line, practicing his reaction, but that seemed too serious. He made a half smile. Drat, he should have practiced in front of the mirror before leaving the house.

The sound of the wheelbarrow bouncing along the brick path only increased his anticipation. He leaned against the wall, pretending to be casually waiting and not as wound up as a schoolboy anticipating the summer recess.

"Isaac," Laura said as she came around the corner, her dark dress already soiled with muck. "I have news."

"You do?" he asked, eager to hear what had her so flushed. "What is it?"

"I've been wearing old clothes of my mother's. I didn't want to ruin anything fancy or new. Plus, how would I shovel manure in a beaded dress with a low neckline?"

"I imagine that would be difficult," he said, trying not to dwell on the vision that flashed in his mind.

"I put this skirt on for the first time this morning, and I could tell there was something in the pocket." She reached into it now and pulled out a torn slip of paper. "Look here."

He shifted his gift to his left hand and took the note with his right.

"Read it," she said.

"'Meet Morton at ten o'clock. Delaware Park.'" He read it again. "Was there anything else?"

"No. I searched through all my mother's old clothes. I found a few coins and a grocery list, but nothing else significant. But this proves that they knew each other. I'm surprised I don't remember him. But this is her skirt and her penmanship. She was meeting him."

"I'll tell Mr. Cannon about it."

"Could I meet him?" she asked. "I'm worried. The zoo and . . . and seeing you every day has been good, but this note." She shook her head. "I don't understand it. And the other night, when I was out with Abel, something seemed, well, it seemed off."

"Did he do something to you?"

"No, he was nice enough. It's just that when I asked him about his business investments, something about his answers felt off. I could be wrong. I don't want to cause a problem if there isn't one. If I asked Mr. Cannon to look into Abel, would he do it discreetly?"

Isaac nodded. "He won't tell anyone about Abel, or about this." He looked again at the faded note in his hand. "I could pick you up, and we could go this afternoon. What time will you be done here?"

"I've been leaving around two o'clock. The animals are all fed and their pens clean by then. It might take me a few minutes to clean up. I'd rather not smell like animals at the meeting."

"I'll phone ahead and tell Mr. Cannon that we are coming together. I'll come by your house at two thirty."

"You can't just come to my house." She sucked her bottom lip, and he became aware of his own lips. Without intending to, he imagined kissing her. When she spoke again, her words were muffled by the desire he felt to take her in his arms. He'd felt the urge before, many times, but each day it grew stronger. He cleared his throat and waited for her to say more. "I'll meet you at the corner of Florence and Parkside. We need to make sure no one sees us. We may have a truce, but no one knows it. Will that work?"

He nodded, his mouth too dry to speak.

"I'll be there." She pointed at the plate in his hand. "What have you got there?"

"I . . ." He forced the words out. "I brought you this." He took the cover off and held it out to her. "We had pineapple upside-down cake last night. I am told it is all the rage. I just . . . I thought you might like it."

"Our housekeeper makes this. We found the recipe in a *Good Housekeeping* magazine." She took the plate, their fingers touching as it exchanged hands. A thousand fireworks exploded, even from so small a touch. Like a fool he stared at his hand. What was wrong with him? He'd touched women before, when dancing or escorting them about, but no touch had ever leaped straight from his hand to his heart like hers did.

"Thank you," she said, looking past the plate at him. "This is so kind. It's as though . . ." She shook her head slowly, an inquiry in her gaze.

In an instant he made a decision. He was going to tell her that he was behind the letters and beg her to give him a chance. How could he not when her eyes were so full of questions and longing? She had to know, and then together they could find a way. Where once he had believed it impossible, he now refused to accept such a conclusion. He kept his eyes up, never looking at their shoes— his Campbell's and hers Bradshaw's—not wanting to think about feuds or chasms. Together they would build a bridge.

"Laura," he said, his shaking voice betraying him against his will. "After we meet Mr. Cannon, can I take you to Centennial

Park on the lake? It's quiet—there are paths and benches no one goes to. We'd be alone and without the smell of animals. We could talk freely. Will you go with me?"

She gave him the faintest bob of her head. It was all the yes he needed; he nearly whooped aloud. Today it was really happening. The truth would be out, and they could be more than childhood friends, more than allies. Her mouth drew him in again, the perfect curve of her upper lip, the slight rise at the corners. If they were more than friends, someday the longing to hold her, and to kiss her, could be a reality.

"When we're there," she said, the quiver in her voice matching his. "I want to tell you something."

"As do I." He looked past her. "Someone is coming. I can hear them whistling."

She turned in the direction of the sound. "It's Mr. Shaffer. Quick, go behind the mound. I don't want him seeing me back here with you. Or sitting around eating cake." She stuffed one quick bite of pineapple cake in her mouth before handing him the plate and giving him a gentle shove toward the manure mound. Then she grabbed his arm, pulled him back, and kissed him on the cheek all in one motion. "Thank you for the cake," she said before pushing him out of sight again.

The pungent smell grew stronger as he crept behind the back side of the decomposing mountain, but he didn't care. He was too consumed by the warmth of her lips on his cheek and the desire to run to her and kiss her in return. It was an urge he could not submit to, and so he crouched behind the mountain, alternating between holding his breath and gasping for air. He looked at the plate in his hands and berated himself for bringing her cake to eat near manure—so odd a pairing.

"Laura." The zookeeper's voice traveled over the mound to him. "One of the gazelles has his horns stuck in the fence. I thought you might like to come and help."

"I'd love to." Isaac could hear excitement in her voice. "I read about a goat who was constantly getting his horns stuck in a fence."

"What was done for it?"

Isaac's legs began to cramp from squatting. He shifted his weight, but it didn't help; his legs still begged to be straightened. He could only hope the story of the stubborn goat would not be lengthy.

"They took a stick and attached it across the horns so he could not find himself in such a predicament again. I believe, ultimately, it is a better idea to fix the fence, but in the interim, it kept him from injuring himself. Or damaging his horns."

"It's an excellent idea." Mr. Shaffer's voice grew softer, indicating to Isaac that they were walking away. The last words he heard were "I'm impressed with all your book learning. It takes real ambition to be so well self-taught."

His heart swelled knowing someone else realized how smart she was. Convinced he was alone, he straightened his legs, wincing slightly from the rush of blood to his limbs. A quick shake and he was feeling better. He wanted to mosey over to the gazelles and watch Laura help the poor creature, but he wasn't sure if he would be welcome, and though he felt no malice toward Laura for being a Bradshaw, he knew that if they were caught together, the rumors would make their unusual friendship more complicated than it already was. A truce with the enemy was a precarious thing to navigate. For now, it was best for him to go and pass the time on his own until he met her at Florence and Parkside later in the day.

———————•———————•———————

Isaac stared at his pocket watch and then brought it closer to his ear. Time was moving so slowly, he feared it wasn't working.

"Something wrong?" Charles asked.

"I'm not sure my watch has the proper time. What does yours say?"

Charles pulled out a simple pocket watch. "It's just past noon."

Isaac closed his watch and shoved it in his pocket. The time was accurate. Still over two hours to get through before he could fetch Laura. Trying to appear relaxed, he leaned back in his chair and put his feet on the desk. "If someone wanted to climb through a second-story window without being caught, how would he do that?"

"Are you planning to rob a home or seduce a woman?" Charles said as though this were an entirely typical conversation.

"It's hypothetical."

"Sure it is." Charles *humph*ed. "I must warn you, as your friend, that sneaking into Laura Bradshaw's bedroom is not a good way to woo her."

"Why would I do that?" He let out an uncomfortable chortle. "That would make me no better than a Peeping Tom."

"You've been acting strange lately, so I wouldn't be surprised." He yawned and stretched. "Elsie has decided that with her mother on the mend, she wants to have the wedding in two weeks. She called me on the phone last night and went over every detail."

"I thought you were going to be married the very day her mother left her sickbed."

"The church isn't available, and Elsie is determined to be married in the church her parents were married in." He smiled; his cheerful grin rarely faded these days. "Maybe you should climb up a ladder, knock on Laura's window, and see if she would consider a double wedding. We could get your parents to cover the expenses, and it would be a victory for all of us."

"Clever idea, but she still doesn't know I'm the letter writer." He took his feet off the desk and leaned forward. "I'm going to tell her today. I've been thinking about it for a couple of hours. I can't decide if it would be better to just blurt it out or to do some grand romantic gesture."

"Are you certain she would want a romantic gesture?"

"No . . . and yes." He shook his head. "I believe she would welcome it—I hope she would—but then she'll think about the rift between our families, and I don't know what she'll do."

"So she likes you?"

Isaac's lips twitched. He tried to hold back a smile, but it rebelled, the memory too sweet and powerful to contain. "She kissed me on the cheek. That has to mean something."

"My grandma kisses me on the cheek, and over on Hertel Avenue, the Italians are always kissing everyone. It means hello, goodbye. I think it can mean most anything."

Isaac's smile fell from his face quicker than a drop of rain in a thunderstorm. "You don't think it meant anything?"

"I didn't say that." Charles shrugged. "It could mean something. It's a shame your letter girl wasn't someone else." Charles rubbed at his scruffy cheek. "You wouldn't have to do so much secret-keeping and guessing."

"I can't change her lineage. All I can do is tell her about the letters, and after that . . . I don't know. There must be a way for us to be together. We're so much better together than we are apart."

"In that case, I vote you do something romantic. It may be your only chance, and it'll make for a better story later."

"You only want a story so you can be entertained while you wait for your wedding."

"Two weeks would go by much faster if I was entertained."

Isaac opened his watch again. Only five minutes had passed. But something he hadn't noticed before caught his eye. On the far side of the cover, a few centimeters from the engraving, was a symbol, shaped like two small letters merged into one. The symbol was so small it could have been mistaken for a dent. "Do you suppose I could find the artisan who engraved this?"

"You might be able to. My cousin is a jeweler, and he always leaves a signature on his work so he can recognize it if it comes back. You should ask him. He knows most everyone's signature."

Isaac stood, watch in hand. "Do you have an address? I'll go now."

"I don't know the street number, but it's the jeweler on Butler Avenue. It's just a small storefront. His name is Richard Carlisle. If his wife is there, she's Rose. Tell them I say hello."

"I will." He left in a hurry, eager to do something meaningful while he passed his time. The moment his father gifted the watch to him, Isaac had known there was a deep meaning to it, only he'd never been able to decipher what it was. The gentle curve of the letters seemed innocent enough. But why those words? And why had his father looked near tears when giving it to him? Yet another mystery to solve.

Charles had an extensive family tree, branches of cousins, aunts, and uncles. He proved an excellent resource in times of need. And today he'd done well again. When Isaac arrived at the small jeweler on Butler Avenue, he was welcomed in with warmth. Richard didn't look much like Charles, other than their matching smiles, but he seemed eager to help.

With a magnifying glass, Richard studied the signature, then had his wife, Rose, look.

"It's one of Cecil Bonetti's," Rose said, her eye still near the magnifying glass. "This signature is a little worn, but it's his. He's never changed his signature. It's been the same from the start."

"Do you know where I can find him?" Isaac's heart beat faster. He could see why Mr. Cannon enjoyed the quest for answers. "It's important. I'd like to see him today if I can."

"He's not far from here." Richard took a scrap of paper from under his counter and drew a map. "You're about ten blocks away. You can't miss it. Cecil does mostly watches. He repairs them and engraves them. He can get anything working again."

"But your piece is working," Rose said. "It's keeping excellent time."

"It's the engraving I hope he remembers. I'd like to ask him about it."

"He keeps impeccable records. There's a chance he will." Richard pushed the watch back across the counter to him. "It's an excellent watch. Very fine quality."

"A gift from my father," Isaac said as he tucked it back in his pocket for safekeeping. "Thank you for looking at it. Charles was confident that if anyone could identify the signature, it was you."

"Charles speaks too highly of us. This city is getting so large that there are new signatures every day. I can't keep half of them straight anymore. I'm glad we knew this one," Richard said. "Tell Charles hello for us. We're looking forward to his wedding."

"I don't think a man has ever been so eager."

Rose laughed, a birdlike chortle. "He's excited about everything. It's how he lives his life."

"Even when he was small," Richard said. "He'd fall and bounce right back up. Never stopped smiling."

"It would do us all well to take a lesson from him," Isaac said, thinking of the many times he'd fallen and stayed down for far too long.

He thanked them again before heading off to find Cecil Bonetti.

CHAPTER 21

Isaac turned the corner onto Florence Avenue and saw Laura standing beneath a red awning with her back against the brick wall of a small café. She waved and stepped toward the street the moment their eyes connected. Gone were her dirty zoo clothes, which had been replaced by an olive-green day dress and matching felt hat. Simple and stylish and utterly attractive.

He jumped out of the Ford, ran to her side, and opened the passenger door. "I brought you something. It's on your seat."

"First cake, and now another surprise?" She smiled before getting into the car. Next to her on the bench seat was a handkerchief. "What's this?"

"It's for you." He picked it up and unfolded it. In the corner, embroidered red and yellow flowers framed the initials *CB*. "Right before your mother died and the factory split, I fell at the park. I bloodied my lip, and your mother handed me this. I took it home and had it cleaned. I planned to bring it back to her, but I never got a chance. I always felt bad about that. I didn't know what to do with it, so I just kept it. Now it's yours."

Laura ran her fingers over the stitching. "Her mama sent this from South Dakota. I remember that when it came, my mother pressed it to her face. I think she was imagining an embrace from her mama."

"And now it's yours, and you can imagine that your mama is here beside you in this automobile." He started the engine, glancing over at her from time to time. She held the handkerchief close, pressed to her heart.

From her letters, he knew that there were times she remembered her mother's death in vivid detail. He could only hope his small gesture would ease some of her struggle if such a memory came. At least she'd have something to hold on to.

"My mother," she said, looking ahead, "spoke highly of you."

"She did?" He'd not even been to her funeral. The company hadn't split then, but things were different, more tense. Changes were happening, only he hadn't known what they were or how lasting they would prove.

"Yes." Her smile was faint and far off. "When I would complain about your teasing, she'd tell me that you'd outgrow it. She said that underneath your wild ways were the seeds of a good man."

"She was a good woman. When I was fifteen, she told me once to not overlook you," he said, remembering the way Mrs. Bradshaw had pulled him aside when he was at a church social and told him he ought to ask Laura to dance. Laura had been sitting by herself, stroking a stray dog and watching everyone else on the dance floor. "She said that you were a deep thinker with a good heart, and that those traits were lasting."

Laura tightened her grip on her handkerchief. "I often wonder what life would be like if she were still here, but those thoughts never help."

"What would help?" he asked, ready to give her the moon if she wanted it.

"This is helping," she said, gesturing toward his gift of the forgotten handkerchief. "And talking about her with someone who remembers her. Mrs. Guskin, my housekeeper, is an extraordinary listener, but she did not know my mother. My father won't speak of her."

"Perhaps it hurts too much."

"He said once that she was nothing but an actress. I don't know what he meant. He wouldn't elaborate." She took the handkerchief from her chest and looked again at the embroidered letters. "We had some good times, all of us together. It all seemed real, not like acting."

Isaac reached across the bench seat and put a hand on her arm. "It was real."

They drove in silence the rest of the way through the busy streets. It took him several minutes to find a place to park. Once he did, he opened her door, and they walked around the back side of the enormous building together.

"I meant to tell you," he said as they walked, "I learned something about my uncle today."

"You did?" She tucked her mother's handkerchief into her pocket. "What did you learn?"

He pulled out his watch and handed it to her, then opened the unmarked door for her so she could enter the hallway that led to Mr. Cannon's office. "My father gave me that pocket watch a couple years back. It was for my uncle, but my father never got a chance to send it to him. I always wondered about the inscription. It seemed an odd choice to have engraved. I supposed it could be making reference to the war . . ."

"*Even apart, we battle together.* It's not what I would have chosen. Do you still think it is about the war?"

"I'm not sure." He showed her the small signature before knocking on Mr. Cannon's door. "I was able to use that to find out who did this engraving. I had time this afternoon, so I went to meet him and see if he could remember anything."

"You're turning into a rather fine detective."

Mr. Cannon, in his ever-frantic way, shoved the door open, interrupting their conversation, and pulled them inside. He shut the door with just as much force. Laura shot Isaac a wide-eyed, questioning look. He only shrugged. She'd see for herself soon enough what sort of a man Mr. Cannon was.

"This is her?" Mr. Cannon said while moving a stack of papers off a chair in the corner and carrying it closer to the desk. He motioned for them to sit.

"Mr. Cannon, this is Laura Bradshaw."

They both greeted each other, and then Isaac, eager to tell Laura the rest of his story, took the lead in the conversation. "I was just telling Laura about my pocket watch and what I've discovered."

"If it doesn't have to do with the case, I don't have time for it." Mr. Cannon picked up a pencil and notepad. "If it does, then share."

"I'm not sure what it means."

"Go on then."

"My father gave me this watch." Isaac handed it to Mr. Cannon and quickly explained about the signature. "I found Mr. Bonetti today. I told him that it had been made for my uncle and asked if he remembered anything about it. He keeps good records. It was purchased and engraved in 1917."

Mr. Cannon scribbled quickly on his paper. His shorthand was illegible.

"He had several notes written in his ledger." Isaac picked up the watch again.

"What did they say?" Laura scooted to the edge of her seat. "Tell us."

"One said, 'Watch engraved for Morton Campbell, paid for by William Campbell.' None of that was a surprise. But then there was a note that said, 'Not to be discussed with Stanley Bradshaw.' Mr. Bonetti said both of our fathers used his services often for gifts for their wives, employees, and the like. And that it was peculiar my father specifically told him not to discuss this watch with Bradshaw."

Mr. Cannon rubbed at his large nose. "Your uncle didn't work for the factory, correct?"

"He wasn't working at all. He was thinking of going to law school but wasn't working very hard toward it. He was younger than my father, and being raised by older parents, he wasn't pushed to grow up. He was twenty-three when he went off to war, but still wandering aimlessly through life. Don't get me wrong—he was a good man. But he wasn't very serious about life."

"The question is"—Mr. Cannon lifted his pencil—"how was Morton connected to the feud? Or was he at all? Your watch seems to indicate that somehow he was, or else why would your father care if her father saw it? Could the inscription be a reference to the battle between Campbell and Bradshaw? Let's say it is. What could Morton have done to become a part of it?"

"In one of my mother's skirt pockets, I found a note that said she was to meet Morton at a set time. I didn't even know she knew him," Laura said. "My father and mother were close. I believed them happily married. But he's been bitter and angry for years now, and he won't talk about my mother. When he does, it's never complimentary. I don't want to believe it, but I think my mother may have been part of it all too."

Mr. Cannon tapped his pointer finger on the desk. "What if your mother and Morton were involved? She may have married for love but lost her way."

"Are you suggesting my mother and Morton were having an affair?" Laura's face paled. "She would never . . . I don't think she would." She turned toward Isaac, horror on her face. "She said she wanted to go and make things right the morning she died. She was downtown, near the war office. Do you suppose it had something to do with Morton?"

"I don't know," he said. He truly didn't. In all these years of rivalry and hate, he'd never considered such a possibility. Uncle Morton was young and carefree, but Isaac had believed him to be morally upstanding. The entire Campbell family was known for being pious and upright. Had Morton wandered from their shared values?

"Until we know otherwise, we will consider it a possibility." Mr. Cannon drew a line across his paper. "It could have looked like this." He put a mark at the start of the line. "Your parents all get along, and the Bradshaw-Campbell company is thriving. Morton and your mother begin seeing each other in secret." He put another mark a little farther along the line. "That would put tension between your fathers if it was discovered and explain Stanley's irreverence for his wife's memory. Morton is drafted into the war." Another dot. "William orders the pocket watch with the intention of giving it to Morton, but Morton dies before it is ever sent. Your mother is killed in the accident. We can presume she was somehow going to try to resolve the tension between herself and her husband, but I'm not sure why the war office. Perhaps she wanted to ask after Morton's address to mail him a letter." He tapped his pencil on the desk. "Hmm . . . Was your father at work when the accident happened?"

Laura nodded. "He was. He only heard about the accident when someone went to fetch him."

"So she went to 'make things right' when your father was not around." Mr. Cannon put a dot and wrote *Mrs. Bradshaw dies.* "Your distraught father would have been extra hostile after his loss and blamed the Campbell family for it. You said things were not good between them from then on."

"The tension started before that," Isaac said. "I wasn't allowed to go to Mrs. Bradshaw's funeral. It all feels like conjecture. There must be something more."

"You've got to go to Niagara. Morton's own words are needed; otherwise we will be relying too much on inference." Mr. Cannon settled deeper in his chair. "Go together if you like."

"My father would never—"

"He's not here," Isaac said, ready to drive north that very moment. "Mrs. Guskin can come. I'll make the arrangements, if you're willing."

"What about your father?" she said. "What will happen if he hears we are together?"

"He can't punish me if we happen to be in the same place at the same time. I'll make a plan."

CHAPTER 22

M r. Cannon's office fell silent as both men waited for Laura to decide whether she would be bold and go to Niagara.

"I'm not sure," Laura said, nervously twisting a metal band she wore on her right hand. "I don't know what my father would do if he found out I'd gone to Niagara. And if he knew I went with you . . ."

"There's a man who is going to be going over the falls in a rubber ball. I saw in the paper that it's supposed to happen in two days. They expect a large crowd. We will simply both be in the crowd. No one can fault us for that."

"That may work. Father doesn't mind me out if I'm with Abel." She grimaced. "He's worried if I don't spend enough time with Abel, it will disrupt his business plans. I promised him—"

Mr. Cannon cleared his throat. "This chitchat is entertaining, but I do have other cases that require my time. I'll do what I can from here. You both find a way to get to Niagara and Morton's letters."

"Mr. Cannon," Laura said, "if I could have a few more minutes of your time, I have a question for you. But I don't have any money."

"I'll cover the cost," Isaac said.

"Go on and ask it. I always listen before I decide if I'll help."

Mr. Cannon looked at the clock on the wall and then back at her.

"My father has been insisting I go out with a man named Abel Fredricks. He's new to the city and has a reputation of being a talented investor and business owner. I don't want to cause trouble, but I am beginning to wonder about him." She avoided looking at Isaac as she recounted her history with Abel and their quickly budding, then stalling, relationship. "The last time we were together, he told me he is working on selling some of his properties in Florida. I have no reason to doubt him, but something doesn't sit right. Abel has got my father convinced he needs to invest every penny he can. My father is even selling off household items so he can invest more. He believes he's getting an exceptional bargain, and he may be, but Isaac knows that his father is also working on an investment opportunity with Abel. Doesn't it seem strange that he would court me and do business with my father's enemy?"

"A good businessman keeps doors open, unless there's a reason to close them." Mr. Cannon shrugged. "Land is in high demand. This economy is big and growing. Everyone wants a piece of it. What is it you want me to do?"

"I don't know exactly. I simply find it strange that Abel came out of nowhere and has so quickly made connections. It all feels very calculated."

"I'm not a good businessman myself," Mr. Cannon said. "I undercharge far too often and have never been great at book-keeping." He stood and walked behind them to a file cabinet. He opened it and grabbed out the files closest to him. "But I have been hired many times to investigate bad business deals." He threw a file on the table. "Heber Downs swindled four thousand dollars by buying fake stock certificates." He threw down another file. "Vincent Marlan lost his home and business after falling for the Ponzi scheme. That one was in all the papers."

"His home and business," Isaac said, his tone somber. "Abel doesn't seem the type of man—"

"They never do. That's why they get away with it." Mr. Cannon returned the files to their spot in the overstuffed cabinet. "You say he's been courting you. Does he seem truly interested in you?"

Laura shook her head. "I don't have a lot of experience with men. He was attentive at first. He was always flattering me. I was surprised because no one had ever paid attention to me before. I did believe his intentions were sincere. But now . . . not much has changed. We go out, we dance and eat. There are times when he is kind and other times when he seems frustrated by my presence."

"I'm a detective," Mr. Cannon said, looking her straight in the eye. "If you want my help, I need the details. Is he kissing you? Promising you a future?"

Heat rushed to her cheeks. "He almost kissed me once, but we were interrupted. He hasn't tried again—I don't know why." She paused. Had Isaac mumbled something about him being a fool? She chose not to look at him and focused instead on Mr. Cannon's shorthand. "We don't talk of marriage, and I don't even know if he is taking other women out. I asked him once, and he gave me a vague answer that wasn't really an answer. May I be honest?"

"Please," Mr. Cannon said, nodding, "tell us everything."

"I don't care for Abel Fredricks. I thought I could in the beginning. I tried to be what he wanted, and enjoyed the thrill of something new, but it has been some time since I've felt any excitement. I now accept his invitations only because of my father's insistence. I've no desire to go out with Abel but feel compelled to until my father's deal is closed. I realize that makes me sound heartless. I do too many things because of my father. But I am not willing to marry the man just so Bradshaw shoes can flourish. Knowing more about Abel could help me know how to get out of this mess. But I need help."

Mr. Cannon picked up his notepad and scribbled a few notes. "Hmm. It follows the pattern I've seen before. Earn the trust of the father, seduce the daughter, make it seem urgent that they invest now."

"I've not been seduced," she whispered, sickened by the thought of giving herself to Abel. "I won't let such a thing happen."

"Poor word choice," he said, not looking up. "I'll do some digging. If he's the famous businessman he claims to be, it shouldn't be hard to discover a bit about his past dealings. And if he's one of those money grabbers, it'll be fun watching him fall. We'll sort out payment later."

"Thank you. And please, don't let anyone know. If he is honorable, then I don't want to tarnish his name with my skepticism."

"You have my word." Mr. Cannon tapped his chin with his pencil. "Are you brave?"

"No. I wish I were," Laura said. "I've been rather sheltered these last few years."

"She's here," Isaac said. "That's a sign of bravery."

"I agree," Mr. Cannon said. "I will investigate Abel's company. I need you two to get to Niagara and get those letters, and I think if we are smart, we could get clues on both matters at once. Laura, go with Abel. Your father would approve, and you can ask questions and see if you can discover more about his dealings. If your father is planning to close this deal next week, and if it is shady business, then we haven't much time. Do you think you could convince Abel to go?"

The very idea of riding all the way to Niagara seated beside Abel made her stomach queasy, but there was no turning back now. "I'm willing to try."

"Very good. Be careful. I expect Abel will turn out to be nothing more than a man eager to climb society's ladder, but there's a chance that greed has tainted him." He opened the door for them. "You have my number. Telephone me if something urgent comes up. If not, we will meet again when you get back."

They left the small, overcrowded office in silence. What had begun with a warped letter had grown into something entirely different. No longer was this about retrieving a goodbye; it was about setting the future free, pursuing justice, and building bridges. Or perhaps they were off course, chasing something that didn't exist. Maybe there were no answers to the past. And was Abel really so bad, or was she merely afraid? She left the office weighed down by questions and fears.

"Do you still want to go to Centennial Park?" Isaac asked when they were seated side by side in his Ford.

When he'd first offered the invitation, Laura had felt the most delightful flutter, like butterflies in her stomach. The entire morning at the zoo, she'd daydreamed about walking the shores of the lake on Isaac's arm. Now, haze veiled the brightness and joy of the morning, leaving everything mottled and unclear.

"We could talk there," she said, sorry for the bleak tone. "If I am to go to Niagara with Abel, there is a lot I must think through."

He nodded and turned the Ford left at the intersection. "I never thought Morton capable of any wrong. He was like a brother to me."

"It's all unsettling," she whispered.

"I don't like the idea of you traveling with Abel," he said. "I have no say over who you court, but I don't trust him."

"I am not excited to go with Abel. I never feel like I am truly me when I am with him." She traced the seam in the seat cushion. "I am more nervous to know what the letters say. I want to remember my mother how she was. I want to go on believing she was as good and kind and beautiful as I remember. I want to understand what happened, but I don't want to let go of those memories."

"She may have made a mistake, but that doesn't wipe out all her good," he said, taking another turn closer to the water.

"What if it is her fault that the company split and everything happened?" She pulled the handkerchief from her pocket and twisted it in her hands, the initials visible and then gone.

"It wouldn't be all her fault. Our fathers were friends—they were part of it."

When Isaac stopped the car near the narrow park that ran along the shore of Lake Erie, they both were slow to exit.

"My father said I look like my mother. Even Mr. Shaffer at the zoo knew I was Catherine Bradshaw's daughter."

"She was a beautiful woman," Isaac said, and she wanted to revel in his compliment and savor the feeling of being noticed by him. But she could not shake off the image of her father scowling as he called his late wife nothing more than an actress.

"Do you think the reason my father hardly talks to me now is because I remind him of her?"

"If it is, then he is wrong to do so. You are your own person."

"His heart may have been broken. She may have shattered it when she betrayed him." She opened her door and stepped out into the sunlight. He joined her, walking beside her on the path near the glistening lake. The blue water was bright and clear, and the grass was green and vibrant. It was a quiet park, unlike the often-busy Delaware Park.

"Nothing she did could justify the way he's treated you. You should not have felt alone all these years."

"I wasn't entirely alone," she said, reaching for the bravery he believed she possessed. "I have had a friend through it all. A very good one."

"You mentioned that when . . . when you were drunk." He said the word with a touch of humor. "You said a few interesting things."

"Oh dear," she mumbled. "I remember some, but the memory isn't clear. It's fuzzy."

"You secretly always wanted to dance with me?" He raised a brow.

"I was a child when I wished for that." She laughed. "You were the boy who was always there. Of course I dreamed of you."

"Are you saying you no longer want to dance with me? I was so sure you still did."

The heaviness grew lighter, the haze clearing as they inched closer to each other with their playful teasing. With no manure to taint the air, only the light breeze, the sparks between them seemed bigger and brighter. Here, away from the fear of rumors spreading, it seemed possible that two people torn apart by life could reach across the divide.

Laura stopped walking and faced him. "I think if I were asked to dance, I would consider it."

Isaac's lips pulled up at one side, his face handsomer than the princes in her fairy-tale book and more desirable than the actors in moving pictures.

"Would you require me to grovel?" he asked, using a word she'd once used in a letter. "Would you secretly be trying to humiliate me?"

"Isaac," she whispered. Did he know? Her breath came quicker. How could he know? "I have to tell you something."

"Not yet." He cut the small distance between them in half. His chest rose and fell as he took a deep breath and let it out steadily. "First, I have something to return to you."

"You do?" she said, his words only half resonating. His proximity unnerved her in all the right ways. "What is it?"

He reached in his pocket and pulled out a yellowed paper, creased and weathered. "I found this a long time ago." As if in a dream, he unfolded it slowly and began to read. His tone was like honey, sweet and pure. "'A wish so small you can't see it at all. A wish to be seen, to be heard, and to be loved.'"

Laura's lip quivered as she listened to her words from so long ago. The poem she'd stuffed in the tree—he had it. He kept reading. His voice and the memories sent tears rushing down her cheeks.

"How?" she whispered when he paused his reading.

Isaac took another half step closer. His hand went to her arm. A hand that was large and safe and warm. "I threw a pinecone at a head-in-the-clouds couple, and I found this. I didn't know who the Wishing Girl was until that day at the Quarry Garden—"

"You came."

"I did." His breath touched her cheek. His words teased her heart. "I came. I didn't know what to do."

"You left. I never saw you."

"I tried to go away and forget it all, but I couldn't. When you wrote again, I could breathe again. I'm sorry. I'm so sorry."

"No." She shook her head. "Don't be. I knew too," she said through her tears. "After the night at the square, I spied on you at the zoo. I saw you get my letter. I couldn't believe it at first."

"You toyed with me." He smiled down at her, and she wanted to melt into his arms.

"I did." She laughed. "I wanted to get back at you. But I couldn't because . . . I cared about you."

His thumb grazed across her arm, and everything in her wanted to be closer to him. The distance between them had existed too long. She wanted it gone—all of it. Long ago his words had stolen her heart, and now here he was, holding it in his hand.

"You knew." His voice sounded as breathless as hers. "And you didn't run."

"No." She pressed closer, her hand daring to go to his arm. "I didn't run. I didn't know how it could ever work, but I couldn't let you go. I worried, but only because I wanted there to be a way for you to stay."

"There is—there has to be." An urgency in his tone chipped at her remaining reservations. She moved her hand from his arm to his shoulder and rested her head against his chest. He responded; his hands came around her waist, and they both sighed. At last, the distance was gone. They'd conquered it. They'd won.

"We'll show the world that no grudge can keep us apart," he said and then pressed his lips to her hair, his touch lingering. With it, broken pieces came together, and painful memories were cushioned by hope.

The blue sky, the sound of the water gently lapping the shore, and the caress of the gentle breeze—she wanted to remember it all. She closed her eyes, praying that this would not be a memory to cling to when life became unbearably hard but rather the first of many beautiful moments.

"Laura." Isaac tightened his arms around her. She lifted her head enough to look up into his face, and he surprised her by brushing his lips against her forehead. Tender and gentle. Being in his arms was effortless. She felt at ease, safe and content. There was no pretending. He was looking at her, and he saw her. The real her.

"I'm sorry I didn't know it was you sooner. I should have been there for you."

In his arms, with their heads so close, she studied her dear friend. His dark eyes and equally dark brows. His hair, which had a small wave from wearing a hat. His lips. She paused on his lips. "You're here now."

"Laura." Her name caught in his throat.

"Yes."

"May I—"

"Yes." She went up on her toes at the same time he bent to meet her. Everything slowed as their lips found each other, and then all her senses shouted at once. The taste of his kiss, the fresh scent of damp air, and the touch of his hands on her back—she should be appalled. It was all so fast, but then again, it was years in the making. Every letter had brought them one step closer to each other, and to this moment.

When he straightened and she came off her toes, his embrace loosened and he grinned. "I always wondered what it would be like to kiss my letter friend."

"Was it all you hoped it would be?" she asked, her heart still beating far more rapidly than normal.

"It was better. But I'm told the second kiss is sweeter than the first."

"Who told you that?" she teased, silently hoping he'd pull her back in close and kiss her again.

"Would you still let me kiss you if I told you that it was my theory and that I made it up?"

"I think you ought to test your theory. And you may want to find out if the third or the fourth is better still."

"If you insist," he said, already moving closer.

"I do." The words barely escaped her lips before he kissed her again.

CHAPTER 23

The sun traveled closer to the horizon as the afternoon wore on. Neither Isaac nor Laura was in a hurry to leave the calm waterfront or the company they had found in each other. They sat hand in hand on a park bench, talking about letters, the zoo, and the miraculous way they'd stayed connected despite physical distance and parental barriers.

Isaac's hands were much larger than Laura's, yet they fit together perfectly. Being beside her with no secrets was a beautiful homecoming.

"Mrs. Guskin will worry if I'm not back soon," Laura said, making no move to stand. "I told her I wouldn't be gone long. She's like a mother hen and probably pacing the house ready to tuck me under her wing as soon as I walk through the door."

"We don't want her worrying. When will I see you again?"

"I was hoping you'd still meet me at the manure pile." Her finger danced gently across his palm. "It's become a tradition I look forward to."

"What about Niagara?"

"I'll phone Abel tonight, and tomorrow I'll tell you what time we will be leaving. That is, if I can convince him to go with me. No matter what he says, I want to go to the zoo tomorrow and tell Mr. Shaffer that I will be heading out of town. He's been so good to me. He says my instincts with animals are keen."

"You're brilliant," Isaac said, honored to be the man sitting beside her. "You could go to school and become a veterinarian."

"I don't care if I have a title. But I do hope to have more than just Tybalt to care for. I think I'd like a dog and—"

"A horse and a cat."

"Yes! And a lamb. There's nothing sweeter than a newborn lamb." She looked out at the gentle waves on the lake. "I rarely share my dreams, but with you, it's different."

"I want to hear them all."

"You've read them in my letters. You know I long for long walks in the park. You even know that I have read too many fairy tales for a woman my age and that I love pineapple upside-down cake."

"I had never tried pineapple cake until I read your letter. The trouble with the letters was that I had to wait days between getting answers. You would mention a secret wish and tease my curiosity. I could write out questions, but I could never see your face when you gave your answers. I much prefer our new arrangement. Besides, you can't hold hands with a letter. With you beside me I can ask a question, immediately hear your reply, and see your face."

"Ask me a question, then, and tell me if my face says more than my words ever did."

"Very well. Will all the animals you take in be named after Shakespeare? Will your dog be Romeo and your horse Juliet?"

"No. I already had a cat named Romeo—I can't use the name again. I think I will name all future animals after letters."

"Letters?"

"Yes. One could be Epistle, and another Sincerely." She cocked her head to one side, an adorable smile on her face. "Maybe one could be Paper."

He watched her eyes, her mouth, her body as she answered. No letter could compare. With her right here in the flesh, he could see the humor written in her every feature. "Your lips, right there"—he touched the corner of her mouth—"tell me you would never really name an animal Paper, and you would choose a better parting than *sincerely*."

"And what does my face say when I tell you that I don't want to go to Niagara with Abel?"

"That you are telling the truth." He tightened his grip on her hand. "Listen, just because Mr. Cannon thinks you may be able to learn more about the business deal doesn't mean you have to do it. It all may be a waste of time anyway." He smiled, hoping his encouraging words would make her decision easier for her. "If you choose to go, I believe you'll make a very good spy, but we can find another way, if you'd rather."

"Would it surprise you if I said I had a lot of practice spying?"

"Yes, I'm intrigued."

"Getting to the zoo so often was not easy. Mrs. Guskin was my accomplice." She let go of his hand and rubbed her hands together nervously. "I don't want my father or yours to make a bad business deal. I hate that their rivalry has them not thinking clearly. It's not like my father to be so impulsive. But Abel is so charming and believable."

He put his arm around her shoulder and waited for her to say more.

"What if we are wrong, and I only suspect him because

I don't care for him and feel he's being forced on me? Are we meddling where we shouldn't?"

"It doesn't hurt for us to ask questions." He'd had similar doubts, wondering if his drive to prove himself had spurred his unease about Abel. It was true that Abel's success had made him feel small. His father's constant praise of the man left him wondering what Abel had that he lacked. And he'd been jealous, ridiculously jealous, of Abel for courting Laura. "If we discover that Abel is an honest businessman, then no one has to know that we were speculating about his integrity."

"You're right." She nodded. "I'll phone Abel when I get home. I'll tell him how eager I am to see the man go over the falls."

"Will he go?"

"If I tell him that everyone important is going, I believe he will."

Isaac stood and held out his hand to her. She took it, leaving the bench. A flock of geese flew overhead in a perfect V. In equally perfect harmony Isaac and Laura looked up at the birds and watched until they disappeared out of sight.

"What will become of us after Niagara?" she asked, still looking up.

He didn't answer. Instead he let her question drift away, like the birds they could no longer see. He had no answer, but he would find one. And when he did, he would offer it to her along with his heart.

"Will Abel be a gentleman?" he asked when the sun moved behind a cloud, casting a shadow over everything.

"I hope he will. He's made few advances. He's not an easy man to read—he's unpredictable. I think that is part of why I question him." She cleared her throat, her unrest obvious. "I have experience sneaking to the letter tree but no experience fending off untoward advances. Let's just hope he doesn't make any."

He scowled, not at her but at her answer. He didn't want her going with Abel *hoping* she would be treated well. Too many men treated women abominably. But no woman, certainly not Laura, deserved to be treated as nothing more than an object to be tossed about, used, and discarded.

"I'll be there. I'll be the obnoxious man who is always underfoot. And if you need anything, I'll jump to your rescue."

"I had no idea you were a knight in shining armor."

"I'm an ordinary man." He shrugged, wishing he had more to offer. "But I would help you if you needed anything."

She touched his cheek, startling him with her gentle caress. "A humble man willing to rise to the occasion is the very definition of a hero. Be as obnoxious as you like. I'll be glad of your presence."

"He can't know about us." He followed her lead and put a hand on her waist. "He can't be suspicious."

"It'll be our secret." She kissed his jaw. "I never expected my life to go from so dull to so exciting all at once."

"After Niagara," he said, reeling her in close, "this will stop being secret."

"'From forth the fatal loins of these two foes—'"

"'A pair of star-crossed lovers . . .'" He kissed her, slow and with all the tenderness he could. "Shakespeare's ending is not our ending. You wrote of fairy tales—"

"My mother loved them."

"How do they all end?"

"'And they lived happily ever after.'"

He took her hand and, as though they were dancing, twirled her around, then brought her back in. "I like those endings better."

———————•———————————•———————

Laura rolled a dress and put it in the dusty traveling case she'd pulled from the attic. It had been years since she last traveled, and now she was going away without her father's knowledge. A rush of excitement mixed with nerves tickled her senses.

"What time did Abel say he would pick us up?" Mrs. Guskin asked, a hint of disapproval in her tone.

"He's coming tomorrow morning at eleven. I want to be packed today so that tomorrow I can run to the zoo and talk to Mr. Shaffer before we go."

Tybalt scratched at his cage.

"Do you think Tybalt will wonder where I have gone?"

"Cook's going to take care of him. He might not be as spoiled as he is with you, but he'll survive." Mrs. Guskin put a hand to her chest. "It's your father I'm worried about—and Abel. I don't know what's come over you. You've never been one to take such risks."

"Think of how many times we've talked about doing something, and now we are." Laura picked up another dress and rolled it carefully. "Father likes Abel, and you're going. Why would he object?"

"Because you're working behind his back, that's why."

"For his own good," Laura said, staying strong even though her insides were wound tighter than a clock spring. "Doesn't it seem strange to you that Abel is interested in me?"

"You've plenty of fine qualities. Any man with half his senses would recognize that."

"I have *none* of the qualities he is looking for. I don't care a bit about being fashionable. I dance decently well, but if he were to look closely at my hands, he'd be appalled by my blisters. There must be a different explanation for why he calls on me. What if he is simply using me to get Father's trust? Half the business-men in this town will follow Father's lead." She paused, dress frozen in the air. It had hurt at first to realize Abel had other motives for taking her out. But she had not been entirely in-nocent either. She had once believed that Abel would be a means to leaving this house. She'd been willing to gamble that love could come later—she'd been wrong. Hearts were not meant to be toyed with. "No matter what Abel is up to, we aren't right for each other."

Mrs. Guskin smirked. "It's that letter-writing Isaac, isn't it? He's got you acting out of sorts."

"Isaac Campbell." She sighed, remembering how it had felt to be in his arms and recalling the touch of his lips. "He's thoughtful, and funny, and he likes me the way I am. He's seen my blistered hands. I'd pick him over Abel any day. If I could pick him, that is."

"You sound like a woman in love." Mrs. Guskin took the dress from Laura's hands and tucked it into Laura's traveling case for her. "You ought to be watching the spectacle at the falls with Isaac, not a man you don't care a thing about. You're ask-ing for trouble."

"I will simply pretend I am in a William Le Queux spy novel. All that novel reading will finally be put to use. I think Mama would be proud."

Mrs. Guskin laughed as she helped her finish packing. Laura had shared her worries about Abel, and she'd even told Mrs. Guskin what the detective had suggested, but she hadn't shared all the details of her afternoon with Isaac. It felt too much like a dream. Mrs. Guskin had proven time and again that she trusted Laura, but would she believe that what Laura and Isaac felt for each other was real?

Once packed, Laura wandered the empty halls of her house. The library with its walls of books beckoned her, welcoming her with its promise of adventure, romance, and knowledge. She ran her hand along the spines, touching the books her mother had brought home.

Had her mother really been secretly spending time with Morton Campbell? She paused near a matching collection of Shakespeare. Had her parents' love story become a great tragedy? What she discovered in Niagara could tarnish her memories. She pulled out *Romeo and Juliet* and fanned the pages. They'd been so young, so hopeful, so foolish.

Her heart beat faster. She slammed the book closed. She was going to Niagara. Fear would not stop her.

She left the library and entered her father's study, where she left a note for him in case he returned before she did.

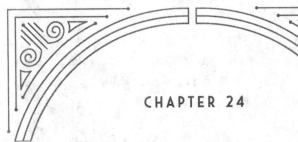

CHAPTER 24

The breeze in Abel's Nash touring car sent the foul odor of his recently smoked cigarette in Laura's direction. She spent much of the drive looking out her window at the rural farmlands, imagining a life in the fresh air of the countryside.

Mrs. Guskin rode in the back seat, saying little as they bounced along the road that led north. Abel had not been in favor of bringing the housekeeper, claiming that their separate rooms at the Clifton Hotel would be enough to keep any gossip down. Laura had stood her ground, insisting that Mrs. Guskin come so she would have a companion in case a business meeting arose and took Abel's attention away. This argument won him over. He'd sighed into the phone and then said he understood and would be happy to have Mrs. Guskin along.

"Did you know that Arnold Lamar is not the first to go over the falls?" Laura said, striking up a conversation. There was no way to learn about his business dealings if they were silent.

"There was a woman, correct?"

"A woman was first—she went over in a barrel. It is said that after she survived, she told the crowd that no one should ever do it again. The article in the paper said it was a steel barrel that was used next, more than a decade later." A farmhouse with two stories and a brick chimney, perched on a little knoll, came into view. A barn with large doors and a rock fence stood beside it. "I don't understand why so many people do things like sit on poles and go over the falls. The next man over died. It seems a waste when he could have led a quiet life."

"Why did you want to watch if you think it's foolish and fear someone might die?"

Oh dear, she'd said the wrong thing. If only she could have stopped the car and escaped to the tranquil countryside. There was nothing easy about conversing with Abel. But running away was not an option, and she was not the quiet woman she had once been. She would see this through.

"It's been so quiet since my father left," she said, scrambling for words. "I heard they expect two thousand spectators, and though I have no desire to go over the falls, I find the idea of watching with others exciting. And it has been such a long time since I've been anywhere." Now she was rambling. She bit her tongue and waited.

"Oh," he said, and nothing more.

She went back to looking out her window. Being with Isaac was so different. With him, she never doubted that her words would be well received. When she'd seen him this morning, she'd wanted to be closer to him, to linger longer.

"You will be safe?" Isaac said before she left the manure pile.

"I will. I'm staying at the Clifton Hotel. Mrs. Guskin will be with me. We won't have a letter tree there—"

"We'll have a letter door," he said, finishing her thought. "I'll find out your room number, and I'll give you mine. I'll slide letters under your door. It'll be like old times."

"I do love letters," she said. "And I will love knowing that you are there."

He pulled her in close then, embracing her with all the fervor of an anxious man.

If only she were in Isaac's Ford now, riding beside him, rather than seated beside Abel in his stuffy Nash. She may have found this outing exciting if that were the case. As it was, the touring car bounced about on the road, jostling her with each bump.

"You would think that with all the sightseers going to Niagara Falls these days, they could fix up the roads." Abel scowled as he drove, an air of annoyance in his posture. "When do you expect your father to return? He's been away a long time."

"Any day now." She'd had only two brief conversations with her father since he left. During the latest call he'd given her reason to believe he would be returning in the next few days. "I know he is eager to return and close his investment deal with you."

"Good. I don't want him to miss out. My agent has all the investors ready to close on their new properties this week."

"Why must they all close at the same time?" she asked, lacing her fidgety hands together to appear at ease.

Abel sighed, and though he smiled, she noticed his hands tightening on the steering wheel. "It's good business to have all the papers drawn up at the same time. If we close all at once, no one will feel cheated. It's just good business."

"How many people are buying land?"

He shot her a sideways glance. "Don't worry. Your father is getting the best deal of anyone. I've only a few acres left, and then all the land will be asked for."

"I'm glad it'll be over soon. The deal has taken up so much of your time. You deserve a break." She tried to picture the women at the clubs and mimic the way they'd smiled. "What will you do with your time?"

"Focus on my other businesses—and on you, of course." He reached a hand across the bench seat and took her left hand out of her lap. No warmth raced through her, only a cold chill.

"Your hands are blistered," he said as he ran his fingers across her calloused skin.

"My mother's flower gardens were her passion," she said, wanting to take her hand back. What would the women in her spy novels do in this moment? They would play their part, believing in their cause. So she let her hand rest in his, despite the revulsion she felt, and prayed the drive to Niagara Falls would hurry by.

The traffic slowed to a crawl as they approached the city limits. The farm country transformed into a small city with busy sidewalks as everyone made their way to the falls. Like ants, they wove this way and that around one another, most smiling and many arm in arm. Laura looked at the men, searching for Isaac, but didn't see him.

The Clifton Hotel was glamorous, with its porches and balconies and white trim. As they approached, Mrs. Guskin let out a low whistle and said, "My goodness, it's beautiful."

Laura blocked the sun and admired the fine hotel. She looked past it at the busy city and then turned and saw a distant view of the falls, mostly obscured by buildings and automobiles.

"Should we walk and get a closer look?" she asked Abel.

"You'll get a good enough look tomorrow when we watch the man go over in his rubber ball." Abel stopped the car and waved at a porter. "We have luggage. Come and carry it inside."

"Yes, sir," the young man said, hurrying toward them. He pulled their traveling cases from the Nash. "I'll carry them into the lobby and then up to your rooms as soon as I know your room numbers."

"We've called ahead—there should be rooms ready for us." Abel ushered Mrs. Guskin and Laura up the stairs and into the lobby.

"It's so fine," Mrs. Guskin whispered. "Look at the trim work on the ceiling. It's like we're stepping into a penny card."

Laura leaned closer and whispered back, "Maybe I'm wrong and Abel is as wealthy and talented as everyone believes him to be."

"He's a snake, even if he is good with business." Mrs. Guskin sneered at Abel's back. "You were right to be suspicious. Under those good looks is a wolf. I'm sure of it."

"Shhh," Laura said, afraid he would hear. She left Mrs. Guskin's side and stepped across the honey-colored wood floor toward Abel, only to pause when a man to her left caught her eye. Tall and broad, he was grinning at her.

———●———————————————●———

Isaac had spent the last half hour pacing the lobby of the Clifton Hotel, watching for Laura and her party to arrive. He was already checked in, and after making small talk with the maître d', he'd been able to discover which rooms Abel and Laura would be occupying. He'd stood a little taller, feeling like a genuine detective. He'd even quietly gone down the hall and left Laura a note under her door without drawing attention to himself.

She waved at him now, a small half wave, but it was an acknowledgment. Under the circumstances he could not expect more, though he longed to be at her side. She returned her attention to Abel, who had not seen him, and soon the two had keys in hand and were being led down the hallway toward rooms 23 and 24. He was in room 8 down a different hallway than them, but at least they would be sharing the same roof.

With them out of sight, he waited, trying not to draw attention to himself. When they returned, he would feign surprise and interject himself into their party.

"Isaac Campbell!"

He looked around, unsure who'd said his name. There, to his utter shock, stood Ruth Bagley.

●────────────────●

Laura stepped into room 24 and immediately saw a letter on the floor. She took her traveling case from the porter and set it on top of the paper.

"I think I'll freshen up," she said to Abel, who stood in the doorway. "I want to hang my dresses so they aren't wrinkled."

"Yes," he said, looking past her into the room. "Does this room suit you?"

"Yes, it's lovely."

"Only the best for you," he said, and if she'd only just met him, she may have believed him terribly sweet. "I have a few phone calls to make. I'll use the phone in the lobby. Meet me when you're ready. We'll go to dinner together—be sure to dress for the occasion. We don't know who we will meet, and it's important we make a good impression. You understand?"

She winced, his words so like her father's, demanding and said with only business in mind.

"I understand." She forced a smile. "I'm eager to see all of Niagara Falls."

"And I look forward to being the one to show it to you." He

backed away from her door. "I trust Mrs. Guskin will give you any help you need."

"Yes, of course," she said as she closed the door and breathed a sigh of relief.

"What are you hiding?" Mrs. Guskin lifted the traveling case up and retrieved the letter before Laura even caught her breath. "Abel could have seen this."

"I know. We'll have to be more careful."

"Go on and read it. I'll unpack and try to find you something *suitable* to wear."

Laura nodded and sat on the edge of the large four-poster bed, with its pink-and-white quilt, and unfolded the letter.

For the woman I miss already,

Charles, my friend, would call me a starry-eyed schoolboy for addressing you in such a way. I suppose I am. Not a schoolboy, but starry eyed.

I am in Niagara Falls, staying in room 8. If you need anything, I am not too far.

As I drove north, I kept thinking of you. I thought how you must love the lush scenery. And I worried about you and wished that you were beside me. Will you think me a fool if I tell you that I was jealous? I'll be glad when Abel is gone.

I will find you soon, and we will accomplish all we set out to do. But be careful. I care about the past and about business, but not as much as I care about you. Whatever happens, be safe, and if you can, meet me at the gazebo behind the hotel. It is in disrepair, but it is private and smells better than the dung pile. I'll be there at ten o'clock.

Take care, dear friend.
The boy with the pinecones

There was no escaping Ruth. She'd seen him, so rather than cause a scene, Isaac crossed the lobby to her.

"Have you come to watch Arnold Lamar go over the falls?" he asked, his eyes still roaming the lobby in case Abel or Laura reemerged.

"I came with my father. We heard that Abel Fredricks was going to be here, and he wants to try to meet with him about business. It's not fair for Abel to leave my father out. Our family's business is as successful as yours." She came closer, her hips swaying with every step she took. "Besides, he can't be serious about that Bradshaw girl."

"You've come here for Abel?" They'd make a fine pair, equally matched in many ways, but he couldn't say so for fear of giving himself away.

"Don't act as though your feelings are hurt. You could have taken me out again. If you asked real nice, you still could." She batted her lashes and pursed her lips, toying with him. "What are you doing here, anyway?"

"I came to watch the man go over the falls."

"By yourself?"

He nodded. "I drove up alone. I needed to get away from the city."

"Well . . ." She brushed past him. "Don't get in my way."

He put his hands up, palms out. "I wish you nothing but the best."

"Thank you. I'll settle for nothing but the best," she said as she hurried for the exit of the lobby, leaving him to wait alone.

Counting knots in the floorboards only kept him entertained for so long. He wandered around the grand lobby. On the far side tucked in the corner were two telephones for guests to use. He thought about calling Mr. Cannon to see if he'd been able to learn anything else about Abel, but stopped himself. The likelihood of Mr. Cannon knowing anything different from yesterday was not high.

A man approached. He didn't look at Isaac, only at the phones. Isaac backed up, stepping into the corner out of sight, but he was still within hearing distance of the phones. It was rude to stand nearby and listen in. He chided himself and took a step away, ready to begin his pacing again, when he recognized Abel's voice.

"I'd like to be connected to Haynesville 233."

Isaac wiped his clammy palms on his pants.

"I'm going to need you to print more deeds," Abel said into the phone and then paused. "At least ten. Word's getting out about it." Another pause. "I'm not worried." Another agonizing pause had Isaac waiting with bated breath. "I'll take care of her. It's another week, maybe less, and we can close the deal. I'd do it sooner, but some of the bigger accounts are still pulling their funds." If only Isaac could hear the other half of the conversation. "I won't let it get too big. I don't want to draw undue attention, but a few more investors won't hurt. Look, I gotta go. I have people to meet. Just make me more deeds and have them ready by next week. I'll pay you when I see you."

Isaac turned away, not wanting to be caught when the conversation ended. He went back to the lobby, leaned against the wall, and pretended to be doing nothing other than watching people come and go. He pulled out his pocket watch. Laura had been in her room for nearly half an hour. She was bound to return soon.

He thought of walking down the hall and sliding another note under Laura's door, but there was more traffic in the halls now than there had been earlier in the day. He would have to hold in his many questions until their ten o'clock rendezvous at the gazebo.

Five minutes later Laura entered the lobby. He stared at her, shocked to see such a change from the woman who had entered earlier. Gone were her relaxed traveling clothes, replaced by a deep blue fringed dress that showed off her legs and neckline. Her face had a fresh coat of makeup, and her hair was twisted and pinned to look like all the women in the magazines.

The plan was for him to notice them, act surprised, and then finagle himself into their party by striking up business conversations with Abel. He knew the plan; he'd reviewed it many times in his head and rehearsed several questions and even practiced the tone of voice he'd use to ask them. But right now, looking at Laura, the only question that ran through his mind was what had happened to the woman he knew.

"Look, Mrs. Guskin," Laura said, a hint of disgust in her tone. She was making the first move instead of waiting for him. "It's Isaac Campbell."

"Ah," Mrs. Guskin said as the two women stepped closer to him. "So you're the notorious son of Campbell."

"I'm . . . yes." He struggled for composure. He knew the

roles they were going to play, but he felt a sting from her tone. "I'm Campbell's son. I didn't expect to see you here."

"Why not?" Laura said with an edge to her voice that would have anyone believing they were enemies. She was good. "Because I'm supposed to be the reclusive daughter of Bradshaw?"

"Laura." Abel's voice entered the conversation. His long legs brought him across the lobby in seconds, and soon the four of them were standing together. "Isaac, I didn't know you would be here."

"I should have had it printed in the paper. It seems my presence is shocking everyone."

"Everyone?" Abel said.

"Both Ruth and Laura have now expressed their surprise." He caught Laura's moment of disbelief. For one second her eyes grew large before returning to her carefully schooled expression. "I know you've been meeting with my father. How is business?"

Abel reached an arm around Laura and reeled her in close to his side. His fingers ran up and down her bare shoulder. "I came up here to spend time with Laura. She's eager to see the falls. I believe it best if business matters are set aside for now. I've been neglecting her too much lately."

Laura smiled up at him.

"Shall we go and explore the town?" Abel asked her. "I hear there are several fine restaurants. We could peek in all their windows and decide which looks the most mouthwatering."

"I'd like that," Laura said, and Isaac almost believed she meant it. But then her eyes met his, and he saw the distress in them.

"I think I'll join you," Isaac said. "I hope you don't mind, but

I haven't had time to see the town or the falls yet. It's been years since I've come up here."

Abel gave him a quizzical look. "I was hoping for some time alone with Laura. You understand, don't you?"

Isaac took a step back. His plans to impose himself on their party were failing. A sideways glance from Mrs. Guskin had him jumping back into the arena. "I didn't mean to intrude. It's only that we've had so few chances to talk, and this seems the perfect opportunity for us businessmen to get to know each other better. Down the road, perhaps we could work together on something."

"Abel's business is thriving," Laura said, tucking her arm around Abel's. "He doesn't need help from you. He owns properties and—"

"Enough," Abel said, cutting her off. "My business affairs are mine alone. Perhaps another time we will be able to meet about business. Enjoy your evening."

Abel led Laura away. Mrs. Guskin followed at their heels. Near the door Abel turned and faced the housekeeper. "We won't be needing you tonight. There is a large crowd—no need for a chaperone. You may have the evening to yourself." He turned again, not waiting for a reply, leaving both Mrs. Guskin and Isaac staring after them.

"Well, I never," Mrs. Guskin mumbled under her breath before turning her back to the door. She walked near Isaac and, in a low voice, said, "Meet me in the stairwell."

He waited a few moments, assuring himself that no one was watching, and then made his way to the stairway. The hotel featured an Otis elevator, and as a result, the stairway was relatively private.

"I don't know you," Mrs. Guskin said the moment the door

closed behind him. "But I trust Laura, and she speaks highly of you."

"You can trust me."

"Abel's never made any advances with Laura. As far as I can tell, he's interested in her simply because of her father's money." Mrs. Guskin studied him a moment before going on. "What do we do?"

"I don't know where they've gone . . ." What would Mr. Cannon do? If Isaac were a detective, what would be the next step? "We could try to get in his room and see if anything in there proves he's up to something. I need more evidence, and with them out to dinner, now is a good time."

"I don't know how we'd get a key." Mrs. Guskin lowered her voice further. "The balcony runs in front of their rooms. We could try to go in through a window."

"I've snuck in several windows before. Mostly at the Bradshaw factory. It's been years, but if I can get a piece of wire, I can do it."

"There are wire hangers in the closet of Laura's room. I can get you one. But how will you get through the window without being seen?" Mrs. Guskin's face was flushed and red. "I don't know if this is a good idea."

"I can't sit around doing nothing." He rubbed his neck. "There are rocking chairs on the balcony. You can sit in front of me, blocking the view."

"It'll still be suspicious."

"The porters all wear uniforms." He looked around. They were in the stairwell of the first floor, but there were stairs leading up and others going down. "I'll go downstairs. That must be where the laundry and workers are. I'll see if I can get a porter uniform. If I'm on the balcony in it, people passing by will think I'm working."

"What of the hotel staff? They will know you don't work here."

"I'll put it on in Laura's room. No one working at the hotel will get a good look at me." He let out a great puff of air. "It's the best chance we have."

"You're right. Go and get a uniform if you can. Meet me in room 24."

Isaac tugged at the ill-fitting porter's uniform. The sleeves were several inches too short, the jacket could not be properly buttoned, and the pants were likely to split if he wasn't careful. But from a distance, he looked the part.

"It'll have to do," he said before taking the wire hanger from Mrs. Guskin. "It'll take me a few minutes to get this through the latch hole and to twist it open. Will you stand guard for me?"

"I told Laura I wanted adventure, but this might be too much for me." She checked to make sure the lock on the room was bolted. "I'll go on the balcony and rock in the chair. I'll watch the street and the balcony, but work quickly."

"If Laura and Abel return, you have to warn me and then find a way to keep them from coming to the room."

"I'll do it."

They both stepped outside. To their great relief, no one else was on the balcony. The street was busy, but no one seemed interested in a porter and an old woman.

Mrs. Guskin moved a chair close to the railing so she could

see over it. Then she started frantically rocking while he un-twisted the hanger and inserted it into the latch hole. It was a tight fit—smaller wire would have been better. He worked it in circles until it finally slid in, and then he carefully started twisting it until the latch was turned to unlocked.

"I've got it unlocked," he said over his shoulder to Mrs. Guskin. "Is anyone looking?"

"No, go on in."

He put both hands on the glass and pushed it up. The window groaned as it opened. Isaac put one foot in, his too-small porter pants making it difficult, but he managed. He ducked his head under the now open window and pulled his other leg and body through.

A mirror above the dresser was the first thing to catch his eye. He saw himself in a borrowed porter's uniform, standing in Abel's room, and could only hope his efforts would prove worthwhile.

CHAPTER 26

A bed, a dresser with a mirror, and a small desk—it was a typical room. Isaac stepped farther into the chamber, searching for anything suspicious. On the desk he found a razor and gentleman's kit. Nothing amiss there. He opened the top dresser drawer only to find it empty, as were the other drawers. Abel's traveling case lay open on the end of the bed.

Isaac took a step closer, his heart racing. Every social rule he'd ever learned raced through his mind—this was a terrible invasion of privacy. Worse than that, it was trespassing. Had he not heard Abel's suspicious phone call, his resolve would have weakened, and he would have turned tail and run from the room. But something wasn't right, and there was no one else to put the clues together except Isaac and Laura. He took another step toward the bed, and then, careful to leave nothing amiss, looked through the case.

It contained clothes, as expected, folded and stacked. He lifted them out and set them on the bed in the exact order they'd been in the case. Beneath them he found a clothes brush, a bronze shoehorn, and a notebook. He nearly whooped when he saw the brown binding. Surely within its pages he would discover exactly what Abel Fredricks was up to.

Just as he reached for the notebook, Mrs. Guskin's head

popped through the open window. "I knocked on the wall. Didn't you hear me?"

"No."

"Well, you should have been listening," she snapped. "They're coming. They're already inside the building. Get out of there."

He looked at the notebook. It was right there for his taking.

"Go to the hall and stall them. Give me two minutes, and I can be out of here."

"Oh dear," she said, but he saw her nod as she hurried off.

He had no time. There could be no dallying. He opened the notebook, flipped through the list of names. There was so much here but no time to make sense of it. Abel's lists of things to do, his potential clients. Isaac paused when he saw Laura's name.

> Stanley Bradshaw, factory owner. No heir. One daughter, Laura Bradshaw. Homely. Reclusive. The city trusts Bradshaw.

The date above the entry was before Abel had come to town. He'd targeted Laura. Someone had given him information about her. It was a defilement, and he felt the sting for her.

He turned to another page, which contained more names and information that meant little to him. Near the back of the book were notes about his Florida land.

> Florida land. Inherited from father, not interested in drilling, selling to highest bidder. Thirty deeds made already, need a week's notice to get more. Interested parties . . .

His father's name was on the list, as was Laura's, with a note that Mr. Bradshaw was getting the most shares and needed to be treated with the utmost care until the deal closed. There was also a scrawled note about which daughters he'd taken out. The notes were extensive, reminders so he could keep the information straight.

The Campbell factory kept good notes as well, but this was different. His father never left annotations about who knew his business dealings, who could talk to whom, or the relationships between the potential buyers. Isaac wanted to take the notebook with him and pore over the other pages, but he couldn't—not yet. If he was caught and couldn't convince anyone of his arguments, he'd be the one in trouble.

The sound of footsteps in the hall moved him to action. He threw the notebook back in the bottom of the case, lifted the stack of clothes, mindful of their order, and returned them. Everything looked right. He put his left leg through the open window. A ripping noise stalled him, but only for a moment. He pulled his body through the window and then his other leg. From his spot on the balcony, he pushed the window closed— there was no time to lock it. He could only hope Abel paid it no heed. Peering through the window, Isaac could see that the door was opening. He ducked low and then crept across the balcony to Laura's room, where she greeted him with a hushed voice and worried expression.

"He could have caught you in there."

Mrs. Guskin put a hand on Laura's back. "I was standing guard. We were careful."

"You?" She looked confused. "This is getting out of hand. I can't have everyone I care about in the middle of this."

"Why did you come back?" he asked, sensing that the time for questions was short. "I thought you were going to dinner."

"We were . . . We are. He forgot his pocketbook in his other pants, so we came back. I told him I wanted to check my face since we were here. I could tell something was wrong by the way Mrs. Guskin was perspiring."

"I am not perspiring." Mrs. Guskin wiped a hand across her brow only to look at her hand, frown, and wipe it across her skirt. "Well, it's a warm day."

"It is warm," Laura said as she stepped to the dresser and picked up her lipstick. Gazing at Laura's pursed lips as she applied a thick coat of red did nothing to help Isaac focus. It only stoked the seeds of jealousy he harbored. "We're going back out, but don't go in his room. He's acting strange. I think he's suspicious."

"Later I'll tell you what I've learned, but I am even more convinced this business deal is a scheme." He took her hand. "Be careful."

"You should go out and act as though everything is normal. It might help him relax. I think he's questioning why you're here in Niagara."

"Where are you dining?" he asked.

"Queen Victoria Place Restaurant. It's upscale. You can't come alone, and you certainly can't come dressed like that."

"I thought you didn't care a snit about fashion."

"I may not care about it, but I still know how it works, and you can't go like that." She smirked. "Besides, you've a rip in the backside of your . . . uniform."

He reached around, and his hand touched the torn seam. "I'll change. I'll find a way to be there." He grimaced. There was no one here to go with. Mrs. Guskin was too old and wasn't dressed for fine dining. "Ruth is here. I could take her."

Laura's eyes found his. "If you must."

"I'd only be asking her so I could be near you and—"

A knock at the door had all their heads turning.

"Laura, are you ready? We don't want to lose our reservation." Abel's voice traveled through the door.

"Get under the bed," Mrs. Guskin whispered to Isaac. "Now!"

He rolled his eyes but obeyed, sliding under the bed like a child caught snooping for Christmas gifts. The long quilt nearly touched the floor, providing the cover he needed. He kept his breath slow and quiet while he waited.

"I got to talking with Mrs. Guskin," Laura said. "I'm ready."

"Good. My window was unlocked." Isaac heard footsteps that were much too large to be Laura's moving across the floor.

"No need to come in Laura's room," Mrs. Guskin said. "I'll make sure all the windows and doors are locked before I go out. This hotel is reputable. I'm sure it's safe."

"I was sure I checked mine, and now it's unlocked," he growled. "I'll have to have a word with the manager."

Isaac looked under the narrow slit between the floor and blanket. His clothes from before were sitting folded in a corner, and the wire hanger was on the floor by the window.

"Let's not worry about the window. I'm sure you just *thought* it was locked." Laura's voice was smooth and velvety. "I want to go out and be with you. Let's enjoy ourselves."

Isaac made a face that only the dust bunnies and darkness could see, hating this game they were all playing.

"Very well, let's go."

He heard the tread of feet leaving the room. They stopped, then started up again.

Isaac waited under the bed until Mrs. Guskin lifted up the blanket. "They're gone. But I think he saw your bundle of clothes in the corner. If you're going to take Ruth to dinner, you'd better hurry. I saw her come back to the hotel while I was rocking on the porch."

"I don't know what room she's in." He stood, brushing at the dust that now clung to him.

"Change your clothes and then check the lobby first—she may be there. I'll take care of your torn pants and sneak them back to the basement." She brushed at his shoulder. "I need you to look after my girl."

"I will."

Isaac changed out of the ill-fitting porter's uniform and into his slightly disheveled suit while Mrs. Guskin guarded the hall and looked for Ruth.

"Have you seen her?" he asked in a hushed voice, eager to get away from this side of the hotel and any suspicion his presence could cause.

"No. Go check the lobby and the large front porch."

It took him five minutes to find Ruth. She was on the porch rocking back and forth, staring off at the horizon. His body reacted to the sight of her, urging him to turn back. The anger he'd felt when she deliberately intoxicated Laura threatened to resurface.

I can do this, he coached himself, *for Laura.*

"Ruth, I was hoping to find you."

"Why?" she asked, not slowing her rocking. "So you can tell me that we are not suited for each other?"

"I am sorry if my words hurt you."

"Think nothing of it. There are plenty of other men."

"Yes, I am sure there are." He cleared his throat. This was more difficult than he'd imagined. "I find that I am restless and hungry."

"There is a kitchen at the hotel. I am sure you could order something."

"I've seen the hotel. I'd like to go out and see more of the city. I have heard the Queen Victoria Place Restaurant is quite fine, but I came to Niagara alone. Would you care to join me?"

"Why are you asking me?"

"Look, you don't have to join me if you don't want to." He turned to walk away. She rushed to his side.

"Fine, I'll go with you. But I've set my sights on someone else, so don't get the wrong impression."

"Not to worry," he said, offering his arm. "It will only be one dinner."

CHAPTER 27

Laura should have felt like a princess—the food and surroundings were extravagant and decadent—but she did not. Isaac sat two tables away with Ruth Bagley across from him. His presence was comforting, but hers made Laura's blood boil with jealousy and sour memories.

"Stop looking over at them," Abel said. "No one will care about your parents' feud here. You came to dine with me."

"You're right," she said, taking another bite of her dinner and hardly tasting it. "When will you buy the house on Seneca Street?"

He wiped at his face with his napkin. "I'm considering other options now."

"You are?"

"Yes. I want to be sure it's the right house."

"You must be sick of living in the hotel." He'd confided in her a couple weeks back about his lodgings. They were temporary, he assured her. "You're so well acquainted in Buffalo now. It'll be nice having a house to host guests of your own."

"Yes, I suppose it will be. I'll have to throw a dinner party right away."

Again, her gaze wandered to Isaac and Ruth. He appeared to be deep in conversation with her, his body leaned forward, eyes focused on Ruth. He'd kissed Laura and spoken of a future with her. There was no reason to doubt his loyalties, was there?

"Ruth's father is here," Abel said. "I think I'll try to meet with him and see if he is interested in making an investment. So stop scowling at them. I don't want to burn bridges all because you're upset over a little joke."

His words smarted. It hadn't been a little joke; it'd been cruel and hateful. She swallowed the rebuttal she so desperately wanted to throw at him and said instead, "You'll have all of Buffalo investing soon enough."

"My father was a savvy businessman."

She used her knife and fork to cut through the steak on her plate. With her head down she asked, "What if the land ends up not being as profitable as everyone believes it will be? You could be living in a city with a lot of enemies."

"What makes you think the land isn't profitable?"

"I didn't say it wasn't, only that it might not be. My father, I know, is selling off items in our house and collecting on his debts. He's ready to throw it all into land he's never seen. He would suffer greatly if the oil you've promised is not there."

"I don't like this skeptical talk." His jaw flexed as he ground his teeth. "I've deeds that verify the value of the land. Don't ever say things like that again. That kind of talk could scare people off. I don't want to hear another word about your worries."

She nodded, afraid of the fire she saw in his eyes. "I didn't mean anything by it."

"Why'd you really want to come up here?" he asked, his features hard and menacing. The suave, thoughtful suitor from before was gone, replaced by this anxious, agitated man.

She took a steadying breath. "My father is eager to invest

with you and is convinced that if I spend time with you, you will let him put in more money than anyone else. That's the truth."

Abel gnawed on a bite of steak. "He's a regular businessman, willing to use anything for collateral, even his daughter. I admire that about him."

"Collateral," she whispered. Tears stung her eyes. She fought them back, refusing to cry in front of Abel. It hurt, though, hearing the truth spoken and laughed at.

"I like your father. We think alike." Abel looked around the room, his eyes landing on Ruth. "I have business to attend to tomorrow. I'll still take you to the falls in the afternoon. I can't have anyone thinking I've brought you here and abandoned you." He leaned closer. "This deal is too big for a tiff with a woman to get in the way. I don't know what you're up to, but it's not more important than what I am working on. I'll let your father invest, but only if you keep whatever crazy ideas you have to yourself. Do you understand?"

She nodded, her courage waning.

"Good. I'm glad we understand each other," he said before flashing a grin at a couple a few tables away. "There's music. Should we dance?"

She wanted to shout no and then turn and run away. But she was a spy, and more than just her father depended on her.

"Yes," she said, taking his hand when he offered it.

The dance floor was small and intimate. As they walked, an older couple commented on how perfectly suited they were for each other. Abel brought her hand to his lips and kissed it, all for show.

"You should smile," he said as he brought her in close. "If you lean against me, we may even be able to make Ruth jealous. I saw her watching me through dinner. She's wondering why I'm with you. A jealous woman will do practically anything."

Laura couldn't relax in his arms, no matter her efforts. His conniving ways were simply too revolting. Where before he'd worn an elaborate mask, he'd now shed it, and his true colors were on display. The touch of his hand, the smell of his breath—his closeness sickened her.

His mouth came near her ear. "You came here for your father and his business. Doesn't he deserve a better performance than this?"

"Excuse me." Isaac stepped onto the dance floor with Ruth. "Do you think this floor can fit another couple?"

"You can see how big it is. Go and dance if you wish."

"It's good to see you," Ruth said to Abel. "My father is hoping to meet with you. We *both* are eager to know you better."

"I am hoping to meet with him too." Abel transformed back into a dapper gentleman. "In fact, why don't we switch partners for a song, and we can discuss your schedule. Laura, you don't mind, do you?"

"Not at all. I'll go back to the table—"

"No," Abel said. "I don't want you sitting alone. It's such a fine night. Dance."

She nodded, hating her complicity, and stepped into Isaac's arms. His touch was gentle where Abel's had been taut and severe.

"Are you all right?" Isaac asked in a low voice.

"I don't ever want to see him again," she whispered. "Don't look at me like that."

"Like what?"

"Like you care about me. He can't know."

Isaac stiffened and straightened his face. "This isn't how I pictured a dance with you."

"We won't count it. I'll let you have another chance at a dance later." She looked past him at Ruth and Abel. "They're suited for each other."

"Both eager to get ahead. Tonight, when you meet me, I'll tell you what I found. Will you be all right until then?"

"Yes. I'll claim a stomachache and ask to go home after this dance. I'll blame you for it."

"If it'll get you away from him faster, then blame me all you like." They made slow circles on the small dance floor until the song ended and she stepped out of his arms.

Ruth was slow to leave Abel. She looked at him with desire in her eyes before going back to Isaac's side.

"I don't know if it's something I ate, but . . ." Laura put a hand on her stomach. "Would you mind taking me back to the hotel? I know it's early, but I'm ready to turn in for the night."

Abel narrowed his eyes. "One dance with Isaac and you're sick."

"I thought it was the food, but maybe it was him." She let the false pain show in her face. "No matter the cause, I think it's best if I retire for the night."

"I'll take you back," Abel said and then asked Ruth if her father was available. "With Laura resting, my evening is open. I could take him for a drink."

"A drink?" Ruth's eyes twinkled. "What about prohibition?"

"Canada, our dear neighbor, does not have the same laws we do. I figured since your uncle is a bootlegger, your father is probably not a teetotaler. Besides, my deals are closing this week.

If your father wants to invest, it has to be quick. Why not talk over a mug of beer?"

"We can all walk back, and I'll ask him." She pursed her lips and then said, "I'm not a bit tired. Would you mind if I joined you?"

"Come along if you wish." When he grinned, Laura felt nauseous. Ruth had wronged her, had humiliated her deliberately, but seeing her so easily wooed by Abel's charms had her concerned.

They settled their bills at the restaurant and made their way back toward the hotel in silence. Isaac bid everyone good night in the lobby and disappeared toward room 8. Laura allowed Abel to walk her back to her room, and Ruth went to find her father.

"I don't like you out alone with him," Mrs. Guskin said the moment the door closed.

"I don't want to be either. I'm going to be sick again tomorrow." She put her hand on her stomach as she walked from one end of the room to the other. She stopped at the window and looked out at the street. "He plans to use Ruth to get her father to invest with him. He'll play games with her heart and her father's money."

"She toyed with you."

"I don't want revenge. Maybe I should, but I feel sorry for her. And I feel like a fool for ever believing Abel sincere," she said. "We have to find out what's going on so we can stop it. I'm supposed to meet Isaac at ten at the gazebo, but if Abel is out with Ruth, I could meet him sooner."

"Where? If he's caught in your room, you'll be in a heap of trouble."

She gnawed on her thumbnail, her eyes still on the street. "If I write him a note, will you slide it under his door?"

"Yes." Mrs. Guskin wrung her hands. "I want to help."

"Thank you," Laura said, pulling her eyes away from the street and onto Mrs. Guskin. "This is proving to be quite the adventure, isn't it?"

"It's not a novel," she said.

"No, it's not. But it'll still have a happy ending. Isaac is sure of it."

"I got a good look at your Isaac while he was climbing in and out of the window. He's a handsome man."

"Mrs. Guskin!" Laura feigned surprise.

"I'm not too old to know an attractive man when I see one. But he's more than good looks, I can tell, unlike that skunk Abel."

"Isaac is a much better man than Abel," she said, already missing him. "He's thoughtful and hardworking, though his father doesn't recognize it. I used to dream of a prince, but Isaac's better than a fairy tale. And worse because we still don't know how we can ever be together. I don't want it to be true, but sometimes I feel like we are Romeo and Juliet, bound for a tragic ending."

"Pishposh."

"That's what he said. He believes there's a way."

"He's wise. Add that to your list of fine qualities. You keep doing the right thing, and everything will sort itself out. Go write your letter."

"I wanted to see Abel leave first." She watched the street until at last she saw Abel and Ruth and an older man who must be her father. "They're gone. I'll write fast."

Dear fellow spy,

I don't like the idea of Abel swindling money from anyone, not even Ruth. When we were alone at dinner, his charm was gone, and deep inside

I knew he was evil. Meet me in the lobby. I will bring a book and pretend to read while I keep watch for you. You should call Mr. Cannon and tell him everything.

I think I know what our next move should be.

Yours,

The girl who longs for a real dance with you

CHAPTER 28

Mr. Cannon answered his phone with a raspy hello, despite the late evening hour. Isaac spoke in a hushed voice and darted glances at Laura every couple of seconds. She was at the other end of the lobby, hiding behind the pages of a book. They had been careful not to arrive together, and they didn't talk to each other in the lobby, other than her saying she'd drop her book if someone was coming.

"Between the notebook and the phone call I overheard, do you think we have enough to turn him in?"

"No, you don't," Mr. Cannon said.

"What else do we need? He's forging deeds. He came to Buffalo with plans to swindle everyone. And the way he's been treating Laura confirms it."

"You need more evidence."

He raked his hands through his hair. "We don't have time."

Mr. Cannon chortled into the phone. "I'm on your side, and I've found a big piece of this puzzle."

"You have?" He sank deep into the seat. "What is it?"

"Don't you think you ought to pay me first?"

"I'll pay you—you have my word." He was ready to grovel, beg, and plead. "Just tell me what you know. Help me stop him."

"Calm down. I already told you I'm a poor businessman. I'll help you." Mr. Cannon's voice grew serious. "I started following Abel backward. Where did he come from? Where was he born? I tried to find it all, but there were no records of him. The post office couldn't find me an address, and I could find no birth record. I put in a call to the land office in Florida but haven't heard back yet."

"How does this help?" Isaac put his hand near the phone to muffle his voice.

"I went to the hotel where he is staying, and a man there told me everything he knew about Abel. He said Abel was drunk one night and told him he was in Saint Louis last and that he didn't plan to be in Buffalo long. I contacted a friend in Saint Louis—well, he's more of a contact than a friend—and he said a man who went by the name Reuben Donnely sold forged deeds to land six months ago. Reuben disappeared after that."

"It's him," Isaac said. It had to be.

"It could be, or he could be copying what someone else did. There are schemes happening all over right now—everyone wants easy money. We need a way to prove that Reuben Donnely and Abel Fredricks are the same person; otherwise I could lose my credibility. I won't settle for conjecture."

"What are you proposing we do? If there are no records and the deeds are forged . . ."

"Use the name around him. See if he looks up. And I'll find out who lives at Haynesville 233. The person forging the documents must know something. Call me again tomorrow morning or tonight if you can."

"Should we call the police?"

"Soon, but not yet."

Mr. Cannon hung up. Isaac sat there a moment, unsure what to do next. Using the name Reuben Donnely around Abel would be suspicious.

So much for his plans to meet Laura at the gazebo and enjoy their budding romance. Until this matter with Abel was settled, there would be no relaxing. Protecting her, and all those investing in Abel, took precedence.

He left the telephone and walked to the counter where a man in uniform was working.

"Do you . . ." He had to remind himself that a spy stayed in character, no matter how it made him look. "I'm wondering if you could tell me where someone might get a . . . a real drink around here."

The man shook his head. "I can't tell you that. I could lose my job. This side of the border is not in favor of alcohol."

Drat. He wiped a hand across his scruffy jaw and tried again. "I am looking for someone. I'm not after a drink. I don't know where to start."

"Very well, Addison Avenue is the nearest wet bar. It's just across the Honeymoon Bridge. That's all I can tell you. The Clifton is a dry establishment." He took a step back. "Someone on the street may be able to point you toward other locations."

"Thank you." He walked past Laura and, without stopping, mumbled that he would be back. His first stop on Addison Avenue proved unproductive. Abel wasn't there. He asked a man on the street for advice and soon found himself on Second Avenue, in front of a large brick building with shops and a diner at street level and stairs that led to a lower level. He took those and let himself into the smoky underground room where men and women sat on couches with their feet up on furniture and cigarettes in their hands.

He looked through the haze. In a back corner he saw Abel, his arm around Ruth. Her father was in a chair beside them, staring at nothing. Isaac had found them. Now what?

"Excuse me," he said in a quiet voice to a man at the bar. "I hate to trouble you, but I'm looking for a man named Reuben."

"I don't know no one's names here." The man's voice was slurred. "I just came in here to get myself a little drink."

"I could get you another"—Isaac put a couple of dollars on the bar—"if you'd ask the room if there is anyone here named Reuben."

"You want me to shout it at the whole room?"

"Yes," he said, wishing he had a better plan. "I'll be over there. After you ask, go back to drinking. Everyone will think you've simply had too much."

The man shrugged and pocketed the money.

Isaac stepped away from him and into the shadows where he could see Abel, but Abel couldn't see him.

The man at the bar stood and steadied himself. "I'm looking for a fella named Reuben."

Abel's head shot up. It was all that Isaac needed. The man from the bar looked around. No one answered him. He waved a hand in the air and shouted, "I think I've had a bit too much. I'd better get another."

A murmur followed. Isaac waited for everyone to forget about the outburst and then left as quietly as he'd come.

He waited on the hotel balcony for an hour, watching the street for Abel to return to the Clifton. When he finally approached the hotel, he staggered. Ruth and her father were with him, all laughing and leaning on one another.

Isaac moved to the hall. He listened as Abel said goodbye to Ruth, making promises to see her again the next day, and then Abel talked to her father.

"I was going to wait until the end of the week. But I'm so excited for everyone to have their land, I might do it sooner. Why wait?"

Isaac gritted his teeth. He'd been counting on having a few more days, but Abel was getting nervous. It was the only explanation for him rushing his deal.

The moment Abel headed for his room, Isaac stepped into the stairwell, keeping his hand on the door while it closed to prevent a giveaway thud. He peeped through the narrow window in the door. Assured that he hadn't been seen, he hurried downstairs to the telephones.

"He's Reuben," Isaac said when Mr. Cannon answered. "And he's getting nervous. I overheard him saying that he might close the deal sooner than planned."

"We'll have to act quicker than he does. I found Haynesville 233. Whoever lives there wasn't home. I looked through the windows, and there *are* deeds being made."

Isaac pinched the bridge of his nose. "Will you call the police? We can't wait any longer. Have them come for Abel. He's in room 23 of the Clifton Hotel."

"I'll call them."

"Thank you."

"It's my job. Tomorrow you will get the letters?"

Isaac had been so consumed with Abel, he'd hardly thought about the letters and Mary Kensington. "Yes, I'll go tomorrow."

They hung up, and then Isaac looked at his watch. It was ten o'clock, the time he was supposed to meet Laura at the gazebo. He walked to the back of the hotel and peered into the moonlit night, wishing she were there. If only Abel was already arrested . . .

A movement near the gazebo caught his eye. He opened the back door. "Laura," he whispered into the night.

"I'm here," she said.

He stepped outside and made his way to her. "I thought that with all that's happened . . ."

"I didn't know if you'd come. But I had to check." Her voice was as light as the breeze. "I was worried."

He felt himself relax, unaware until this moment that every muscle in him had been tense and on edge. But she was here and safe.

He reached a hand out in the dark, and she took it. He pulled her close. She came willingly, falling into his arms. "Don't worry," he said with his cheek pressed against her hair. "It's going to be over. The police are going to come, and they'll arrest Abel. Mr. Cannon is calling them now and telling them everything we know. Our parents' businesses will be safe, and you'll never have to go out with that man again. It'll be over."

She pulled her head away from his chest. "You have to write about it. It's the next move. Write an article and give it to the paper. Use your name. It's your story."

He let her words percolate.

The excitement in her voice was contagious. He felt his heart beat faster. He could do it. Their years of letter writing had not only brought him her but also gifted him with a love of details and talent with words.

"Write it tonight before anyone else can take your story." She grabbed his hand, pulling him back toward the hotel. "You've got to do it."

He stopped her. She looked up at him, searching his face.

"I've never had someone believe in me. My father is always telling me to run off and enjoy myself. But you . . . you look at me, and I feel like I can do anything."

"Because you can," she said. Her hands wandered up his arms to his shoulders and stopped at his neck. She pushed herself up on her toes and kissed his cheek. "You, Isaac Campbell, can do this."

Their lips found each other, and without saying a word, he thanked her for believing in him.

"Let's go inside so we can be here when the police come. I know they'll have questions," Isaac said, leading her from the dark and back to the hotel.

"I'd rather stay by the gazebo," she said as she followed him.

"I'd prefer that too." He held the door open for her, and they were greeted by dim electric lights. "I think we should go to the lobby."

She let go of his hand. "Do we go as strangers then?"

"You!" Abel's voice met them in the narrow hall. "I thought you were sick!"

Isaac took a step in front of Laura. "We were both getting some air, that's all. We ran into each other."

"You filthy liar. I saw your clothes in her room. I know you followed me to dinner. I'm no idiot." He put a hand on the wall, steadying himself. "You won't ruin what I'm doing. I won't let you."

"It's late," Laura said, her voice gentle. "You should go to bed. Tomorrow we can talk about everything."

"No. Tomorrow everyone is signing papers. They're buying their land, and I'm getting out of here." He stepped closer.

"Don't," Isaac barked. "Don't come any closer."

CHAPTER 29

Commotion in the lobby drew Abel's attention. He looked over his shoulder and stumbled toward the noise. "Did you call them?" He swore, and his eyes blazed. "You did this." He pointed a finger at Laura.

Laura and Isaac said nothing, waiting for Abel to make the next move. He headed for the back door, pushing past them. Isaac grabbed Abel's shoulder before he could flee. Abel was large and strong but also drunk and clumsy. He staggered forward a step before falling to the ground. Isaac stepped over him, his muscles flexed and taut, ready to tackle Abel and pin him down until he could be cuffed and taken away. Laura stepped against the wall, unsure what to do.

"Tell the police where we are," Isaac yelled, spurring her to action. "Quickly."

She rushed past them and out of sight. Behind her, she could hear the sound of Isaac and Abel scuffling. "I need help!" she screamed into the lobby. "Come quickly!"

The moment she heard steps in her direction, she went back to Isaac and Abel, just in time to see Isaac grab Abel's hand and fling him to the ground. Abel groaned but got back up. He swung at Isaac, missing with his first blow, but his second connected.

Isaac winced, but it didn't slow him. Isaac's next swing was full of force. Abel teetered backward and then, like a bear, came running at Isaac.

Isaac bent low, avoiding Abel's fists, and pulled Abel's legs out from under him. Abel was down again. Everything happened so quickly that Laura could hardly keep up. The two men took turns throwing punches, and then footsteps, ones she didn't expect, soft at first, grew louder. The clicking of a woman's shoes tapped toward them.

"Don't hurt him." Ruth, a blur of color and tears, raced past Laura. Isaac paused, startled, giving Abel a chance to swing. Abel's fist connected with Isaac's chin, forcing Isaac's head upward, and then down he went, his eyes finding Laura's as he crumpled. In two long strides, Laura was at his side.

"Stop this!" Laura shouted at Abel while pulling Isaac back to his feet.

Abel's eyes blazed, and he growled. Laura's heart raced, but she stood her ground, refusing to leave Isaac.

"Abel Fredricks, turn yourself in." At last, the police were there. For one moment, she felt relief, but then her eyes found Abel's again.

Abel sneered and wrapped a menacing arm around Ruth. She cried out, but he only tightened his hold. With her as a shield, he started for the back door.

Another officer entered the hall. He shouted for Abel to stop and threatened him with his gun. But Abel kept walking. Laura grabbed Isaac's hand, squeezing it tightly. "He can't take Ruth. Keep talking to him. Don't let him leave," she said.

Laura gave his hand one more reassuring squeeze before letting go. As swiftly as she could, she ran back toward the lobby and out the front door of the hotel into the moonlit night. Then she ran around the side of the building, not slowing until she approached the back door.

She could hear Ruth crying out in fear, begging for mercy.

"Ruth had no part in this." Isaac's voice drifted into the night air.

"Shut your mouth," the drunk Abel said. "If you and that little snit had minded your own business, none of this would have happened."

Laura looked around her, suddenly afraid. Her plan to run for the back door had been impulsive, but what now? She could hardly beat Abel in a battle of brawn. She pressed a hand to her forehead, berating herself for her foolishness. But she was here now, and if Abel came out that door, she had to stop him.

The abandoned gazebo had become a resting place for discarded items. Perhaps she could arm herself with something there. She left the side of the building and crept across the path to the gazebo. When her resolve weakened, she thought of Ruth's scared eyes next to Abel's serpent ones. He was a deceiver, and if he got away, he'd deceive again.

A cracked pot too heavy to swing, a chair with no back—neither would work. Her hands shook. She'd wanted to help, but unarmed, she could do nothing. With so little light, she felt around the gazebo with her hands, digging through the heap until she found a flowerpot. It would have to do. She left armed, nervous, and ready, returning to the back door where she could again hear the scuffle inside. The police, Isaac, and Abel all yelled at one another. Ruth did nothing but whimper.

Laura waited, crouched near the side of the back door. Minutes passed, but nothing changed. And then the door opened, and she saw the back of Abel's head as he backed away, ready to run, with Ruth still crying in his arms.

He was going to get away. She swung with all the force she could muster, jaw clenched and heart pounding.

A thud. A cry. And then Abel was on the ground at her feet, and Ruth was free. Laura stared—she'd stopped him. Abel Fredricks would not toy with another woman or lure more trusting businessmen with his farce. She looked at her shaking hands; she'd done this.

Isaac grabbed her hand, bringing her back to the moment. "It's okay," he said. He pulled her into his arms. "He's alive and will get a nice long sentence. Ruth is free. Don't worry." He shifted her in his arms so he could look in her face. "You were amazing. You were so brave."

"I had to stop him," she said before laying her head on his chest.

"And you did." He pressed his lips to her hair. "I thought you'd run off. I thought you were afraid, but you were thinking more clearly than the rest of us."

"I was afraid." She took a slow breath and then shut her eyes and listened to the beat of his heart. "I'm not afraid anymore."

It took two hours for the police to get statements from everyone and for the hotel's guests to return to their rooms. When at last the night was quiet enough that the sound of the rushing falls could be heard, Laura and Isaac moved to the balcony, where they sat slowly rocking beside each other. It was late, after midnight, but neither Laura nor Isaac could sleep.

"It could have been me," Laura said. "I could have been the one he grabbed, not Ruth."

"She'll be all right. And Abel's gone."

"I should have warned her. It happened so fast."

"She wouldn't have listened." He took her hand, and like an old couple they sat in stillness. A breeze rustled the papers in his lap. "I called the paper. They are expecting my story. If I leave to bring it to them now, they think they can have it in the paper tomorrow. It'll be the front page."

"Front page!" She covered her mouth, muffling her voice. "That's exciting."

"I'm going to use my name, like you suggested. And everyone will know that you stopped his escape."

"Our names will both be on the page." She tipped her head back and looked at the stars. "Will you be all right, driving this late?"

"I'll be careful."

"I rode up here with Abel." She bit her lip, realizing she no longer had a way home.

"I'll come back. I'll be here by morning, and we can go see Mary Kensington together."

She smiled into the darkness. "If Abel hadn't come, I may never have written to tell you that I'd found another key to my cage. We might still be writing anonymous letters to each other. Because of him, well, all of this . . . the article will come out tomorrow, and everyone will know that you and I are not . . ."

"Enemies," he finished for her. "They'll know that we stopped Abel together."

"I don't know if it will be enough to convince my father to stop hating your father."

"Tomorrow morning, before we see our parents, I want to get

the letters from Mary Kensington. I think it best if we have them before we go home." He leaned his head back against the chair. "There will be no secrets tomorrow."

"My father will be proud, won't he?" She wanted reassurance. "We saved everyone from Abel's scheme."

"I hope both our fathers are proud." He laced his fingers through hers. "I don't know what mine will think of us."

She nodded, plagued with the matching fear.

"The article may have my name on it, but we did this together," Isaac said. "I never would have suspected him without you, or even written the article. We did this together."

"You know," she said, afraid that when they returned to Buffalo, their quiet moments together might cease. "We have been here a day and not gotten a good look at the falls yet. I think tomorrow I would like to go see them with you."

⸺•⸺

True to his word, Isaac returned before the sun came up. He'd gotten his story to the press in time for it to run in the morning paper. Laura had been alarmed by the dark circles under his eyes but grateful to know he was safe.

"The press manager said they don't normally take stories this late, but they wanted to be the first to break the story." He pulled the paper from behind his back and handed it to her. "Look," he said, pointing, "Isaac Campbell."

She took it, her heart soaring from the joy of his success.

They were in the small breakfast room at the hotel, practically alone thanks to the early hour. She began reading aloud.

Financial Scheme Thwarted

In the years since the Great War, prosperity and financial abundance have sparked the rise in investments. The quest for easy money has, likewise, resulted in a rise of fraudulent activities, and our fair city is no exception.

A man going by the name of Abel Fredricks came to town, his motives vile and his prey, our city's businessmen and their daughters.

She looked up and found his eyes. "This writing is excellent. I am as enthralled by it as I would be a novel."

He looked down at his plate. "That reminds me. I have to tell you something about your books."

"What about them?"

"I asked Mr. Cannon when I first met him to help me know who was buying them. I had hoped I'd be able to talk the buyer out of it."

"You don't have to worry. My father won't sell them now that there is no deal with Abel."

"He already has. Mr. Cannon told me this morning that he finally tracked the buyer. The cook let him in yesterday. He took the whole collection."

The whole collection. She said nothing—there were no words. The loss was too great. Those books had been her mother's. They'd been the piece of her Laura had been able to keep.

"I'm sorry," he said. "I didn't mean to ruin breakfast. I wanted our first meal in public to be a good one."

"It's not your fault," she said, struggling to comprehend her loss. "My mother loved her books. I know I told you that in my letters. But she really loved them. She was always looking for a great novel or a book about animals for me. She loved fairy tales and Shakespeare. Books and words were what we shared. If the books are gone, and the letters tell a different story of my mother, I'll have nothing left of her."

"I want to read Morton's letters. I want to know what my uncle left behind, but if you say so, I will forget they exist. We don't have to open them. I don't want your memories to be tainted." He took the paper from the table and set it on an empty seat. "You should eat while it's warm. Think about what you want to do."

She nodded and ate, only because she knew she should. Her appetite was gone, overshadowed by fear of what was ahead and an aching heart. Pretending the letters did not exist was not an option. She would always know they were out there. She would always wonder. Hiding from the past wouldn't change it.

"I want to know the truth," she said after eating the last bite of ham on her plate. "I'll go and see if Mrs. Guskin is ready, and we can be on our way."

"Laura," he said, his voice tentative.

"I want to go. I'm choosing it." She didn't pretend to smile. Isaac was the one person she didn't have to pretend for. "I'm scared, but I *want* to go."

"All right," he said. "I'll be in the lobby waiting for you."

She left him and found Mrs. Guskin, who put her motherly arms around Laura the moment she saw her face. "Oh dear, it was a long night, wasn't it?"

"I hardly slept," she said and covered a yawn. "I kept thinking about Abel. I can't believe it took me so long to see through his acting. I feel like a fool."

"He was clever. The important thing is that you did see through it—that's what matters."

"I'm glad it's over." She stepped out of Mrs. Guskin's arms and sat on the bed. "Isaac wrote a story for the paper about it. Everyone knows we worked together to stop Abel. I guess Father might not have seen it." She frowned then. "Isaac heard from Mr. Cannon that Mother's books have already been sold. They were picked up yesterday. When we go home, the library will be empty."

"Oh no." Mrs. Guskin shook her head. "You'll have to start again."

"What do you mean?"

"Buy a book, first one and then another. It might take you a while, but you'll find a way. Buy one and bring it home, put it on the shelf."

"It won't be the same."

"It doesn't have to be." Mrs. Guskin picked up Laura's comb from the dresser and put it in the traveling case. "It'll still help you feel close to her. Someday you can tell your daughter how your mother loved books, and she'll know because you'll have a whole room full of them."

"What if the letters tell a different story of her? What will I tell my future daughter then?"

"You'll tell her that your mother loved books. That part doesn't have to change."

"I'll try to remember that," Laura said, hoping it would all prove as easy as Mrs. Guskin made it seem. "Isaac is ready to go."

"Go on without me. Pick me up when you're done there. I'll stay in this room and get it packed up, and then I'll take a nice long nap."

"Are you sure?" she asked.

"Yes, don't worry about me. I think you and Isaac need to be alone with whatever you find. Remember"—she put a hand on Laura's arm—"to be good to each other. Your mother and his uncle made their own choices. You get to make your own too."

"Thank you." She accepted all of Mrs. Guskin's advice and then said goodbye with the promise to be back as quickly as she could.

CHAPTER 30

Isaac was in the lobby waiting for her, his hands in his pockets, pacing back and forth. She watched him a moment before greeting him, admiring his dark hair and long stride—such a handsome man. Her heart felt tight, as though it were in a vise. She loved him in a way she never could have imagined. What if she lost him? Fear tightened the vise. She pressed her hand to her chest. Her pinecone-throwing man was worth the risk.

"Isaac," she said, and he pivoted toward her, his blank face transforming into a smile.

"Ruth was just here," he said.

"She was?"

"Her father was too. He thanked us for everything."

"Is Ruth all right?"

"She's upset about last night, and she's embarrassed. She said to tell you thank you for what you did. And she said she's sorry for what happened at the square."

The day they'd watched the man on the pole felt like a lifetime ago. "It's forgiven."

They left the hotel together, not hiding from anyone. Isaac offered his arm, and she took it. They walked toward his automobile like a courting couple, proud to declare themselves to all the world.

The ride to Mary's house was short. A mile into the country-side, a small white house came into view. The yard was over-grown, and the fence was leaning. But the grass was green, and the view lovely. Laura sucked in a deep breath of air. It was moist and warm and fresh.

"It's beautiful, isn't it?" Isaac put a hand on the small of her back as they walked up the path to the front door.

Isaac knocked, and she stood beside him, her hands clammy and shaking.

When the door opened, a woman in her thirties with a long brown braid and a questioning gaze greeted them. "Can I help you?"

"We're looking for Mary Kensington," Laura said when her eyes connected with the woman's.

"You came to the right place." She untied her apron as she stepped back into the house. "Come on in and tell me what I can do for you."

"We received a letter from you. It had to do with my uncle Morton," Isaac said as he stepped over the threshold.

Her hand stilled on her apron strings. "Morton Campbell?"

"He was my uncle."

"Oh my, I'm so glad you've come." She tugged at the apron, finally getting it free, and threw it on the back of a chair. "When my sister came back from the war, she had all sorts of luggage with her. But she was sick."

"I'm sorry to hear it," Isaac said.

"We got so busy nursing her, we never went through her things. We asked about her time as a nurse in the war, but it made her cry, so we stopped asking. We were afraid that dis-tressing her would make matters worse." She paused. Her eyes glistened with tears. "I thought when she was better, she'd tell us about it."

"About the war?" Laura asked. She spied a small boy just outside the window throwing a stick for a dog. So naive to life's hardships. Carefree in a way adults could only long to be.

"About the war," Mary said. "And . . . and about Morton and the baby."

"Morton and the baby?" Isaac said, repeating her words.

"She came home expecting. Whenever we asked her about it, she would sob and refuse to answer. She never got better. She delivered the baby and died two weeks later. We never knew the father's name. I know we should have insisted she tell us. But we only cared about her getting well."

"What makes you think the baby is Morton's?" Isaac asked, his eyes on the dark-haired boy in the yard.

"I didn't at first. I guessed his father was a soldier, but I didn't know for sure. Whoever he was, he hadn't come home with my sister, and I didn't think it right to go searching for him in case she'd run away from him."

"I understand," Laura said. "We don't blame you."

"Her luggage was tucked away in the attic and forgotten. I never opened it. I regret it now—I regret so many things. It hurt, just looking at it, so I put it away. I had a baby to take care of, and everyone gossiping. I wasn't thinking clearly." She wiped at her cheeks. "I'm sorry, I should have asked you to sit." She motioned with a shaking hand toward the low sofa near the window. "Please, sit down."

They both obeyed, sinking low into the floral sofa, and waited for Mary to say more.

"I didn't open her luggage until a few months ago. Her son,

his name is Albert, was asking about her, and I just wanted to feel closer to her. I finally went to the attic. Both Albert and I were ready."

"My uncle's middle name was Albert. It's a family name."

"I never knew why she chose the name. We were close when we were young. I spoke to her every day until she went overseas to be a nurse. Her leaving felt like a betrayal. I hated that her life was happening so far away and was angry with her. I hardly wrote her while she was gone."

"I'm sure she understood," Laura said. "She must have known that you were just missing her."

"I hope so. I did finally write, and I told her I was sorry. But with the war going on, there were months between letters. I hadn't heard from her for a long time, and then she was back and about to have a baby." Mary looked older than her true age as she told the story. There was a heaviness in the air as she spoke of the past.

Laura scooted to the edge of the sofa. "Was she in love with Morton? Did she ever mention him?"

"She wrote once of having a surprise for me and how she couldn't wait for the war to end so she could come and live by me and have a family. There were no details. But that was her way. She loved surprises. Now I believe it was Morton she loved. When I finally went through her luggage, I found a letter from the war office. It was written to a Mrs. Campbell. But there was no first name. I started trying to piece it all together myself." She spoke quickly. "I would have hired a detective, but I didn't have money, and I was afraid. I love Albert. I didn't want to lose him—"

"They were married?" Laura asked, interrupting Mary's rambling. "She wanted to surprise you with her new family?"

"I believe so."

"But Morton died," Isaac said and pressed a hand to his forehead. "I wish I'd known about your sister. I would have come to meet her and would have helped if I could."

"I'm sorry I didn't go through her things. I should have. I didn't mean to keep Albert from the rest of his family. After all, he's your cousin. I hope you can forgive me."

"A cousin." Isaac's voice trembled. "It's not too late. We know now. We'll do right by him."

"If you'll wait here, I'll go fetch the letters. When I found them, I knew I had to deliver them. I wrote to Mr. Campbell because he was the only William Campbell I had ever heard of. I'm so glad you've come." Mary stepped out of the small living room, leaving them to look around as they waited. Yellow wallpaper with red birds gave the room a cheery feel.

"Do you suppose your uncle was really in love?" Laura whispered.

"I don't know. When I saw him, he was usually over for a game of checkers or to get me to go out on the lake with him. My parents were always lecturing him and trying to get him to grow up and settle down."

"Did they want him going to war?"

"He was drafted—he went because he had to. He was upset about going. It makes me feel better, believing he found love there."

Mary returned with the letters before Laura could respond. "I have three that I'm hoping you can help me with."

Isaac took them. They had no addresses. There was only a simple name across the front of each folded letter: Isaac Campbell, William Campbell, and the Bradshaws. "I can help you with all of these. I'm Isaac, my father is William, and Laura is a Bradshaw."

Mary smiled, a sense of peace filling her features. "You've made that easy. I feel better just putting them in your hands."

Mary insisted they read the letters in private. She pointed them toward a path in the grass that led to a little rise with a bench on it. "My father put it there for my mother. She loved the view. It's the perfect place to remember your uncle. I'll be here when you get back. Albert and I have chores to do."

"Do you think we ought to read all the letters?" Isaac asked when they were alone on the well-worn path.

"Let's start with the one to you," Laura said. She paused at the top, put a hand on her forehead to block the sun, and looked out at the rolling farmland. "I could live in a place like this."

"Would you miss anything about the city?"

"I would miss the zoo and the letter tree," she said. "And the park, and you. My mother was from a small town. She used to talk about how everyone knew one another and how they'd help if someone was in need. It sounded so simple."

"Not simple, blissful," Isaac said as he stood beside her, neither rushing.

Laura was the first to take a seat on the hand-carved bench. Isaac sat beside her, draping his arm around her as though it were the most natural gesture in the world.

"I've been thinking." He tapped the letters against his leg. "About us. And I have a proposal."

"A proposal?" She flinched, surprised.

"Not that kind of proposal!" He shook his head. "Not that I would never ask, I just, I'm not asking you . . ." He took a deep breath. "Can I start over?"

"Yes, do start over."

"When I dropped the article off at the paper, the president of the paper was there. He offered me a job. A steady job. I was waiting for everything to settle before I told you." He took another deep breath, and she held hers, eager for what he'd say next. "I always thought the only thing I could do was work at the shoe factory. I thought I had to be like my father. I even clung to the same hate he had, believing I needed to follow him."

"And now?"

"I don't want to inherit his hate, and I don't think I want to run a factory. I want to be ambitious like he is. He's got plenty of fine qualities. He's a good man, albeit imperfect. What I'm trying to say is, no matter what these letters say, whether or not they contain magic words that can heal the divide between our families, I am going to make a life away from the hate."

She closed her eyes, imagining a world where it didn't matter that he was a Campbell and she was a Bradshaw. A world where they were free to make choices on their own, to pick the higher road.

He took his hand away from her shoulder and stood in front of her. "I wouldn't make much, not at first. I'd be as poor as a pauper, but with time, I could save up, buy a little house. Or I could go somewhere else. I could show another paper the articles I've done. I could get a recommendation and go anywhere. I could get a house with a hill and a bench and animals . . . What do you think?"

"I think your plan is liberating. It's brilliant. My father feeds the hate. Every day he has to feed it more and more to keep it alive. It's stolen so much from him." She ran her hand over the seat of the bench. "You're smart to get away from it. It doesn't need to steal your life too."

"Why do you look sad?" he asked, sitting again.

"I've dreamed of a way to get away. I don't mean to be sad—I am happy for you." She nudged him with her elbow. "I'm more than happy for you. You're going to be a writer."

"Laura, I . . ." He turned toward her on the bench. "I told you about all that because I wanted you to know that now there is a way for us. I can't propose—I know it's too soon for that—but someday . . . I, well, I might. I was just . . . I was trying to tell you that we don't have to be nervous opening these letters. No matter what they say, they can't keep us apart."

"You might ask me to marry you one day," she whispered, the rest of his words meaning nothing.

He took her hand. "Yes, of course I'm going to ask you. You have been there . . . always. There's no one else for me. There never has been."

"Let's read these letters," she said, sniffling. "And then let's get back to Buffalo and tell everyone that the feud ends with us."

"And then I'll get to work writing articles and saving money—"

"And then you'll climb to my window and take me away."

His shoulders shook as he laughed. "I'll climb any tower you like. You just say the word."

He tore open the first letter, the one addressed to him, and read aloud.

Dear Isaac,

I've been thinking about you while I've been overseas. I always loved playing games with you and causing mischief. You were like a little brother to me. Now that I'm sick, and they say there's a chance I won't recover, I've been thinking about the kind of example I was for you. I should have been a better one. I didn't take anything seriously. I tried to get out of work and was willing to let everyone else take care of me. Your father was always trying to help me see the importance of work, but I never did—not until I came out here.

I only came because I was drafted and couldn't get out of it. I begged your father to go to the war office and tell them I was needed at the factory. He was willing, but Bradshaw wasn't. I even went to his wife and asked her to help. I wanted to go on being aimless.

Isaac stopped reading and handed the letter to Laura. "Will you read it to me?"

She took it but didn't start right away. "He went to see my mother. It says so right here."

"That doesn't mean they did anything improper. Your mother was kind. He may have simply believed she would help him."

"My father might not have seen it that way."

He nodded. "Morton was so fun, but he was not always thoughtful. I wish we could just ask him what exactly happened."

"There may be more here." She found where he left off and continued reading, hungry for information.

When I got here, I found a cause I believed in. It changed me. Don't go thinking I couldn't still lick you at backgammon. I still enjoy a good game every now and then, but I am a better man now than I was before. I'm a husband, and soon, I'll be a father. I wanted to be a good one. If I don't come home, be a good man, and help teach my child to live for a purpose.

I may not be there to ride the elephant with you or see what you will do with your life. But I hope you don't wait as long as I did to find meaning and purpose.

Our family isn't good at saying it, but I love you, and I miss you.

Your uncle,

Morton

"He sounds like a caring uncle," Laura said after finishing the letter. "He would have been a good father."

"I wish I could have seen him again," Isaac said. "I never thought he'd die. He was so young and carefree. It didn't seem like anything could hurt him."

"It's strange that your father was always encouraging him to be more serious while he's encouraged you to be more carefree."

"My father was so upset when Morton died. He tried to keep me from his grief, but I remember him storming about the house. He was different. He was so angry and hurt." Isaac squinted under the bright sun. "I think he tried to make up for pushing Morton so hard by doing the opposite with me."

"What will they think of Morton being married and having a child?"

Isaac looked in the direction of Mary and Albert, who were carrying armloads of firewood and stacking them in a pile near the side of the house. "It'll be like a piece of Morton has come home. Will you read yours now?"

She nodded.

Dear Mr. Bradshaw and daughter,

I received word about Mrs. Bradshaw's death, and it has troubled me.

I didn't write sooner because I didn't know what to say. Being so far away made it easy to pretend like the news was not real. But I'm afraid if I don't say something now, I will never be able to.

I am sorry for her death. I blame myself. Before leaving for the war, I visited Mrs. Bradshaw on multiple occasions and begged her to help me avoid being drafted. I thought if she went to the war office and declared me an essential worker, then I wouldn't have to go. She was sympathetic to my pleas, promising to speak to you. Later she told me that you wouldn't help because you'd offered me a job a year ago, and I hadn't taken it.

I was angry when she said it. I let my temper boil over, and I told her I blamed your whole family for not stepping in and saving me from the draft when they had the power to. She said she was sorry. But I didn't accept her apology. I didn't know I would never see her again. When I heard she died near the war office, I felt certain she was there because of me.

It's my fault she died. I never should have asked any of you to speak up on my behalf. I was irresponsible. I wasn't a good worker, and I didn't take life seriously enough. I don't know how I can make it right. All I can do is tell you the truth of what happened and pray you will forgive me for the part I played.

The army has changed me. If I come back alive, I will show you I am a better man. And if I can pay restitution, I will.

In sorrow,
Morton Campbell

As the words of the letters settled like rain, the pieces of the past drifted together. Her mother's death was indeed linked to Morton Campbell, but it was an accident. Her mother had not been the villainous actress her father accused her of being. She'd been alone with a man, but she'd not been unfaithful. She was the good-hearted woman Laura always believed her to be.

"I never should have doubted her," she whispered. Isaac

leaned against the back of the bench. Together, they silently let the past wash over them.

Morton Campbell, the carefree uncle, had tried to avoid his duty. He'd died, but first he'd lived and loved. A loss for each. A Bradshaw loss and a Campbell loss. Both left brokenness in their wake. Both losses brought hurt and anger.

Laura left the bench and walked a few feet away. They needed to go and face their parents, show them the letters and see how the dust would settle.

Isaac came beside her. He took her hand and, without saying a word, led her from the hill.

CHAPTER 31

Mary, with Albert by her side, wished them well as they prepared to leave. They embraced one another and promised
to return soon. Laura felt a kinship with the strong, determined
woman who'd so fearlessly faced life. Loss had left its marks, but
she kept fighting, and Laura admired her for it. Isaac was especially gentle and kind to Albert. The bond between cousins was
instant.

They rode back to Niagara Falls in near silence. Mrs. Guskin
was packed and ready when they arrived at the hotel. Isaac excused himself for a moment while the women discussed the
morning. Mrs. Guskin responded to Laura's tale with sympathy
and compassion.

"The letters could change everything. They could bring our
families back together," Laura said. "And now there is Albert
to think of. How could anyone stay angry when there is a child
looking up to them?"

"I've learned a few things," Mrs. Guskin said. "Sometimes
folks don't want to let go of their hate, even if they know they're
being watched. They hold it tight, like they would any other
vice."

"You don't think they'll forgive each other. Don't you think
my father will be grateful to know that his wife was faithful to

him, and Isaac's father will take comfort knowing his brother was not angry about going off to war?"

"I hope they see it that way. But your father is a stubborn man, and his hate has become habitual. You need to think about what you'll do if he doesn't forgive Campbell."

"Isaac and I will remain star-crossed lovers," she said with a frown. "We'll be stuck on opposite sides of a fight that will never be won."

"None of that nonsense. You'll just be awfully poor as you set out on your own. But plenty of people have done it before. I don't know why so many people are afraid of being poor."

Mrs. Guskin had a way of shining a new light on Laura's woes. For now, she would have to take it all one day at a time. There were too many unknowns to guess at the future. Isaac hadn't officially proposed, and their fathers' reactions were only presumed.

It was there on the porch that Isaac found them. He was smiling as he climbed the steps. "I called the paper. They want me to stay in Niagara and write a story about Arnold Lamar. The reporter they sent has another story to write in the city. If you don't mind, we will all be seeing the falls together."

"You know I've been wanting to see them." Laura grinned, all other worries set aside.

"Let me escort you both, and we'll get a better look." He leaned close to Laura and said, "If you can, let's forget about our parents and enjoy the daredevil. After all, this is our first real date."

"You don't count the manure pile?"

"I count it all, but those encounters were more like half dates than a real first date. Come on."

He walked with an extra jaunt in his step as they made their way to the falls. The streets were bustling, everyone moving in the same direction like a herd of migrating bison. Laura tried to look past the crowd, but she still couldn't see the oft-talked-about falls. Five minutes later, they stepped away from the city buildings, and their view opened to majestic splendor. Words did not do it justice.

"It's beautiful," Laura said, gawking at the thundering current and the sparkling mist that filled the air and covered everything in a watery sheen. Rainbows danced all around as sunlight filtered through the vapor. The crowd was large. There were thousands of people all around Horseshoe Falls and American Falls, some down on the rocks, others on the rim. Some had binoculars and spyglasses. All were awed by the same masterpiece.

Isaac pulled out pen and paper. He took notes and asked spectators questions as they waited for word that Lamar was approaching the falls. Lamar's ball, with him in it, was put in the river a half mile up. No one knew how fast it would travel, so they all stared with bated breath.

"He's nearing the falls," a man with a megaphone shouted five minutes later.

A hush settled over the crowd. The only sound was the powerful flow of the falls as it crashed from the peak into the swirling pools below. Mrs. Guskin grabbed Laura's hand and whispered, "I can't watch. I've never understood these stunts."

"Don't look," Laura said. "I'll tell you what happens."

A black object came into view. It floated on the mighty river. For one moment only, it looked peaceful in the water, and then—*whoosh*—it flew over the side, where it danced in and out of view as it fell to the depths and was sucked into the churning pit below, disappearing from sight. The crowd gasped. Everyone leaned closer, looking into the river below, watching and waiting. Some prayed. Others stood with their mouths agape. Was the man inside alive? Would they be able to pull him from the whirlpool at the bottom? Each heart raced with excitement and fear.

The popular *Maid of the Mist* boat circled near the bottom of the falls, so close that those aboard were drenched by the spray, as it readied to spring to the rescue.

"I don't see him," Laura whispered to Mrs. Guskin. "He's in the water below, but I don't know where."

Mrs. Guskin kept her eyes closed, but her mouth offered a silent appeal heavenward.

Abnormally long seconds passed.

And then, like a bouncing child's toy, the ball burst from the depths, freed at last from the hungry water. The crowd cheered, and the rescuers on the *Maid of the Mist* made quick work of reeling in the man and contraption.

Isaac scribbled notes as quickly as he could. Mrs. Guskin opened her eyes and breathed a sigh of relief.

"That was foolhardy," she said as she wiped moisture from her forehead.

"It was," Laura agreed. "But since he survived, it was sort of exciting."

The crowd was slow to leave. The spectacle had come and gone too quickly. They lingered, admiring the falls and clinging to the exhilaration that had been in the air, not ready to go back to their ordinary lives. Laura understood. She, too, felt no desire to hurry back to Buffalo and the unknowns that awaited her.

Standing beside Isaac, Laura listened as he asked the spectators what they thought of the feat. It was an hour later before he was ready to leave.

"Shall we go?" He shook his hand. "I'll have to learn to write notes faster. My hands are sore."

"Mrs. Guskin can teach you shorthand," Laura said, looking again at the grandness of Niagara. "She can write faster than anyone I know."

Mrs. Guskin blushed. "Stop singing my praises. I'm not that fast."

"She is," Laura said. "She's just being modest. I wish we could stay here. The falls make everything else seem small."

His hand went to the small of her back. "We don't have to hide behind the falls. We have the letters. We'll find a way."

She nodded, following him. With each step the sound of the falls dimmed.

The three conversed easily as they headed south from Niagara to Buffalo. They relived the moment of wonder at the falls, speculated on the sentence Abel would receive, and even shared stories about Morton. The closer they got to Buffalo, the longer the silences in their conversation grew. In Niagara they had felt so hopeful and free, but in Buffalo Laura and Isaac were still the children of the feud.

At Laura's house they shared a quick goodbye, not nearly as long and drawn out as Laura would have liked. But Isaac was eager to get to his house and face his father.

"I could go with you," Laura offered.

"I think it best if I tell them about the paper and the letters and Albert." He squeezed her hand. "I'll come by later, if that's all right."

"My father still isn't back," she said. "Mrs. Guskin won't mind. Come as soon as you can."

Once alone, Laura crept into her house and slowly made her way to the library. It was foolish going there, knowing it would sting to see the empty shelves. She stood outside the door, trying to remember how it looked before it was so starved. With her eyes closed, she could see the rows of books and could almost smell the fragrance of paper and binding glue. And then she thought of her mother and the way her eyes sparkled when she brought home a new book.

"Come with me," her mother would say. "Help me find the perfect place to put it."

Laura opened her eyes. The past faded. She stepped into the room and looked at the empty shelves. Where Shakespeare should have been, there was nothing but dust. The spy novels, romances—all of them were gone.

Each volume had been her friend. In her moments of loneliness, she'd come here and visited her old comrades. Elizabeth Bennet, Margaret Hale, and Lucy Snowe were all gone, and she'd not even said goodbye.

Begin again, Mrs. Guskin had said. Buy one book and then another.

Laura walked around the room, running her hands over the empty shelves. It was a loss, a deep one. And her heart ached because of it. When the pain of the empty shelves became too much, she sought solace in the privacy of her room.

Like a sullen child she sank onto the floor, back against her bed, head tilted up toward the ceiling. *I can do this*, she told herself. *I can start again*. She said it again and again until the words became her resolve. She turned to stand, only to catch sight of the corner of her fairy-tale book tucked beneath her bed. The last book her mother had ever bought. With unwarranted urgency, she pulled it out and held it close.

When at last she stood, she went to her window seat and opened the cover. She turned one page and then another, each filled with princes and princesses, magic and romance. Her mother did not feel as far away. Her memory felt close. When she'd turned the last page, Laura closed the book and retraced her steps until she was once again standing near the empty library.

"Where should it go?" she said, her voice echoing. "Where would it look best?"

Slowly she circled the room, stopping at a low shelf near the window. "Right there."

She stepped back and looked at the book. It seemed so small and alone in the large room, but it was a start. So often she'd felt alone, much like this book looked. "I'll get others. I'll bring you friends."

Before leaving she paused at the door, closed her eyes, and thought again of her mother.

"Laura!" Mrs. Guskin's voice boomed through the hall. Laura snapped to attention.

"What's wrong?"

"You'd better come and get your bird. Cook says she's tired of listening to his horrid chatter, and if you don't come and get him, she's going to open the back door and let him out."

"Oh my." Laura tried not to laugh as she retrieved Tybalt from the far corner of the kitchen. She did her best to keep a straight face as she thanked the cook for feeding him.

"That animal ought to have his mouth washed out," Cook said. "Get him out of my kitchen."

"Were you using your sea language?" she asked Tybalt as she lugged his cage through the house and back to its spot in her room. He pranced around, showing no remorse as he gnawed at the door. "One of these days someone really is going to just let you go." When he cocked his head and looked at her with innocent eyes, she stopped chiding him and let him out.

She put him on the back of her chair, then sat across from him so she could see him.

"I know you want to hear all about my time away," she said as she unpinned her hair and let it fall over her shoulders. "I don't know where to start. I suppose all that matters is that Abel is in jail, Mother's death was a tragic accident, the falls were beautiful, Morton left behind a child, and someday, if Isaac asks me, I'm going to marry him."

Tybalt's head shot up.

"Don't be so surprised. We've been in love a long time, only we didn't know it before." She pressed a hand to her heart. "But it was always him. He's going to come back later tonight, so don't think me rude, but I'm going to close my eyes and see if I can catch up on sleep. You should too. And remember to be on your best behavior when he comes. Save your sea mouth for later."

●━━━━━━━━━━●

Isaac waited as his father read the letter addressed to him. Isaac had wanted to read it himself, but his conscience kept him from unfolding the page. And so he waited.

His mother sat trembling beside his father. She had a handkerchief out, ready to wipe whatever tears were going to come.

His father finished and handed the letter to his wife without telling its secrets to Isaac.

"This is why you went to Niagara," his father said.

"I went because I was concerned about Abel *and* to get the letters." He pulled out his letter and handed it to his father. "He wrote me, too, and he wrote the Bradshaws. I read that letter with Laura Bradshaw. We both wanted to understand what happened. We finally believe we do."

His father took the second letter and read it. His dark brows furrowed together, but Isaac wasn't sure whether it was from grief or anger or surprise.

Isaac tapped his thumb on the arm of the wingback chair he sat in and thought back over his parents' reaction when he'd returned home.

His father had greeted him with a paper in hand. "What's this?"

Isaac had stopped his father with a raised hand and then begged him to hear the whole story. It'd taken him several attempts to properly tell about Abel. He left out his letters to Laura—there would be time for those details later. He told of Mr. Cannon, of Mary Kensington, and of Abel's forged documents. But he still wasn't sure how his father felt, and so he waited, eager and anxious.

His father looked up from his letter. "You want to know what happened? I'll tell you. Morton was young. He got the draft letter and didn't want to go. Bradshaw wouldn't declare him an essential worker no matter how many times I asked. He could have kept Morton from going, but he wouldn't. He said that Morton had declined the job he'd offered him before, and it wasn't fair to declare Morton essential when he wasn't. We argued about it up until the day Morton left. A rumor started that Morton had been seen at Bradshaw's house when he wasn't there. Bradshaw believed it and said that it was further proof Morton wasn't worth having around. He wouldn't listen to reason."

"Morton is the reason the factory split," Isaac said quietly. "You fought over his draft letter."

"Bradshaw only cared about proving he knew business. He was stubborn and dug his heels in. He was trying to show us that he'd done what was best for the company. When his wife died, he became a different man. Ever since, being the best is all that matters to him. He's a stubborn fool. Splitting with him was the best decision we made."

"But he was your friend," Isaac said. "He made a mistake. A horrible one, and his wife ended up dying—"

"It was his fault she died. If he'd just gone to the war office and stopped the draft, she wouldn't have been going and trying to speak for him. He killed Morton and his wife."

Isaac's insides knotted. He'd imagined a glorious reunion of friends, a healing. "This changes nothing," Isaac said to no one but himself. "You are going to keep hating him. You have a nephew you knew nothing of. You have Morton's own words, and that still doesn't change anything."

"Stop making it sound like your father is doing something wrong." His mother twisted the handkerchief she held. "It's best we leave things as they are."

"But I don't want to," he said, his voice rising. "I don't want to hate Bradshaw. I don't want to hate anyone. Morton asked me to be a good example for his son. I'll start by washing my hands of your hate."

He left his seat and walked to the wall where the framed

photograph of Morton hung. Isaac looked at Morton's roguish smile and playful eyes. "Morton fell in love—you read his letter. He was glad he went to war and for the life he found. He would hate knowing what we have all become." His hands fisted at his sides, his whole body tense. "He found himself in Europe. He told me to work hard and find my own way too."

"You have everything you need here—" his mother began, but he cut her off.

"I am going to work for the newspaper. They liked my writing and have offered me a job. I'd like to stay here and save money, but I'll leave if it's best. I plan to work and save, and then I'm going to marry Laura Bradshaw."

CHAPTER 32

Heavy footsteps and a slammed door interrupted Laura's nap. She sat quickly. It was her father; he was the only one large enough to make such a racket. She groaned, not ready to face him.

Stalling wouldn't help. She stuck the letter from Morton in her skirt pocket and searched for her father. He was in the living room, pulling off his boots.

"Father," she said. "I need to talk to you."

"I don't have time," he said. "I have to find Abel."

"He's in jail." She tried not to gloat, but it was difficult when she felt such elation knowing Abel was no longer a threat to her or anyone else. "He was going to sell everyone forged deeds to land in Florida. It's all in the paper. Isaac Campbell wrote about it."

Her father's hands froze on his laces. "In jail."

"Yes, and if you'll listen to me, I'll tell you exactly what happened." She tried not to smirk, but it was difficult when she could hear the strength in her own voice and knew how shocked he must be hearing it too. He'd left a weak daughter at home and returned to a strong, determined woman.

He wasn't exactly an amiable audience, but he sat through her retelling. His face was stoic and dark. When she finished by sharing that she and Isaac had gone to Niagara Falls not only because of Abel but also because of Morton, the anger she'd expected surfaced.

"I don't want to talk about Morton. That man and his family ruined everything."

"I know that's what you believe," she said, not backing away from him. "And I can see why. But I think you're wrong." She handed him the letter. "He wrote this as he was dying. He wrote Isaac and Mr. Campbell too. I don't think he was the villain you believed him to be. Either way, he died, leaving a son behind."

Her father surprised her and took the letter. For a long time he held it, not opening it, not speaking. The silence was uncomfortable. It begged to be filled, but she waited. He still didn't open it. He stood, letter in hand, and walked away.

When he was out of sight, Laura sought out Mrs. Guskin for advice.

"Give him time" was the only advice she offered. Which was hardly advice at all.

"Will you watch for Isaac, tell him I can't see him tonight? Tell him I'll try to see him soon." It hurt, the idea of turning Isaac away, but her father was unpredictable. She spent the evening in her room, looking out at the park, counting the stars and re-reading old letters from Isaac.

Tybalt swore a few times, but even his unruly mouth didn't make her laugh. She knew what she wanted but not how to get it. Isaac would be penniless; he'd be starting from nothing. It could be years before he'd be able to buy a home. Even then she would have to wait for him to ask. If her father wouldn't let him in, how could he?

After an hour of thinking, she was no closer to the answers. All she knew was that she was not going to wait for a prince to come rescue her. She'd tried that with Abel—never again. She wanted Isaac. She loved him. But she wouldn't cower in the corner waiting for him.

From her window, she saw Isaac walking on the sidewalk, his gait so familiar. Oh how she wished she could run to him and stroll the park on his arm. As it was, she had to act quickly. She tapped on her window and then swiftly opened it.

He looked up at her and waved. "Hello, fair lady. Should I climb up and sweep you away?"

"My father is home," she said. "I can't meet you. You have to go."

"I need to see you." The humor left his face.

"I can't." She shook her head. There was a noise coming from somewhere in the house. "I'll leave a letter in the tree as soon as I can," she said before closing the window and stepping toward the sound.

She was careful to keep her feet quiet and to avoid the boards that creaked. The sound led her to the library. She crept close to the door and peered inside. Her father, the man she'd begun to believe was void of heart and feelings, sat on the floor, his back to the wall, letter in hands and tears on his face.

He wiped his cheeks as he looked around the now empty library. His anguish permeated the entire room. Laura could feel it in her own heart. And then, as though the years had never happened, she crossed the floor and wrapped her arms around him. He stiffened but didn't brush her away.

"I'm sorry," he said as he rocked back and forth. "I was wrong."

"It doesn't matter," she said, allowing him to lean into her strength. "She always loved you."

"I yelled at her. I wouldn't listen to reason. I thought she'd . . . I accused her of terrible things." His jaw tensed. "It's all my fault. I blamed her, but it was my fault."

She let go of him and crouched so they were face-to-face. "Father, don't do that. It was a misunderstanding. Everyone erred, but it can be made right. Mother believed in forgiveness."

"No," he said. "I can't."

"You can't what? Say you're sorry? Be friends with Campbell?" She fought her own rising anger. "Mother died. We lost her. Morton died. Haven't we all lost enough?"

"It's not that easy."

"Yes, it can be." She stood, placing her hands on the empty bookshelves. "You gave your anger seven years. You gave it your happiness and mine. You even gave it Mother's books. Stop feeding it. Don't let it take anything else. Let it starve and die."

He wadded up the letter in his hand.

"You can do what you want," she said, strong and unwilling to follow his lead. "I'm done with it. I'm going to be friends with Isaac Campbell. I'm going to go to the socials and the zoo. The hate does not get to take my life."

He looked at his feet, still refusing to meet her eyes.

"I want you to be a part of my life." Her own tears came. "I want a father. I want the father I had when I was little to come back. But I can't keep waiting. This isn't what Mother wanted for me."

"I don't know . . ." He grimaced. Whatever words he wanted to say weren't coming easily.

"Listen to me," she said, each word slow and clear. "I forgive you. We can put more books on the shelves. We can fix what's broken."

He looked up then, and their eyes met.

"I'm sorry," he said again.

"I know. And now we have to decide what to do next. I had a long night last night. I'm going to go to bed. Tomorrow when I wake up, will you eat breakfast with me?"

He nodded before burying his head in his hands again.

———•———

Dear Love,

Is it all right if I call you that? I know I should wait until we've been on at least two real dates to use such a strong endearment, but our romance has been far from conventional.

The first thing I did when I woke up this morning was find your article in the newspaper. Your words took me back to the falls. I could see it all in my mind. I could even hear the water crashing and feel the mist. It was a fine article.

I did not think we would be back to writing letters again. Then again, I don't know if I ever want to give it up entirely. I think I will always love letters, but if I had to pick between letters and your presence, I would pick your presence.

My father is hurting. I can't explain it exactly. He is wrestling with himself. I think it is hard for him to remember who he was before the hate set in. But he is trying, and I admire him for that. He sat by me at break-fast this morning. We were mostly silent, but he was not unkind.

I told him I planned to come to the zoo today, and he didn't tell me not to. He nodded his head and then took a sip of his coffee. That may seem insignificant, but it was not. Tonight I plan to ask him if he is up for a game of checkers. We played often when I was small. If he says yes, then I might cry happy tears.

I've enclosed money for you to give to Mr. Cannon. My father was agreeable when I asked for it. He is embarrassed that Abel lured him. He would like you to thank Mr. Cannon for him.

I saw you yesterday, and already I have a thousand questions for you. It would be so much easier to ask you in person, but I don't know when I'll see you. When you do write back, will you tell me what your family said about the letters and about Albert? And tell me all about your job. Write me the longest letter ever so I feel like I am right there with you.

Do you remember when we were at Centennial Park and you tested your theory? I have a theory of my own. When I see you next, I think we ought to test it.

Missing you,
Me

Isaac sat at the base of the letter tree, legs stretched out in front of him, back to the tree. He'd nearly laughed when he pulled the letter out. Here they were again. Writing letters.

His parents had softened some. His announcement that he planned to marry the daughter of the enemy had alarmed them at first. His father had even shouted that he would not permit it.

But Isaac had refused to budge on the matter. There was no compromise to be found.

"I am going to marry her," he said. "Don't you remember her? She was quiet and sweet as a child. How could you hate her? She had no part in any of this."

"It's not a family you should marry into." His mother fanned herself with her hands. "You're not thinking clearly. I can have another party. We can fill the house with women."

"I don't want a house full of women. I want Laura." He stood to leave the room. From the corner of his eye, he saw them look at each other.

"Don't walk away," his father said. "It's only right for parents to worry and to ask you if you've thought it all through."

"I have." He left then. By the morning they'd been more pleasant, trying to subtly ask him to wait, to rethink his plans and sort out other matters first.

He'd put his open pocket watch on the table. "*Even apart, we battle together.* I know you meant fight Bradshaw, but I wonder if you could change the meaning and choose to have it mean that you and I will always care for each other and fight the same foes. I *am* going to write for the paper and marry Laura. I won't be here like I have been. But I want us to be on the same side."

"Morton died before I could send it." His father picked up the watch and looked at it. "I'm glad I didn't send it."

"You are?"

"I read his letter. He didn't want us to fight over his leaving. He had no regrets, except believing he'd come between us and of course not being able to be there for his wife and child."

Isaac nodded. He'd guessed that Morton's letter to his father said something like that, and he had hoped the words would pierce his father's soul. A cry from the grave to change course.

"I will try," his father said, closing the watch and putting it back in Isaac's hand.

Now Isaac pulled the pocket watch from his pocket as he sat at the zoo, reading Laura's sweet address many times—*Dear Love.*

It was nearly nine o'clock. He'd finished his response letter and decided to walk over by the manure pile for old times' sake. The stench, strong as ever, greeted him. Foul and welcoming.

"Isaac."

His heart leaped. She was there, leaning against the wall. No shovel, no wheelbarrow.

"I thought . . . I hoped you'd come." She grinned. "I came to deliver a letter and to talk to Mr. Shaffer. He's going to let me volunteer again. I can't come as often as before. I want to spend time with my father and with you."

"Will your father allow you to volunteer?"

She blushed. "I told him I was going to. I didn't ask, and he didn't stop me."

The wind blew stronger, and the stench engulfed them. They both smelled it and laughed. Isaac grabbed her hand, pulling her away from the pile.

"Come and walk around the zoo with me. And if you happen to walk by a particularly beautiful maple tree, you might want to reach inside. I've heard you like letters."

"I love letters." She took his hand.

"And I love you," he said, feeling the truth of it deep in his core.

For the first time, they looked at the animals together. When someone stared, they smiled back. They'd let them talk. Let them gossip. Isaac and Laura were done hiding.

The foxes wrestled and put on a show. Isaac kept taking his eyes off them and looked instead at Laura. Her eyes were twinkling with delight. The sea lions, the gazelles, the bears—they saw them all. She peppered him with facts about each animal, making this walk through the zoo more fun than any before.

"Laura!" Mr. Shaffer yelled from across the path. "The gi-raffes arrived."

Laura tugged on Isaac's hand. "Come on. I've always wanted to see a giraffe up close."

A large circus truck pulled up beside the zoo. There were ten men, ready to help the animals if they spooked. Someone yelled at Isaac, telling him to mind the gap on the left. He stood tall, arms up, and then they opened the bed of the truck, and Laura gasped with delight as the tall animals came into view.

"Meet Arthur and Joanne," Mr. Shaffer said. "Laura, grab one of those branches with leaves on it. See if you can lure them out."

The giraffes were stubborn at first, refusing to step off the truck. Laura walked closer, waving the leaves in front of them. "Come on out, come see the zoo. It's the finest zoo in the coun-try." Her voice was soft and singsongy. If he were a giraffe, Isaac would follow her anywhere. "Come on, come and see."

They took a step out, and then another. Everyone stared wide-eyed at the zoo's new additions. They followed Laura as she talked to them and led them away from the truck and into their new enclosure. Cheers erupted when the gate was closed behind them.

"I see why you like giraffes," Isaac said to Laura. "I think we ought to get a giraffe one day."

"No," she said with a laugh. "But we will have to come to the zoo often." She stiffened. "Have I told you I have a bird? He's a macaw and uses awful language."

"You've mentioned him. I'm eager to meet him."

"He will go with me wherever I go."

He put a hand on her shoulder, and his fingers wandered

to the back of her neck. "I think I can handle a bird. Didn't you write that you had a theory you wanted to test?"

"We will have to leave the giraffes to test it. It's a theory better tested without an audience."

"I think I like testing theories with you."

Moments later they stood beneath the magnificent branches of the letter tree, Isaac placing one hand on her waist, the other on her cheek.

"Your theory?" he whispered.

"I've always believed this spot a romantic one. A perfect place for two people to share a private moment and . . ." She blushed. "A kiss."

His heart swelled as he bent to meet her lips and test her theory. As he held her, he could not help but feel grateful for the letter tree's grandeur and providence.

Before letting her go he whispered, "I love you, my Wishing Girl."

CHAPTER 33

Life found a pleasant normal. Letters and an occasional nine o'clock meeting at the zoo with Laura. She was still adamant that her father needed time before Isaac could come by her house, but she seemed happier every day and was not afraid to meet him in public. They got plenty of strange looks, and rumors were flying through the city about the son of Campbell and the daughter of Bradshaw. But Isaac couldn't have cared less.

They'd even gotten Mary to bring Albert to the zoo. Mr. Shaffer let them stay after the zoo closed, and Laura helped Isaac take Albert in to meet Big Frank. When he lifted Albert up beside the giant elephant, he'd felt as though he were keeping a promise to his uncle.

Isaac had a desk at the paper. He knew everything that was happening in the city and had even convinced his parents to read what he wrote. His father had praised his work and then asked if Isaac could do an article on the Campbell factory. Their relationship was mending, one stitch at a time.

Charles sat in a chair across from Isaac at the newspaper office. "Are you going to court her forever? A letter here, a stroll there."

"It hasn't been that long, and it's complicated. Why aren't you married yet?"

"Her mother got better, and her father got sick." He groaned. "If your parents are all healthy, you should get married now. Otherwise, you could end up like me—waiting forever."

"That is incentive. You look miserable."

"I am." He pouted. "I have tried to see this as a good thing. But I can't. It's torture. No man should have to move his wedding back this many times."

"I am sorry," Isaac said. "You could get married by his sickbed."

"I suggested it." He groaned. "Enough about my pain. When are you going to bring Bradshaw and Campbell together? Not the factory, of course—I doubt they'll ever merge."

"I've been thinking about it. I have an idea, but I don't know if it'll work yet. I know I have to accept that they may never be friends again, but I'd like to find a way for them to stop being enemies."

"Realistic." Charles picked up the draft for a new article. "You're pretty good."

"Thank you. I never fit at the shoe factory, but here I do. I looked at an apartment today. It's small, but I think I can afford it on my salary."

"You are thinking marriage," Charles said. "I knew you were. You'll probably end up a married man before I will."

"Don't be jealous," Isaac teased. "Maybe God is teaching you patience."

"I always believed God had a sense of humor."

Charles left not long after, and Isaac was alone with his

work. As quickly as he could, he finished his assigned articles and then he wrote from his heart.

———————●———————————————●———————

A Feud, a Friend, and a Future

Seven years ago, a large shoe factory, the Bradshaw-Campbell factory, split into two separate companies. Since then, both have competed to make the finest shoes. Their success is seen throughout the city. Look at a neighbor's feet, or glance down at your own, and you have a good chance of seeing a pair of shoes made by one of these great companies.

But some ask: Why did the company split? The truth is, pain split the companies apart. Friends, who were like brothers, refused to speak. Their children were kept from each other. The hurt and loss was so deep, it created a crevasse between two good men and their families.

He looked at the words on the page. They were raw and real and vulnerable, but they were the truth.

His father wanted an article about shoes, and he would get one. A human-interest story that Isaac could only hope would soften hearts.

He wrote a paragraph about the thin thread that bound two unsuspecting hearts together, and how it grew thicker and stronger with each passing year. Then another about discovering the identity of his pen friend. His beautiful, one-of-a-kind love story, born of grief and sorrow, came together on the page.

> And so, what was once broken is coming together again. The road has been long, marred by rocks and ruts, but the course has been sure.
>
> Shakespeare wrote once of feuding families. His tale was a tragedy. But the Bradshaw-Campbell feud is not a play; it is real. And in real life, two people in love can change the story.
>
> And so, after all these years apart, the owners of the two great companies will be meeting at Delaware Park at five o'clock to shake hands and share in the brotherhood they once knew. Their fine example should inspire us all to mend the broken parts of our lives.

The editor read the article silently after Isaac completed it, his face expressionless. Isaac nearly grabbed it back and told him to forget the whole thing. It was a silly idea; no one wanted to read about a family's problems.

"I like it," the editor said and walked away with it.

⎯⎯⎯⎯⎯●⎯⎯⎯⎯⎯⎯⎯⎯●⎯⎯⎯⎯⎯

Laura's father beat her to breakfast the next morning. He had the paper open, reading as he ate. "Looks like the price of automobiles will be going up."

"Oh," she said before starting her meal. "Anything else interesting in the paper?"

He turned the page. "Isaac has another article in here."

"Read it, will you? His articles are always my favorite."

Her father grunted but obliged, a sure sign he was warming to the idea of her and Isaac being friends . . . and someday more.

"It's about the company," he said, once again sounding callous. "How dare he write about my company. It's not his to discuss."

"It affected all of us." She took the paper from him and read the story aloud, stopping from time to time to see her father's reaction. His face was softening as she read, the truth so gently written, so full of hope, it was hard to remain angry. She got to the last paragraph and stopped.

"Might as well finish it," he grumbled. "You read that much already."

She cleared her throat. "'And so, after all these years apart, the owners of the two great companies will be meeting at Delaware Park at five o'clock to shake hands and share in the brotherhood they once knew. Their fine example should inspire us all to mend the broken parts of our lives.'"

"I'm not going." Her father stood and threw his napkin on his half-eaten meal. "He can't trick me like that."

"It's an invitation, not a trick."

She said nothing more but spent the day counting down until five o'clock. At 4:49 p.m. she heard her father come home with something in his hands.

"If I have to shake Campbell's hand, I might as well try to set everything right." He handed her the thick envelope. "I couldn't buy the books back. But I want you to have the money from them. You can use it to buy more books or to start your life with . . . with the Campbell boy, if you want. It's yours. Your mother would have wanted you to have it."

She didn't count it or care how much there was. It was the gentle look in his eyes that she wanted to capture, bundle up, and keep always. After staring at him for an uncanny amount of time, she threw her arms around him, accepting his truce with her whole heart. "Thank you," she said. "Come on, let's go to the park."

"I still don't think it was right of him," he said as he followed her away from the house and across the street. The crowd was large, full of curious gawkers. Her father waved at them as he made his way to the center of the crowd, but under his breath he muttered about how ridiculous it all was.

Isaac wove through the crowd toward her. "I didn't expect this."

"Everyone loves a good spectacle. Remember the crowd at the flagpole sitting? And this is much more exciting. Are your parents coming?"

"My father said no at first, but he's here. He's over there." He pointed into the crowd, and she gasped. Her father was already at William Campbell's side. Campbell stuck out his hand, and her father took it. They shook. Their hands remained together, bobbing up and down as they talked.

"I wish I could hear them," she said, staring at her father.

"Whatever they're saying, it's the right thing. They look like old chums again. Do you think they mean it?"

"I do." Her father looked younger, standing beside his boyhood friend. "I think my father has been wanting this for a long time. He just didn't know it."

"Do you think this crowd needs something else to talk about?"

"I think your article gave them plenty of dinner conversation."

"I don't think it's enough."

"What do you have planned?" She looked away from their fathers and tried to read his expression.

"I was thinking now might be a good time for me to ask your father if I can officially court you."

"I think you should come over to the house tonight and ask him then. Your chances of getting a yes are higher in private. He's not big on being a spectacle."

"Tonight then." He took her hand as they watched the miracle in front of them. "Will you walk with me in the Quarry Garden?"

"Yes," she said and followed him away from the crowd. "I have wanted to walk with you in the Quarry Garden for a very long time."

"I have had that same wish." They were in no hurry. They walked slowly, strolling in the open air of the park like the many couples she'd watched from her window.

She stopped walking and pointed to a large rock just inside the entrance. "I was standing near that rock when I was waiting for you."

"I know, I saw you." He pointed behind him. "I sat over there while I waited for you to leave. I didn't think there would ever be a way for us to be together. It seemed impossible."

They stepped along the rocky path, arm in arm, no barriers between them. When they came to the edge of the pond, they stopped walking. She touched his cheek, the end-of-day growth tickling her fingertips. "Have I told you that you're my favorite person?"

"In your letter you called me love, so I had hoped."

"I did call you love." She kissed his cheek and then his jaw. "I will love you always."

"And forever," he whispered back. "I have a question."

"What is it?" She was in his arms, looking into his eyes.

"Will you dance with me?"

"I have always wanted to dance with you." She put one hand on his shoulder and the other hand in his. They danced to the wind, slowly making circles in the shadow of the limestone, moving closer to each other until he bent and kissed her, then picked her up and let out one elated whoop.

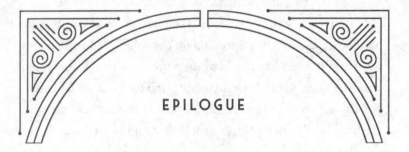

EPILOGUE

THREE MONTHS LATER

H old the ladder still," Isaac said to Charles as he climbed higher. It was the middle of the night, and they had only a sliver of moonlight to see by.

"This is the most foolish idea I have ever heard. I thought I did a lot of stupid things while courting Elsie."

"You did," Isaac said. "And I helped you with some of them."

"I should be home with her. *My wife* is probably wondering where I am."

Isaac looked down from his precarious spot. "You like saying the word *wife*, don't you?"

"If a man is going to get married, he should be fully committed to his wife. There is no shame in a man loving his wife."

"Enough with the lectures," Isaac said. He climbed up another rung. It shouldn't have been this hard, but with a stack of books in his hand and a dark night sky, the ascent was precarious. "I'm almost there—just hold it steady."

"I will, unless you get all mushy."

Isaac ignored Charles and continued his climb. He paused to catch his breath at the top and then knocked on the window as loud as he could.

"Storm's coming," a man's voice called out.

"I have the wrong window." Isaac started making his way back down as quickly as he could on the wobbly ladder. Charles was laughing too hard to hold it steady. Two rungs down, the window came open. Isaac made himself as small as he could. He did not want to face Mr. Bradshaw at this unholy hour, in the dark, while attempting to reach his daughter's room.

"Isaac?"

He popped back up at the sound of Laura's voice.

"It's me," he said as he made his way back up. "I wanted to bring you a gift, but I heard a man's voice. I can . . . I can go."

"It's only Tybalt. He sounds like a sailor. I don't know who, but the man must have been interesting. You do know it's three in the morning, don't you?"

"He's a lovesick puppy," Charles said.

"Oh." Laura leaned out her window and looked down. Her long braid swayed like Rapunzel's. "Hello, Charles. How is your wife?"

"She's well," Charles called back.

"I am so happy you're finally married."

"It's been a week of bliss. I heard her brother is sick now. I'm glad we got married when we did."

Isaac adjusted his grip on the ladder. "Do you think you could just hold the ladder and let me do the talking?" he asked Charles.

"Go ahead, lover boy. Pretend I'm not here."

"I've brought you something," Isaac said, forgetting Charles and giving Laura all his attention. An angel could not be more beautiful than she was, leaning out her window with a touch of moonlight around her.

"A present?"

"I saved enough, and Mr. Cannon got me the name of the man who bought your mother's books. I couldn't afford them all, but I got you a stack of them."

"Isaac," she whispered. "Did you really?"

"Yes." He handed them to her. "I got three Shakespeare, two Jane Austen, and"—he tried to read the spines in the dark—"I can't remember the author of the other two."

"My father gave me the money from the books, but I was saving it for setting up house . . . if I should ever need it."

"You will." He grinned. "And now you'll have a few books to start your library with."

"When do you suppose I'll be setting up house?" She had the books pressed against her heart. "I like being prepared, that's all."

"Could be a long time if you have an illness run through your family tree," Charles said.

"Charles, you're not supposed to be here," Isaac said before going up one rung higher. His and Laura's faces were nearly level now. "I talked to your father today."

"Was he grouchy?" She set the books down and leaned against the windowsill.

"No, he was cordial."

"He's doing better, but he still has bouts of sadness. I think he misses my mother."

"He said as much. He said for me to treat you better than he treated her. He wants you to be happy." Isaac cleared his throat. "I was waiting. I wanted to be sure he would give me his blessing." Isaac reached in his pocket. "You told me once you wanted a man who would climb to your window and take you away."

"I remember."

"I am at your window, and I want to share my life with you."
With one hand he held the ladder, and with the other, he offered
her a simple ring. "Will you marry me, Wishing Girl? Come away
with me?"

"Yes," she said. "I will marry you, my dear pinecone-
throwing man."

She leaned out far enough that she could kiss him. Charles
made a gagging sound, but it didn't stop them. "I don't think I
want a prince anymore," Laura said. "I want a journalist with a
tiny apartment." She kissed him again and then pulled back. "I
have a present for you too. I was saving it, but now seems a good
time."

She disappeared for a second and then was back, a pot in her
hands. "I was by the letter tree and saw a tiny sapling. It was only
an inch high. I brought it home and plan to take care of it so
wherever we go, we'll have a letter tree."

Isaac tried to talk, but his throat was tight. Like a fool he
clung to the ladder and fought off the tears of happiness that
tried to escape. "I can think of nothing finer than a letter tree."
Charles shook the ladder. Isaac had to grab hold of the windowsill to steady himself. "What are you doing?"

"I'm just reminding you that I'm here. Save all the mushy
stuff for later."

"I'd better go," Isaac said to Laura. "But don't worry, I have
all kinds of mushy stuff ready for tomorrow."

"I can hardly wait." She stayed by the window, looking out at
the starry sky as he climbed down.

Soon, he would be marrying his letter girl.

AUTHOR'S NOTE

Dear reader,

I am an author, but I began as a reader and always will be one. When I read a novel, I love knowing what is fiction and what is fact, what sparked the idea for the story, and who helped it become a finished project.

And so I will tell you more about *The Letter Tree*.

First, what is factual.

The Buffalo Zoo and Delaware Park, right beside it, are real locations. The zoo really had an elephant named Big Frank, and it is the third-oldest zoo in the nation. The other animals are fictitious and may not match the actual Buffalo Zoo animals of 1924. I chose animals my children loved seeing when we lived in Buffalo and frequented the zoo.

The Quarry Garden is no longer there but used to be part of the beautiful park system. There are lovely old homes near the park, but I don't know if a Bradshaw family ever lived in them. Niagara Falls is a real location, of course, and several daredevils have gone over it. Because of my timeline, I fictionalized Arnold Lamar (basing him loosely on the man who went over Niagara Falls four years later, Jean Lussier).

AUTHOR'S NOTE

The financial schemer Abel Fredricks was fictional, but during the twenties there were many financial scams. One famous incident of fraud had to do with selling counterfeit land deeds with the promise that oil was underground.

There was not a Bradshaw/Campbell shoe factory feud, but the idea for feuding shoe companies came from the Adidas/Puma feud (a.k.a. the Dassler brothers' feud) that took place a couple of decades later in Germany. Part of their dispute had to do with whether it was right to keep relatives out of the war.

I have done my best to represent the era, clothing, and lifestyle of the 1920s as accurately as possible. If I have erred, I apologize.

And now, on to how I got the idea for *The Letter Tree*.

I wanted to write a story that featured a feud before I ever started drafting this novel. So often hate keeps people apart, and exploring that and watching characters rise above it appealed to me. I researched old feuds and thought about classic stories that featured rival families or businesses. But hate alone was not enough to start the story.

Then the pairing of *Romeo and Juliet* with *You've Got Mail* took shape. I thought it would be fun to mash them together and throw them in a different era. And *The Letter Tree* went from an idea to a story!

But I did not complete it alone. I had a quick deadline for this book and a busy summer planned. My whole family helped me find time to write (we took in a new foster baby, so life was double busy). My husband, who is always my biggest fan, encouraged me to make this novel a priority. I'm so grateful for the best home team around!

My agent, Lesley Sabga, was quick to offer help when I

wanted it and was always there to answer my texts and tell me that she believed in me. She is a joy!

My new editor, Laura Wheeler, makes writing fun. Every writer needs an editor like her. The entire team at HarperCollins has been fantastic. My line editor Whitney Bak filled my margins with encouraging praise and helped sort out my grammatical mess.

This book had some amazing readers step up and agree to trudge through my sloppy early drafts. Thank you to Katelind, Amy, Bailey, Eva, Alyssa, Kami, Kaycee, Jess, Adele, Stephanie, Leah, and my mom. You are all lifesavers!

I started writing almost seven years ago when I was looking for a creative outlet. My husband suggested I write a novel, and I felt much like Isaac in *The Letter Tree*. A whole new part of me came alive. I found a God-given passion and a love for the written word. I am grateful we all have unique talents and pray I always use mine for good.

Thank you for reading, for following, for reviewing, and for supporting me as I continue my writing journey.

Happy reading!

Rachel

DISCUSSION QUESTIONS

1. Laura's life became more solitary after losing her mother, requiring her to be creative with how she filled her time. Have you, like Laura, ever had a lonely "season"? How did you navigate it?

2. Isaac is twenty-three at the opening of the story and wrestling with the expectation of working for his father, despite it being unfulfilling. Thinking of your own upbringing, were there times when you struggled with expectations placed on you?

3. Laura and Isaac have been friends for years via letters without knowing each other's identities. In what ways did this allow them to get to know each other? In what ways did it inhibit their relationship?

4. Laura's father attempts to matchmake her with Abel. She is not enthusiastic about this arrangement but tries to make it work. Do you think her reasoning was faulty, or can you understand her rationale?

5. In the Quarry Garden Isaac recognizes Laura, and though he wants to reveal himself, he decides to remain anonymous. Do you think he should have approached her? Do you agree with his reasoning?

6. When Laura's father is out of town, she chooses to volunteer at the zoo knowing that he won't approve of her choice. Where do you think her new confidence came from?

7. Mrs. Guskin proves a loyal friend to Laura. Who are the mentors in your own life?

8. In Niagara Falls, the couple work together to bring down Abel. Do you agree with their decision to potentially put themselves in harm's way to do so? What makes a cause worth standing up for?

9. The Bradshaw/Campbell feud unravels as the story closes. By the end of the book, Laura and Isaac understand enough to know they don't want any part in the hate their parents have clung to. Why is it difficult for the fathers to let go of their animosity, even after they understand what really happened?

10. Fairy tales and happy endings seem just out of reach for much of the story. In what ways did the challenges Isaac and Laura face work to bring them together?

Rachel Fordham is the author of *Where the Road Bends*, *A Lady in Attendance*, *A Life Once Dreamed*, *The Hope of Azure Springs*, and *Yours Truly, Thomas*. Fans expect stories with heart and she delivers, diving deep into the human experience and tugging at reader emotions. She loves connecting with people, traveling to new places, and daydreaming about future projects that will have sigh-worthy endings and memorable characters. She is a busy mom, raising both biological and foster children (a cause she feels passionate about). She lives with her husband and children on an island in the state of Washington.

Learn more at rachelfordham.com
Instagram: @rachel_fordham
Facebook: @rachelfordhamfans